Sam Parks, a.k.a. Sam Gale, moved from the US to the UK to pursue her love for writing. Now she's settled there, writing romantic stories and going for long walks with her golden retriever Kirby. In the little spare time she has between writing and editing books, she likes to play D&D with her friends and dress up like she could stumble into a Ren Faire at any moment. She also reads as much as life allows, documenting her reading and writing on her YouTube channel.

www.samanthaparks.com

tiktok.com/@samparksbooks
youtube.com/@searchingforsamantha
instagram.com/searchingforsamantha

Also by Sam Parks

<u>Roll for Romance</u>
You've Got Chain Mail
Date Knight

The Summer House in Santorini
The Summer Wedding in Santorini

DATE KNIGHT

SAM PARKS

One More Chapter
a division of HarperCollins*Publishers*
1 London Bridge Street
London SE1 9GF
www.harpercollins.co.uk
HarperCollins*Publishers*
Macken House, 39/40 Mayor Street Upper,
Dublin 1, D01 C9W8, Ireland

This paperback edition 2025
First published in Great Britain in ebook format
by HarperCollins*Publishers* 2025

1

Copyright © Sam Parks 2025
Sam Parks asserts the moral right to be identified
as the author of this work

A catalogue record of this book is available from the British Library

ISBN: 978-0-00-873934-8

This novel is entirely a work of fiction. The names, characters and incidents portrayed in it are the work of the author's imagination. Any resemblance to actual persons, living or dead, events or localities is entirely coincidental.

Printed and bound in the UK using 100% Renewable Electricity
by CPI Group (UK) Ltd

All rights reserved. No part of this publication may be reproduced, stored in a retrieval system, or transmitted, in any form or by any means, electronic, mechanical, photocopying, recording or otherwise, without the prior permission of the publishers.

Without limiting the exclusive rights of any author, contributor or the publisher of this publication, any unauthorised use of this publication to train generative artificial intelligence (AI) technologies is expressly prohibited. HarperCollins also exercise their rights under Article 4(3) of the Digital Single Market Directive 2019/790 and expressly reserve this publication from the text and data mining exception.

For the Fellowship.

AUTHOR'S NOTE

Dear reader,

This book takes place in the same world as my previous story, *You've Got Chain Mail*, though reading that book first is not necessary. For those who have read it, you've already had a taste of the magic that is Phil and Amy, and I can't wait for you to read their story.

This book is especially close to my heart for a lot of reasons, some of which may be difficult for readers who can relate. Whilst it is a rom-com at heart, there are some heavier themes at play. Specifically, one of our main characters, Phil, is a carer for his grandmother Ethel, who is in the early- to mid-stages of dementia. This was hard to write – my own grandfather with dementia passed away as I was writing the first draft of *Date Knight* – and if that's a possible trigger for you, I want you to go into the story with your eyes wide open.

However, despite those heavy themes, this is still a relatively light-hearted story, and I just know you'll fall as hard in love with Phil and Amy as I have. Thanks so much for reading, and I hope you enjoy the book.

Love,

Sam

CHAPTER 1
YORICK PROUDHOLLOW

Yorick Proudhollow pressed his dagger into the cleric's neck, his arm pinning her against the stone wall. It wasn't often that he got to be the group's muscle, and even less often that he was evenly matched with his opponent.

"Yorick!" Morgana reached for his shoulder, but he shrugged her off. She stepped back in line with the others who looked on in horror, not helping Yorick, but not stopping him either.

"She knows something," Yorick hissed. "Don't let her fool you."

The cleric, a gnome just an inch or two taller than Yorick, was putting on a good show, her eyes wide in a show of fear, her hands pressed flat to the crumbling brick behind her, her mouth trembling. To be fair, he'd gotten in a good few hits before the others had caught up to him. But it was warranted; he'd seen the tattoo of a twelve-pointed star peeking out of her tunic back at the tavern. The amulet around her neck and the holy tunic and the smell of incense wouldn't fool him, even if the rest of his party was convinced she was innocent. If he weren't certain, he wouldn't have chased her out. And if she weren't guilty, she wouldn't have run.

They'd been hunting The Twelve for months now, trying to work out who was behind them. They knew it wasn't the Queen's adviser Lord Arnault or his minions; Yorick and his friends had defeated him. But in the aftermath of what they'd hoped was the final battle, as they'd mourned the friends and fellow adventurers they'd lost, Yorick had received a letter, supposedly from his long-dead mother, with a twelve-pointed star stamped into the wax.

Yorick instantly went into a frenzy trying to solve the mystery. They'd sent *him* the letter. They'd targeted *him*. And though he'd confirmed his father's and younger siblings' safety, he didn't like being baited. Used.

Weeks later, having exhausted every lead they had, one finally panned out; the delivery boy who had brought the letter had been handed it by a woman in a pub with a "weird sparkly star tattoo". And after staking out the pub for days, Yorick had watched an unfamiliar gnome stand up to leave, her cloak catching on her top just long enough to show the outline of a twelve-pointed star.

"Tell me what you know about The Twelve," Yorick demanded now, using his free hand to hold the wax seal, long dislodged from the letter, to the young woman's face. He was trying to be intimidating, something he didn't often attempt due to his stature, but she seemed unfazed.

"I don't know what you're talking about," she insisted, closing her eyes and wincing away from Yorick's blade, which pressed so hard into her neck that her skin yielded. If he slid it even a fraction of an inch, he would draw blood.

"Liar!" he spat.

"Yorick, maybe let's take a beat," Calamity said, and that made him pause. The rest of the party – the honourable Ser Liam Prize, ex-Queen's Guard Captain Morgana, Gorlag the barbarian, and their newest initiate, the druid Eden – could be a bit too restrained sometimes. But Calamity was a trigger-happy, pyromaniac, half-demon sorcerer. If *she* didn't approve of what he was doing, maybe he should reconsider.

But he didn't get the chance.

The cleric must have seen his resolve waver, because the slightest of smirks tugged at her upper lip. *Yes,* he thought. *I knew it.*

But at that same moment, Yorick felt a nudge at his feet as thorns erupted from the ground, twisting around his legs and his torso, holding him in place.

A look of confusion crept over the cleric's expression, which spread instantly to Yorick – why was she confused? Had she not been the one to cast the spell? – but before he could figure it out, the roots reached Yorick's hands, causing them to tense, dragging the blade across the cleric's skin just enough to nick her artery.

It took six long seconds for the cleric to die. Yorick remained trapped in place, and the cleric trapped beneath him, watching in horror as the blood drained from her neck and the light from her eyes, until the spell holding him ceased as suddenly as it had taken over him, the roots withdrawing into the gaps between the paving stones. But by then it was too late. Yorick dropped to his knees to catch the cleric's body as it fell.

"What's wrong with all of you?" he yelled at his friends as he cradled it. "Why didn't you help?"

"Did you not do that on purpose?" Liam asked, rushing over to place his hands on the wound, but none of his divine healing magic made an ounce of difference. The cleric was dead.

"Of course not," Yorick spat. He looked over his shoulder at the others, who stood there in horror. His eyes landed on Eden, whose hands hung limply at her sides. He could still see the remnants of her druidic magic pulsing over them.

"You did this!" he shouted, his face hot with anger.

"You were going to kill her, clearly!"

"My hand was steady until your godsforsaken roots got a hold of me!"

He watched as the colour drained from Eden's face as she realised what he meant, then rushed to the ground next to Yorick. But no matter how much magic she and Liam channelled into the body, the life force had already dissipated.

"No!" Yorick wailed as he turned on Eden, pushing her away. "I had her right where I wanted her! She smirked at me! She was giving away the game!"

"What was it you thought you saw?" Calamity asked, helping the elf to her feet.

"She had a twelve-pointed star tattooed on her shoulder. I saw it in the pub."

Calamity and Morgana exchanged a loaded glance. They didn't believe him.

"Go on," Yorick said, pointing at the body. "See for yourself."

Calamity nodded at Liam, who gingerly sat the cleric up and drew back her cloak. She was wearing a loose-fitting tunic underneath, which he pulled to one side to expose her shoulder.

As they pulled back the fabric, they revealed one point, then three, then five, until they could see the tattoo in its entirety. Just as Yorick had known, it was a twelve-pointed star that perfectly matched the seal in his hand. And now that he looked at it more closely, the tattoo seemed to shimmer in the warm evening light.

CHAPTER 2
PHIL

"I told you!" I crossed my arms and sat back in my seat so suddenly I nearly tipped backward, though I thought I played it off. Amy rolled her green eyes at me from where she sat across the table, mimicking my posture.

"It's literally my first game," she said. "How was I supposed to know?"

"I don't know, maybe listen to the people who have been playing for longer than you?"

Amy waved one finger in the air in a circle to indicate the rest of the group. "I was! And every single one of us thought you were full of shit. So I did what felt right."

"And you got someone killed in the process!"

"Well, if you'd waited five seconds before holding a knife to her throat, I would have used the spell on you instead, and everyone would still be alive."

"And she would have gotten away, and we still wouldn't have gotten any information."

Amy narrowed her gaze, her jaw tensing. Then she turned to look down the table at the others, who all sat watching us with varying looks on their faces. Amy's older brother Jack, also my best friend, was wincing. It was exactly what his D&D character would do in a conflict between friends, too, which was hilarious because he'd tried so hard to make his character different to himself. His girlfriend Morgan even drew his paladin character Ser Liam as an identical tall, blonde-haired man.

Speaking of whom, Morgan was pressing her mouth into a thin "none of my business" line as she watched the fallout from the game; this was similar to her fighter character's approach, too.

Grey's eyes were widened in interest, not unlike their half-orc barbarian.

Chloe's smile was one I recognised instantly from two decades of friendship: pure glee. Just like her tiefling sorcerer Calamity, she was chaotic as hell, and I loved her for it.

Even Morgan's dog Pablo, a little teddy bear of a thing, looked down the table at us with interest from where he sat cosied up in Grey's lap.

I looked in the other direction to find Fatima, our game master, smirking.

"You," I said, turning my ire to her. "You knew what you were doing having me roll that perception check in secret."

"What does that mean?" Amy asked her brother, but I put a hand on the table between us and answered her myself.

"It means she was being underhanded. She wanted you all to doubt me. You didn't know I rolled a natural twenty on my perception check, so you all thought I was seeing things."

Jack's mouth fell open as he turned to Fatima. "You created inter-party conflict *on purpose*?"

Fatima just shrugged.

"You messy bitch," Chloe said, but she was smiling approvingly, twirling a strand of her long red hair around her finger. She lived for this kind of drama, in real life as much as in Dungeons & Dragons.

"But still," I said, looking again at Amy, whose posture went instantly defensive. "That's no excuse for PvP violence."

She frowned. "PvP?"

"Player versus player. Friends don't cast spells on friends without enthusiastic consent."

"How the hell was I supposed to know that?" she asked, throwing her hands in the air. "Allow me to repeat, it's literally my first game. Ever."

"Yeah?" I asked. "Is it also your first day on Earth, *ever*?"

She scowled at me, then leaned forward and reached out for the tin I'd brought, which now sat almost empty in front of me. She grabbed the last lemon bar, the one I'd been saving to have on the way to the pub. By the time I realised what she was doing and went to swat her hand away, she'd already absconded with it, and my hand hit the side of the tin instead, smarting slightly. Amy stuck her tongue out at me, and I returned the favour. She took a comically large bite of the lemon bar, her eyes locked on mine the whole time as she chewed.

"You're both so astoundingly mature," Grey said, scooting back from the table. "Let's continue this en route to the pub, shall we? I think we could all do with a drink."

Everyone else muttered their agreement, and I watched as they packed up their dice and character sheets. Or rather, I watched Amy as she ate the lemon bar and watched them pack up. A strange look flashed across her face – she almost looked sad – before she started clearing up, too.

"Thanks," she said to Fatima, pushing her borrowed set of dice and character sheet towards her.

"You can keep this," Fatima said, pushing the character sheet back to Amy. "Unless you want to make a different character? You don't have to use Lauren's hand-me-downs if you don't want to, I just thought it would be helpful for you to have a starting point."

Chloe's currently off-again girlfriend Lauren had joined the party for a few sessions, but they'd agreed before their last on-again bout that maybe it was a bad idea, and so the character had conveniently been on a separate mission for a while.

Amy's brow pinched together. "You want me to come back?"

Fatima laughed softly. "Yeah, of course. The invitation was to join the campaign, not just the session."

Amy looked up at the group, her eyes landing on mine for a long moment. It was like she was trying to sense whether I wanted her there or not. Which was ridiculous, given that I was the one to suggest to the others that we invite her. Not that she knew that.

Given our history, I wasn't surprised at her scrutiny. I tried my best to soften my expression, my chin dipping slightly in a nod as I scooped my own dice and character sheet into my bag.

"I mean, it's not like I've got anything better to do," she said, then seemed to consider the implication of that. "God, how sad is that?"

"Hating on nerd culture is a bit clichéd, Ames," I said as I rose from my seat. "And besides, you're a part of it now."

FATIMA HAD SPRUNG for an air con unit last year, which made summertime gaming sessions infinitely more tolerable. It also made the first step out into the still-hot evening infinitely *less* tolerable, and the short walk to the pub fairly miserable. It was made even worse by the beard I'd grown over the last few months; I was half tempted to shave it just for the hotter months.

It was only just June, not even technically summer yet, but it was already sweltering, even at half past eight. At least the sun was beginning to set, promising a temperature drop, and painting the sky a vivid pink that matched the scrunchy holding up Amy's long blonde hair. Her ponytail bobbed from side to side as she walked a few paces in front of me, arm in arm with Chloe.

"I need one of those fans that you can wear around your neck," Chloe was saying to her, and I pulled out my phone to add it to the running list of gift ideas I had going. Her birthday was in July, so she'd have to suffer a little while longer.

As I opened my phone, I noticed that I had a message from Anil. I felt a Pavlovian twitch of panic – Anil looked after my grandmother Ethel when I was out, and anytime I saw his name on my phone, my nervous system insisted on jumping to the worst-case scenario. My brain knew it was nothing; that I would have missed calls if anything were wrong. But until I opened the message and saw something innocuous, I wouldn't know for sure.

> ANIL
>
> Class got cancelled on Saturday. Do you want me?

Anil had looked after Ethel every Saturday night for over a year until a few months ago, when he'd started a weekend certification course in a nearby city. Amy had been staying with Ethel on Saturdays instead.

I lifted my chin to look up at Amy and nearly ran into her instead – she was stood completely still in the middle of the pavement, staring down at her own phone.

"Fuck's sake," I said, stopping just a fraction of an inch from her. "Watch it."

"I believe you're the one that nearly ran into me?" she sneered without looking up from her phone.

"Yeah, because you stopped dead in my way."

"Whatever," she said, literally waving it off as she fell into step beside me. "Question for you. How late do you think you'll be on Saturday? Dad wants me to do a site visit with him on Sunday morning, and it's obnoxiously early."

"I didn't know you were doing site visits?" Her dad was a contractor, and I knew she'd been working for him, but the last I'd heard she'd just been doing a few hours a week of admin.

Amy sighed. "Yeah, well, Dad's notes are impossible to read, so I told him if he wants me to put together his quotes he needs to take me with him. I think the eight a.m. call time is just to punish my insolence."

"Sounds about right," I said, chuckling. "Well, you're in luck. Anil's free on Saturday, so I don't actually need you at all."

I watched Amy out of the corner of my eye, surprised when her mouth drooped in a frown. Then I watched as she forced herself to smile instead.

"Perfect. That's my Saturday night back."

For all the cons in the heat, the beard had its pros, too. Namely, it made my facial expressions harder to read, which was especially important if Amy were going to be spending more time with the group. As fun as antagonising her was, I wasn't always the best at keeping a straight face, and the facial hair helped disguise the grins when they popped up.

Not that I'd had to try very hard to keep a straight face after tonight's game. Was attacking me very on-brand for her as Amy? Of course it was. But it wasn't exactly helping to further the mission. And yes, I'd been the one to suggest she join us, but I was beginning to regret giving her another channel to use to drive me crazy.

I watched her from across the table – we were at our usual picnic table in the pub's beer garden, which was really too small for seven of us, but Jack had pulled Morgan onto his lap so we could all fit. Amy was at the end of the opposite bench from me, laughing at something on Chloe's phone.

Chloe and Jack were my two best and oldest friends. I'd

known them since the first day of secondary school, which was my first day living in town after growing up until then across the border in Wales. Ethel had become my guardian after my parents both died in a car accident when I was eight, and eventually we'd had to move from my mum's hometown back to Ethel's house so she could go back to work, and I'd had to start at a brand new school. And if I hadn't met Jack and Chloe that first day, if they hadn't started talking to me without even introducing themselves as if we'd always been friends, my life could have looked very different.

Of course, Amy had come into my life not long after. It had started with me hanging out at Jack's, Amy nosing her way into things as much as possible. But when their mum Patricia had found out Ethel was raising me alone, she'd made it her personal mission to look after us. So the Evanses had become like a second family to me – Patricia had even started teaching me to cook when I was a teenager – meaning Amy and I never went long without seeing one another. Of course, I knew even then that she had a crush on me, but it had always felt innocent. Unserious, even.

Then Jack, Chloe, and I had all gone to different unis, which was when I'd met Grey, despite the fact that they were from the same town as me. I met their best friend Fatima, too. And then we'd all moved back to the same town after uni, and they'd been my people ever since. Between Ethel, the Evanses, and my friends, I'd never once had the opportunity to feel lonely. And for a kid who had lost his parents so young, that was saying something.

For a nearly thirty-year-old who was a full-time carer for his nan with dementia, it was still a godsend.

"Oh my god, that's definitely you," Amy said, handing Chloe's phone back to her, no doubt in response to something like "you as a sleepy kitten based on your rising sign".

Grey, Fatima, and Morgan were talking about something

across the table in front of me, but I wasn't listening; I was trying to figure out what Chloe was saying that was making Amy's mouth quirk up in that very specific way.

"Maybe Amy should go out with him," Fatima said, and Amy and I both snapped our heads to look at her.

"With who?" she asked, grimacing. "There's no way you know my type."

"It's *whom*," I muttered under my breath; she rolled her eyes at me in response.

"Some new teacher at Fatima's school," Morgan said, passing her own phone to Amy. "But I get red flag vibes."

"No way," Fatima insisted. "He's really lovely. And great with his students."

Amy looked down at the phone, and I felt a pinch in my gut as her eyebrows shot up, as if she were impressed. "Okay, I'm listening."

Fatima leant in as she took her phone back. "He just moved from Surrey to be closer to his family, and he teaches classics."

Amy frowned. "I thought you taught at a primary school? Who's reading Virgil at age ten?"

Fatima shook her head. "It's a private school. Goes all the way through sixth form."

"Okay, okay," Chloe said, waving her arms between Fatima and Amy to interject. "Let's cut to the good stuff. When is his birthday?"

"How am I supposed to know that? I met him like a week ago."

"Twenty-ninth of November," Morgan said, holding her phone out, showing his Facebook page. It was hard to tell from where I sat, but I supposed he didn't look obviously hideous. "And he's in some group called 'I Hate Coriander'."

"Ooooh, a Sagittarius," Chloe squealed. "Just like Morgan!"

"Fire sign power couple, Sag and Aries," Fatima said.

"Just what I need," Amy said, her voice thick with sarcasm. "No, I don't date fire signs anymore."

I watched them volley back and forth about Amy's astrological compatibility with this random man, and it was like they weren't even speaking English anymore for how little I understood them.

"You should invite him to the quiz then," Amy said. "So I can meet him with no pressure."

"What quiz?" I asked. I hadn't heard about any quiz.

"The pub quiz," Grey said, tapping on the flyer in the middle of the table. I picked it up and read it; the pub would be having a summertime quiz series on Tuesdays starting the next week.

I stopped paying attention; I didn't have Ethel cover on Tuesdays. Plus, pub quizzes weren't usually my thing; people always expected me to be good at the sport or history questions from the way I looked, when really I barely knew how many players per side there were in rugby sevens. (There were, I'd embarrassingly learned in a uni pub quiz, seven. Hence the name.)

Had I been a normal person my age, it might not have felt weird to have weekly pub quizzes, weekly D&D games, weekly film nights, and sporadic weekend plans. But between all of Ethel's appointments, Anil's schedule, and having to keep up appearances of going on dates, my calendar was getting downright unruly.

I tuned back in briefly to find that the rest of the table had moved on to talking about their costumes for the fantasy festival we were going to in a few weeks. I should have been paying attention as I was making half those costumes. I'd been sewing since I was eleven, when Ethel had taught me to tailor my own school uniform, and recently I'd become the de facto costume designer for the group. It was probably my fault – we'd gone to America for a Ren Faire last year, and I'd volunteered to make the costumes for that – but for the fantasy festival, things had gotten a bit out of hand.

I'd taken updated measurements last week, so I could afford to check out of the conversation until they made up their minds. So instead I was focused on Amy, who had taken Fatima's phone again and was looking down at the picture of the guy they wanted her to go out with. I felt my jaw tense at the idea of it; maybe it was just overprotectiveness from knowing her since she was little, or maybe ... no, it was definitely just that, I told myself. It would be hypocritical to be jealous, given that she looked after Ethel every week so I could go on dates, right?

I pulled my own phone out to distract myself.

"And not a single phone in sight," Jack said sarcastically, which alerted Chloe to what I was doing.

"Ooooh, gimme!" she said, holding her hands out. "Swipe time!"

I groaned. "Not now, Chloe."

Amy frowned. "Swipe time?"

"It's Thursday," she said, still holding her hands out towards me. "Phil needs to find his date for Saturday. Thursday is prime swipe time for that."

"No way," I said. "The last time you ended up matching me with someone I dated in school." I was watching Amy's face, which had gone a bit red, maybe from the beer she was drinking.

"It's not my fault you've been through the majority of this town's eligible population."

I wanted to remind her that the only reason I went out with so many people was because she and Ethel were obsessed with me finding someone to settle down with. As long as I kept meeting up with new people, they stayed off my back. If I were intentionally keeping those people at arm's length, or if I sometimes pretended to go out on a date when I actually just went to the cinema alone, that was quite frankly none of their business.

I didn't have the mental bandwidth to date properly with everything else I had going on.

Chloe was right, though; I did still need something to do on Saturday.

It had been months since I'd actually let myself go on a proper date. I'd met up with Hinge matches, sure, at the only good bar in town. And until a few months ago, I'd gone home with some of them from time to time. I was only human, after all. But once Amy had taken over Saturday night shifts with Ethel, I'd thought it would feel too weird to come home from a hookup to find Amy in my lounge.

But Amy wouldn't be there on Saturday night. And based on the tension I felt in my chest every time Amy looked my way, I could do with a proper night out, and all that entailed. And I knew there was one person I could message for a true no-strings-attached evening.

PHIL

You free Saturday?

Poppy's reply came in less than a minute.

POPPY

Sure am. Usual time and place?

CHAPTER 3
AMY

My horoscope had warned me that morning that I'd make some controversial moves, but I hadn't thought it would be in a game of Dungeons & Dragons.

I knew Phil wasn't trying to punish me for the unintentional p on p – or whatever he'd called it – but watching him on his phone knowing he was looking for a date made my stomach churn unpleasantly. I tried to focus on the conversation the rest of the table was having, but they'd started talking about some festival they were going to in a few weeks.

It was easy to forget around my brother Jack's friends that they were, in fact, *his* friends. Especially with Chloe and Phil, whom I'd known most of my life, and who treated me like part of the group. But Chloe was like that with everyone she met, and Phil ... well, he and I had enough tension in our shared history that I could never quite work out if he actually wanted me around or not. Though I didn't hate the idea of being able to annoy the shit out of him in-game if I carried on playing. And then there was Jack's girlfriend Morgan, who was far too good for him, but if she didn't realise that, then I wasn't about to be the one to tell her.

I hadn't spent much time with Grey and Fatima until moving home ten months ago, but they were lovely to me, too. Grey was Phil's best friend from university, and their biker vest and buzz cut, the latter of which changed colour regularly, were a direct contrast to their golden retriever personality. Their bestie Fatima seemed like my kind of girl – whip smart and hilarious but incredibly pulled together – but I hadn't spent much time with either of them, so they didn't feel like my friends, really.

Plus, there were fairly regular reminders that I was not, in fact, part of The Group, like the nerd fest they'd been talking about. I'd been home for months before they decided to go, and they talked about it in front of me all the time, but they'd never even casually mentioned that I could come. Not that I wanted to; I didn't really understand the appeal of meeting up with thousands of other people wearing nerdy costumes. But I was jealous of the fact that they were doing it together, and that they were so excited. They'd even started talking about another trip to America next year for a different Renaissance Faire, and it was everything I could do to ask questions and act interested without letting on how envious I was.

At least they wanted me to be a regular part of their D&D game. As much as I'd resisted, it had actually been fun, pretending to be a different person with magical powers. And if I got to use those powers to antagonise Phil, even better.

I set my beer down on the table in front of me practically untouched and pulled out my own phone to distract myself, earning a groan from Jack.

"Chill out," I said. "Some of us are actually getting notifications. Don't be jealous."

"Everyone who would text me is around this table," Jack retorted. "Unless Mum and Dad chime in."

"I'm not sure that's the flex you think it is."

"And I'm not sure you having something else to pay attention to right now is the flex *you* think it is."

I rolled my eyes. Jack and I mostly got along these days – we had been pretty close since he'd moved home from full-time travel a few years ago – but sometimes we couldn't help but slip back into big brother/little sister mode.

I looked down at my phone, instantly wishing I hadn't bothered to pull it out at all. The one notification I did have – which was a miracle in and of itself, because despite my big talk I didn't actually have anyone else who might message me anymore – was yet another email from Chris. I swiped to dismiss it as quickly as possible; even just looking at his name made me feel sick to my stomach.

"Everything okay?"

Phil was studying me from the other end of the picnic table.

"Yeah, why?" I widened my eyes and looked around as if his question were baseless.

"You just looked tweaked," he said, shrugging, and I tried my best to keep my face neutral. I shook my head.

"Nope."

"Okay, well," Phil said, bringing his hands to his knees and standing up from the table, "I've gotta get back to Ethel. But I'll see you nerds next week."

"You're not coming to the quiz?" Chloe asked, an exaggerated pout on her face.

"Probably not."

He made his way around the table, giving each person a hug, including Jack. Even as kids, they'd always given each other proper hugs when saying goodbye. But then he got to me, and I realised I would have to hug Phil, otherwise it would look extremely suspicious. He seemed to have the same realisation at the same time, pausing as he turned from Chloe to me.

"See ya," I said, standing up and determining to keep it as

casual as possible. I reached out just my right arm for a side hug, but he did the same with his own right arm, meaning we ended up reaching past one another in a way that made a full hug inevitable.

It's not that hugging Phil was unpleasant. In fact, it was quite the opposite; he was only a few inches taller than me, and I knew from experience that I could just about tuck my head under his chin, my cheek against his chest. I didn't intend to do that, but it was as if my body remembered what it was like to hug him properly, even if we hadn't done so in months. Years, maybe. In fact, I wasn't sure if we'd hugged like this since that night five years ago.

He pulled me into him, his arms wrapping around my back just tight enough, his chin propping on the top of my head. Despite the heat, he wasn't sweaty, and he smelled fresh, like unscented soap, and a little bit earthy. I resisted the urge to breathe in deeply, but only just.

"Sorry for the change of plans this weekend," he said, not yet pulling away, and I could feel his voice against my temple as it reverberated through him.

I opened my eyes and realised Jack was watching us, his eyes narrowed. I wasn't actually sure how long I'd been hugging Phil, but clearly it had been long enough.

"It's fine," I said, pulling back. "I'll see you next week like you said."

"Don't forget, we're camping next week," Morgan said.

"Oh shit, yeah," Phil said, looking apologetic. "And Anil's staying with Ethel all weekend."

"Oh yeah, sure," I said, trying to hide any shred of disappointment. I really did like hanging out with Ethel, so I was sad not to see her two weeks in a row. But more than that, I was surprised at how bummed I was not to be playing D&D next week. I caught Morgan's eye briefly, and she frowned at me, though I wasn't sure why.

As Phil turned to leave, I suddenly remembered that I had something with me that I'd planned to give to Ethel.

"Hey, wait," I said, reaching down for my bag and digging out the stone I'd bought online last week. "Can you add this to the windowsill?"

He looked down at the pink and black crystal I held out to him. "What's this one then?"

"Rhodonite. It's supposed to be good for using other senses to help with memory."

I couldn't quite tell with his beard in the way, but I was pretty sure his mouth quirked into a slight smile. "Sure," he said, plucking it from my palm.

"You've gotta charge it though," I said. "Under the new moon tonight."

Phil rolled his eyes, but the smile didn't dissipate. "Utter hogwash, all of it," he said, but I knew he'd do it anyway. I was pretty sure it hadn't been Ethel or Anil dusting the ones I'd put on the windowsill so far.

"Interesting," Chloe said as I sat back down and narrowed my eyes at her. She liked to make pointed comments about Phil and me from time to time – hell, even Jack had gotten involved since I'd moved home last year – but Chloe knew better than anyone why that would never happen.

Better than anyone but Phil, that was.

~

I walked back to Fatima and Morgan's house with the others, then took Jack's car home, promising to pick him up the next morning before work. We didn't technically share the car – it was his beloved Land Rover that he'd fixed up by hand – but he acted as if we did, which was annoyingly generous of him. As I drove myself home, I mentally tallied up how much money I still needed to save before I could get a car of my own. Not that my social life was particularly busy, but it was annoying to have to rely on Jack's schedule, or Mum's at a pinch. It made me feel even more like a tag-along than I already did.

But I was constantly balancing in my mind the cost of a car versus the cost of getting my own place. Not buying – I had no idea where I wanted to be long-term, and I was tens of thousands in savings away from being able to afford a deposit – but just to get out from under Mum and Dad's thumb. They were good to me, but Mum especially could be a lot.

I'd moved away about three years ago, after it became abundantly clear that my social life in my hometown was dead. The only school friends I had that hadn't moved away had settled down, and we had precious little in common anymore. And after things went south with Jack's friends – with Phil, specifically – I just wanted to be anywhere else. So I'd moved in with my uni mate Niamh in Manchester, got a job, and started building a life. I'd even met someone, thought I'd fallen in love, and moved in with him.

But then we'd broken up. I actually preferred to say I broke up with him, because that's technically how it had happened. But he hadn't exactly asked me not to, and I'd found him in bed with my supposed best friend, so maybe it would have been more accurate to say it was mutual? Either way, I'd come home with my tail between my legs, and I'd been in a sort of stasis since then. I'd picked up enough virtual assistant work and admin hours at Dad's contracting business to build up a tiny bit of savings, but I had very little else going on in my life, which was incredibly depressing if I let myself think too hard about it.

I pulled into the drive and parked behind Mum's Subaru, grateful that at least I wouldn't have to walk down to Jack's to get the car in the morning. He technically lived on the farm with us, but on his own slice of the land about a quarter mile further down the drive, in a house he'd built himself when he'd moved home a few years ago. Then again, none of us lived on the farm, really. Dad's brother John owned the farm and his own house over the hill, and Mum and Dad lived in the old stone farmhouse. Not that we saw much of Uncle John; his house was even further away than Chloe's parents' house, which wasn't quite visible from ours.

I walked through the front door, unsurprised to find Mum watching TV in the lounge.

"How was your game?" she asked as I slipped off my shoes and dropped Jack's keys on the hall table. "Did you win?"

"I don't think it's the type of game you win," I said, walking into the lounge and sinking into Dad's armchair since he was nowhere to be seen.

"What kind of game is it then?"

"The kind where I annoy Phil to no end apparently."

"Well, you always were good at that."

I laughed. "How was *Masterchef*?"

"Good. My money's on that Brin."

"If you say so," I said, though I'd already stopped paying attention, thinking instead about the notification I'd dismissed earlier. It was the third email I'd gotten from Chris this week, and I needed to deal with it eventually. But after the way things had ended, with me having to leave Manchester to get away from the whole situation, I just didn't want to open up that can of worms.

Though I was already thinking about it plenty, so he'd kind of already won, hadn't he? Maybe I could just do a reading to figure out what this was all about instead of actually having to talk to him?

"What do you think?" Mum asked, and I blinked myself back into the room.

"Sorry, about what?"

"Head in the stars again?"

"Something like that," I muttered. Mum was the last person I would tell about Chris reaching out; she didn't know exactly what had happened between us, and I just knew she'd tell me to give him another chance, which was *not* an option.

"I asked if you wanted to come along to one of the rewilding expeditions this summer," she repeated. "We're short on volunteers, and I think you'd really enjoy it."

Mum had volunteered for the local rewilding trust for years now, and she was so serious about it. I was pretty sure the scope of their work extended to planting wildflowers on verges, but she acted like it was this intense job.

"I really don't think I would," I said. Jack had been her little flower child, paying rapt attention when she named every plant and every bird on our camping trips growing up. It had never really appealed to me.

"Suit yourself," she said, then turned her gaze back to the TV and turned up the volume. I hated how disappointed she sounded, but the last thing I wanted was to start volunteering with Mum and stay stuck in the same holding pattern I'd been in for the last few months. Living with my parents, working crappy online jobs whilst having to beg my own father for hours at the family business, tagging along with my brother and his friends when they hung out.

Not that I had any idea what I should be doing instead, of course.

I said goodnight to Mum and took myself upstairs to my childhood bedroom where, even after months, most of my belongings still sat packed in boxes around me. I didn't want to get too comfortable in my situation, because I didn't trust myself to be able to get anything done if I did.

I undertook the most aspirational version of my bedtime routine, every skincare step giving me a few seconds where I didn't have to deal with the emails waiting for me. But eventually I ran out of K-beauty products, and I sat down on my bed, bracing myself for whatever nonsense Chris was bringing with him on his way out of the woodwork.

From: chris.arden@hammondandgreenwood.co.uk
To: amythearies@googlemail.co.uk
Subject: URGENT - please don't ignore this

    I assume you've got me blocked everywhere else, and I don't blame you. But this is now extremely time sensitive. We're coming through your little town on Saturday, and there should be no reason why you can't meet up at some point. Any time is fine. But it's urgent that we speak in person. You have my number. Text me a time and place, or I'll come to the address I still have for your parents.

I could taste bile in the back of my throat as I read the email. The casual condescension of "your little town," the threat to show up at Mum and Dad's house, the insinuation that I had nothing better going on than to meet up with my cheating ex-boyfriend on a Saturday night...

Okay, that last part wasn't untrue exactly, especially now that Phil had cancelled on me, but how dare he anyway.

Mum and Dad would be a problem. Well, really just Mum; she'd taken my breakup harder than she had any right to, despite never having met Chris. So letting him show up at the house was *not* an option. But Mum was nosy enough that going out to meet him would be a challenge, too. Wouldn't she notice if I was out at an odd time? Given how pushy she'd been about me meeting up with old school friends or letting myself be set up with her friends' adult children (most of whom I'd also known since school), all of which I'd firmly rejected, going out would absolutely raise her suspicions.

Except, I was always out on a Saturday night, wasn't I? Or *in*, rather, but at Phil and Ethel's instead of at home.

"Shit," I muttered, knowing my hands were tied; I'd have to do exactly what he wanted me to do if I wanted to minimise the damage. So I typed out a reply:

From: amythearies@googlemail.co.uk
To: chris.arden@hammondandgreenwood.co.uk
Subject: RE: URGENT - please don't ignore this

    Don't be so dramatic, Chris. It's not a good look on you. Saturday night, 7PM. The Old Coffer.

Sent from my iPhone

It would have to do – it was the only nice bar in town, and a drink felt much more palatable than a meal.

Fuck. What the hell did he want? Why was he going to be in town? And importantly, what should I wear to communicate both that I was completely unbothered about his existence, *and* that I was better than him in every way?

I'd just started mentally cataloguing every item of clothing I owned when my phone lit up again on the nightstand. I swallowed hard and took a deep breath, assuming Chris had already responded with something else underhanded and condescending.

But it wasn't an email from Chris. It was a text from Phil; he'd sent me a photo. I didn't know what to expect, but I was already smiling as I tapped the notification.

My screen filled with an image so dark I could barely make it out, but when I squinted, my smile widened. It was a pink and black rhodonite freeform on the plastic table in Ethel's garden, charging under the new moon.

CHAPTER 4
PHIL

I walked up the driveway outside the house, squeezing between the cars parked out front. My beat-up blue Ford Fiesta was parked dangerously close to Ethel's vintage Healey; it was the only way for them both to fit. She hadn't driven in a couple of years, but she still smiled at it every time she walked past it, so it was worth having to squeeze myself like a tube of toothpaste every time I needed to drive somewhere.

Though, given how hard it was for her to get in and out of the Fiesta these days, I probably needed to think about getting something bigger, like Anil's big van, which was parked on the street in front of the house. It would almost certainly mean having to move the Healey, or even sell it. I couldn't think about that yet though. One thing at a time, one foot in front of the other.

I took my time walking up the front path, bracing myself to slip back into carer mode. It was still weird, being anxious to go inside; I'd used to be so excited to come home when I was younger. Ethel had always had something delicious for dinner and something for us to do together, whether it was watching a film or playing Texas Hold 'Em at the dining table. When had that changed?

Probably around the time she stopped being able to live independently, I thought. She'd had her fall nearly three years ago, breaking her ankle, and whilst it had healed reasonably well, her memory seemed to have taken the real hit. I learned later that it was normal for a physical injury to trigger neurological symptoms, but it had caught me off guard at the time. What had just seemed like quirky forgetfulness before eventually grew worrying, and when she'd had a panic attack at Tesco because she didn't know where she was, I'd finally caved and asked for a referral. That was when they'd confirmed what we'd feared: Ethel had dementia. Over the last year it had just gotten worse and worse, and the whip-smart woman who had kept me on my toes my whole life was melting away in front of me, and my life had completely changed because of it. It was weird to think that just a year ago I'd been bored caring for Ethel. I'd really only been there as a precaution, and because I didn't *need* to work full-time as long as I lived with her. But now my days were full of more and more hospital appointments, therapies, and trying to keep her busy so she didn't decline further. All whilst trying to keep us both alive, make enough money to cover our essentials, and try to have some semblance of a life.

I paused when I got to the front door, turning to the dwarf hawthorn planted on the right side of the path. The white flowers were starting to drop, flowering having peaked in May, but they still smelled just as fragrant, the sweet almond scent greeting me at the door for a couple of months every year. I cupped my hand around one, inhaling deeply.

"Hey, Mum," I said quietly. I always associated spring's flowers with Mum, whilst the autumn berries we harvested each year were Dad. It made sense; their ashes had been feeding the tree for nineteen years now. We'd chosen the hawthorn tree because, even at age eleven, I'd been able to tell how similar the fragrant blooms were to Mum's perfume. And whilst I had no memory of it myself, Ethel insisted that Dad's favourite cocktail had used hawthorn cordial. It had been our way of bringing Mum and Dad with us when we'd moved out of the home I'd grown up in, and even now it still felt like they were there every time I came or went.

I opened the front door to the familiar sound of the *Masterchef* intro; it had finished hours ago, but Ethel liked to watch the new episodes over and over. She was sat in her rocker in front of the TV, dressed for bed, and whilst she looked up and smiled at me as I came in, she quickly turned back to watch someone pull a tart out of the oven.

"It's going to be soggy on the bottom," she said to me, pointing at the screen, as if she was predicting it instead of remembering it. These days, I genuinely wasn't sure which it would be.

"Amateur," I agreed, then pressed a kiss to the top of her head.

I passed a stack of mail on the hall table as I headed towards the kitchen, which reminded me of everything I needed to do the next day. Ethel's pension payment had been wrong last month for some reason, and I needed to see if her next appointment letter for the occupational therapist had come through; they were hoping to start more regular appointments at the hospital.

Then there were Anil's account details to change since he'd moved banks. Ethel was probably eligible for an NHS nurse, but I liked the flexibility of someone who could change their shifts around as needed, and the consistency of having the same person every time. Even if it did cost me – I paid Anil well, but given that I refused to even touch Ethel's bank accounts, I'd been slowly depleting what was left of my trust over the last few years. Ethel had put my parents' life insurance payout and the money from their house into the trust I'd gotten access to after uni, but because I'd lived with her since then, it had gone a long way. I was technically my own trustee now that I had power of attorney for Ethel since her diagnosis. I knew it would run out eventually. But again, I couldn't think about that.

I didn't have my head completely in the sand. Most of our bills came out of Ethel's account automatically, just as her pension went in. I added up all the paper statements each month, and by my math, we were just about breaking even in that account. So I didn't even look at it; I didn't want to even be tempted, if there did happen to be more money in there, to use it on things like craft supplies or groceries. I could pay for those things myself, whether out of my trust or with the money I earned doing ad hoc data entry jobs through an online agency. I only had a few hours for work most weeks, but that was enough for everything I needed (and most things I wanted), and it was flexible enough that I could scale it up or down as needed. Though, of course, scaling it up so I could afford more would mean that I then had to let some things fall by the wayside, or find more support, which of course cost more money. I'd become used to those kinds of trade-offs, but it didn't make them easier, and I wasn't about to put Ethel's care on the chopping block for the sake of a little extra cash.

I walked into the kitchen to find Anil washing up from dinner.

"Slay any dragons tonight?" he asked when he saw me, his arms covered in suds up to the elbows.

"Not tonight," I said with a laugh. "But Amy caused some drama."

"In the game or in real life?"

"In the game," I clarified, "though I wouldn't put the real-life drama past her."

"That's my girl," he said with a laugh. They'd only crossed paths a handful of times, but they'd gotten on like a house on fire. Everyone seemed to get on with Amy like that; she had a way of adapting herself to whoever was around.

"Get in line," I muttered.

I stepped in to help Anil, drying once he'd washed; we really did need a dishwasher, didn't we? We ran through the evening together, and I was relieved to hear that it had been uneventful, and Ethel had been mostly with it.

"It was a good day," Anil said.

"And you remembered to up the beta blocker dosage?"

"Sure did," Anil replied, knocking his knuckle against the white binder on the worktop next to the landline. It was open to the medication schedule, which I'd updated just that morning. I'd started the binder when I'd first hired Anil, wanting to make sure I had everything documented; it was the only way I felt comfortable leaving Ethel with him. I doubted he referenced it much anymore, but it was still nice to have, especially when Amy had started staying with her, too.

"Just a thought, man," Anil said, "we should think about adding a second bath per week for a while. I've noticed a few blemishes I think more baths could help. And she seems to enjoy them."

I froze with a plate in my hand. The suggestion made perfect sense, of course, but it caught me off guard, too. Ethel had made it very clear in her earlier stages that she didn't want me bathing her or helping her use the toilet; she wanted me to hire people to help with that. I only had Anil on Thursday and Friday nights though, and Saturdays when he wasn't on his course. Although...

"Actually," I said, "my friends wanna start doing a pub quiz on Tuesdays. Do you wanna add another night into the mix? At least for the summer?"

"Hell yeah," Anil said, smiling at me. I got the sense that he really liked spending time with Ethel, which made it much easier to leave her with him.

"Perfect. I'll send you the details over the weekend when I figure out what the plan is."

As I sent Anil on his way and headed back into the lounge, I realised my pocket was heavier than usual, and I remembered the hunk of rhodonite Amy had given me. I pulled it out and examined it.

Here at home, I could let the smile crack across my face as I looked it over. Our windowsill was littered with shiny rocks of various hues, all of which had different purported healing properties. It was all a bunch of nonsense as far as I was concerned, but Ethel liked the way they looked, and I'd always been touched by how much Amy cared for her. How much she cared about everything, actually.

I stepped out into the back garden, dragging the plastic dining table off the raised stone patio and into the middle of our small patch of grass so it would get as much moonlight as possible, then placed the crystal dead centre. I stepped back and snapped a photo, then sent it to Amy.

I watched as the message quickly went from delivered to read, and I was only a little disappointed when she didn't respond.

The next evening, I sat across from Poppy talking about Ethel. She was an occupational therapist, and she was giving me a list of questions to ask when we had Ethel's next appointment. They were mostly the same as what I'd found online, but I was grateful she was talking me through it anyway.

Poppy and I had been out dozens of times over the last few years, mostly as respite from the hell that was our local dating scene. It was a small town, which meant that almost everyone I matched with was someone I knew or recognised, and there was really only one good place to go for drinks. It was exhausting to have to ask the same four questions over and over again: What do you do? Are you from around here? What do you do for fun? And, of course, the old classic: how is someone like you single?

No, Poppy and I already knew all that about each other. She was an OT, she'd lived here her whole life but had gone to the posh school Fatima now taught at, she loved old films, and like me she had no emotional bandwidth for a relationship. She was a single mum whose kid spent weekends with her dad, which meant Poppy had one night a week where she wasn't working or parenting. It was perfectly symmetrical to my situation, so despite the fact that we had zero long-term interest in one another, we got dressed up every now and then and pretended like we did.

And if sometimes we ended up back at Poppy's, well, that was fine too. She was a beautiful woman, tall, with long blonde hair and a dusting of freckles across her pale cheeks. In brief moments of uncharacteristic self-awareness, I could recognise the parallels to another leggy blonde I knew. But most of the time, I was happy to ignore that particular coincidence.

It had been a while since I'd gone back to hers, though, or to anyone's for that matter. About ten months, in fact.

As Poppy told me about a particularly chaotic shift she'd had during the week, my attention felt suddenly pulled towards the front window, as if my gaze were magnetised. The sun was still out and wouldn't set for a while still, and the lighting inside was low and moody, so I could see outside perfectly.

Standing just to the side of the door, her face frozen in surprise, was Amy.

It was a shock to see her, but I found myself smiling immediately. She looked beautiful in a white knit top that tied together twice at the front, her chest and stomach bare beneath, her long tanned legs visible through the holes in her jeans. The setting sun caused a sort of halo effect around her blonde hair, which was perfectly straight and hanging all the way to her hips instead of in its usual messy ponytail.

I stared at her for a long moment, wondering what she was doing there and waiting for her to look around and see me, but her gaze was fixed on something on the other side of the bar from where Poppy and I were sat. I tried to follow her line of sight, but the best guess I had was a table at the back where a couple sat on one side of a four-top. It was one of my biggest pet hates; save the PDA for home and actually look one another in the eye, for fuck's sake. And there was plenty of PDA: the clean-cut guy had his mouth all over the neck of the petite blonde next to him, her chin-length hair giving everyone full view of what was going on. She had her hand on the side of her date's face – or her fiancé's, I supposed, given the giant rock on her left ring finger.

I looked back to Amy – could this be what had her so upset? Who were they? – and I saw a tear roll down her face.

Poppy was mid-sentence when I rose, abandoning my drink and walking across the bar without looking away from Amy. Despite my D&D character, there had been very few times when I'd involved myself in real life drama. But nothing in the world could have kept me in that seat when I saw Amy start to cry.

CHAPTER 5
AMY

That conniving bitch.

I could barely see through the tears forming in my eyes, but the sparkle glinting off the diamond ring on Niamh's hand cut through it all. Niamh, my ex best friend. The woman who had welcomed me to Manchester with open arms. Who had ushered me into the friend group, set me up with her friend Chris, and then fucked him for months behind my back. And now she was sitting in a bar in my town, making out with him like she wanted to rub it in my face. Like the fact that they were engaged now made any difference to the way they'd hurt me.

My horoscope that morning had said not to be afraid to get my hands dirty, and I'd assumed that was referencing meeting up with my nasty ex-boyfriend for whatever desperate reason he had. But now, all I felt was gross, watching the two of them all over one another. I'd need a lot more than the amethyst pendant around my neck to deal with the level of toxic energy in that bar.

I felt Phil's presence before I saw him, and I'd barely processed that it was him before I was in his arms. It wasn't until my face felt wet against his shirt that I realised I was actually crying. At least Niamh and Chris had been too preoccupied to see; that would have been humiliating.

In theory, it should have been embarrassing to have Phil see me like that, too, but for whatever reason, I didn't feel embarrassed. Maybe I was too preoccupied by the fact I'd just been forced to watch one of the greatest betrayals of my life play out in real time.

"Who are they?" he asked after he'd held me for a moment.

"My ex-boyfriend and ex best friend." I knew he knew the basics; Chloe had gotten me drunk enough to tell her a couple months after we'd moved home, and Jack had let slip a few weeks later that he knew. So I only assumed the whole group was well informed of how pathetically my time in Manchester had ended.

"Well shit," he said, and I took that as confirmation that he did, in fact, know.

"Shit indeed."

"Were you expecting them?"

I couldn't help but laugh at that. I pulled back from the hug, but he didn't quite let me go. "I should have been. Chris said he needed to see me. I should have known she'd be behind it. He wasn't even bothered to see me half the time when we were together."

"Idiot."

"I can't do this, Phil." I heard my voice strain into a whine, which I normally would never let happen in front of him – my greatest fear with Phil had always been that he would think me childish – but something about the way his hands grasped my arms or the sympathetic look on his face made me feel like I didn't need to try to hold it together. "I thought I would be okay to see him, to find out what he wanted, but I don't think I can handle both of them. Especially not if they're engaged. God, she'll be fucking insufferable as a bride."

"You don't have to do anything you don't wanna do. Just go home. I can take care of it."

"How's that?"

He shrugged. "I'll walk in and tell him you don't want to see him. Easy as that."

I let out a huff of laughter through my nose and shook my head. "No, if they think they've gotten to me, they win."

"But they *have* gotten to you," he said softly, and somehow it didn't sound judgmental. "And that's okay. You're allowed to have feelings."

Except no, I wasn't. Everyone in my life had made that abundantly clear. Phil himself had made that clear five years ago. I'd been the dramatic one growing up, wearing my heart on my sleeve, and I'd learned that it was hiding those feelings that made other people tolerate me.

I looked in through the window again to see that the making out had eased, and they were just staring into one another's eyes. God, they really did look perfect together, with their expensive shirts and their shiny hair. How I'd ever thought I'd fit with either of them was beyond me.

But by staying away, by letting Phil fight my battle for me, I would be proving them right. They'd already taken so much away from me. The people I'd thought were my friends had taken their side in the fallout, and I'd had to move home with my tail between my legs.

No, I refused to cower outside like a scared puppy.

I was at least five minutes late by now, and as I was debating what to do, Niamh looked up from her love bubble, her eyes meeting mine almost instantly. Her face broke into a huge grin, and she waved chaotically like a child, beckoning me inside. She seemed genuinely happy to see me, but all I felt was rage. The bitter taste in my mouth grew stronger as I realised I definitely couldn't walk away now.

I took a deep breath and turned around so I could wipe my

eyes without her seeing. *Don't let them see you sweat*, I told myself. *Embody your inner bad bitch.* They needed to see just how unaffected I was by what they'd done – even if I had in fact been deeply affected. They needed to realise they weren't the main characters in my story, or anyone else's for that matter.

And suddenly, I had an idea that was just unhinged enough that it might work, given the Gemini I had standing next to me.

I turned back around and smiled at Niamh, who was standing up from the table, channelling as much enthusiasm into the expression as I could. Then I looked at Phil, who instantly frowned deeply enough that it caused the shape of his beard to change entirely.

"You wanna help me fight fire with fire?" I held my hand out to him, palm up, and he took a long time to decide what to do with it, looking back and forth between it and my face.

But clearly he decided he was up for a little drama, because he not only took it but laced his fingers through mine.

He opened the door for me, and I was barely inside before I heard an ear-piercing scream that I knew from experience was Niamh's. She was rocketing towards me before the door had even shut behind me. She completely ignored Phil and wrapped her arms around me, squeezing me tight despite the fact that I made no move to reciprocate the gesture.

Chris had once said we looked alike, which was ironic in hindsight. It was also untrue; we both had blonde hair and green eyes, but where my hair was waist-length and straw-coloured and unkempt, Niamh's was a perfectly highlighted platinum kept in a tidy bob. Where she'd grown up in designer clothes, I had always tried to imitate her as best I could via the high street. I'd never felt more "not like other girls" in my life than when I'd hung around with Niamh and our other friends – or rather, *her* friends, I supposed – despite the fact that I knew *she* was the anomaly. And whilst I would have staunchly defended her right to designer clothing and expensive jewellery to any man who dared denigrate it, it did feel oddly out of place in my hometown after ten months apart. Like she was the villain in a Hallmark film come to try to drag her boyfriend back from the local bakery owner he'd fallen for.

"Who's this?" Niamh asked in her Irish lilt as she leaned back from the one-sided hug, finally acknowledging Phil and our still-clasped hands.

"Phil," he said, holding out his other hand to shake hers. She shook it.

"Oh. My. God." She turned her head back to me slowly and dramatically, her mouth hung open. "*The* Phil? Are you telling me you finally got with your brother's hot friend?!"

I felt my face go instantly scarlet, and I didn't dare look over at the smug smirk I knew Phil would be wearing.

"Sure did," he offered, and nope, I was absolutely not going to look at him. I could hear the taunt in his voice. Sure, it was no secret that I'd had a thing for him growing up, but as far as he knew, that night five years ago had been the end of things. I'd worked very hard to give that impression, anyway. So this was about as humiliating as it could get.

"That's so exciting. How long have you been together?"

"About ten months," Phil said, almost too quickly; quickly enough that it took me a couple of seconds to realise that was almost the exact amount of time it had been since I'd moved home. He was implying that I'd been so unbothered that I'd jumped straight into a new relationship. *Good boy*.

"Well, it sounds like we're celebrating all around! Come sit. Champagne on me!" She flagged down a passing waiter and ordered a bottle of something I'd never heard of.

"Just water for me, thanks," Phil said as he pulled my chair out. "I'm on call for my nan, and I've already had one this evening."

"Oh, that's so sweet," Niamh said, sitting down next to

Chris, who still hadn't said a word. "Chris is on water too, so he can drive us back later. Is your nan okay?"

"He's her full-time carer," I offered, determined to get involved with the conversation so I didn't seem like a startled deer in their presence.

Niamh cooed, bringing her hands to her heart. "That is SO lovely, isn't it, Chris?" She turned to her other half, who looked so uninterested in being there that I almost felt bad for her. Almost, but not quite. "Chris, say hi. Phil, this is Chris."

"Good to meet you, man," Phil said, so casually I was actually impressed, given his anger on my behalf outside. They shook hands across the table.

I felt something graze my skin on the side furthest away from Phil, and it made me jump before I realised it was his hand; he'd snaked it around my waist. I turned back towards him to find he'd brought his face in close enough that his beard tickled my ear.

"This okay?" he whispered, and I nodded subtly, trying to conceal the gulp in my throat. I looked down at the table, but I could feel him smile next to me. He was locked in, alright. I was the one who would need to keep my shit together.

"Now, I'm so sorry," he said, turning back to Niamh and Chris. "Remind me, how do you two know Amy?"

I felt my eyes go wide as he said that, but I bit back my smile. Damn, he was good. And I could tell his attempt to catch them off guard had worked; the two of them looked at one another in confusion, and Niamh stammered a bit as she answered.

"Well, Amy and I lived together in Manchester, isn't that right?" She looked at me as if for confirmation.

"That's right."

"And she and Chris dated for a bit too, though I think it was pretty casual, wasn't it?" She and Chris were nodding like a couple of bobbleheads.

Again she looked at me to affirm what she was saying. It was egregiously revisionist to describe it that way – we'd moved in together, for fuck's sake – but I didn't need to correct her. I could fill in the gaps for Phil later, and she knew what she'd done. I could see it in the panicked look in her eyes as she waited for my reply. I settled for squinting my eyes slightly in reproach until I saw a flush spread across her pale cheeks.

"More or less," I said, my voice light and even. I chanced a look at Chris, who was narrowing his own eyes at me. He knew what I was doing, making sure Niamh felt bad, and he was trying to do the same to me. I wouldn't let it work though.

"Oh!" Niamh exclaimed, loud enough that the table next to us looked over in annoyance. "Sophie and Maya say hi, by the way. We all miss you so much."

Sophie and Maya were our other flatmates, and Niamh's uni friends. I hadn't heard from either of them since the day I'd left town, so I doubted they'd actually asked Niamh to say hi to me.

"That's lovely," I said mildly. "Tell them hi back."

We talked for a couple of minutes about the things people always talk about when they meet: Chris bragged about getting promoted at the consulting firm he worked at, and Niamh used an absurd number of acronyms when describing her marketing job, and they talked about the summer holiday they had planned to the French Riviera. Chris was predictably condescending about the part-time data entry work Phil did around caring for Ethel, but I wasn't having it, and I played the part of the proud girlfriend well. It wasn't hard; I'd always thought Phil was a better person than most for how dedicated he was to Ethel. Otherwise though, I let Phil carry the conversation until the waiter came with two flutes of champagne and two glasses of water.

"Well, we've got exciting news to share," Niamh said, "though I'm sure you've seen it on socials already."

I pursed my lips and shook my head. "I haven't really

looked," I said, refusing to acknowledge that I had them both blocked.

"Well..." she said dramatically, then held out her left hand as if she hadn't been talking with it since we'd arrived.

I was so enormously proud of both Phil's and my performances of Unimpressed Man and Unimpressed Woman. I chanced a quick look at him and saw that, like me, he'd creased his brow in confusion, as if the Mount Everest on her finger was the most pedestrian thing we'd seen.

"Oh," I said, sounding underwhelmed, "is that news? We'd already seen the ring – you didn't exactly try to hide it – so I just assumed your news was something else."

Niamh's face fell in disappointment. "Oh, could you see it from outside?"

"I think they can see that thing from space," Phil said, somehow managing not to make it sound like a compliment. "But congrats."

"Thank you," Niamh said, visibly shaking off the awkwardness of her failed announcement. "Anyway, we'd love for you both to be there."

All my impeccable control went to shit as I tipped my head back and laughed. A full-on belly laugh that would have put the jolliest of Santas to shame. It was a good few seconds before I looked up to see that all three of them, Phil included, were looking at me as if I'd broken out in the Macarena.

"Wait, seriously?" I asked, leaning forward to prop my arms up on the table.

"Well yes," Niamh said, taking my hands in hers, and it was everything I could do to not recoil. "You were so instrumental in us getting together."

It was such an outlandish thing to say that I was almost certain she was having me on. Instrumental? If that were true, I should have been their fucking maid of honour. Was it possible that she genuinely didn't know how fucked up her actions had been?

"We'd be honoured," Phil said, reaching around my waist to pull me back away from Niamh and into his side, and I bit my tongue to keep from laughing again. I knew Phil wouldn't be caught dead at anyone's wedding, much less theirs. "When's the big day?"

"The seventh of September at Chris's family's place."

I resisted an eye roll; Chris's family lived in a listed manor not far from Manchester, with enough land to get lost in. His family were unbearably posh, with their waxed Barbour jackets and pedigree spaniels, and their membership at a wellness club dear enough to not list their prices online. I'd only been to the family estate once, and it had been the most fish-out-of-water experience of my life, but I had to admit it would make a beautiful wedding venue.

Just as Niamh launched into an obviously oft-repeated monologue about their wedding plans, I felt a buzz on my left hip. It was Phil's phone in his pocket. I looked up at him to see a panicked look on his face as he answered.

"Everything okay?" he asked, then paused as a muffled voice on the other end of the line said something.

"I'll be there soon," he said, ending the call and pushing away from the table quickly enough that his chair almost tipped backwards.

"Is something wrong?" I asked, standing with him, my hand on his arm in an uncharacteristically intimate way, though the way we had just been pressed together made it feel inconsequential. "It's not Ethel, is it?"

"Afraid so. Anil can't find her new beta blockers, and she needs them before bed." He looked down at Niamh, who had her brow knitted together in concern, and Chris, who looked frankly relieved that the evening had come to a premature end.

"Sorry, folks. Congrats and all, but we've got to call it." He looked back at me again. "You good to walk?"

"We can drive you!" Niamh offered, but Phil waved her off.

"It's okay, it'll take as long to direct you there as it'll take us to walk. But thank you, and lovely to meet you." He grabbed my hand and pulled me towards the front door, and I spared a casual wave back at Niamh as we left.

"See you at the wedding!" she called, and I just pressed my mouth into a thin smile in response.

"God they suck, saying you were instrumental in their twisted little love story," Phil said as soon as we'd rounded the corner outside the bar. He slowed right down, mouth wide as he laughed.

"Yeah, they're the worst," I said, tugging at his arm. "But come on, don't we need to hurry?"

"Oh, no," he said, shrugging me off, and I frowned; apparently the physicality of our little ruse was over. "That wasn't Anil. That was Jack."

I stopped in the middle of the pavement and scowled at him. "Jack? As in, my *brother* Jack?"

Phil laughed. "Yeah, he rings me at half seven every Saturday and pretends to be Anil in case I need an out. I haven't used it in a while, but it came in pretty clutch, didn't it?"

I laughed – I'd never felt more grateful to my brother. But before I could ask more questions, I saw Chris appear over Phil's shoulder, looking around as he left the bar. I grabbed Phil and hissed for him to keep moving, grasping his hand as he tried to wrench it away.

"Amy!" Chris called, jogging after us. I pretended to see him for the first time, turning around as if in surprise.

"Everything okay?" I asked, faux concern in my voice. "Did you need us to chip in for the champagne?"

"We've got it," he said, sounding as smarmy as he looked.

"No, I just wanted to ask you to please actually come to the wedding."

I couldn't help but break character yet again. After all, I didn't really care what Chris thought of me, which is why I'd been fine to come tonight to begin with. The emotions, the act; it had all been for Niamh's benefit, not his.

"And why the hell would I do that? Is that really why you came all the way here?"

"It would mean a lot to Niamh."

"And it would have meant a lot to me for her to not fuck my boyfriend, and yet..."

"Please," he said, catching my eye, and maybe for the first time ever, including when we'd dated, I saw nothing but earnestness in his expression. It was slightly unnerving.

I squinted sceptically. "You really love her, don't you?"

"I do," he said without hesitation. "Not that that makes a difference to you. But I couldn't let you leave thinking it was a throwaway comment, her wanting you there. She's been talking about it for weeks, but she didn't think you'd say yes."

I looked at him for a long moment, not sure how to respond. I didn't want to see them get married, and I didn't actually give a shit about making Niamh feel better when she couldn't even acknowledge how fucked up her behaviour had been.

But it made me miss the life I'd had. I missed Sophie and Maya, even if they didn't actually miss me. It had been a hell of a long time since I'd been invited to something and felt like my presence was actually, genuinely wanted.

"I'll think about it," I said finally. "You know where to send our invitation."

Chris snorted. "Seriously?"

I groaned. "Fuck's sake, Chris. What now?"

He gestured to Phil, who was standing behind me, and I only just noticed that his hands were placed lightly on my hips. Had I really not noticed that happen?

"What?" I asked defensively. "It's not like you and Niamh weren't all over each other in there. Don't tell me you've become a prude in the last ten months."

Chris scoffed. "You really expect me to believe you're with this *townie*? No way. He's not coming with you. Plus ones are for actual partners."

I felt Phil's grip tighten on me, and I placed my hands over his in response. That condescension wouldn't fly, especially not about Phil.

"Come on, Christopher," I said, evening my voice and levelling my gaze at him. "You can't be bad in bed *and* this much of a twat. You have to choose."

His sneer was instantaneous. "Oh, I chose alright."

The double meaning stabbed sharply into me. But instead of reacting with the hurt expression I was sure he was after, I kept my face as calm and neutral as I could.

"If you want me there for Niamh's sake," I said, "you'll send an invite for both of us. Now fuck off back to your fiancée, Chris. You two deserve each other." Then I imagined crossing my fingers that Phil wouldn't kill me for what I was about to do.

I pressed up onto my toes, spun around in Phil's grasp, and brought my hand to his face. We only had a fraction of a second to do this if we wanted it to look natural – hell, even then it would look performative at best – but thankfully, Phil didn't hesitate.

He leaned in and pressed his mouth to mine, and the rest of the world disappeared.

CHAPTER 6
PHIL

Five years ago, I'd nearly kissed Amy Evans.

She'd come home for the summer holidays before her last year of uni, and her mum Patricia had invited Ethel and me over for a barbecue. Jack was still off globetrotting with his evil soon-to-be-ex girlfriend, and whilst Chloe had done a good job of keeping tabs on Amy whilst he'd been away, it had been more than a year since I'd seen her when she walked through her parents' back door into the garden.

Years later, I could still remember exactly what she was wearing – a sage green linen playsuit that perfectly matched her eyes, with white Converse trainers – and the way her blonde hair bunched together, held in a low, loose ponytail with a white satin ribbon. Long gone was the kid who had followed us around for years. It was like it was the first time I'd ever seen her, and I nearly dropped the pavlova I'd made. I'd had to hit the booze immediately to avoid saying something out of pocket.

Unlike when we were growing up, instead of her following Chloe and me around, we gravitated to her. Uni had made her a hell of a lot more confident. She was funny and self-assured and whip smart, and maybe she'd always been that way and we'd just failed to realise it, but we certainly realised it then.

It was only a few weeks, but the three of us became inseparable. We went to outdoor films, rode her Uncle John's quad bikes all over the place, and hung out by the pond where Jack would eventually build his house. She dragged us into her summer fun, and we were just happy to be along for the ride. It was like having Jack back, but different, because where Jack was easy-going and affable, Amy was incisive and instigative.

I also wasn't wildly attracted to Jack.

I'd known that Amy had liked me growing up. It was perfectly normal; I was her brother's best friend, and I'd spent an inordinate amount of time around theirs. But as far as I knew, she'd grown out of her crush when she'd gotten old enough to realise that the weird guy who spent most of his time baking and sewing with the mother figures in his life wasn't actually very cool.

But as the summer went on, it became clear that she hadn't, in fact, grown out of it. And as it turned out, I'd grown into it. Chloe could tell, and she tried to warn me that it might end badly, but I didn't listen. How could I, when faced with someone as mesmerising as Amy?

By the time our last hurrah of the summer came around – another family barbecue that ended with her parents and Ethel inside and the three of us on the drink out back – we'd shared more than a couple lingering looks that told me it was probably safe to make a move. Chloe, possessing a pair of eyes and more than a single brain cell, excused herself, and it wasn't long before Amy and I had found ourselves sharing a sun lounger, looking up at the sky, where there was supposedly a meteor shower on. But I was too intoxicated to see it, both from the beer and from the nearness to Amy. I was certain I'd had more than twice as much to drink as anyone else, trying to psych myself up to risk our newfound friendship.

The critical moment came, and I turned my body to face her fully. My free arm draped across her waist – she was wearing that same sage green playsuit – and she turned to me, too. I brought my other hand to her face, running over her jawline with my thumb. God, she was beautiful. She smiled into my hand and kissed my palm, her face flushing pink, as if underneath all that bravado she was still uncertain whether I'd reciprocate. But reciprocating was the only thing on my mind. I smiled – was this really, truly about to happen? – and brought my face slowly towards hers.

But just a moment before our lips met, she hiccupped, and I could smell the booze on her breath. I pulled away slightly and looked over her shoulder at the pitcher of Pimm's, which had still been mostly full just before Chloe had left, but was now down to the dregs.

I dropped my hand. "Fuck."

"What?" Amy asked, her voice sharp with surprise, and she recoiled from me.

"I can't do this."

Those had apparently been the worst possible words to say, because Amy reacted instantly to them, jumping up from the sun lounger and wrapping her arms around herself as if to hide from me.

"You're such a dick, Phil," she said as she hunted around for her shoes, which she'd kicked off at some point.

"Why?" I asked, sitting up and watching her in disbelief. "Because I don't want to take advantage of you?"

She stopped what she was doing and turned on me, flinging her arms out to the sides so forcefully that the one shoe she had found went flying again.

"Is that what you think? Fucking hell. What do I have to do to get you to see me differently?"

She said the last part almost as an aside, already moving towards the door, abandoning her shoe hunt.

"Well, never mind," she said as she reached the door, stage whispering, presumably so the others inside wouldn't hear her. "Just forget this summer ever happened, okay?" And then she was gone.

~

I spent a lot of the next few years wondering what exactly had gone wrong that night. My best guess was that she'd thought I still viewed her as a kid or something because I'd said I didn't want to take advantage. But she never gave me the chance to correct her. Almost overnight, our relationship whiplashed from hot and heavy to complete strangers, and I didn't speak to her at all for the next year. She moved home after uni once Jack was back, and I started to see her every now and then again, but true to her word, she acted like that summer had never happened, so I tried my best to do the same.

At the worst of times, I wished I hadn't stopped. I wished I'd kissed her anyway, trusting that I hadn't misinterpreted the signals she'd sent me over the preceding weeks. But most of the time, I felt like I'd done the right thing, even if it hurt like hell every time I saw her.

Then she'd moved to Manchester, and I only heard secondhand updates about the asshole she was dating. Plus, Ethel had her fall at around the same time, and a relationship felt like the lowest possible thing on my priority list. So I tried to wish the best for Amy, even if it was far from home. Far from me.

And then she'd moved home again, after the messiest breakup I'd ever been privy to, and yet again it was like she was a different person. Though this time it wasn't necessarily for the better; everything that had happened in Manchester had clearly knocked that confidence I'd loved to see in her. We still bickered, and to my chagrin I still felt high every time she was around. But where she'd always been happy to insert herself into whatever the rest of us were doing, it was like suddenly she needed an engraved invitation to everything. It was why I'd made Fatima invite her to play D&D; no matter how many times Jack, Chloe, and I mentioned it, she never seemed to understand that we were inviting her along. That we wanted her there.

∽

I WAS PRETTY sure she'd forgotten all about that night together; maybe she had been wasted and it was lost to the haze of uni blackout nights, or maybe enough had happened in the intervening period that it didn't even register anymore. And if she could pretend it hadn't happened, so could I.

But now I was kissing her, and it was everything I'd ever dreamt it would be. Not the part about doing it in front of her ex-boyfriend, or on the street, obviously. But her lips were soft and warm just like I'd imagined, and my hands fit perfectly just above her waist where her top rode up slightly, and her fingers wound through my hair at the nape of my neck as she arched into me, and ... oh god, I was gonna need to stop this soon, or she was going to feel just how much I wanted this.

In the end, though, it wasn't that which stopped us. It was someone clearing their throat. I assumed it was Chris, desperate to have the last word, but as Amy and I jumped apart, I was mortified to see that Chris was long gone, and it was Jack and Morgan standing there, eyes wide and smiles splitting their faces.

"Oh my god," Amy said, turning her back to all of us and covering her mouth with her hands.

"Hey, mate..." I started, but I actually had no idea what to say, so I just trailed off awkwardly.

There was a long moment of silence before Morgan

screeched and lunged at Amy, wrapping her in a hug, and Jack laughed.

"Hell yes!" he said, bringing me in for the classic man gesture of clasped hands, arm around shoulders, singular pat on back.

"It's about time!" Morgan said, swaying Amy back and forth in their hug, and we caught eyes over our respective embraces, both equally confused by their responses. Though perhaps we shouldn't have been; I'd been getting a lot of wink-wink, nudge-nudges from Jack over the last year where Amy was concerned. Maybe she'd gotten the same.

"How long has this been going on?" Jack asked, stepping back and gesturing between Amy and me.

"Less time than you'd think," I muttered.

"It's not what it looks like," Amy said, then cocked her head. "And what are you guys doing here anyway?"

Morgan pointed at the bar. "It's the only good place for cocktails around here. Wanna join us? Ooh, double date!" She clapped her hands together in glee.

"We were just going, actually," Amy said, pulling me away by the arm. "Let's go talk, yeah?"

"Yeah, wait a minute," Jack said, holding up his phone. "Why did you answer my rescue call?"

Just then the door opened again, and Chris and Niamh walked out. Instinctively, I reached for Amy's hand, probably out of some ill-placed protectiveness, but she grasped for me too.

"You're still here?" Niamh asked, rushing over, leaving Chris by the door. "You sure you don't need a lift?" Then she seemed to notice who had joined us. "Oh, hi, Jack!"

"Niamh?" he asked, scowling at Amy now. "You were here with Niamh?" Then realisation dawned over his face as he answered his own question about the rescue call.

Amy nodded exaggeratedly, her lips pressed into a line.

"Yep, and Chris is here too," she said, pointing over Jack's shoulder, where Chris was already walking away. "They're getting married."

Jack nodded back, his eyes wide, seeming to catch on. "Got it," he said. "Well, congrats, I guess."

"Oh, thank you," Niamh said, placing a hand on Jack's bicep, and he recoiled slightly at the same time Morgan's face dropped into a frown.

"Let's go, babe," Chris yelled, and Niamh cantered off to meet him.

"See you both at the wedding!" she called over her shoulder to Amy and me as she left.

"Is this for real?" Jack asked, sounding almost hopeful as he looked down at our hands, which were still clasped together. Even then, neither of us dropped the other's hand. What did that mean? "Is this what you've been doing on Saturday nights all this time?"

"Absolutely not. Can we just talk about this later?" Amy asked through a sigh, sounding exasperated. "I need to get home so I'm ready for that site visit in the morning."

She turned to smile at me, stepping in to give me a hug goodbye. There was nothing weird about that on the surface; we hugged all the time these days. But she rested her head on my chest in a way she didn't normally, then brought her lips to the side of my face.

"Can we talk about *that* later, too?" she whispered, then stepped away, and finally our hands broke apart.

I nodded, gulping as I did, before she turned and walked away. I watched her go for a good few seconds before Jack cleared his throat again, and I turned back to him.

"Listen, man, I get it. You wanted to feel it out between the two of you before telling me. Morgan and I did the same thing when we got together." He looped his arm around Morgan and pulled her close. "But for what it's worth, I love this for you both."

"Seconded," Morgan said, lacing her fingers through Jack's. "Now come on, let him go after her."

She pulled Jack towards the bar, and they both waved as they went. Then I was stood on my own on the pavement, wondering what the actual fuck had just happened.

I watched the door for a while, wondering if someone else would come out and keep the circus act going – maybe Poppy, whom I'd left inside on her own, or hell, even Ethel at this point – but it stayed shut, and my thoughts finally came back to me.

I'd just kissed Amy Evans. Like, actually. In real life. Not in my dreams. And it hadn't been a near miss. Her mouth had touched my mouth. Her body had pressed against my body.

But she hadn't kissed me because she'd wanted to. She'd kissed me as a punchline to her back-and-forth with Chris. And despite what Morgan had said, I was almost certain she didn't actually want me to go after her in that moment. So instead, I just started walking home, trying desperately not to let my mind fill in the gaps of what might have happened if I *did* go after her. After all, I had five years of experience getting carried away imagining being with Amy; I didn't need any more.

CHAPTER 7
AMY

I'd known from the moment I'd walked away from Phil, Jack and Morgan that it had been a mistake not to set the record completely straight, but I couldn't help myself; after so many years of being obsessed with Philip Owen, we'd finally kissed, and he hadn't recoiled in disgust. So sue me for enjoying on a perverse level the five seconds where people actually believed we were together.

I could have done without those people being Jack and Morgan, but I figured I could just clear things up with Jack at family dinner the next day. So I let myself put it out of my head as much as possible when I got home, collapsing onto my bed and looking up at the glow-in-the-dark stars Jack and I had pressed onto the ceiling decades ago.

I'd been home for all of ten minutes when my phone buzzed. I nearly leapt on it, hoping it would be Phil, but it wasn't. It was one of my flatmates from Manchester:

MAYA

> Niamh just said you're coming to the wedding?!?! YAY!! Let's catch up soon xxxxxxxxx

I smiled down at my phone, pleasantly surprised she'd texted, before remembering that I wouldn't in fact be going to the wedding. There was no way I could show my face alone after Chris had tried to call my bluff with Phil. So I didn't respond, tossing my phone onto a mess of clean washing on the chair in the corner.

I tried to forget the whole ordeal, but that proved impossible, and after ten minutes of replaying that kiss in my mind, analysing every hand placement and every sensation, I knew I needed to change tack. So I decided to let the fates deal with it instead.

I walked over to my dresser where my crystals were scattered, adjusting the position of a black obsidian tower, which was supposed to be protecting me against harmful energies. Based on what had happened with Niamh and Chris, I wondered if it needed cleansing, so I lit a sage bundle and rested it and my amethyst pendant in the metal bowl in the centre of the dresser surface before passing each of my crystals through the smoke from the sage. Being thorough couldn't hurt.

Once that was done, I picked up my tarot deck and decided on a single card for clarity. I needed to shut my brain up somehow, and typically a reading did just that. Once the cards told me what was what, it was easier to just let it go. Usually, anyway.

I channelled my energy into the deck as best I could as I shuffled, asking the deck for the truth behind that kiss, stopping when it felt right. Then I drew the top card and placed it in front of me on the dresser. The Knight of Swords lay upside down in front of me.

I'd started reading tarot in university, when a friend who ended up being otherwise inconsequential gave me a reading that shocked me to my core with its accuracy. She'd also told me I was something called a Starseed soul – someone who felt out of place because I was a reincarnated space alien – so I took everything she'd told me with a pinch of salt. But I had in fact felt out of place my whole life, like I was constantly trying and failing to fit in, and I'd always been drawn to the stars. So I decided to lean into the parts of astrology and tarot that felt right to me, eventually including crystals. Since then I'd mostly just dabbled in the mystical, but it was one of my favourite parts of my life, even if no one else around me understood it. It made me feel grounded, and like I could make sense of the things that happened to and around me.

The Knight of Swords was an ominous choice, though. When reversed, it symbolised a disregard for consequences, the inverse of nobility. Had it been ignoble of me to kiss Phil? Except, he'd technically kissed me, hadn't he? Was he the ignoble one? What was nobility anyway, and did I actually give a shit if it was noble if it got the job done? If it didn't hurt anyone?

See, this was the problem with one-card spreads. Really I should have asked for more specificity. More insight. But I was tired, and the sun was finally setting, and I could deal with things tomorrow.

DAD HAD LET me go with him on the last few quote visits so I could ask the client clarifying questions in person rather than having to beg Dad for those clarifications. It was especially important on this visit; it was the biggest project he'd ever gone for, and there were a lot of moving parts. A developer from London – a caricature of a finance bro named Tim – had bought an old care home in a suburb called Kenchester and was turning it into flats. It was absurd how much of a stereotype he was; he and Dad even had an extended conversation about how hard it was to find good workers, and whilst I knew from experience that Dad was talking about needing apprentices and young people, I was pretty sure Tim had meant it differently.

The development was huge – there would be nearly fifty units by the time it was done, according to the plans he'd had drawn up – and he had plans for some of the surrounding commercial properties, too, since the development would be relatively isolated. And he was looking for a contractor to manage and execute the entire project, including the future phases. Dad walked around the entire time like a cartoon character with dollar signs in his eyes. But he nearly had a stroke when I told Tim he should think about using vinyl in the bathrooms rather than tile.

"We'd make way more money off tile," Dad insisted when we were back in the van after the visit, shouting over the death metal blaring from his speakers any time the engine was running. I'd made the mistake of reaching for the volume knob once, and he'd nearly taken my hand off.

"Yes, but we don't actually need a tiler for anything else on that project," I said as calmly as I could, and I took great satisfaction from the way his jaw relaxed slightly. "Jerry and Luke can install the big stone panels for the shower surrounds, and the kitchen guys can handle the backsplash since it's just a continuation of the worktops. Plus, the cost of the tile might be higher, but our profit margin is way higher on the LVT."

Dad frowned. "Is that right?"

I nodded, and Dad glared at me as if paralysed by my flawless logic. At least, that was what I told myself.

"Fine," he said, which was the closest he ever came to ceding victory in an argument.

"You know, this job is gonna be massive," I said, chancing my luck. "Loooooads of admin."

He just grunted in response.

"Wouldn't that be easier if you had someone full-time to handle it? Or even twenty or twenty-five hours a week instead of five? If your systems were more integrated, your processes would be more efficient."

"I might hire someone," he said, "if I felt there was someone reliable who could do it. Someone a bit more committed to putting down roots."

"Dad, I'm literally begging you for this work. Would I do that if I had one foot out the door?"

"Unpack the boxes stacked in your room and then we'll talk," he said, then turned the music up even louder – I wasn't even sure how that was possible – and ignored me for the rest of the drive. *Oh well*, I thought. It was more than I usually got out of him.

When we pulled into the driveway at home, we could see Jack and Mum doing garden work, lugging something through the gate and piling it onto the flatbed that usually sat parked behind Dad's workshop. It looked like remnants of Mum's greenhouse stacked there. As we got out of the van, Jack walked through the gate covered in dirt and sweat with a huge plexiglass panel held over his head, shouting for us to move. Mum followed behind with a single pole, maybe a metre long, in one hand.

"You're home!" she said, dropping the pole to the ground and wrapping me in a hug. I cringed in anticipation of getting dirty, but her dungarees were completely clean, confirming that she was using Jack as her workhorse.

"Yep, as planned," I said tightly. "What are you doing?"

"I've planted everything out from the greenhouse, so that ratty old thing could finally come down. Now your father can buy me a new one for Christmas."

"Can I now?" Dad asked, turning around from where he'd attempted to get inside without being roped into the conversation. But he always paid attention when Mum talked about spending money. "Don't we have anything else you'd rather spend that money on?"

"Since you're both here," she said, ignoring him, "what would you like for family dinner later? I'm about to pop out to the shops." Mum had declared last week that Sundays would be family dinner days in an attempt to feel less like ships in the night.

I shrugged. "I'm not fussed. What's easiest for you?"

"Pizza?" Dad asked, and yet again Mum pretended he hadn't spoken at all.

"Remind me," she said, turning to Jack, who was on his way back from the truck. "Morgan's not veggie or anything, right?"

Jack shook his head. "She's not. Why, is she invited?"

"Of course," she said, as if it was the most obvious thing ever. As if it hadn't always been just the four of us. "You did invite her, didn't you?"

"I didn't, but I think she's free." He bent down to pick up the pole Mum had dropped. "Does that mean Phil's coming too?"

Despite the heatwave, my body went cold as ice. *Shit*. I glared at Jack, trying to convince him through my eyes alone to roll back what he'd said, but he was oblivious as usual.

Mum frowned. "Why would Philip come? Unless you're in a throuple now? It's fine if you are."

Jack doubled over with laughter. "Mum, who taught you the word throuple?"

"I know things," Mum said with a shrug.

"Well, you'll be sad to hear that I am not in a throuple with Phil. I don't particularly fancy sharing him with Amy."

SHIT SHIT SHIT.

"Shut the fuck up, Jack!"

"Language, Amelia!" Dad yelled.

"Wait, what am I missing?" Mum asked, looking back and forth between Jack and me. Jack finally met my gaze and gave me a guilty look, and then the twat scarpered off towards the truck with Mum's discarded greenhouse pole.

"Nothing," I said quickly. "Jack doesn't know what he's talking about." But I might as well not have said anything.

Mum gasped. "Are you and Philip together, darling?" Her hands were clenched in fists just below her face like an excited kid. "Is this finally happening?"

"It's really not," I said, just as my traitor brother came back.

"Come on, Ames. I know you were keeping it low-key, but you can't hide it forever. It's not like he needs to meet the parents or anything."

I took a deep breath and decided that, no matter how fun it was to pretend the kiss had meant something, I had to set the record straight once and for all.

"Phil will not be coming to dinner," I insisted, "because he's not my boyfriend. And even if he were, it would be no one's business. I would like to eat whatever is easiest for you to make, Mum, and I'd like you all to back off, please."

I turned on my heels to walk inside, passing Dad, but he put a hand out in front of me before I could make it to the step.

"Amelia Celeste," he said in his patented dad voice.

"What?" I knew I sounded huffy, but I couldn't help it. I could have run Jack straight through with that greenhouse pole.

"Try again."

I swallowed every ounce of my pride and softened my voice, turning towards him but not quite meeting his gaze. "Yes, Dad?"

"Please don't speak to your mother that way."

"I'm sor—"

"—but..." He spoke low enough now that Mum and Jack couldn't hear. In fact, they seemed to have gone back into the garden. "Are you really dating Phil Owen? Because if so, I suppose I owe you an apology."

I frowned. "How's that?" I racked my brain for any time Dad had shown an interest in my dating life, but naturally I drew a blank. It was Mum who was constantly on my case about putting myself out there.

"I've been assuming you were on your way out. That moving home was just a pit stop for you. But if you're putting down roots, I've clearly misjudged the situation."

I felt instantly conflicted. My resolve to correct their misunderstanding dissolved in the face of a rare apology from Dad, especially if there was a chance it would get me what I wanted.

"I'm not planning an escape, I promise." That was true, at least. I didn't have anywhere else to go, and I did like the work I was doing for Dad. I liked the idea of working for him, and of carrying on the family business, in a way Jack never had. Was I completely, irrevocably committed to living in my hometown forever? No. I had nothing else holding me here, which I suppose was his point. But what twenty-five-year-old did feel that level of certainty?

"Then let's try it," he said with a decisive nod. "Twenty-five hours a week, like you said. For three months. *If* it works, we can discuss something more permanent. Save the big ideas for then. You need to show me you can get stuck in first."

Despite how it had come about, I couldn't help but smile. It was what I'd been asking for all along. Just a chance to show that I did want to be here, and I could make a difference at the company.

"Deal," I said, holding up my right hand. Dad actually cracked a smile as he shook it, and I tried not to wince when he gripped a bit too hard.

"Oh, Amy," Mum called as she and Jack came through the gate with their next load of rubbish: another massive panel for Jack, and two smaller poles this time for Mum. "You've got post. Something fancy." She reached into her dungaree pocket on her chest and pulled out a white envelope.

I frowned as I looked it over; it didn't have a stamp, meaning it must have been delivered in person. But once I saw the blue biro addition to the address, I understood. I tore through the custom "N&C" wax seal and pulled out the contents.

Mr & Mrs Declan Kelly
Request the pleasure of your company
At the marriage of their daughter
Niamh Orla Kelly

To

Christopher Henry Arden III
Son of Mr & Mrs Christopher Arden Jnr
on the seventh of September, two thousand twenty-
four at two o'clock in the afternoon
The Arden Estate, Manchester

~

BY THE NEXT AFTERNOON, things had escalated. I got a text from Chloe asking me if I'd ever planned on telling her Phil and I had gotten together, and I knew Jack had taken that conversation with Mum as permission to spread the news to the rest of the group. Which was a problem, first of all because it wasn't true, and second of all because the other person involved was completely unaware of how bad it had gotten. And when I went downstairs to work at the kitchen island to start on the Kenchester job quote, I heard Mum on the phone with Ethel, and I knew we'd reached DEFCON one. I pulled out my phone to text Phil, unable to avoid it anymore.

AMY

I'm so sorry. This wasn't me, I promise. Jack can't keep his mouth shut. Can we talk?

I knew Phil might still be at the art centre with Ethel like every Monday – I may have memorised her schedule from the binder over the course of our Saturdays together – but I hoped I'd get to him before the others, and before Ethel said something.

The reply came just a few moments later:

PHIL

Free whenever you are.

"Mum, I'm taking the car for a bit!" I yelled, running so quickly that my socks slipped on the kitchen tiles and I nearly slid into the front hall. I didn't even listen for a response as I pulled on my trainers and grabbed the car keys off the hall table, doubling back only to grab the discarded wedding invitation as well.

CHAPTER 8
PHIL

Amy didn't message me on Sunday, and I was determined to let her make the first move, so I didn't reach out either, instead settling for staring at my phone instead of getting any work done. The only time I managed to focus on anything else was Monday morning, when I made some very lopsided pain au chocolat – I'd always been able to lose myself when cooking and baking.

Monday afternoon, as we walked through the door from Ethel's class down at the art centre, the landline rang. I knew it was almost certainly for Ethel; the only people who had the number were her friends and telemarketers, and even now she loved having them on. Even when she was having a bad memory day, it worked out nicely, because she'd just spin them round in circles until they gave up. Sure, we'd ended up with a set of expensive kitchen knives and a window washer we probably didn't need given that we lived in a bungalow, but I had to admit those knives cut like a dream.

She walked into the kitchen to answer, and I listened long enough to be able to tell it was a friend rather than a salesperson, then turned my attention to the corset on the coffee table.

It was still in parts; I needed to sew all the panels together, insert the boning, and then shape it. It was for one of Chloe's outfits for the festival, and it had me seriously considering a "no corsets" rule moving forward. I understood why makers online charged so much for them.

But then my phone buzzed, and I realised I had four different messages, all about the same thing. The most recent was from Amy:

> **AMY**
> I'm so sorry. This wasn't me, I promise. Jack can't keep his mouth shut. Can we talk?

A pit formed in my stomach as I opened the next most recent message, which was from Amy and Jack's mum Patricia:

> **PATRICIA**
> I'll pretend to be okay with the fact that you two didn't tell me yourself! 😊 Anyway, I suppose you're officially invited to family dinners, which I'll be reinstating for Sunday evenings. I know you're off on that camping trip next weekend, but the weekend after you can help me cook. Ethel obviously invited too. LOL

I was pretty sure she thought LOL meant "lots of love," despite Jack correcting her several times. I blinked down at the message, trying to piece together what had happened. Why had Amy still not corrected everyone? It was one thing to pretend in the moment outside a bar, but it was another thing to actively lie to her family.

My mind was spinning, but I didn't have a chance to calm down, because the oldest message, from nearly an hour ago, was from Chloe:

> **CHLOE**
> Seriously?????? This is how I hear???? FROM JACK?????

I sighed; okay, that one would need some attention. I texted back immediately:

PHIL

> I promise it's not what it sounds like. I need to talk to Amy, but I promise you're not desperately out of the loop.

The last remaining message was from Grey, sent just a few minutes after Chloe's, and I let out a somehow even deeper sigh when I read it. Despite Chloe being furious that she'd found out about Amy and me through the rumour mill – and despite the fact that it was just that: a rumour – she'd clearly been doing her part to keep it spinning. Grey's message read simply:

GREY

> NICE.

At that point I was surprised it hadn't been shared in our Wench, Please group chat. In fact, it would be so easy to dispel the rumour en masse, I thought. But for some reason, I couldn't quite bring myself to do it before talking to Amy. Before understanding why she'd let it get this far.

So instead, I ignored Patricia and Grey's messages and texted Amy back.

PHIL

> Free whenever you are.

I'd just decided to get the sewing machine out and get stuck in, hoping to distract myself until Amy rang, when Ethel came out of the kitchen, a sad look on her face.

"Hey, what's wrong?" I asked, leaping out of my seat and rushing to her side, taking her arm and guiding her towards her chair. Maybe she'd just learned one of her friends had passed away? I wondered if I should start screening her calls.

She sat down and looked up at me, her already quite wrinkled face further creased in concern. I squatted down next to her, holding her hand in both of mine.

"Philip, my love, I know I don't have the best memory these days."

"That's an understatement."

She swatted my arm. "Cheeky git."

I grinned at her. She preferred to keep things light-hearted, and I had to admit it felt better for me too.

"But really," she said, going serious again. "A lot of things get lost to the Great Sieve that is my brain, but I feel pretty confident that I'm not so far gone I would have forgotten if you'd told me something important."

I narrowed my eyes. "What are you on about, Ethel?"

"That was Patricia on the phone. She said we're invited round for family dinner now you and Amy have finally gotten together."

I groaned. "Ethel, it's not like tha—"

"When were you going to share that with little old me? I know I'm old and senile, but you can't just keep major secrets from me! And with how much shit I give you about finding someone?"

"Okay, that's a bit dramatic," I said, standing up. "You're not fully senile yet."

"It isn't!" she said, standing as well. I didn't like how quickly she bounced up, putting all her weight on one foot to walk over to me.

"Come on, Ethel," I said, gesturing towards her feet. "You're gonna break an ankle again if you're not careful. Last time you were a nightmare for the ten weeks you were in that boot." It had also escalated a lot of her dementia symptoms, but that wasn't helpful to mention.

"Who's being dramatic now?" she asked, doing what looked to be an attempt at the can-can as if to prove her point.

"That is so unnecessary."

"I had no idea you two were a couple, Philip. I feel like a fool."

I sighed, less in frustration than in pity, though I daren't let Ethel know that. "I promise," I said, "if there was something to tell you I would. This whole thing has blown massively out of proportion. We're not actually together."

"Well, maybe you should tell her that," Ethel said, pointing around me. I turned to follow her gaze, and I couldn't help the way my breath hitched when I looked through the open bay window at the front of the room, past the crystals that dotted the low windowsill, to see Amy walking up the front path.

I let her in through the front door, and Ethel immediately pushed past me.

"So good to see you, Amy," she said, wrapping Amy in a hug. "And I should be very cross with you, I know, but I'm just so happy for you both."

Amy's face went red as she caught my eye.

"I'll leave you two lovebirds to yourselves," Ethel said suggestively as she pulled back, disappearing into the lounge.

I reached into the kitchen for the tin holding the leftover pain au chocolat, then led Amy outside into the garden, where the table was still pulled into the middle of the grass from when I'd charged the crystal a few days ago. Instead of moving the table back onto the patio, I pulled the plastic chairs onto the small lawn so we could sit there, further away from any eavesdroppers. I felt a chair leg sink into the grass as I sat.

"Want one?" I asked, pulling the lid off the tin and showing Amy the pastries.

"My favourite!" she gasped, removing one delicately from the tin and immediately sinking her teeth into it. I was particularly satisfied by the crunch it made as she bit into it, but then she moaned in pleasure, evoking a very different idea of satisfaction that I quickly banished from my mind.

"So, Ethel heard," I said. "Your mum told her we're together, and she got mad that I hadn't told her."

"I know," Amy said, her mouth still half full, burying her face in her spare hand. "I swear I told Mum we weren't together, but she thought I was just being secretive. Trying to throw her off the scent."

"Let me guess, Jack?" That guy pretended to be chill, but he could be messy as hell when he wanted to be.

"Yup."

"Listen, about the kiss—" I started, resolved to get to the bottom of things. Had it meant as much to her as it had to me?

"I know," she said, cutting me off. "You were my knight in shining armour with that one. It was probably a bad idea, I know, but Chris just looked so smug, and when he called you a townie..."

I tried not to feel disappointed that she'd brushed it off so quickly. "Yeah, that guy was a prick. I'm not sure what you ever saw in him."

"Honestly? Not much," she admitted, and I frowned.

"How does that happen?" I couldn't imagine for a second that Amy would have had a hard time finding a boyfriend, and she could have done much better. In fact, she couldn't have done much worse, from what I'd seen. I knew the broad strokes of what had happened in Manchester, but I wanted to hear it from her.

"Honestly, it was Niamh who pushed me on him. Looking back, I think she thought he would never like her back, so she was trying to live vicariously through me. And we did all have fun together."

"Were you all friends then?" It was hard to imagine Amy with another group of friends like ours, but she'd lived there for two years after all.

"I was friends with Niamh first from uni," she said. "We were on the same business admin course. It was why I moved to

Manchester. I just wanted to leave, and she had a place there where I could live with her for cheap. She helped me cobble together some part-time jobs so I could support myself."

"Why did you want to leave?"

She shrugged. "All my friends from school had either moved away or settled down, and I just didn't really have a life here anymore. I wanted to start over."

I wanted to tell her she did have friends, but I knew that wasn't strictly true. Things between us had soured a couple of years before she'd left, and it had taken her and Jack a while to form a friendship after he'd moved home. I might have wanted a new start too if I were her.

"Anyway, Chris was friends with our other flatmates, and we all hung out together a lot. I could feel them pushing me on him, and honestly, he can be really charismatic and attentive when he wants to be. So yeah, I guess I liked him. It got weird the moment I moved in with him, though. When it was just us, it became painfully clear that we didn't really have a lot in common. I realised pretty quickly – within a couple of months – that he was cheating on me, and honestly, I know it sounds terrible, but I was kind of relieved. I had a reason why it hadn't worked, and I could move back in with Niamh. She didn't need the rent money, so she hadn't filled my room still.

"But a few weeks later I caught them together, and I realised they'd been sneaking around for a while. And when I tried to talk to our other friends about it, it turned out they all already knew."

I fought back a scowl; it made me furious to think of people treating Amy like that. She could be spiky, sure, but she was one of the most thoughtful people I knew. It was a mystery to me how someone so wonderful could end up surrounded by people who were so awful.

"Anyway," she said, physically shaking it off, and I resisted the urge to reach out and cover her hand with mine. "That's why I wanted to pretend around them. They clearly got off on hurting me, and I didn't want to give them the satisfaction."

"I'm glad you didn't tell me all this beforehand," I said, my jaw still tight. I brought my hand to my chin to loosen it. "I'm not sure I could have been so civil to them."

"Well then I'm glad, too," she said, smiling weakly. "Your complacency was perfect. Niamh was so confused."

"Happy to be of service," I said. "But that kiss—"

She cringed. "Yeah. Sorry about that."

"I mean, I kissed you, technically," I said with a shrug.

"Semantics. I put you in that position. I didn't really give you a choice, did I?"

Oh, I chose, I thought. But it was too close to what Chris had said, so instead I asked, "So what now? We seem to be in a bit of a mess."

"And look what arrived," she said, placing an envelope on the table between us. I could tell just from the weight of it hitting the table that it was a wedding invitation. A bit of chocolate from her finger smudged onto the white paper as she placed it down.

"Fuck," she said, hurriedly trying to wipe it off but just smearing it further.

"That was fast."

"They hand-delivered it," she said. "And look at the names."

It had her name and address written in beautiful calligraphy, and then my name, first and last, added in blue biro next to it, as if it had been scrawled hastily before delivery. I laughed.

"I hadn't expected to be invited by name." I looked over at her and found her looking down at the envelope with a strange expression on her face. She almost looked ... longing?

"Amy," I asked, leaning forward, "do you wanna go to this thing?"

She shook her head vehemently. "Definitely not. I mean,

showing them they didn't hurt me is one thing, but subjecting myself to celebrating their love is another thing entirely."

"Because you know I'd go with you if you wanted me to," I said without thinking, and her gaze snapped up to meet mine. Her brow knitted together in consideration.

"You would?"

"Yeah, I would," I said. *I'd do anything you wanted me to,* I didn't say.

"That'll be fun to explain to our families," she said, laughing. "Once we tell them we're not actually together, and then fuck off to go to a wedding in three months' time."

I laughed too, and nodded. Then I saw movement over Amy's shoulder, and I looked up to see Ethel standing at her bedroom window, shamelessly watching us. She made a kissy face when I looked at her, and I rolled my eyes, shooing her off. Amy turned around to look just as Ethel darted away.

"Oh my god," she said. "She's incorrigible."

"She's been on my case for so long to find a girlfriend," I said. "I think this might be the happiest day of her life."

Amy and I were both smiling, but our smiles faded in tandem as the implication of what I'd said sank in. That if that were true, she'd be crushed to learn that we weren't actually together.

"Was your family happy?" I asked. "When they thought we were together?"

"Honestly," Amy said, "Mum was so excited you'd think I told her she was going to be a grandmother. Absolutely uncalled for."

I couldn't help but smile. Patricia was like a second mum to me. We'd spent hundreds of hours together in the kitchen over the years; she'd taught me everything I knew about cooking. Even up until last year, I'd regularly gone over just to see her.

"And your dad?" I asked, less confident about Alan's reaction. He'd always been pleasant enough, but he was a tough guy, and we had exactly nothing in common.

Amy's eyebrows shot up. "Um, well, he actually gave me a job."

I frowned. "Sorry, what?"

She nodded. "You heard me. He found out we were together – or, well, Jack said we were – and he gave me the job I'd been asking for. Said if I was putting down roots, he'd obviously misjudged me. So now I've got a three-month trial to prove it wasn't a mistake."

"Well shit," I said, sitting back in my seat and sinking further into the grass as a result.

"Chloe's pissed we didn't tell her."

"Yeah, I picked up on that," I said. "Grey, too, which means Fatima almost certainly knows."

Amy let out a sigh. "Wow. So that's reached just about everyone, hasn't it."

"Seems like it," I said quietly, my gears spinning. I was having what I was almost sure was a really, really bad idea. But as I looked up at Amy, she looked almost sad. Was it wishful thinking that maybe she was sad for the same reason I was?

"Can I say something stupid?" I asked, and I didn't miss the way her gaze flicked instantly to mine, her eyes widening slightly.

"I suppose I should be used to it by now."

I rolled my eyes. Even now, of course she was throwing barbs my way. "Fuck off," I said, making her laugh.

"Go on, what were you gonna say?"

I sucked in a breath through my teeth, gathering courage. This was either going to be the most embarrassing moment of my adult life, or ... well, or it wouldn't be.

"What if," I said, and she sat up a bit straighter in her seat, bolstering me, "what if we didn't correct them?"

Her mouth fell open slightly for just a second before she

snapped it shut again. I could tell she was trying to keep a straight face.

"Say again?" she asked, and was it just me, or was she fighting a smile?

I cleared my throat before continuing. "I mean it," I said. "Chloe and Ethel have been on my back for ages about finding someone, and clearly your family is happy about it too. So maybe, at least between now and the end of your trial with your dad, we just ... let them believe it?"

I said it like a question, and really it was. Because I heard myself, and I was ridiculing myself internally even as I spoke. It was absolutely unhinged, the idea of pretending to date someone to keep Ethel and Chloe off my back. Never mind Amy, the woman I'd thought about every day for five years. Whose family was like family to me. Whom I couldn't just casually *date*, because our lives were so entwined that a breakup would have catastrophic consequences ... right?

But I didn't take it back. I didn't turn it into a joke. I just let it hang there between us, watching as Amy's own gears spun behind her eyes.

I imagined having three months where I didn't have to hand Chloe my phone for "swipe time", where no one at Ethel's social groups tried to set me up with their grandkids, where I could hold Amy's hand whenever I wanted to. I'd need to come up with a solution for the very specific kind of tension I always felt after too much time around Amy, but maybe that would be worth it for the rest?

I watched Amy, wondering what her own internal battle looked like. Eventually she sighed and shook her head emphatically. "Bad idea."

I forced out a laugh, half relieved that my stupid idea hadn't worked, and half hurt that she agreed it was stupid. But she wasn't done.

"I couldn't do that to you," she said. "It's way too much."

I frowned. "What do you mean do that *to* me? It was literally my idea."

"Semantics," she said again.

"Jesus fucking Christ, Amy," I said, leaning forward and hanging my head in my hands. This woman annoyed the hell out of me sometimes. "It's not semantics, alright? I said it because I was genuinely suggesting it, and I kissed you outside that bar because I fucking wanted to."

She looked at me wide-eyed, her face flushing, and I felt myself backpedal immediately, deciding I'd better add a qualifier.

"I wanted to help you put those twats in their place. And now I think we can help each other."

She breathed out slowly through her mouth, holding my gaze. It was like she was trying to see if I'd fold; trying to call my bluff. But I wasn't going to, no matter how ill-advised the idea was. Not if there was a chance she'd take me up on it.

"Fuck it," she said, and I grinned. There was the fiery girl I knew.

"Fuck it," I repeated.

"We'll need to set ground rules," she said. "And we'll need to figure out an exit strategy that doesn't explode our whole lives. But if we stay on the same page, it could actually work."

"Definitely," I said, nodding my head.

"And if at any point it's not working, we stop. No big deal."

I smiled, trying to keep it cool and casual. "Exactly. We can just see how it goes. Easy peasy."

"Lemon squeezy," she said back, her own smile tentative, like she couldn't quite believe we were actually having this conversation. Despite having had the mad idea, I was right there with her.

I reached forward and grabbed her hand, holding her gaze. It was genuinely absurd, what we were talking about doing. Lying to the people we loved most. Ignoring our catastrophic shared history. I needed to make sure she was genuinely on board, so I narrowed my eyes at her, waiting.

"So ... we're doing this for real," she said.

I nodded, and I couldn't help but grin. This might be a terrible idea, but I was pretty certain it would be fun.

"Amy Evans," I said, taking a deep breath, amazed that I was saying these words after everything we'd been through. "Will you be my fake girlfriend?"

CHAPTER 9
YORICK PROUDHOLLOW

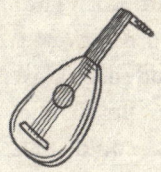

Days later, Yorick was still angry about the incident with the cleric, but his annoyance was eased by the fact that he'd been proven correct. Plus, Eden clearly felt remorse – she'd apologised so many times that Yorick was starting to feel like the one in the wrong. But more importantly, she'd also managed to come through for them with a lead.

Since defeating Lord Arnault months ago – Morgana had taken his head clean off with her sword, so they were certain he was out of the picture – Yorick and his friends had learned that he had been one of an actual council of twelve, each seeking an artefact of great power, with the intention of ascending to take over the world. Yorick thought that was horribly clichéd, but villains were rarely as original as heroes in his estimation.

The party had destroyed a mind control artefact called the Supremacy Sphere when they defeated Arnault, but they still didn't know who any of the other eleven were, or what artefacts they sought. With the cleric dead, they didn't know anything. The only lead her death provided was the tattoo itself.

Unlike any representation of The Twelve they'd seen before, this tattoo shimmered, no matter the light. Eden had known immediately what it was: whatever ink had been used, it had been infused with astral diamonds.

The astral plane was the space between worlds, with portals to other places more wonderful and more terrible than the material plane. A tattoo infused with its rarest material implied a force or entity involved with The Twelve that was further-reaching – and likely more powerful – than any of them had encountered before. Suddenly, Lord Arnault looked tame in comparison to the types of beings they could be up against.

The only intel they could find on the trade of astral diamonds pointed them to a travelling group who often set up camp deep in a nearby forest; a forest known for being dangerous to traverse due to its density and its ferocious wildlife. Gorlag now led them through that dense wood, bushwhacking through the thick undergrowth, followed by Eden, who was navigating them, and Yorick. Calamity walked behind him, probably keeping herself calm lest she start another forest fire with her magic, and Morgana and Ser Liam could be heard bringing up the rear, the clatter of their armour at odds with the sounds of nature waking up around them. It was getting dark; if they didn't find the encampment soon, they would need to make a camp of their own. And given that this forest was notorious for the packs of wolves that roamed it at night, that could be a problem.

"I'm sorry again about the cleric," Eden whispered to Yorick. "You were right. I should have trusted you."

"Trust is earned," he admitted, "and we haven't worked together for long enough for you to trust me implicitly."

"Still," she said as she paused to examine the moss growing up a tree, then redirected Gorlag with a tap on their shoulder, "I'm not used to the way you all do things. I'll try to follow your lead a bit more."

Yorick smiled to himself. He was so rarely deferred to – whether it was his diminutive stature or his accommodating disposition, he wasn't sure – and it felt nice. But he knew that he could stand to make more of an effort with Eden, too. Trust worked both ways.

Suddenly Eden froze, and Yorick nearly ran into one of her long legs.

"Do you hear that?" she whispered, pointing into the forest. Yorick tried to focus, but it took a moment for him to hear what she had heard. When he did, though, he was amazed he hadn't heard it before. Clearly audible over the rustle of leaves and the chirping of insects were the unmistakable sounds of people: laughter, the clatter of dishes and cutlery, the thwack of someone chopping wood. He could even smell the smoke now, and something meaty cooking over the fire.

"Nice one," he said to Eden, smiling up at her as she beamed. They all turned to head in that direction, Yorick's stomach grumbling in anticipation of whatever he could smell.

But just as the orange blaze of a campfire flickered into view between the trees, a bird perched on a nearby branch began to squawk and flap its wings. It set off an almost identical-looking one on a tree a few paces away, and then another one beyond that. Within a couple of seconds, there was a cacophony of cawing, and the din of the encampment went quiet.

Then the rustling in the underbrush intensified, and a panic settled over Yorick. Because the people in the camp were now the least of their worries.

CHAPTER 10
AMY

In the cruellest of ironies, my teenage dream of being Phil Owen's girlfriend had come true, but I didn't get to enjoy it, because it wasn't real. In fact, it started out downright clinical, with the creation of four rules.

Rule one was mine: no unnecessary PDA.

"Don't be naive," he said, rolling his eyes. "Have you never seen a rom-com? There will be mistletoe somewhere."

"Phil, it's June. We couldn't be further from mistletoe."

"Then a one-bed trope at the very least."

My mouth went dry at the thought of sharing a bed with him. I couldn't think of why that would come up, but he was right – if we didn't think about it, the universe would almost certainly force us to deal with it at one point or another.

"That's why I said *unnecessary* PDA," I said. "I don't need you hanging all over me." I pulled a face, hoping to communicate disgust at the idea, but really, I just didn't want to get confused like I had the other night at the bar. I wasn't convinced I'd be able to keep things straight if the snuggling and hip hugging and kissing became a regular occurrence.

Phil looked affronted but agreed anyway; no unnecessary PDA.

Rule two was about dating other people. For the duration, we would be exclusive. This meant I couldn't date anyone, of course, though that was no skin off my back given my complete lack of romantic life. But it also meant Phil had to give up "swipe time" and his Saturday night dates.

He agreed to this more readily than I'd expected, saying that it really didn't make sense to let it continue in a small town like ours if we'd any hopes of maintaining the illusion.

Which brought us to rule three.

"We haven't exactly spent a lot of time together, just the two of us," I said. "When are we supposed to have gotten together?"

"You heard your brother," Phil said. "As far as he knows, we've been spending every Saturday together when you've been here with Ethel."

That was true, though there was one witness who could contradict that.

"Won't Ethel know that's not true?"

Phil's face fell. "I mean, I hate to say it, but..."

"You think she won't remember?" Yikes. It did suck to admit, but it was probably true.

"Probably not. We can fix it when it comes up if she does, but I suspect she won't look that closely at it anyway."

I tapped my finger against the table, thinking. "So when did we get together?"

We decided to keep a shared note on our phones called "Our Lore". If either of us made something up about the relationship, we would add it to the note so the other person didn't get caught off guard. So when we decided we'd been together for just two months – any longer and it would have been rude not to fill in our friends and families – into the note it went.

And then finally, the fourth rule, which was the most

practical, but somehow felt the most uncomfortable to talk about. When we broke up after my trial with my dad ended, we'd need to do so in a way that didn't make either of us the bad guy. That made it plausible that we could continue to exist as friends. So we'd work together for the next three months to come up with something that made sense.

By the time we'd agreed on our rules, I had to leave; I hadn't exactly gotten permission to drive Mum's car, and I knew she had book club in an hour. Phil walked me inside where I said goodbye to Ethel, and she thanked me for the pretty new crystal, requesting a blue one next time. I immediately thought of blue calcite and kicked myself for not having brought it sooner; calcite was the stone of the mind, and I was pretty sure I had a blue one on my dresser. I promised her I would bring it on Saturday.

"I'll be camping," Phil reminded me, and my smile slipped. That stupid fucking camping trip. "But why don't you come to the pub quiz tomorrow?"

I scrunched up my nose. I hadn't realised those plans had solidified; no one had told me. "I'm rubbish at trivia."

"So?" he said with a shrug. "Me too. Besides, the point isn't to show off our general knowledge. It's to hang out. I think it would make sense for my girlfriend to be there, don't you?"

Ethel watched our conversation, looking back and forth between Phil and me as we spoke, her face a picture of glee. I felt a pang in my side – would it feel like betrayal every time we pretended in front of people we loved? If so, it would be a looooong summer.

"I guess we could use it to hard launch, if you're ready for that."

"Absolutely," he said, almost too quickly.

"Okay, deal," I said, then gave Ethel's arm a pat and moved to walk past Phil and leave. He reached out and grabbed my hand as I walked past, pulling me back to him. My breath caught in my throat as he caught me with a hand around my waist and levelled his gaze with mine. For a moment, I thought he would kiss me again – would he flagrantly break our first rule so soon? – but instead he just pulled me in for a hug. Like he'd done dozens if not hundreds of times over the years, but for some reason it felt different. Like he was holding me differently.

"See you then," he said softly, and then he released me.

~

THE FATES HAD EVEN LESS of an idea what to make of the situation than I had; every reading I did over the next few days seemed to say something different. I drew major arcana over and over, which I usually found helpful because they steered my interpretation so heavily, but with cards like an upright Emperor (authority, structure, order) next to a reversed Hierophant (rebellion and subversiveness), my interpretations were all over the place. To be fair, we had tried to impose as much structure and order as possible – on my part, at least, it felt like a helpful way to keep it distinct from a real relationship – but my emotions were still all over the place, which didn't help my readings.

My horoscopes were no more helpful, but the one that popped up on my phone the evening after I'd seen him was ominous as hell:

The higher your hopes, the farther you can fall if they don't happen. Be realistic.

Great. Even my random horoscope app was telling me this was a terrible idea. But I was usually such an over-thinker that I figured I was due a bit of cognitive dissonance, so I decided to pretend like everything was fine.

Dad had asked me to write up a job description for my trial

period, so I tried to get started, but just as I opened my laptop, my phone buzzed with a text from Phil:

> **PHIL**
> Daily Phamy lore drop #1. When you asked me out for the first time (because you definitely were the one to ask me out), I thought you were making fun of me somehow and said no.

I laughed out loud. Honestly, it was more likely to have been the other way around, but fine; we were making things up anyway, weren't we? And I didn't hate the insinuation that he had some sort of emotional stakes, even if it was only in this fictional relationship we were concocting.

I checked the shared note, and sure enough Phil had added that tidbit as the first entry.

> **AMY**
> Is Phamy our ship name? I don't know how I feel about that.

> **PHIL**
> Embrace it. I've already doodled it all over my journal.

> **AMY**
> Fine. But I get to drop lore too.
>
> You realised your mistake very quickly and were then the one to ask ME out, and I said no back out of spite. So instead of a first date, we just made out angrily in your front hallway.

> **PHIL**
> Honestly? That feels right.

I tried to turn my attention to my job description, but unsurprisingly, I failed. I'd spent every day of my preteen and teenage years fawning over Phil to no avail, and then after what had happened five years ago ... well, needless to say, I found it hard to believe that we were documenting relationship lore, fake or not. So much of the angst I'd felt about him over the years had been about how embarrassing he'd found me. Now, even if it was all for show, he was not only *willing* to be associated with me, but even *contributing* to that appearance. It was strange and bittersweet.

The only thing that managed to snap me out of thinking about it was when my phone buzzed again, this time with a notification that I'd been added to a group message called "Niamh's Hen Party!!!!! " I wouldn't have thought anything could stop me reaching for my phone constantly, but that did the job.

THE NEXT DAY, as I tried to work on the quote for the Kenchester job, my focus was even worse, knowing I'd be seeing Phil in the evening to hard launch the relationship. Jack messaged me to say he was excited I was coming along, and I knew everyone had heard about Phil and me anyway, but I was still nervous. It would be the first true test of our acting skills.

Phil messaged midway through the day this time:

PHIL

Daily Phamy lore drop #2. We've outlawed the game Ticket to Ride in our relationship because you get mad every time I take a route you need, regardless of whether I need it too.

AMY

Fine, but we've also outlawed Cluedo because I once caught you cheating by looking in the envelope as I was coming back from the loo.

We broke our first rule almost immediately on Tuesday evening when Phil flung his arm around my waist as we walked into the pub. He did ask if it was okay, to be fair, but I wasn't sure it qualified as necessary. I wasn't mad about it though; like at the bar on Saturday, being held by him felt somehow stabilising. So I snaked mine around his middle, too.

Chloe was the first to clock us – unsurprising given that she was craning her neck to watch the door – and the rest of the group erupted in cheers when they saw us walk up with our arms around one another. This of course made my face and neck go fully pink.

I sat down in one of the two empty chairs they'd pulled up, and Phil reached down to grab two of the legs, pulling it so forcefully towards him that it made a loud scrape against the floor, until my side was pressed fully to his. Chloe and I exchanged a wide-eyed look – apparently she was just as giddy as I was over the whole thing, if not more so.

But even with the physical contact – and Phil did initiate a surprising amount of it, mostly casually like an arm on the back of my chair – I felt surprisingly at ease. Despite their initial uproar, the group was acting ... well, normal. Like Phil and me being together was already old news. And whilst my pride was a little hurt that they didn't want every sordid detail of our supposed love affair, it did feel nice to know that they were comfortable enough with it to just accept it as canon with no real question.

Our team – Presti-quiz-itation, named by my very hilarious and not at all cringey boyfriend after a D&D spell – managed second place in the quiz, which meant we could have a free round the next week. Naturally, this made us decide to commit to the whole summer series.

I'd come with Jack, so Phil and I had to say goodbye in front of everyone, and that nosy bitch Chloe was absolutely watching from a few feet away as he pulled me in for a kiss on the cheek, whispering to ask if it was okay before he pressed his lips to my skin.

When he pulled back, I reached into my shorts pocket and gave him the little blue calcite for Ethel. I was surprised when he asked of his own accord if he needed to charge this one.

~

HIS MESSAGES STARTED EVEN EARLIER the next day:

> PHIL
>
> I have your daily lore drop, but I feel I need to open with the fact that the others now assume you're coming on the camping trip this weekend. And the fantasy festival next month, actually, but we can deal with that later.

"Fuck," I whispered at my phone. Mum had tried hard to instil a love of all things outdoorsy in us, but unlike my brother Mr Outdoorsman, I'd never understood the appeal of sleeping in a tent, no matter how many times I'd been forced to do it. The festival would probably be more fun, but in the meantime, I wasn't thrilled about having to traipse through the mud for the appearance of dating Phil.

But, whilst it would have been nice to get an actual invite, I didn't hate the idea that my presence was assumed. Even if I was almost certain Morgan had been the one to instruct Jack that I should come, remembering the way she'd looked at me on Thursday after reminding Phil about the trip.

> AMY
>
> Looks like we'll be encountering that one bed trope sooner than expected.

PHIL

> Seems so. You okay with that?

Was I okay with that? Holding Phil's hand was one thing, but spending the night together? That was another thing entirely. But he double texted before I could sort out my response.

PHIL

> Actually nvm, I've got a really small tent, and Jack says yours is small too. So I think we can get away with sleeping separately.

I tried to ignore the duelling emotions of disappointment and relief doing battle in my gut.

AMY

> Are you with my brother rn??

PHIL

> He's got the day off so we're playing video games. He's out talking to Ethel right now though, so I've got plenty of time for…

> Daily Phamy lore drop #3. The angry hallway makeout happened on your birthday weekend. I know we said two months, but I thought it would be helpful to have exact timing.

AMY

> Why my birthday weekend?

I didn't disagree that we needed to know when exactly we'd gotten together, but it was slightly depressing that I'd had so little going on for my twenty-fifth birthday weekend that I could have plausibly been at his.

> **PHIL**
> It was the first weekend after I last answered Jack's emergency call.

> **AMY**
> Been ending your dates yourself like a big boy, have you?

> **PHIL**
> Bonus lore drop: your pet name for me is "big boy."

> **AMY**
> Big boy is what does it for you? Really?

> **PHIL**
> Hey, come up with something better and we'll talk.

I deleted the part of the shared note that said "Amy's pet name for Phil is big boy", but it reappeared almost as soon as I'd removed it.

~

I TRIED to tackle the mess that was Dad's invoicing. I'd planned to do it across Thursday and Friday, working a half day each, but since I was apparently going to be spending Friday wandering into the wilderness, I had a full workday ahead of me. But not before Phil could send through what had quickly become my favourite part of each day:

> **PHIL**
> Daily Phamy lore drop #4. We haven't used the L-word yet.

That one made me frown. When would that come up with anyone else? But I didn't hate the idea of defining just how serious we were. We'd known each other long enough that, without doing that, the others might assume we were basically married immediately after getting together.

> **AMY**
> Seems sensible. But to clarify, we absolutely have had sex.

> **PHIL**
> Well obviously. I'm only human. But maybe let's skim over that detail around your brother?

> **AMY**
> BTW, found my tent in dad's workshop, and it is indeed too small to share.

> **PHIL**
> Mine too! Look at us, avoiding the one bed trope like a couple of pros.

> **AMY**
> Yes, my vast fake dating experience has prepared me for this moment.

> **PHIL**
> Really? I learned from cheesy Christmas rom-coms where they get snowed in at the local B&B run by a poorly disguised Santa.

> **AMY**
> You and Ethel really need to stop watching those.

> **PHIL**
> Or maybe you need to START watching those with us…

My head went pleasantly fuzzy at the thought of Phil, Ethel, and me watching cheesy films together come Christmas, but then I remembered that we'd be long broken up by then. So instead of egging him on, I left his last message on read.

DATE KNIGHT

THE NEXT DAY, I sat in the front seat of Jack's Land Rover Defender, exchanging looks of horror with Phil through the rear-view mirror as he huddled in the middle seat. Jack was belting in what I think was meant to be a harmony with Fatima, who was sat directly behind me. They were both completely tone deaf, though, so they could have been attempting to sing the same notes. I couldn't be sure.

"What even is this?" I yelled to Morgan, who sat behind Jack, looking only slightly less shellshocked than Phil and me.

"The soundtrack for the musical episode of *Buffy the Vampire Slayer*. They're obsessed."

I breathed out as slowly as I could, attempting to centre myself through the noise. I decided to distract myself by texting Phil; I'd been thinking of what to contribute to our fictional history. He'd have to hide his screen well, but Morgan was staring out the window, presumably trying to dissociate, and Fatima seemed thoroughly engrossed in her Broadway debut.

AMY

> Daily Phamy lore drop #5: we've watched every single Meg Ryan film together in my attempt to educate you on non-Christmas rom-coms.

PHIL

> Hey, initiating the lore drops are my job! What if I already had one ready?

AMY

> Go on then, what are you waiting for?

PHIL

> Daily Phamy lore drop #5: we've watched every single Meg Ryan film together in your attempt to educate me on non-Christmas rom-coms.

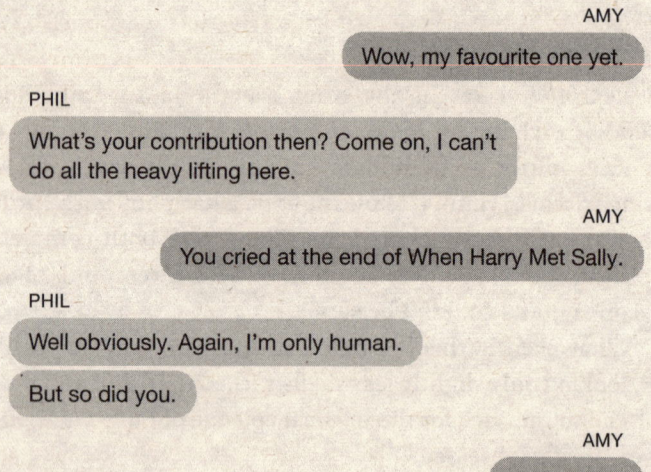

A few hours later, I was slogging along the trail, remembering acutely why I hated camping, and we hadn't even made it to the site yet. My boots were so covered in mud that it was starting to soak through my socks – how was it so muddy when it hadn't rained in weeks? My backpack was so heavy with my tent, chair, and everything else that I was sure I was sinking twice as far into the sodden ground as I otherwise would.

Jack kept apologising for not realising the trail was so muddy, but I wasn't mad at him. Not for that. For wanting this bullshit for a birthday celebration? Sure. For having a hot best friend that I was so obsessed with growing up that I jumped at the chance to be his fake girlfriend, resulting in being on this cursed trip to begin with? Sure, I could find a way to make that his fault. But he was carrying all the food and booze for the weekend in his backpack, so I couldn't really complain.

But once we got to the camping spot, a sheltered area at the edge of a disused reservoir, I started to get it. The ground was dry here, so once I got my sandals on, it was actually really nice. Phil and I set up our tents close together because that felt like an obviously couply thing to do, and the tent was much easier to set up than I'd remembered. Then we sat in our camp chairs and watched everyone else together. Phil was clearly having a great time; I could see his smile, even behind his beard.

"You gonna keep that?" I asked, lifting my hand to touch it, but deciding that was too intimate and bailing at the last second.

He brought his own hands to his face and rubbed the beard self-consciously.

"What, you don't like it?" He looked genuinely distressed by the thought.

"I didn't say that." It was the closest I could get to "actually it makes you somehow even hotter than you've always been" without shrivelling up in shame.

"I knew it," he said, stretching his legs out and looping his fingers together behind his head. "The beard does it for you."

"I also didn't say *that*." I'd very intentionally chosen *not* to say that, thank you very much.

Once everyone had set up camp and Jack had managed to get a small campfire going, we all dragged our chairs around it and got out our dice and character sheets. Fatima handed me the extra set of hers I'd used last time.

"We'll have to get you your own set," Phil said as he settled in next to me.

"I don't want to buy any until I know I'm sticking with it."

"Well, you're locked in for at least three months," he said quietly, leaning in close so the others wouldn't hear.

"That wasn't one of our rules."

"Is now."

"Fuck's sake," I said sarcastically. "Pub quizzes, camping trips, D&D campaigns ... what other activities have I unwittingly committed to?"

The next morning, I woke up nice and late to the screeches of Chloe and Morgan jumping into the reservoir. I'd never been here before, but I could tell from their shrieks that it must be frigid. Still, growing up with an older brother had taught me that I'd end up in that water one way or another, so I changed into my swimming costume and a pair of shorts before leaving my tent. After a side quest to take care of the usual morning business, I was greeted by Phil with a camp mug of coffee.

"What was that about no L-bombs?" I asked, taking it happily. "Because I might be about to drop one if you keep handing me coffee."

"Noted," he said, clinking his tin mug against mine. Then he leaned in close to my ear and lowered his voice so it rumbled all through me, despite the fact that everyone else was down by the water. "Can I greet you good morning?"

"Uh, sure?" I didn't know what that meant beyond just saying "good morning", but he'd just caffeinated me, so I supposed I could go along with it, especially since Jack was sat over by his tent not-so-subtly watching us.

I felt his hand run along my back and wrap around to my opposite hip, pulling me towards him as he brought his lips to my temple.

"Good morning," he said with a smile. "Did you sleep okay?"

"Surprisingly so," I said as calmly as possible, clearing my throat, grateful again that Phil and I hadn't had to share a tent if even an innocent "good morning" gesture had me this flustered. "You?"

He nodded. "Yeah, fine." He lifted his mug towards the water, where Grey was attempting to drag Fatima off the small dock. She was putting up a good fight, but now Jack was headed over too, presumably to help Grey, so she wouldn't last long. Phil didn't move his arm though.

"You gonna go for a swim?"

"Not if I can help it," I said with a grimace. "You hear how high-pitched they've gone? That water's twelve degrees at most."

"You'd better stay clear of Jack then," Phil said, just as Jack helped Grey hoist Fatima overhead and chuck her in.

∽

I managed to stay dry most of the day somehow, even when Phil tried to entice me in, but as the temperature rose throughout the afternoon, the reservoir looked more and more tempting. Jack, Grey, Morgan, and Phil went for a hike, and I stayed behind with Fatima and Chloe, who were helping me think through what other characters I could play whilst we sunbathed on the dock.

"Honestly, a wizard would be helpful," Chloe said. "Especially as we get to higher levels, they're really powerful."

"Is level eight not high?"

Chloe shook her head. "It goes all the way to twenty."

Fatima tipped her head back and laughed, almost maniacally. "You're not getting to level twenty," she said. "That would be a nightmare to run. You'll be lucky if I let us get past twelve."

I liked the idea of a powerful magical character, but I wasn't sure how that would work with the numbers I'd been given. "I've got my highest score in wisdom, right?" I asked. "Would that work for a wizard, too?"

"The wisdom bonuses are coming from your race," Fatima explained. "Lauren probably picked a wood elf because the wisdom bonus went well with being a druid, which uses wisdom for casting spells. But a wizard uses intelligence."

"I like being a druid," I said, not realising until right then that it was true. "It feels mystical."

Chloe smiled. "Very on brand."

"You should just tweak the build," a voice said from behind me, making me jump. I looked up to find Phil towering over me, apparently back from the hike. "Change your subclass and subrace."

"I have no idea what that means," I said as he crouched down next to me, putting a hand on my shoulder for stability. He'd changed out of his hiking gear and back into his swim trunks, and I took advantage of the privacy of my sunglasses to check him out.

I hadn't seen him shirtless in years, and his tangle of chest hair had grown, a dark shadow over his barrel chest. He'd never been particularly chiselled, but I had no doubt he could pick me up and throw me around if he were so inclined, which was dangerous given how close I was to the water. I had to admit it very much did it for me, and I let my eyes wander, following the trail of dark hair to where it disappeared into his swim trunks, which stretched tight across the tree trunks he passed off as thighs.

"When we're back," he said, "look up Circle of Stars and Astral Elf. You'll love it."

"If you say so." I looked reluctantly back up at his face, where he wore a cheeky grin.

He pointed at Fatima. "Now you. I heard you were talking shit about me."

Fatima shrugged. "I mean, you looked pretty slow earlier."

"Put your money where your mouth is."

Fatima sprang instantly to her feet and dove into the water in one fluid motion, emerging into a precise front crawl.

"Oh and babe," Phil said, turning to me, letting Fatima increase her lead. "At this angle, I can see through your sunglasses."

I stared mortified at him, my entire body flushing as I realised he'd seen me checking him out. Then he stood up and cannonballed in, taking off after Fatima in a ... doggy paddle?

Plea for rescue? Whatever it was, it was inelegant at best when compared to Fatima's expert stroke.

"Oh, he *like* likes you," Chloe said, and I looked round to see her smiling as she watched the race.

"What are you on about?"

"Circle of Stars is a druid subclass where you cast magic based on star charts and constellations."

My mouth fell open. "Oh shit."

"Oh shit indeed. And Astral Elves are literally described as having stars in their eyes. He's thought about that."

"Wouldn't that be a bit too much of a self-insert?"

"I mean, Morgan's character is literally called Morgana. I feel like we're past that."

I couldn't help but grin as I wondered how much time Phil *had* put into thinking about that. Given that we hadn't talked about it at all, it meant he'd been thinking about my character – thinking about *me* – when he didn't have to. For an actual boyfriend, it would have been below the bare minimum. But for a fake boyfriend ... yeah, it was kind of cute.

"Where did the others go?" I asked Chloe, ready to change the subject.

"Jack and Morgan are over there," she said, pointing to the other side of the reservoir, where they sat on top of the hill side by side. Jack had his tablet out, no doubt sketching a house – he'd made being an architecture student at least half his personality – and Morgan sat reading a book.

"But tell me," Chloe said excitedly, scooting closer to me, clearly not ready to let me brush past what she'd said. "How long has this Phil thing been going on? I can't believe neither of you told me!"

"A couple of months," I said, trying to sound as casual as possible. "And I don't know, maybe because you guys have proven that you can't keep your mouths shut?"

"Yeah, but that's them," she said, gesturing vaguely towards camp. "I was *there*. That summer when you two spent every free moment eye fucking each other and then it just ... didn't happen."

I felt my stomach plummet at the reminder of that summer. That night. I'd spent so long trying to forget about it; trying to rewrite what had happened in my mind. I'd been so drunk, but I'd also been so certain that it was finally going to happen. And I'd been so angry afterwards, most of all at myself.

"I don't want to talk about that summer," I said, shaking my head. "It wasn't the right time is all."

"I don't know," Chloe said. "I really thought it would happen. I guess you were really young still."

I couldn't help but sigh in frustration. I hated that excuse. "I'm five years younger than you lot. It shouldn't be weird at this point. Sure, it would have been weird if he'd liked me back when I was fifteen. Even then I knew that deep down. But that summer, we were both adults, just like we are now."

Chloe held up her hands in surrender. "You're right. I agree. And for what it's worth, I agreed that summer, too."

"Plus," I said, not quite ready to let it go, "that's basically the same age gap as Morgan and Jack." I waved towards them sat up on their hill, the light shining perfectly down on them like a storybook cover.

"Yeah, they're disgustingly cute," Chloe said, "but I'm sure they'd kill for the shared history you and Phil have. You got there in the end, didn't you?"

I huffed out a breath, not sure what to say. Because to everyone else, yeah, it looked like we'd overcome that awkwardness. But really, I knew that deep down Phil must still see me as a kid. It was why he hadn't kissed me five years ago, and who knew, maybe it was why he'd never looked twice at me in the years since then.

Or maybe he had actually liked me back then like I'd

thought, but he didn't anymore. My years in Manchester had changed me, after all, and not necessarily for the better.

But to Chloe, and to the rest, they just saw what they thought was a happy ending to the whole thing. I hadn't thought of that downside yet somehow, for all the ruminating I'd been doing. It felt slightly invalidating; as if all the hurt feelings and mixed signals were being paved over by the fact that we seemed to be past it. As if I couldn't feel hurt about it anymore. Just like Niamh, hoping her happy-ever-after undid all the hurt she'd caused to go after it.

"I don't know," I said finally. "Sometimes that shared history feels like pressure. Like, what happens if it doesn't work out? He's been part of the family since he was eleven. That's one messy breakup."

"Jesus," Chloe muttered. "Nothing like planning for the breakup whilst you're in the relationship."

You have no idea, I thought.

"Look," she continued, clearly winding up for a pep talk. "I've seen you moon over him most of your life. I understand why you're anxious about it. But if you're too close-fisted, your fear will turn into a self-fulfilling prophecy."

I sighed. She was right; Phil and I had the summer together, and I didn't want to make it weird by stressing about things that were actually nonissues. We didn't have to worry about the fallout from our inevitable breakup because we both knew it would happen, and we could work together to keep it from getting messy.

Chloe looked out at the reservoir suddenly, and I could hear splashing nearby, but I couldn't bring myself to look at Phil in that moment, so I just kept my eyes fixed on the dock in front of me.

"For what it's worth," Chloe added, standing up, "I may ship Phamy, but I'm team Amy at the end of the day."

I laughed. "Phil calls us Phamy too. Is that seriously our ship name?"

"Don't change the subject," she insisted. "I'm trying to be sentimental."

I held my hands up in apology. "Sorry. Go on."

She took a deep breath before slipping back into serious mode. "I mean it, Amy. Phil and Jack are my best friends, but you're my sister. And no matter what happens, that won't change."

I smiled up at her, genuinely touched. She was right; she was like my big sister. She'd been there for me when Jack had been away, and even after what had happened with Phil. She'd always had my back.

For a moment, I seriously considered telling her the truth. Maybe having someone else who knew the situation would help make it less of a mindfuck.

But then she had to go and betray me.

"Now!" she yelled, lunging for me, and I realised too late what was happening. She grabbed one foot as Fatima grabbed the other, and I felt a familiar pair of hands around my waist. I fought back, screaming through my laughter for them to put me down, but it didn't work. Of course it didn't. So I relaxed and let them chuck me off the dock and into the reservoir, only regretting that decision when I hit the icy water.

CHAPTER 11
PHIL

I'd made a huge mistake going into the camping weekend. I'd asked Anil to message me every couple of hours to let me know how he was getting on – it was my first overnight away in months, and Ethel's needs had evolved a lot in that time. But now I was just having mini heart attacks each time my phone buzzed, only to find a text from Anil saying something inane like "all good here" or "still doing fine".

"Thanks again for moving the campsite," I said to Jack as I turned the potatoes over on the fire.

"Mate, I'm just sorry I didn't think of the signal issue to begin with. And this spot's way better anyway."

He took the tongs from me when I was done, then handed me the pot of beans he'd decanted. Camping food wasn't glamorous, but I was looking forward to a jacket potato after a long day. All we'd had for lunch had been peanut butter sandwiches and crisps, so I'd packed two potatoes each for dinner. I hadn't been the one to have to carry them, after all.

"It's a good spot, isn't it," I said as I looked out at the dock, where the others had set up their chairs to avoid the smoke. The sun was still high – it was nearly the solstice, so it wouldn't set until nine-thirty-ish – but we were headed into golden hour, and I couldn't help but watch Amy as she tipped her head back and laughed at something Chloe had said. She looked over then, and she was far enough away that I couldn't be certain, but I was almost sure she was looking right at me.

I could feel her eyes on me more than ever, and it was hard to know if that was new, or if I was only just now noticing it because I was spending more time looking at her. It reminded me of that summer a few years ago, which I didn't love, but it was also exciting. I mean, I'd literally caught her checking me out earlier, which had felt ... nice, maybe? I didn't actually need her to be attracted to me, but it didn't hurt.

I could feel everyone else's eyes on us, too. They weren't being obnoxious about it, and I didn't blame them. I'd never brought a woman around them before. It also didn't bother me as much as I'd thought it would, maybe because it was a performance rather than the real deal. But the scrutiny didn't go unnoticed.

Once the potatoes were done and the beans were bubbling away, we called everyone over for dinner, and they all dragged their chairs back up the hill.

"No cheese?" Grey asked, the last one to emerge from the water to get their food, turning the corners of their mouth down.

"Do you fancy a hunk of cheddar that's been sat outside for thirty-six hours in a heatwave?"

"True," they said, happily accepting the beans and spring onions they were offered instead.

Amy sat in front of Chloe, who plaited her hair into pigtails as they waited for their food to cool down a bit. Fatima was scrolling on her phone, also appreciating the signal, and the volume was low enough not to be obnoxious. But what *was* annoying was Chloe echoing every sound as it came up.

"How is there even signal out here?" Amy asked.

"It's the 5G chip implanted in my head, obviously," Grey said, sitting down next to her on a towel on the ground.

"Of course," Fatima said without looking up. "Because you're a government experiment, not a real person."

"Damn right," Grey said, blowing on their food. "And don't you forget it. I'll be invaluable in the inevitable robot uprising."

Jack came over with a round of drinks, and Chloe squealed and nearly spilt her hot beans down Amy's back when she realised it was cans of her favourite mead.

"Careful," I said. "That's my girlfriend you nearly scalded."

"That's so weird still," Chloe said, but I saw her check over Amy to make sure she hadn't actually spilled anything on her.

I caught Amy's gaze and tried to decipher what I was seeing. She looked caught, like a deer in the headlights. For someone so self-assured, she would need to work on her acting skills if we were going to get away with this for three whole months. This was light work; our friends could have been much more ruthless with their teasing, and I suspected they would be at some point. And if she caved and told one of them...

Funny, every time I'd thought about things going wrong, it had been between Amy and me. I hadn't thought about how everyone sat around me would feel finding out we'd been lying to them. If I found out any of them had pulled this, I'd be miffed at the very least. Chloe would be pissed, that was for sure, considering how annoyed she'd been that we hadn't told her we were together.

"Hey, look at this," Fatima said, looking down at her phone. I assumed she'd found another possible option for next year's group holiday. After we'd enjoyed last year so much, we'd decided to go to another Renaissance Faire in America. But I would have to break the news to them at some point that I couldn't go after all. Ethel needed me too much these days.

"Have you seen these?" Fatima asked, passing her phone to Chloe.

Chloe watched the video for a few seconds. "Oh yeah! They look amazing."

Amy held her hands up over her head without looking back, her hair still half-finished. "Lemme see!"

Chloe passed the phone to her. "It's one of those fantasy balls where everyone puts on big ballgowns and dances to orchestral covers of pop songs."

"They have them in big manor houses and stuff," Fatima explained. "Even castles sometimes. This company is the one I keep seeing. They've just announced their dates for the second half of the year."

I'd seen videos of them – they looked incredible, if a bit like a thinly veiled excuse for cosplay content. But who would appreciate solid costuming if not me?

"That's sick," Grey said, leaning over to watch the video with Amy. "We should go."

"When are they?" Morgan asked.

Fatima took the phone back and scrolled for another moment. "Looks like there's one in Manchester in September, London in October, France in November, and Scotland in December."

"Ooh, Manchester!" Morgan said with a gasp, looking at Fatima. "We could go see Greg's new game shop!" Greg was a friend of theirs with a shop in the city; Morgan had helped design his branding last summer.

"Manchester could be good," Jack said. "Morgan and I are away for a lot of October."

"And it would be easier than trying to go far in November or December," Fatima said. "I imagine they won't line up with school holidays. But they're on Saturdays, so we could easily get to Manchester and back in a weekend."

I caught Amy's eye again, trying to judge if the mention of going back to Manchester was triggering anything, but she was just pursing her lips in consideration.

"When in September?" she asked.

"The seventh, at eight p.m."

Amy and I widened our eyes at the same time. It was the same day as the wedding. It was also the week our fake relationship was due to end.

"Whad'ya say?" I asked.

She shrugged. "I don't see why not?"

"RIP your fingers," Fatima said to me, and I froze.

"Sorry, what?"

"Come on," Chloe said, "all that will be infinitely easier than the stuff he's making for the festival. Chain mail? I mean, come on."

"Or you could just buy your dresses like normal people," I suggested. I genuinely hadn't thought about the fact that I'd set a precedent, and they'd be expecting me to dress them every time we went to one of these things. I wished I could go back to the me of last year and throttle him for offering to make all the Ren Faire costumes. I'd had so much spare time then, but Ethel took a lot more time and attention to care for these days. Between her and the costumes I was already making for the festival, I wasn't convinced there were enough hours in the day.

"Fine, I'll buy my own dress then," Jack joked. "But actually, this sounds amazing."

"I can get tickets now if everyone wants," Fatima said, pointing at her phone. "It's still early bird, so they're forty quid each. They'll sell out, so we can probably resell them if we can't work the rest out."

Everyone took their phones out then, even Jack, checking they were free. We all were.

"You sure about this?" I asked Amy, trying to give her one last out.

"I think so?" she said, but she didn't sound sure.

I wasn't sure if her doubt was stemming from the wedding – maybe she actually wanted to go, after all – or from making plans with our friends so close to our breakup date. I smiled as reassuringly as possible. "I'll do whatever you want to do."

"Awwwwww," Chloe cooed, "this is still really weird, but so cute. You in then, Ames?"

Amy nodded in response, but she was still looking at me, still smiling, when she answered. "I'm in."

⁓

BACK AT HOME, Amy and I kept up the daily texting. We were swapping lore drops more and more, but now that we'd covered the important bits like timelines, they were getting increasingly ridiculous. By Tuesday, we'd added half a dozen new gems to the Our Lore note, including the fact that I'd apparently once promised Amy a kidney if she needed one.

We did the pub quiz again on Tuesday, and we came in second place yet again, securing our drinks for the next week. The PDA felt more and more natural each time, though we had a near miss when saying goodbye at the pub. She turned to kiss my cheek, and her mouth ended up dangerously close to mine. It was all I could do not to turn my face to kiss her for real.

We saw each other again on Thursday for D&D, after another few additions to Our Lore, and the updates to Amy's character were perfect. I tried not to feel too proud that she'd done exactly what I'd suggested.

Then our first Saturday night as a couple came around, and with Anil still on the break from his course, I told her I wanted to take her out. It only felt right for our first date night, especially knowing most in the future would be spent at home with Ethel. And whilst this wasn't a real relationship, I had an apparently quite posh predecessor to outdo, so I made a booking at the most Michelin-esque restaurant in town.

> **AMY**
> When you say "out out", what does that mean in terms of wardrobe?

> **PHIL**
> I'm wearing something other than jeans and a T-shirt.

> **AMY**
> Well shit. I'll bust out my ballgown then.

She wasn't wearing a ballgown when she knocked on my door, but she was in a purple satin dress that barely hung from the dainty shoulder straps, low enough at the top and sides that I could very clearly see she wasn't wearing a bra.

"You look great," I said once I'd cleared my throat, and she smiled in a way that told me the effect had been intentional. I didn't know what to do with that information.

"Thanks," she said, swaying slightly so her dress flicked out to the sides, and I noticed she was in sandals.

"I hope you're not wearing flats on my account," I said. I'd never seen her in heels, but given how nice her dress was – I could tell it was bias cut from where I stood – I wouldn't have been surprised if she'd busted some out.

"Absolutely not," she said, pushing past me into the hallway. "The biggest benefit of dating a short king is that it's socially acceptable to not wear heels with a fancy outfit."

"Short king? Really? I'm five eleven. And a half."

"Sure, big boy."

I laughed. "You need the bathroom or something? I'm ready if you are."

She frowned at me as if I'd spoken in Klingon. "If you think I will ever walk into this house and not say hello to Ethel, think again."

"Fair enough," I said, standing aside for her. It was always nice to be reminded how much the Evanses loved Ethel, especially when I was so in the weeds caring for her.

I followed Amy into the lounge, where she bent over to hug Ethel, and yep, she was definitely braless under there. I closed my eyes and took a deep breath, reminding myself that I only had that image because she was hugging my *grandmother*.

We walked just a few minutes to the restaurant I'd picked out, discussing the fantasy festival, which she was also now slated to attend. Despite my existing workload, I couldn't help but insist on making her outfits, too. She agreed, as long as I made her other outfit "way better than everyone else's".

When we got to the restaurant, Amy stopped out front before I could open the door for her.

"Phil, this place is really fancy," she said, frowning.

"Don't worry," I tried to reassure her, "you look amazing."

"It's not that," she said, waving me off. "Have you been here before? It looks a bit dead."

I looked through the front window at the white tablecloths and the million and one utensils at each place setting. The food was really well reviewed, and I had been looking forward to the consommé. But I had to admit the atmosphere was non-existent, and I'd already had to prepare myself for the fact that it would cost us a week's worth of my data entry work.

"No," I said honestly. "Not usually my scene."

"Then why did you bring me here?"

I shrugged, but I could feel my face going red, and I knew I'd missed the mark. Yet again, I was grateful for the beard to hide the flush.

"Because it's our first date."

"Of a fake relationship."

That stung for some reason I couldn't quite place, regardless of how true it was. Could I not put effort into hanging out with her just because she wasn't actually my girlfriend?

"And plus," Amy continued, "you're not dating Blair

Waldorf. You're dating me. When have you ever seen me in a place like this?"

"I hate that I understand that *Gossip Girl* reference. That's years of my life I'll never get back."

She rolled her eyes. "You're just mad it wasn't Dorota. Now focus. Does this feel like what I would like?"

I considered that for a moment – I hadn't actually been thinking about Amy at all when I'd chosen the restaurant. I'd been thinking about Chris, and his stupid slicked-back hair, and the fancy wedding stationery. If I'd been thinking about Amy, I might have thought about the quad biking and swimming and day drinking we'd done together over the years. But then again, I wouldn't have picked Chris for that version of her, so what did I know?

"I don't know what you like anymore," I admitted, shrugging as I ran my hand over my beard. "Based on who you dated last, I suspect you got accustomed to a much higher dining standard than usual."

Amy nodded. "You're right. Chris took me to a lot of fancy places. And he always insisted I wear heels, even though he is actually shorter than you, because it made him feel powerful to have a tall woman on his arm. And he'd talk *at* me about work over meals like the one we would undoubtedly be served in there." She pointed into the restaurant.

I bit at my lip. I hated that Chris had treated her like that. That he hadn't appreciated her for who she was. She'd lost so much to those assholes, and how she was still so bright was beyond me.

"Phil," she said more softly, reaching for my hand, and I happily let her take it. "You've known me for most of our lives. If you erased everything you knew about me from the last three years, and this were a real first date, where would you have taken me?"

"Definitely not here," I admitted easily.

"Where then?"

I barely had to think about it at all, because I'd spent a summer five years ago figuring out the answer to that question. And I did know Amy. She was funny and showy and competitive, and she was always up for anything. I loved all those things about her.

"Honestly?" I asked, and she nodded encouragingly. "Chippy and bowling."

Amy squeezed my hand so hard in response I had to yank it away.

"Now that's more like it. Let's get the fuck out of here."

We walked nearly half a mile along the river to get to the bowling alley, stopping when we were almost there to buy paper parcels full of food: large cod and chips for me, and a jumbo battered sausage and chips for her. Not everything from Manchester could be discounted, apparently, as Amy ordered gravy to go with her chips.

We smuggled the food into the bowling alley, though smuggled was probably a strong word given that the entire business seemed to be staffed by pimply fifteen-year-olds who couldn't have cared less what we brought in. Hell, I'd worked there myself as a kid for one very smelly summer.

We ordered a whole pitcher of some disgusting blue cocktail, and I let Amy refill my glass when it was empty, trusting that Anil and Ethel would be fine. Amy was catching a lift home with Jack later from mine, and I noticed that she practically chugged the first drink, needing a refill almost instantly.

We got very, very tipsy over the course of the first game, which I won by just a few points. During the second game, we played where we took turns copying each other's "trick shots", though that was probably an overly generous way of describing the increasingly creative ways we managed to score zero points. Amy nearly wet herself when I decided to spin the ball like I'd once seen in an old Disney Channel film, and I asked her

"Are you ready for spin time?" before chucking the ball directly in the gutter. Amy technically won that game, though it felt like blind luck more than anything, and I took a selfie of us in front of the score table on the screen, Amy holding her ball up like a trophy. I only noticed later that I wasn't even looking at the camera, but at Amy herself.

As we walked back to mine, we kept bumping into each other as if magnetised, which was probably from the blue pitcher more than anything else. At one point Amy rebounded off me so hard that she almost ended up in the road, so I insisted that she walk on the inside. And if my hands lingered on her waist a little too long as I moved her around me, that was probably just the blue pitcher, too.

Amy insisted on walking me to the door despite the fact that Jack was parked across the street, scrolling on his phone.

"Lore drop," she said as we got to the front door, and I fumbled with my keys. "Sometimes I let you win when we play games because it makes you so happy."

I scoffed. "As if I didn't just let you win that last game."

"You absolutely did not!" she said, shoving me just hard enough that I took a step back. When I came forward again, I may have overcompensated with a little step forward, bringing me just a tiny bit closer to her.

We were both quiet for a moment, and I wondered if, like me, she didn't want the date to end. Or maybe she was hoping for a specific ending – was that wishful thinking on my part?

But the booze I could still taste was too reminiscent of the last time I'd thought she might want me to kiss her, so I changed course in my mind.

"Is this okay?" I asked. "Are you getting what you want from this?"

She seemed to really think about her answer.

"Yeah, I think so," she said, but again she didn't sound so confident. I wondered where all her bravado and certainty had gone. Maybe, like me, she'd just gotten more jaded as she'd gotten older. Less certain. "Things are going well with Dad, anyway."

"That's good," I said, and I was happy that things were going the way she wanted, even if I didn't fully get it.

"But I guess time will tell," she added. "What about you? Are you getting what you want?"

I had to actively remind myself of the reasons I'd had for wanting to do this. Reasons other than just wanting to be around her. Wanting nights like this. Wanting to make things up to her for how badly I'd fumbled it five years ago.

"Yeah, everyone's been off my back," I said. "But like you said, I guess time will tell."

Time will tell an awful lot, I thought. Like if this was all a terribly misguided idea to begin with. But even if I didn't get what I wanted from it, as long as she did, it wasn't a waste of time. Not to me.

"Well, we've got plenty of it," she said. And she was right; we still had exactly twelve weeks until our new expiry date: the fantasy ball. "You think you have it in you?"

The answer came easily. "Definitely."

I looked at her for another long moment and admitted to myself that I couldn't prolong this tipsy proximity any longer. My two options were to kiss her or say goodbye. And as tempting as the first option was, as much as it felt like fighting gravity not to lean in and find out if she tasted like those damned blue cocktails, I wasn't quite ready to crash and burn. And plus, Jack was *right there*. Sure, he'd seen us kiss once before already, but I wasn't sure I wanted to let it happen again on purpose.

So I said goodbye instead, and told her I'd see her on Tuesday for the pub quiz. But when she moved to leave, I couldn't resist the chance to pull her in and press a kiss to her forehead.

She looked slightly startled when I pulled back, but not unhappy, and I took that as a win. Then she stepped away, and I watched her go, craning my neck to make sure she got to Jack's car okay. Then I turned back towards the door, my eye catching on the hawthorn blossoms to my right, catching the moonlight as if they wanted to make sure I knew they were there. That they'd seen everything.

"I know, Mum," I said with a sigh, pushing the door open at last. "I don't want to hear it."

CHAPTER 12
YORICK PROUDHOLLOW

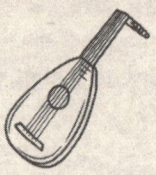

Yorick wove between Ser Liam and Morgana, who were fighting back to back against four wolves surrounding them, and Calamity, who had let her magic loose, trees be damned. One wolf snapped its jaws in his direction as he passed, but it narrowly missed him. He took out his lute, and as he began to play, he dodged around Gorlag, who was cleaving straight through two of the wolves with their great axe. There was a row of shrubs in his way, and he thought about taking shelter behind them, but he needed to be able to see to help.

"Need me to toss you?" Gorlag asked between swings.

"Seriously?" Yorick asked. Gorlag managed to shrug as they struck again at the wolf in front of them. "No, I'm fine on the ground, thank you very much."

He always felt a bit silly plucking out a tune in situations like this, but there was something to be said about the way Yorick's friends seemed to hit harder and aim better when he did. So he turned towards Eden, hoping to inspire the arrow she had nocked to strike true, ideally into the heart of the largest wolf in the pack, which was headed straight for her.

Eden closed her eyes for a moment, and Yorick watched in

amazement, his fingers nearly faltering on the strings, as her skin began to glow. Pinpricks of light appeared on her, creating the perfect picture of the archer constellation on her skin as she pulled back on the string and then released. *That's new*, Yorick thought as he tried to keep up the tempo.

The shot didn't just strike true, it felled the beast in one. The arrow pierced the wolf's chest so sharply that it stuck out the creature's back as it collapsed mid-pounce, landing just inches from Eden, who stood illuminated before it, already aiming her next arrow.

"This way!" a small voice cried, and Yorick looked over to see a child standing at the edge of the camp. It was hard to see through the trees in the fading twilight, but it seemed that a crowd of people was gathered around just beyond the child, watching the party fight. Yorick first wondered why they were just standing there. He then wondered why they were able to. Why hadn't the wolves attacked them?

"The camp is protected!" he called to his friends as he began running towards the child, who waved one arm in huge circles, beckoning to them.

Yorick wasn't particularly fast, but he and Calamity were the closest to the camp, and they made it in just a few seconds. Eden had been behind them, but she suddenly appeared before them, still studded with starlight. She was just barely still in the forest, her bow raised in front of her as if to cover them.

Yorick could feel the moment he passed into whatever circle of protection there was, though it wasn't immediately clear if this was the result of magic or of mutual agreement between the wolves and these people. Perhaps it was a bit of both.

Morgana and Liam, hot on Yorick's heels, stumbled into the clearing next, sinking to their knees as soon as they were safe. Yorick sat up and focused his eyes into the darkness of the forest, where he saw Gorlag running towards them with three wolves hot on their heels. When they were just a few feet away from the barrier, one of the wolves took its chance, lunging forward and closing its jaws around Gorlag's calf. They let out a hideous scream, a roar so ferocious Yorick might have thought it another predator, and they landed half inside the clearing, reaching out for help as the wolf dragged them backwards.

Liam grabbed onto one of Gorlag's hands just before it slipped away, and together with Morgana he managed to pull Gorlag a few feet closer in. A few of the people who had been standing around finally rushed over to help, too. But the wolf was strong, and clearly up for a game of tug. Until Eden's arrow pierced its head right between the eyes, and its jaws released.

The party pulled Gorlag the rest of the way into the camp, even as they cried out and clutched at their bleeding leg. Their weight knocked over those carrying them, and even Eden finally fell to her knees. They all took a long moment catching their breath, and Yorick's eyes actually started to flutter closed as the heaviness of the protection settled over him.

WHEN HIS EYES opened an undetermined amount of time later, the sky was fully dark, the stars bright and clear. But he could only see the very centre of it, because ringed around his vision were people standing over him, looking down. He bolted upright, and the circle of people scattered. He looked around, trying to figure out what had happened, but a sinking feeling washed over him at what he saw – or rather, didn't see.

He was still in the camp. The fire was still burning, and the smell of something delicious still wafted over to him. But his friends were all gone.

CHAPTER 13
AMY

Despite how much shit I'd given Phil for his cinematic preferences, I'd seen enough cheesy rom-coms myself to know that I was on a slippery slope. Fake dating was harder than I'd expected, and I still couldn't help but get caught up in the excitement.

I chalked up the butterflies I felt all through our first date to the copious amounts of dodgy cocktails, so I resolved not to drink as much moving forward. I didn't need to get carried away with myself; I'd learned five years ago what that could do. Relative sobriety proved quite easy after that, as Anil's break from his course was up, so our Saturday nights would be spent at Phil's with Ethel. And as much as I loved her, she definitely helped quash any romantic energy I felt.

Those evenings in ended up looking exactly as I would have hoped. Phil had always been a great cook – he'd learned from Mum, after all – so when he made me homemade sweet potato gnocchi the first week and pulled pork mac and cheese the second, I decided maybe the whole arrangement had been a great idea after all. At least he was keeping me well fed.

And whilst Ethel changed the energy between us, she was

always hilarious to be around. Every Saturday we did something fun: board games, crafts, and even doing her physio workouts together, which showed me just how poor my core strength was.

Then Ethel would go to bed.

I'd expected, after that first date, for that to be the awkward portion of the evening, but I was surprised at how routine it felt. We would wash up from dinner together, and then I'd sit with Phil whilst he crocheted chain mail or stitched together sequin fabric for a costume, and we'd end the night with a film or a show, taking turns choosing. Each week we'd sit closer and closer together on the sofa, and by July it felt perfectly natural to drape my legs over his and feel the weight of his hand on my knee. But we must have both been on edge after that first date, because we didn't have any more sustained glances or lingering-at-the-door moments.

Until one night, when Phil helped me up from the couch and told me to spread my legs.

"Excuse me?" I asked, my mouth hanging open.

"I said spread 'em, Evans," he said, smirking, but he pulled a small retractable measuring tape out of his pocket. "I've officially got everything I need for your festival costumes, so I need your measurements."

I rolled my eyes. "You don't actually need me to spread my legs though, right?"

He shrugged. "I don't technically need your inseam, no. Both your costumes involve skirts."

"Then I'll be keeping my legs firmly closed," I said, holding my arms out to the side. "Otherwise I'm all yours."

Still, when Phil knelt on the ground in front of me and looked up at me with those bright blue eyes, close enough that his beard tickled my belly where my shirt rode up, I nearly crumbled. *Stay strong*, I told myself, looking up at the ceiling. *That is not your man.*

I felt him wrap his arms around my legs, bringing him even closer, and for a moment I could feel his breath on my exposed skin. I stayed frozen in place, willing myself not to meet his gaze. But then I felt him draw the tape across my ass, presumably to measure my hips, and a full body shiver went through me.

"Easy there," Phil said, and I shot a withering glare down at him. I found him smiling up at me with so much mischief in his eyes that I couldn't help but picture him knelt in front of me in a very different context.

"Okay, that's enough," I said, stepping back, though he held the tape tight, not letting me go. So I reached down and grabbed it out of his hands, wincing as it retracted and the metal end hit my knuckles.

"You want a costume?" Phil asked, standing up. "That means made to measure, kiddo."

"Then I will measure myself," I said, extending the tape again and wrapping it around my hips, roughly where he'd had it.

"A bit lower," he said, reaching out to adjust it, but I smacked his hand away.

"Use your words, Philip."

He sighed. "Lower in the back. It needs to be the widest part."

I glared at him, but ultimately obeyed, getting the proper measurement so Phil could take a note on his phone. Then I repeated the process for my bust, underbust, and waist – there was no way I would have survived Phil taking those – and then handed the tape back over so he could take my shoulder and skirt length measurements.

I was beyond desperate to pull focus from my body, so I sat back down on the sofa and pulled my knees to my chest. "Can I ask you a D&D question?"

Phil nodded. "Yeah, of course." He sat down too, turned with his back to the arm of the sofa so he faced me.

"Where did you get the idea for my new character build?"

I'd applied Phil's suggestion exactly as he'd given it, changing my subclass and subrace but nothing else. He was right; they were both cool as hell, and right up my alley. Instead of turning into animals, I could turn into constellations. And Fatima and I had already started discussing some cool backstory elements to incorporate. I hadn't even meant to tie into the whole astral diamonds subplot, but it had worked out perfectly.

Phil smiled, but not smugly this time. He looked almost ... embarrassed?

"Honestly," he said, "I thought of you as soon as I heard about them."

"Which was when?"

"Um, well, we only started playing D&D like four years ago? Fatima has an online subscription so we can use digital character sheets, and when I was building my character on there, I clicked around to see the different options."

I blinked at him, confused. "And you thought of me?" I didn't know why that tied my stomach in knots so badly; maybe because four years ago I'd been nursing a serious grudge against Phil. "Why?"

He shrugged. "Well, Astral Elves are literally described as having a starry gleam in their eyes because of their connection to the astral plane. And Circle of Stars, I mean, come on. Literally turning into a constellation, and using the stars to divine the future? I take it you saw the part where you can use a crystal to power the star chart?"

"It's really cool," I admitted, which was a sentence I'd never thought I'd say about Dungeons & Dragons. But here we were. "Thank you for suggesting it."

"Thank *you* for playing with us," he said, smiling softly,

before narrowing his eyes. "Even if your character is almost as insufferable as you are."

⁓

WE WERE SEEING MORE of each other than ever without even trying, with the pub quiz every Tuesday, D&D every Thursday, and date night every Saturday. I'd finally started crashing his film nights with Chloe and Jack on Fridays, too, mostly because one week Chloe walked from Jack's cabin to the house in the pouring rain to drag me down there. I'd been worried about the dynamic, just the four of us, but it was the same as it had always been: comfortable.

I did wonder how Phil managed to do everything he did without burning out. The more time we spent together, I realised just how much he did for Ethel. He worked as much as he could, but so much of his time was spent shuttling her to appointments and looking after her. Then there was everything he did for his friends – he'd been obsessively shopping for the perfect gift for Chloe's birthday, which was still weeks away, and he never showed up to a D&D session without baked goods in hand. Adding our fake relationship into the mix was more than I would have been able to handle. I just hoped he would say something if he needed to take a step back; I certainly would have been happy to help out more.

We eventually stopped adding things to Our Lore, but that was okay, because we were at the point where we were living it instead of having to come up with it retrospectively. Sure, ours lacked the emotional milestones other relationships might have had, but I still had plenty of anecdotes for Chloe and Morgan when they asked, and it was nice to take away the pressure of making up what were essentially lies.

I also started checking Phil's horoscope along with mine and sending it to him each morning, and I made a hobby out of analysing how ours might be referencing or playing off one another. One day mine said that all the pieces were falling into place for me whilst his said to trust that everything was as it should be, and I actually giggled aloud in the kitchen at the symmetry, making Mum glare at me as she boiled the kettle.

That was when she'd put her foot down and insisted that both Phil and Ethel start joining us for family dinners on Sundays, which he'd been avoiding for the entire time we'd been "dating". So the next Sunday, they came over mid-afternoon so Phil could help Mum cook – she'd messaged him directly to demand his help, apparently – and I walked with Ethel over to Uncle John's farm to see the cows. She stood at the fence mooing for a solid five minutes to make them come to her, and I got a delightful video on my phone of them all congregating in front of her like she was their messiah. Then we came back for dinner, all seven of us including Morgan crowded around Mum and Dad's dining table, Morgan's dog Pablo sniffing for any dinner casualties at our feet. I'd expected things to feel different now that Mum and Dad thought we were dating, but like film nights and pub quizzes and everything else so far, it all felt delightfully normal.

I was slowly realising two things.

First, that people who did get together with someone they'd known their whole life were incredibly lucky. It was so natural, bringing our families together like we had so many times, and like Chloe had said, we did have so much shared history to fall back on. Silences were rarely awkward, because we knew each other almost as well as we knew ourselves. It was funny; Phil and I had never been all that emotionally intimate growing up, but it was like that intimacy had been achieved through osmosis anyway. Like spending time in close proximity had given each of us all the context we needed for how the other thought and behaved.

There was an ease to that, but it was also infuriating.

Because if we knew each other so well, why had it always been so hard to understand what he was thinking when it came to me? Why had things blown up so spectacularly before? I could only assume it was because we weren't actually together that things were this easy, and all the angst and hurt feelings had resulted from trying to force our relationship to be something it wasn't.

And that was the second thing I was realising: that our relationship was, despite all the antagonism and rivalry over the years, a friendship. I'd never considered Phil to be *my* friend, but it was so obvious to me now that that was exactly what he was to me.

I now knew why people were so risk-averse with those friendships. At the worst of times, I felt certain that this fake relationship was even riskier than a real one, and that when it ended, everything that currently felt so natural and right would be compromised. Permanently changed, and not necessarily for the better.

THREE WEEKS before the fantasy festival, Jack and Morgan took off for another camping trip. Fatima was away visiting her sister, so I was looking after Pablo, and I decided to stay out at Jack's cabin. It was easier to get work done there, and my trial for Dad was proving that he desperately needed me full-time. He'd basically abandoned all the admin now that I was on board, and no matter how well I came across to him and to clients, I was still learning the construction industry, so everything took me twice as long as it probably should have. And there was even more work to do on the operational side of things than I'd initially realised. How he'd lasted this long without someone in my role was beyond me.

I'd pretty much completely stopped my virtual assistant

work to focus on the work for Dad, trusting that the extra time now would make him see how dedicated I was, and how important the work was, and that he'd bring me on full-time at the end of my trial as a result. As long as I worked hard, he'd hire me. I'd make sure of it, and I'd sic Mum on him if he didn't.

Now that I had the quotes in from our suppliers, I tried to focus on building the timeline for the Kenchester job, knowing we had just a few weeks until the final meeting. But my mind kept wandering to Phil, wondering what he was doing, even though I'd seen him less than twenty-four hours ago, and I'd see him again in less than twenty-four hours, too, and we'd texted just a few minutes ago about him being in crunch mode for the festival costumes. It was so cliché, thinking about my stupid crush all the stupid time, and I felt like teenage Amy all over again, obsessed about the same fucking boy. Except that boy was now a sexy bearded man, and it was harder than ever to stop thinking about him.

But after what he'd said about my D&D character, and how even years ago, seeing something about the stars made him think of me ... was he thinking about me now? Working on *my* costume since I wasn't there? Was my face permanently lodged in his mind, like his was in mine?

Get a fucking grip, Amy!

I was so fed up with being distracted that I tromped all the way back to the main house, Pablo in tow, to grab my tarot deck and take it back to the cabin with me. I'd avoided doing readings about our arrangement since that first week, because I knew on some level that no reading could be specific enough to quell my anxiety. But I had been free-floating in this relationship for long enough now that I needed a bit of reorientation. So I sat on Jack's back deck overlooking the pond, and I closed my eyes and felt the summer evening breeze on my skin. Then I started shuffling, channelling all my uncertainty and anxiety and desire for answers – and sure, maybe for other things, too – into the deck.

I'd never actually used this particular six-card spread, but I'd seen it online, and it felt like just what I needed. It involved identifying the intentions and energy of both parties – first me, then Phil – and then our shared energy and the fated outcome. So I focused on the key moments of our arrangement so far – showing him the invitation, walking into the pub hand in hand, kissing him outside the bar...

Okay, maybe that last one should be omitted, I decided. It was a bit *too* evocative.

The first card I drew, representing my conscious choices, was an upright Seven of Swords. Trickery, deception, strategy – this made sense, given the nature of our arrangement.

The second card was equally unsurprising: an upright Hermit, indicating that the energy I brought to the arrangement was one of searching for truth and enlightenment. It felt a bit obvious – why else would I have been doing a reading if not for answers? – but I supposed it probably applied more existentially too.

As far as Phil's conscious choices went, I was surprised to see an upright Two of Cups, signifying unity and partnership. Didn't that go against the entire premise of what we were doing? Maybe he was so good at faking it that even the cards were confused. Or maybe I was the one confused, and that was finding its way into the reading.

My hand trembled slightly as I shuffled and drew the next card, which would tell me Phil's energy towards our relationship. His unconscious drive. It was what most eluded me when I thought about what we were doing.

But when I pulled my hand and saw an upright Page of Wands on the deck in front of me, I couldn't help but smile. The card symbolised excitement and exploration. Freedom, even. And given everything that had happened in Phil's life, the hard reality he dealt with every day caring for Ethel, if our fake little relationship was bringing him any sense of freedom and joy, that was a win. Even if it made things more complicated for me.

Another upright card came up next: the Wheel of Fortune to symbolise our shared energy. How I interpreted this card changed a lot from reading to reading; sometimes it felt more explicitly related to change and evolution, whilst sometimes the cyclical nature of the Wheel felt more relevant. Either would have worked; our relationship had definitely changed, and yet there was a cyclical element to it if I thought about five years ago. But as I looked down at it now, the orange of the Wheel drawn out by the warmth of the wooden deck, I couldn't help but think of the inevitability the card sometimes represented. I'd certainly felt that with Phil before. But then again, I'd been disappointed before, too.

The fact that every card had been upright so far was like a slap in the face. Usually that meant the situation was straightforward, but it didn't feel that way to me. It was like the cards were telling me, "You're hurting your own feelings, sweetie." And I didn't appreciate that very much, actually.

The sixth and final card, representing the outcome, was naturally the one I was most nervous about. Were my fears right, and I was heading straight for more hurt? Would we blow up our lives and the relationships we held most dear because we hadn't thought things through? Or would we be able to just step back when the time was right like we'd so optimistically assumed when we'd agreed to it to begin with? Either way, the inevitability implied by the Wheel made a lump form in my throat, and I held my breath as I drew the last card.

When I saw The Lovers appear upright, I nearly chucked my whole deck in the pond.

∼

DATE KNIGHT

Jack came back from his camping trip the next day in a new car. In this context, new meant a slightly less ancient and slightly longer, but otherwise identical, Land Rover Defender, even down to the paint colour.

"Wow," I said sarcastically as he got out, standing on his front stoop holding Pablo. "What an upgrade."

"It's longer in the back," he said. "Morgan and I wanna do more car camping so we can take this little guy." He came towards me in a crouch, waving his fingers and making cooing noises at Pablo, who was wagging his tail so hard his whole body was wriggling. I handed him over reluctantly.

"What did you do with the old one? Trade it in?"

Jack shook his head just as Dad drove it over the hill, pulling in behind the new car.

"I don't know, Jackie," Dad said, getting out and chucking the keys to Jack. "It still rides great, and I miss it, but I think your mum would kill me. You'd better sell it."

He wasn't wrong; he had his Jeep, his work van, and his flatbed truck littering the drive.

"How much?" I asked, surprising myself with the question. It would solve a lot of problems for me to have my own car, though I doubted I could afford it; Land Rovers were massively overpriced, even on the used car market. And plus, I'd been saving up to move out, and whilst I had a nice little nest egg going, even a cheap car would all but wipe it out entirely.

"I was gonna give it to Dad for five," Jack said, and my mouth fell open.

"Five thousand?!"

Jack shrugged. "He sold it to me for not much more, and I've driven it like hell since then. I already paid cash for the new one."

If I hadn't driven it so much myself over the last ten months, I'd have thought it was falling apart or something at that price.

But I knew it was in good condition. The opportunity was too good to pass up.

"I'll buy it," I said before I could convince myself not to. "That way I don't have to keep borrowing yours."

"Whaddya say, Dad?" Jack asked, smiling. "You've got first right of refusal."

Dad was grinning ear-to-ear, which was a rare sight. "You mean I don't have to wait for princess to finish her hair to leave for site visits? Hell yes. Sell it to her."

I rolled my eyes. "That was one time, Dad, and it was because my hair was literally stuck inside Mum's ancient hair dryer. I couldn't have gone to work like that if I'd wanted to."

He held up his hands as if to say, "That's your business", then turned and started up the hill again towards the house.

"All yours, sis," Jack said, tossing me the keys. "Treat 'er right."

"I'll try," I said, already thinking about all the ways I could make the beat-up old car incrementally more comfortable. Some cute seat covers, maybe? Something weird hanging from the rear-view mirror? But that didn't matter now, because I was free, and that meant I had somewhere to be.

I was going to see my boyfriend.

WHEN I GOT to Phil's, I was barely out of the car and on the front path before he came through the front door.

"Look!" I said, pointing over my shoulder at the car.

He nodded, looking confused. He'd seen the car countless times. "Jack let you take the car for a bit?"

I shook my head. "Nope, it's mine now."

He reeled back. "Wait, really? He sold you the Defender?"

"Yup," I said, popping the P for emphasis. "I figured it was about time I got a car."

"That's amazing," he said, smiling at me, but he didn't look as excited as I'd hoped, and I felt instantly embarrassed. Of course he wasn't excited; he hadn't been expecting to see me until later. I'd jumped a million steps ahead in my mind, thinking I could spend more time around his without having to wait for Mum or Jack to be free to drive me, whereas he clearly thought we were spending plenty of time together already.

"Is something wrong?" I asked, bracing myself. Phil sighed and smoothed his beard with his hand, and as he stretched his face I could see how deep his eye bags were. He looked exhausted.

"Honestly, I'm just a bit burnt out," he said, his voice low and gravelly. "I'm buried in these costumes, Ethel has to start doing a second round of physio each week, and I'm trying to take on more work to cover the Manchester trip."

My heart sank. I'd been spending my time doing tarot readings and putting in extra, unpaid hours for Dad when Phil was drowning over here.

"Why does she need more physio?"

"She's just not very stable, and they're worried about falls. She doesn't help herself by acting like she's as spry as ever. So they want me to bring her in twice a week now, and we've been referred to a water aerobics class."

"Ooooh, water aerobics. I volunteer to take her to that," I said, mostly joking, and I felt a surge of satisfaction when Phil cracked a smile.

"In all seriousness," I said, pushing past him towards the front door, "put me to work. What can I do?"

He followed behind me, and I could see from his reflection in the glass of the front door that he was shaking his head, but I went inside anyway.

"There's nothing," he insisted as he pushed the door shut behind us, but I could see through the door to the lounge that there was a huge pile of half-made garments on the sofa, the sewing machine and accompanying detritus taking up most of the coffee table. It was my turn to shake my head.

"I know how to hem," I said. "Let me help with the costumes."

"I'm not that far along," he said with a wince. "Nothing's ready to be hemmed."

"Well, start making a pile, and I'll help on Saturday. And every day until the festival if I need to. I've got wheels now." I smiled and held up the keys again. I was relieved when he started nodding.

"Okay, sure. Yeah, that would be really helpful."

"Done," I said, walking into the kitchen, where the sink was piled high with dishes. "And I'll sort this."

The tips of Phil's ears went pink. "I was gonna do that now."

"And now you can do something else instead," I said, turning on the tap to get the hot water running. "Go be with Ethel."

"She's having a rest."

"Then go get started on that pile."

He was quiet for a moment as I started filling the washing-up bowl with water, but I could feel his eyes on me, and I had to force myself to keep a straight face. I nearly dropped a plate when he was suddenly right next to me, his hand on my waist.

"Thank you," he whispered, the ends of his beard tickling against my ear. And then he pressed a kiss to my temple, long and firm, pulling me tight to him.

"Don't mention it," I said quietly when he pulled away. But as he walked out of the room, leaving me elbow deep in soapy water, I might as well have been giggling and kicking my feet with how huge my smile was.

CHAPTER 14
PHIL

I was genuinely uncertain how I'd made it through life without a fake girlfriend before. Amy started coming over almost every day, sometimes hanging out with Ethel whilst I did other things, and sometimes doing the other things so I could actually spend time with Ethel instead of just moving her around from place to place. I was getting so much more done. The costumes were actually getting finished thanks to Amy's mediocre but invaluable hand-stitching skills, and honestly, they only needed to last a day anyway. The house hadn't looked so tidy since I'd moved back in with Ethel after uni, and Amy had even been driving us to appointments since it was easier for Ethel to get in and out of the Defender than the Fiesta.

She'd been adding more crystals to the windowsill too, a new one in hand almost every time she came over, and the light would hit them just right each afternoon, casting beautiful colours onto the carpet and tablecloth. It was like she was making our life brighter even when she wasn't there.

I'd also been able to do three paid jobs in one week, the most I'd done in months, usually working across the small dining table in the bay window from Amy as she worked for her dad. I'd now earned enough for the rental Fatima had found in Manchester for the fantasy ball. It was turning out to be an expensive summer, though at least now I was splitting the accommodation costs with Amy.

I was excited for the ball, actually, not least because I'd be there with Amy. But I also knew that our little arrangement was due to end shortly after, once her trial with her dad was up and she had gotten a permanent job with him. Which, of course, I had no doubt she would do – she was talking about it nonstop, and I could tell she genuinely enjoyed it. But I knew it would crush me to have to break up, even though we weren't actually together. I was tired of censoring myself around her, having to pretend that I didn't feel all the things we were pretending to have between us. I'd even found myself thinking about what to get her for Christmas before remembering we'd be long broken up by then. So yeah, thinking about the ball was already bittersweet.

And besides, I hadn't even finished the outfits for the fantasy festival next week, and already the girls were sending me inspiration pictures for their ballgowns. My fingers ached at the thought.

"Just tell them no," Amy said from where she sat cross-legged on the floor one afternoon, stitching the hem of Grey's tunic. "You've made so many for them over the last year. Can't they just reuse them?"

I laughed. "Yeah right. Rewear the same dress to multiple photographable occasions? Plus, Morgan's the only one I've made a gown for before. Nothing else is dressy enough."

"Not even this?" She nudged the red sequin abomination poking out of the middle of the pile that had accumulated between us as we worked. It was Chloe's Fairy Godmother dress for the day we were all going as *Shrek 2* characters – Grey as the titular ogre, Fatima as Fiona, Jack as Charming, Morgan as Puss in Boots, and me as Donkey. I'd even managed to whip up a Dragon costume for Amy, though I'd never admit to her how much that had added to the task of finishing the lot.

"It's a bit campy, isn't it?"

Amy shrugged. "You say that like it's a bad thing." She looked around the pile a bit more. "What about this one?" She pulled out a pale pink draped dress, which had taken me a painful amount of time despite its simplicity.

"Her yassified Witch-King of Angmar outfit?"

"Whatever that is." She tossed it to the side. "My point is, you've done so much for them. If they don't have something to wear out of the wardrobes you've made them so far, they can buy something."

She said it so matter-of-factly, but I wasn't so sure how it would go down. I knew nobody would be actually angry at me for saying no, but making costumes and baking for D&D nights had been my main contributions to the group for so long.

But I knew Amy was right, too. I couldn't keep doing this. And just over a month and a half wasn't enough time to make gowns for a fantasy ball. So maybe this *was* the thing that needed to give.

I tried to picture what I could do with all the energy I'd been throwing into costumes over the last few weeks, and beyond a good long nap, my imagination was only filled with things Amy and I could do together. Maybe it was her near-constant presence, or maybe it was because we hadn't done anything super couply lately. But I cut myself off from going down that route, like I always did, because it only ever led to one type of imagining. And I saved that for when I was alone, and she was far enough away that I couldn't get myself into any trouble.

Plus, I knew that realistically there would be plenty to fill that time. Hell, before Amy had started coming around more, the house had gotten so filthy I'd almost been too embarrassed to let her in. And then there was the inevitable truth that Ethel's mobility and independence would continue to decline...

"I think you're right," I said, and she smiled the shit-eating grin I'd learned was reserved for when she was proven correct. "I'll tell them tonight that they can buy their own outfits, and Atelier Owen is on hiatus."

"But not for me," Amy said, and I knew instantly that she was joking. "I still need something fabulous as payment for all my flesh wounds." She held up her thumb, which was wrapped in a plaster from where she'd stabbed into it enough times with the needle to constitute a proper wound.

"You can fuck right off," I said, making her laugh, and I relished the sound as it bounced around the bright lounge.

But little did she know, I did have plans for her. Plans that involved breaking my new "no corsets" rule. Plans for a dress so perfect that seeing her in it would almost certainly make my life – amongst other things – much harder, given that she wasn't actually mine. But I couldn't get the idea out of my head. Now I only had to figure out how to pull it off without her noticing.

~

THAT SATURDAY, Anil texted me to say that his class had been cancelled again, so he was free for the evening if I needed him. I didn't even hesitate before taking him up on it. I was excited to go out with Amy, but I also needed a bit of time with Chloe. She'd declared that she just wanted to do something basic for her birthday – Jack had suggested an escape room, and she'd accepted with zero thought – which was extremely uncharacteristic. Something was off, and I wanted to get to the bottom of it.

As soon as I'd texted Amy to let her know we'd be going out, I gave Chloe a buzz. I knew she'd likely be playing video games at any given moment, so she was one of the only non-medical-provider people in the world I would ring instead of text. Otherwise, I'd have to wait for a save point to get a response.

"Yo," she said on answer, and I could hear what I was pretty sure was the *Silent Hill 2* soundtrack in the background. "What's up?"

"You and Lauren still on-again?"

"For now," she said with a huff that told me it might not be that way for long. "I could do with a third-party opinion, but all we ever do is play games and fuck."

I could have done without that image. "Well, how about tonight? Double date?"

The music stopped, and I figured she'd paused the game. "Wait, really? Because Lauren and I are already supposed to hang out later. Don't you get my hopes up."

"Yeah," I said, shrugging as if she could see it. "Anil's free to stay with Ethel, so let's go out the four of us."

"You beautiful bearded bastard!" she cried. "I owe you one. I'll pick a spot and text you in a few."

"Yeah, yeah," I said. "I'll add it to your tab." But she'd already ended the call.

A FEW HOURS LATER, Amy and I walked hand in hand into the most overstimulating place I'd ever seen in my life. It was an adult arcade with video games, axe throwing, karaoke rooms, and crazy golf. Sound effects ricocheted around the room, I could hear a horrible rendition of "I Will Survive" coming from the supposedly soundproofed karaoke booth, and every few seconds there was the distinct thud of an axe lodging into a wooden target, all on top of the Eurodance pumping out of the speakers. I'd had a couple of dates suggest we meet there over the last couple of years since they'd built it, but I didn't love the idea of handing a potential weapon to a first date, so I'd vetoed it, and thank god. I wished I'd done the same with Chloe.

Chloe and Lauren were already sat at a high table in the bar area with an almost empty pitcher of something pink. I hugged Chloe and nodded at Lauren, instantly getting the weird vibes Chloe was picking up on.

"How long have you been here?" I asked over the music as Chloe and Amy hugged.

"Just ten minutes," she said, and my eyes must have gone wide or flicked to the pitcher unconsciously.

"There was a lot of ice."

We might have made conversation, but I was pretty sure that was impossible given the decibels of the surrounding noise. So instead we paid for a round of crazy golf, during which Chloe kept foisting cocktails on Amy and me in the name of "maximising happy hour". Amy and I had fun as always, but it was painful to watch how weirdly competitive Lauren was being, and how desperate Chloe seemed to win her approval, cheering for her like a football WAG and asking her every five minutes if she wanted a drink. I could tell Amy was curbing her own competitiveness in an attempt not to come across like Lauren, and I wanted to egg her on so she wouldn't hold back, but she probably wouldn't have heard me over the din.

We found a quieter corner after we finished, and I was left with Lauren whilst Chloe and Amy were in the loo. It was strange, because the moment we started talking, she seemed perfectly normal. She asked me about the D&D campaign, and she looked almost disappointed when I revealed Amy had taken over her character; apparently, Chloe had withheld that tidbit. We talked about all the costumes I'd been making, too; I told her about the chain mail I was crocheting for Grey, and she joked that she had a friend with a suit of armour if I didn't manage to finish in time.

I'd been around Lauren plenty over the last year, so it

shouldn't have come as a surprise, but Chloe either gushed about her to the point that I already knew every detail of her life, or made her completely off limits. So it was nice to be reminded of the fact that she was just a normal, pleasant person when she and Chloe weren't making each other crazy.

And they definitely made each other crazy. We tried axe throwing next, and Lauren critiqued Chloe's form every single time to the point that Chloe nearly threw the axe at her. If Chloe wanted a vibe check, I'd need to make sure I told her what I thought when she didn't have a sharp object in her hand.

I was surprisingly good at axe throwing, it turned out – I'd never been particularly sporty, so I'd assumed my hand-eye coordination would be shit, but I won the game by a country mile. I looked over at Amy when I made one particularly impressive hit, the axe lodging in the target just half an inch north of a bullseye, and she was looking at me like I was the fittest person on the planet. At least, that was how I chose to interpret the fact that she was literally biting her lip at me.

"Nice shot, big boy," she whispered as I passed her, her hand on my bicep, and I knew she was joking, but I felt a shiver pass through me so strong it made my eyes roll back a bit.

Unfortunately, Chloe seemed to have heard Amy's pet name, and she and Lauren proceeded to call me "big boy" for the rest of the round until it lost all suggestiveness.

After axe throwing, Amy and Lauren went together to brave the queue for another round, and Chloe and I gravitated towards the table tennis. I picked up a paddle and served gently to her, but she spiked it back so hard it had a dent in it when I went to retrieve it.

"What the hell?" I asked, grabbing a different ball and serving again. Her return was much gentler this time, though at great expense to her, I could tell.

"Sorry," she said. "I know it's not going well."

I sighed. "You want my opinion?"

"You know," she said, "I genuinely don't think I need it. It's not good, is it. Unlike you and Amy, who are disgustingly cute of course. I'm surrounded by love, and it's killing me. I swear it's half the reason I keep crawling back."

Amy and I hadn't been particularly affectionate or flirty, I didn't think. But I didn't like that Chloe was feeling so isolated. I promised myself I'd find a way to spend more time together, though I had no idea when that would be, given my distinct lack of free time.

"But seriously," Chloe said, "it's such a mindfuck. We have buckets of chemistry, but we fight all the time."

I shook my head. I'd yet to see those buckets of chemistry, to be honest. "I mean, you're far from your best self around her. I've never seen you bend over backwards like that for anyone before."

"Back at ya," she said, sounding almost defensive. "I've never seen you with anyone the way you are with Amy."

"Is it a bad thing?" I asked, suddenly panicked that everyone had been watching Amy and me date – or at least pretend to date – as if they'd been watching a car crash.

She shrugged. "I mean, I don't know. I'm a little worried it won't end well."

I rolled my eyes, prepared for a repeat of the warning she'd issued five years ago. That Amy had always had a thing for me, and that I needed to be careful, because I could really hurt her.

"It's not like that anymore," I said, focusing my gaze on the ball. "I know she had a thing for me growing up, but we're both adults now."

Instead of returning the volley, Chloe caught the ball the next time it came her way. "I know that," she said. "That's not what I'm saying."

"What then?"

She sighed. "It's you, Phil. You're the one that's been obsessed with her for years. Sure, back then I was more worried about her. But if you think I can't tell how into her you are, you're crazy. And if it doesn't work out, you're the one I'm worried about."

I pinched my lips together, staring her down. I refused to let myself get worked up to the backdrop of "Blue" by Eiffel 65.

"You've got too much to lose, Phil. Just be careful."

I hated how much sense she was making. And she had no idea how right she was. Had the relationship been real, I might have been able to brush off her concern. But given that we weren't actually together ... well, I was almost certainly on the path to getting my feelings hurt. Especially since we'd yet to discuss our breakup strategy.

I nearly told Chloe everything right then and there, Eurodance soundtrack be damned. But Amy and I had agreed we couldn't tell anyone, so I had no choice but to change the subject.

"Yeah, well, *you've* gotta be careful with these drinks," I said, picking up the dented ball from earlier and lobbing it towards her empty cup. It bounced off the rim and away from us. "Even I need to switch to water now."

"That's because you're a lightweight, big boy," she said, waggling her eyebrows suggestively, and I felt my face flush.

"Okay, that's enough of that," I said firmly, squaring up to give her a taste of her own medicine, but Amy and Lauren returned to save me from taking the bait. Lauren handed Chloe a cocktail identical to hers, complete with a bag of popping candy clipped to the side. Amy handed me something clear and fizzy with a slice of lime in it.

"It's fizzy water," she said in my ear, and I could have picked her up and ravished her right there on the table tennis table for sparing my liver. Instead, I settled for snaking my arm around her waist and kissing the top of her head, right at her part.

I stiffened slightly when I realised what I'd done – this definitely didn't count as necessary PDA, and we'd been pretty good at avoiding that so far – but she didn't seem to mind. In fact, she was smiling up at me when I caught her eye.

It wasn't necessary, but maybe it wasn't unwelcome either. At least, a man could hope.

∽

LATER THAT NIGHT, I was feeling smug about how well I was balancing everything. I'd come home and felt more energised than usual, and I decided to take advantage of Ethel being asleep to cook myself a nice meal. The arcade nachos hadn't really done it for me, and I had some veg in the fridge that was on the verge of going bad.

Over the next couple of hours, I lost myself in the process of making the perfect vegetable and ricotta ravioli. I made and rolled out the pasta by hand, pureed the veg into a fluffy paste, and cooked the little parcels to a perfect al dente, smothering them in a brown butter and thyme sauce. I ate alone at the dining table, knowing the only thing that could have made it better was if I'd been sharing it with Amy.

I was just doing the washing up when I heard a thump from the direction of Ethel's bedroom, and my heart stopped. I was racing down the hall before I even realised I'd reacted, and I flung open her door to find her in a pile on the floor.

"I'm fine," she insisted as I bent to help her up, clamouring to fend off her shooing me away so I could wrap my arms around her torso.

"You sure?" I asked, getting her upright and then sitting her down on the bed, watching how she bent and where she placed her weight. She grimaced slightly as she sank into the mattress, but she didn't seem to be compensating as far as I could tell.

"Yes," she insisted, waving me off again. I took a couple of steps back so she wouldn't get overwhelmed and flipped on the light.

"Maybe we should put some of these lights on sensors so they turn on when you get up," I said, looking around. "The doctor told me shadows can mess with your depth perception."

"I said I'm fine," she said again, louder this time, and I could tell she was getting agitated. She'd been moodier lately, and I knew it was a symptom, and she was feeling more and more lost in her own mind. But it still felt frustrating, given everything I was doing. How hard I worked to try to keep her safe. I had to breathe deeply for a moment so I didn't snap at her. She didn't deserve that.

I took out my phone and made a note to mention this at her physio appointment on Tuesday. It was better safe than sorry, right?

"What were you getting up for?" I asked. "Can I help you?"

"I just needed some water," she said, pointing at her bedside table where I always left her a glass. I realised only then it had been knocked over, and the water had spilt all over the wood and carpet. I rushed out for a towel, then knelt down to soak up as much as I could. As I picked up the glass, I saw it now had a large chip in the rim. I supposed I'd need to start giving her plastic instead of glass, though I already knew she'd complain that she didn't like drinking out of it. Maybe I could get her some of those cups made of the nicer, thicker, heavier plastic.

Once I'd found the chipped piece amidst the carpet piles, I went to get her another drink. I braced myself for her to complain about the plastic novelty cup I'd bought at the Ren Faire last year, but she just drank the water down greedily, not noticing what I'd served it in.

"Are we seeing that beautiful lady of yours tomorrow?" she asked as she finished.

"Yep, Amy's going to pick us up around three in her big car, so you don't have to ride in mine, and we'll go back to hers for dinner." I wondered if I should cancel, but I figured I could make that decision in the morning based on how she seemed.

Ethel frowned, and I thought maybe she didn't like the Defender as much as I'd thought. But as I tucked her in, she looked up at me, and I could tell as I met her gaze that things weren't quite right.

"Amy?" she asked. "I thought you were going out with Ellen?"

It felt like all the blood drained from my body at once. I'd known it was only a matter of time; everyone who'd known my dad told me how much I looked like him, and I'd known Ethel's memory would only get worse. But it was the first time she'd ever mistaken us.

I tried to remember what the doctor had recommended for when this happened – I knew I wasn't supposed to correct her, but I wasn't supposed to pretend to be him, I didn't think.

"We're seeing Amy tomorrow," I said, "but I can try to find some pictures of Ellen if you'd like."

"No pictures," she said. "Have her come by. I miss her."

"Yeah, me too," I said, blinking back the tears forming in my eyes. I didn't want to upset her more. "Night, Ethel."

"Goodnight, Michael."

I left her light on and closed her door gently, pretty sure she was already asleep by the time I made it out of the room. I walked past the mess I'd been tending to in the lounge and straight to the front door, where I opened it quietly and perched on the threshold, the metal cold against my bare feet.

I reached out and touch the greenery-covered branches of the hawthorn tree, the flowers long gone to the summer heat, and the tears finally tumbled down my cheeks and soaked into my beard.

"I can't do this," I said quietly to my parents. "I'm not meant to be doing this alone. Not now."

It wasn't fair. Surely I'd reached my quota for hardship when my parents had been taken from me. But yet here I was, without them, at the ripe old age of twenty-nine, unable to manage even a part-time job and a fake relationship around caring for my grandmother. My whole life was about getting from one day to the next, despite knowing that things were only going to get worse. And if what I'd built my life around deteriorated, if the person I orbited around stopped existing in the way she always had, what did that mean for me?

But I didn't have a choice. I had to do it, precisely *because* I was alone. Because I was the last line of defence.

This was why I hadn't let myself get serious with anyone since Ethel's diagnosis. I just didn't have the emotional bandwidth; I wasn't capable of holding it together. It was like I could only do one thing well at a time, and if things were going well in my love life, fake or not, they weren't going well with Ethel. And Ethel was the only family I had left, so I had to put her first, no matter the cost. I knew that.

Except now I had something valuable I wasn't so sure I was willing to part with.

CHAPTER 15
YORICK PROUDHOLLOW

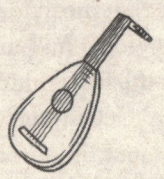

"Move aside!" someone called, and the observers standing around Yorick parted for a young man.

"Where are my friends?" Yorick asked. The man smiled warmly as he looked Yorick over as if checking him for injuries.

"The half-orc was with our cleric having their leg checked over, though they may be done now. The rest are with Laszlo. Are you hurt?"

Yorick paused for a moment to take a mental inventory, but no, he hadn't been hurt in the fight. He shook his head.

"Good," the man said. "Laszlo will want to see you now."

"Laszlo?" Yorick asked. "Is he your leader?"

The man chuckled. "Something like that. He knew you were coming, at least."

Yorick frowned. He still felt the warmth and the sense of safety that had hit him when he'd stumbled into the camp, but now he wondered if that were keeping him off his guard. Should he be worried?

The man helped Yorick to his feet then began to walk away, waving Yorick after him. "Right this way."

Yorick followed him past dozens of barrel-topped wagons, some open in the back with wares and supplies on show, others with groups of people or family units sat together, others still closed up tight. They were festooned with bunting and banners and colourful garlands, with bells and coloured glass lights hanging from the corners and the doorways. The man walked Yorick towards the largest wagon, parked in the centre of the rest, in what looked like the exact middle of the clearing. A grizzled old man stood in the open doorway. Everyone was tall to Yorick, but he was pretty sure this man was exceptionally tall even by human standards.

"Come in," he said, stepping aside so Yorick could enter the wagon. When he did, he saw his friends sat around a low table with mugs of steaming liquid in their hands. Even Gorlag was there with a freshly bandaged leg.

"Yorick!" Eden cried, rushing over to him. "Are you okay? You were out for a while."

Yorick nodded. "Were you not?"

She shook her head. "No, we were all up almost straightaway. But don't worry, we insisted on waiting for you to talk business."

At this, Yorick took in the wagon properly. It was dimly lit but extremely comfortable, the walls lined with tapestries and artwork. Rich rugs covered the wooden floor beneath the eclectic furniture, which included the table the party was sat at, a plush armchair Laszlo now occupied, and a four-poster bed lavishly furnished with blankets and cushions of every colour Yorick could imagine.

"Thank you for your hospitality," Yorick said, turning to Laszlo. "We don't wish to intrude, but we were looking for you."

"I know," Laszlo said with a nod.

"You do?" Yorick asked as he hoisted himself up into the chair closest to Laszlo.

"The cards told me. You're looking for information about The Twelve."

Yorick's mouth fell open as he looked around at his friends, whose expressions mirrored his. They'd agreed to open with questions about the astral diamonds, and only bring up The Twelve if they seemed agreeable.

"How do you know that?" Calamity snapped, but Laszlo didn't bristle at her tone. He just laughed. "He didn't tell us that," she added, directly to Yorick.

"I told you, the cards told me."

"The cards?"

"The cards," he repeated, producing a deck from – well, Yorick wasn't sure where from – and riffled it slightly. "And I'll answer your questions as soon as you all complete a reading. Just one card each."

Liam frowned. "Why?"

Laszlo shrugged. "It's good to know who I'm dealing with. And the information the cards deem relevant will tell me a lot about who you are."

The group looked around at one another, all of them seeming equally unsure what to do. All except Eden, who looked visibly excited.

"I'll go first," she said, and Laszlo beckoned her closer. She went to kneel before him, almost as if in supplication. She grasped the crystal she wore around her neck. Yorick had seen her use it each morning, placing it before a light to project a map of the night sky so she could divine any omens the stars had for her. But now she seemed to grip it more for comfort than for any magical purpose.

"Tell me when to stop," Laszlo said as he began to shuffle the cards, so quickly they blurred before Yorick's eyes, but the movement never looked frenzied. After a few seconds, Eden nodded. Laszlo stopped shuffling, then revealed the top card, placing it on his knee before flipping it over. Eden's face visibly brightened when she saw a One of Stars, but then was less thrilled when Laszlo explained that it foretold unexpected consequences and chaos. Morgana went next, getting a One of Swords, and Liam received an Eight of Glyphs. Calamity seemed almost embarrassed when she received The Dark Lord, though Yorick wasn't sure why. Gorlag, on the other hand, seemed thrilled with the Master of Swords, though they asked if they could change it to Master of Axes, making Laszlo tip his head back in booming laughter.

When it was Yorick's turn, he knelt hesitantly before Laszlo the way the others had, though it was probably unnecessary; he could have just stood. In fact, when he nodded and Laszlo drew his card, he couldn't actually see it at first. He could only see Laszlo frown down at it.

"It doesn't always mean you're a puppet or a spy," Laszlo explained as Yorick pressed up onto his feet. "Sometimes it just means you're out of control."

"I'm perfectly in control, thank you very much," Yorick said through his teeth, but he could feel heat building on his face, and he didn't actually feel very in control. He tried to focus on the card, but he had to blink several times to clear his vision.

On the card was a figure terrifying and uncanny enough on its own; a pale mask and long talons made it look otherworldly, reaching out as if trying to escape the card. But it was only after reading the name that Yorick noticed the strings connected to the shoulders and arms.

It was a marionette.

CHAPTER 16
AMY

The next weekend, I had to cancel date night. Mum had been trying all summer to get me to go on a rewilding expedition with her – "expedition" felt like an extreme word for a day spent gardening, but whatever – and I'd finally committed to a day just to shut her up. Apparently it would go on all day, and since Mum was running it, she had to stay to the bitter end. Phil insisted he needed the time to finish the costumes anyway – I knew he felt bad putting me to work – so I didn't really have an excuse. I was sad not to see Ethel, but I'd seen her on Thursday when I'd driven her and Phil to her physio appointment, and I'd see her for family lunch the next day.

I'd assumed we'd just be chucking bee bombs on the side of the motorway or handing out biodegradable leaflets or something, but Mum was busier than I'd ever seen her in the week leading up to it, and I started to get a sense of the scale. By the time we pulled up outside the garden centre on Saturday morning in the flatbed, I had a much greater appreciation for how hard she worked.

Apparently, we'd be rewilding a piece of disused farmland about forty-five minutes away. The garden centre had donated loads of supplies, and there were so many volunteers going they'd hired a coach to take everyone, which Mum took great care to tell everyone was a zero emission, fully electric coach.

More surprising, though, was who my company would be. As I sat by the window a few rows back, waiting for the other volunteers to filter in and praying I wouldn't get stuck next to a chatty friend of Mum's asking about my new boyfriend, I nearly squealed when Chloe, Morgan and Fatima climbed into the coach.

But Chloe looked less than happy.

"Don't even," Chloe said, holding up a hand before I could properly greet her. "I don't wanna be here any more than you do."

"Just think of the bees, Chlo," Morgan said as they slid into the seats opposite me, Fatima settling in beside me.

"Oh yeah," Chloe said, visibly cheering up. "I'd forgotten about that amidst the distinct lack of caffeine."

"Your mum promised her coffee," Fatima explained, "and apparently we have to wait until we get to the site."

"Oh, diddums," I said in a baby voice, and Chloe stuck her tongue out at me. "I didn't even know you guys were coming." I'd seen Chloe at film night the previous evening, and she hadn't said anything.

"She got me on the way out last night," Chloe said through a pout. "Threatened me with telling my parents the next time I was over so they could come say hi."

Chloe's avoidance of her parents was the most mysterious thing about being her friend. I'd met them loads of times over the years – they lived on the next farm over and had loaned Uncle John equipment a couple of times, as well as letting Jack borrow their forklift when he was building his house – and they'd seemed nice enough. But Chloe insisted there was more to it, so we didn't probe.

"And we were supposed to have girls' day," Morgan added, "so Chloe insisted that we come along too."

I felt a pang of jealousy; I missed girls' nights and brunches and outings with Niamh and Sophie and Maya. I'd been watching them all in the group chat arranging Niamh's hen do for a few weeks' time, and I had to remind myself constantly that I didn't actually want to be there, and they probably didn't actually want me there, either.

"Don't even," Fatima said, putting her head back against the seat and closing her eyes. "I'm still mourning brunch. I had my order ready."

"You should come with us next time," Morgan said, catching my eye, and I smiled, but I knew it was probably a pity offer. She'd been the one to ask Fatima to invite me to play D&D, I was pretty sure, and to prompt Jack to invite me camping.

"Maybe," I said as the coach lurched into motion.

Over the drive, I listened as Chloe and Fatima argued about which video game soundtrack was best, and Morgan talked about her and Jack's plans for their big autumn road trip up to the Isle of Skye in the new Defender. Most of the others on the coach looked to be at least twice my age, some of whom I recognised as Mum's friends. The women in front of me, neither of whom I'd met before, were talking about their grandkids, both of whom apparently worked in tech, and it was hilarious listening to them trying to determine whether they did the same thing when it was clear neither of them knew what any of it was.

Fatima and I talked about our recent sessions, too – I told her that if I'd known there was tarot in D&D, I might have joined sooner. I didn't tell her that the reading she'd given me in-character was a bit too similar for my comfort to the reading I'd done myself, the Knight of Swords in real life mirroring the One of Stars Laszlo had pulled for Eden. Still, I was loving my character, and loving how collaborative everything was. I could

DATE KNIGHT

tell Phil got annoyed with me sometimes, but honestly, that was a bonus.

The coach pulled off the A road onto a small dirt track, where we parked alongside a digger, two horse boxes, and half a dozen flatbed trucks full of plants, ours included.

As we got off the coach, there was a woman standing next to a car with a giant catering carafe and a stack of paper cups. Chloe ditched us immediately to queue for her promised coffee. She came back with what looked more like a cup of tar, though she didn't seem to mind it.

Then Mum called the chaos to order. She gathered the few dozen people she'd recruited around her and explained that the six-acre piece of land had been used for farming for decades, then for grazing for the last few years. When the landowner had passed, his kids had donated a chunk of it to the rewilding trust Mum worked for, but it needed a lot of work.

"As many of you know," she said, "the pigs have been doing their job for the last few months. Now, if we just left the land alone, it would turn into a high canopy woodland with negligible biodiversity and few valuable habitats." I had no idea what that meant in a practical sense, but it was clear from the way she said it that it would be a bad thing. It was actually quite impressive how knowledgeable and passionate she was, and I wished I'd taken it more seriously.

"So today we're focusing on coppicing, digging another pond, and introducing local tree and shrub varieties cultivated over the last year by our wonderful partners at the local nursery." She pointed to an older couple stood behind one of the flatbeds, and everyone clapped.

"How long have they been working towards this?" Chloe whispered to me, and I shrugged, a bit embarrassed that I couldn't answer.

"All this work should help increase heterogeneity—"

"Ew," Chloe whispered, making Morgan cough-laugh into her fist—

"—and allow this land to contribute to the local ecosystem. Now, everyone go to your stations you've been assigned, and if you're not sure where you're meant to be, come see me."

The four of us wandered over to her, queueing behind a few other lost souls.

"Dibs on a chainsaw," Morgan said when we got to Mum, but she shook her head without looking down at her clipboard.

"Only the people who brought the chainsaws get to use them," she said. "I can't be held liable if one of you chops your fingers off. No, Morgan, you and Fatima are on planting duty. You can go see Desi by the truck." She pointed at another person armed with an identical-looking clipboard, and Fatima linked her arm in Morgan's as they walked off.

"I've got a special job for each of you," Mum said, smiling, and I couldn't help but smile too. It was fun seeing her in her element. "Chloe, how do you feel about bees?"

I watched as Chloe's caffeine-deprived face pulled up in excitement. "You know damn well how I feel about them, Patricia!"

Mum laughed. "Well, you get to help put in the bee boxes. You can go see Jess at the horse box."

Chloe skipped off, leaving just me. I was bummed I wouldn't be with any of them, but I was actually getting quite excited about the day, despite the fact that it was already hot enough for sweat to prick at my brow.

"And me?" I asked, trying to lean over and see what was on Mum's clipboard.

"You remember what your favourite job was when we were building that barn at Uncle John's a few years ago?"

I gasped. "The digger?"

Mum nodded. "The digger."

I clapped my hands together. I loved using the digger – it

made me feel so powerful. And the best part was that the digger I could see on the other end of the lineup was a nice enclosed one, meaning it would most likely have air conditioning.

Mum rode in it with me out to the pond site, and I spent most of her orientation trying to get the cold air going. By the time I did, she'd given me the brief for the pond: no real shape requirements, no more than thirty centimetres deep, gentle slopes. Then she hopped out to walk back to the group, where the trucks were beginning to disperse with the saplings.

I spent the next hour happily digging, starting with the centre so I could get the depth right before sloping outward, even pulling up a true crime podcast on my phone to listen to. I could barely hear it over the engine, even at full volume, but it added a nice escape from my thoughts, which were mostly focused on what to get Chris and Niamh as a wedding gift since I wouldn't be at the wedding itself. Phil had told me not to get them anything, but I liked the idea of using a gift as a subtle jab. Maybe something that said Mr & Mrs Arden on it, despite the fact that I knew Niamh wouldn't be changing her name? Though my feminist principles wouldn't quite let me go there.

The podcast was also a necessary distraction because I knew how easy it was to start thinking about Phil when my mind was unoccupied, and given that I didn't have construction timelines to distract me or tarot cards to tell me what to think, I felt that topic was better left unexplored for the day.

I was about a quarter way around the pond when the digger's air con gave out. I had my water bottle with me, and Mum came to check on me and bring me a refill after an hour or so, but by lunchtime, I was so delirious that not even real-life murder could hold my attention. Instead, my thoughts drifted first to Ethel, wondering what crystals I should source next from the website I used. I was almost sure I'd become their biggest customer over the past couple of months. And she needed a boost; this week they'd given her a hydrocortisone injection in her back, because apparently she'd started showing symptoms of arthritis there.

But of course, it wasn't a very big leap at all from thinking about Ethel to thinking about Phil. He'd seemed more anxious than usual this week. I figured it was probably because of the festival coming up; yes, there were the costumes to finish, but I also knew he didn't love leaving Ethel overnight, especially with her back hurting.

Or maybe he was stressed about the trip for the same reason I was: the sleeping arrangements.

I'd had Fatima send me the listing for the house they'd hired just a short walk from the festival, and I'd pored over it trying to figure out what the sleeping arrangements were. There were two king beds and two superkings, and both the superkings could be unzipped to be two beds each. I had already packed a bag with single fitted sheets so we could discreetly take the bed apart, but I didn't even know for sure if we'd be in the one remaining superking after Fatima and Grey split one. Surely Chloe would be in a king on her own, which should have meant there was a fifty/fifty chance we'd get the one that zipped apart, but I also knew Phil had planned to be alone when they'd booked it, so did that mean we'd have a smaller bed? Not that a kingsize was small, but that extra width made a huge difference when I thought about spending two entire nights next to Phil.

It wasn't that I didn't want to share a bed with him. No, the problem was that, on a deep, physical level, I very much *did* want to. It was nearly all I could think about, and when I did ... well, let's just say imagining that had kept me busy more than one night in the last week, and I'd made good use of the memory of him kneeling down to take my measurements.

But I was almost certain Phil didn't feel the same. Not only had he proven five years ago that he didn't feel the same way then, there had been plenty of opportunities this summer for him to make a move if he'd wanted to. And every time our performative PDA escalated, I felt him clam up like it made him uncomfortable, like last weekend at the arcade with Chloe and Lauren.

But still, I wasn't imagining the chemistry we had, was I? I hadn't dated many people, but I'd been with enough to know what good chemistry felt like, and I'd never had it with anyone as strongly as I had it with Phil. Every time we were around one another, it was like we were magnetised. Like we couldn't possibly not brush against one another, or stand that little bit closer. Even before this summer, when we'd yelled at each other about stupid things or gotten overly competitive at a family barbecue, there had always been an electricity between us; an undercurrent that I couldn't have ignored even if I'd wanted to.

And honestly, I didn't want to anymore, especially as I got to see new sides of him. He'd always been Jack's funny best friend to me, and though I'd known on some level that he was a nice guy, I'd seen firsthand all summer that he was the most selfless person I'd ever met. He put the people he cared about first, and he worked tirelessly to take care of them. I'd seen his practical side right alongside his goofy side. For the first time, I felt like I knew him as an entire person. And unfortunately for me, I liked that entire person more than ever.

And yeah, okay, he was hotter than ever with that goddamned beard. He'd been growing his hair out for the festival, too, giving him an unkempt look that was unfortunately really doing it for me.

So if we happened to be sharing a bed at the festival, would that be the worst thing? Would it be horrible if his hands found me in between the sheets, or mine him, and if our bodies drew together in the darkness? I could almost feel his breath on my skin, his weight on top of me, his—

I snapped myself out of my heat-fuelled delirium when I realised I'd been digging in the same spot for a good few minutes, creating a hole nearly a metre deep. I switched off the digger – the rumble of the engine wasn't exactly helping me calm down. Jesus, I needed to get laid – by Phil or someone else – stat. Clearly I was a liability. The digger needed a warning: DO NOT OPERATE WHEN HORNY.

So far, I'd managed to bridge the gap since Chris and I had broken up with just my little blue vibrator and a fantasy of whatever Henry Cavill role – Geralt of Rivia, Clark Kent, Gus March-Phillipps – did it for me in that moment. Now though, it seemed the proximity of our fake dating – which was still very much *fake*, I reminded myself – had made it so I had no filter when it came to my thoughts about Phil. Every time I closed my eyes at night, I was inundated with the million and one dream scenarios I'd concocted over the years, which I had tried so hard to bury after he'd rejected me five years ago. The last thing I needed now was getting into bed with him after a few too many meads and a day of blurring the lines between reality and fantasy.

I pulled myself together before switching the digger back on, just long enough to replace the dirt in the hole I'd created, taking care to tamp it down well. Then I turned it off again and climbed out, the midsummer breeze hitting me and giving me instant relief.

I stepped back to admire my handiwork. The pond wasn't very gently sloped on one side, but I figured that was probably okay as long as the wildlife had some easy ways in. If not, Mum would tell me and I could fix it. But first, I needed to get some food in me.

And maybe douse myself with cold water, based on how dire things had just gotten. Where was an ice-cold reservoir when I needed it most?

I grabbed my water and left the digger where it was as I walked back towards the coach. There I found a woman who must have been at least Ethel's age hanging out the side of a work van, handing out cartons of food from a cold bag.

"Herbivore or omnivore?" she asked me as I walked up.

"Omnivore's fine."

She handed me a brown box with a napkin on top, and I thanked her and walked around to where people were congregating around the trucks. I saw Morgan and Fatima sat in the back of one of the now-empty flatbeds with their own boxes – Morgan's brown like mine, Fatima's white – and walked over to join them. I climbed into the bed, then opened my lunch to find a ham and cheese sandwich and some salted crisps. Chloe joined us a moment later with her own identical box, looking even more exhausted than she had earlier.

"Your mum was very thoughtful assigning me to the bee group, but I really hate those bee houses."

"Really?" Morgan asked through a mouthful of crisps. "Why?"

"They're the same as those bug hotels you can get with all the tubes, and they always get full of spiders. And I don't like holes anyway."

"Honestly, this is gruelling work," Morgan said, looking down at the dirt under her nails, then ignoring it to reach into her box for her sandwich. "Maybe we should run off into the forest to get out of this afternoon."

"Oooooh, and live off the land and start a coven," Chloe said, a bit too excitedly. "Amy can teach us witchcraft."

"I don't know anything about that," I admitted, "but I can do a mean tarot reading."

We did ultimately get assigned to another task for the afternoon, but Mum must have seen how exhausted we were – embarrassing really, considering how unfazed the older volunteers seemed – as she assigned all four of us to measure for the deer fencing that would be installed to help protect the new tree shoots. I was almost certain it wasn't a real job, and that she already had the measurements she claimed to need, but I was grateful, especially since it just required walking around in a specific route with a measuring wheel. Plus, there was just one wheel, so we got to stay together the whole time.

We started the walk with Morgan detailing the fantasy book she'd just finished in excruciating detail; even if I'd wanted to read it, and it did sound good, I didn't need to anymore.

"You ever notice that none of those love interests are blonde?" Fatima asked. "Kind of goes against the shadow daddy aesthetic, I guess."

"Oooh, wonder how Jack feels about that," I said, then instantly regretted it; nothing like your boyfriend's little sister yucking your literary yum, right?

But Morgan just winked. "Hey, my book boyfriends are my business. What Jack doesn't know won't hurt him."

"How are you guys by the way?" Fatima asked, and again I watched Morgan for any flick of her eyes towards me, or any awkwardness, but she just smiled.

"We're really good," she said, her voice almost dreamy. "I'm excited about going travelling together this autumn."

"That's big," Chloe said, "given all the travelling he did with his ex." Jack and his ex had travelled full-time together for years, and that relationship had fucked him all the way up, to put it lightly.

"Yeah, I mean, I'm a bit worried about that," Morgan admitted, a half frown appearing on her face. "Not because I think it'll be the same, but I'm just worried he'll freak out if his precious independence feels threatened. And given that we'll be stuck in the car together for a month, we'll be pretty codependent for a while."

Honestly, I would have thought the same thing after the mess that was his previous breakup, but I wasn't worried. Anytime Jack wasn't with Morgan, he only ever seemed anxious to get back to her.

"Well, that's far from full-time travel," I said, "but even then, you're right. It wouldn't be the same. I'm surprised he hasn't asked you to move in yet so you can be attached at the hip constantly."

"I know, right?" Chloe said. "He's playing it very cool."

"Tell me about it." Morgan groaned. "I wish he would. Don't get me wrong, you're a great housemate, Fatima, but you're just not as good in bed."

Fatima laughed. "Maybe he'll ask once you're back from travelling and he sees how easy it is to live with you. But you realise you'll need your licence if you're gonna move to that cabin."

"True," Morgan sighed. "And I really don't fancy learning to drive. But I'd still want it."

"And that's that on true love," Chloe said. "Thank god he found you."

"Hear, hear!" I said. "He's had so much bad relationship baggage for so long, it's nice to see him so happy."

"I suppose you're the queen of overcoming relationship baggage," Chloe said, and it took me a moment to realise she was talking to me. I frowned.

"Wait, what? What's that supposed to mean?" As far as I knew, Phil hadn't had any long-term relationships to qualify as baggage.

Chloe shrugged. "Just that Phil's been through the town's population of eligible women twice over, and that must be hard."

I didn't know how to respond. No, it hadn't been hard, but would it have been if we were actually together? Was it just the pretence of the relationship that kept it from being a problem?

"Everything going okay between you two?" Fatima asked.

"Yeah, great," I said, but I wasn't convinced myself. It was all starting to feel very ... real. And intense.

If we'd actually been together, I suppose our relationship progress would have been ideal. And maybe that was why I was feeling so confused: because it was progressing like an actual relationship, if a bit fast. But the truth of what it was kept undermining my feelings. I wondered if he was feeling the same, or if he was keeping his emotional distance.

Then Morgan asked for an update on Ethel, and suddenly I had a lot more to say, both because I was grateful for a change of subject, and because I'd become way more involved with Ethel over the summer. I told them about her physio updates, and the arthritis, and how she'd managed to remember the names of some of the crystals I'd given her, and the somewhat sad but ultimately hilarious attempt at a joke she'd made the day before, where she'd ended up calling Phil a bellend, and we still didn't know what the punchline was supposed to be.

"See, that's why he loves you," Chloe said. "Ethel is the most important thing in the world to him, and you clearly care about her."

I felt myself tense up just the slightest bit, and Chloe caught it instantly, her eyes going wide. "Holy shit, have you two not dropped the L-bomb?"

I tried to play it cool; I hadn't expected the lore we'd made up about this to actually be needed. "Please, we've been together for like five minutes."

"Uh, yeah, and you've been *avoiding* being together for like five *years*."

"Don't remind me," I muttered. I wracked my brain for anything I could throw out to change the subject, but ultimately it was Morgan who saved my ass.

"Oh my god!" Morgan gasped, pointing at the hedge line several metres away. We all snapped our heads to look, and I saw a tiny muntjac deer poking its head through the greenery. It was rare to see them out so long before sunset, and we all froze to watch it as it snuffled around for a moment before darting out of view.

Morgan and Chloe turned the conversation to some rabbits they had at the local rescue, and I was relieved that the spotlight had moved off me. Eventually they started talking about rescheduling their girls' day, and I was surprised when their revised plans seemed to include me by default.

I'd been so desperate for friends after moving home that I'd agreed to play Dungeons & Dragons, for fuck's sake. And my willingness to get involved seemed to be paying off. But when things with Phil fell apart, which was an inevitable part of this whole arrangement, would my newfound friendships crumble with it, just like they had in Manchester? Phil and I had promised each other we'd find a way out of the relationship that didn't blow up either of our lives, but we hadn't talked about it at all yet. My life looked so different now than it had just a month ago. There was so much more to lose than I would have thought possible; so much more than I'd ever had in Manchester. Time with Ethel, my relationships with Morgan and Fatima and even Chloe... I wasn't sure I was willing to sacrifice any of it.

Phil and I were more than halfway to our breakup, and I didn't feel confident anymore that we'd do it gracefully. So I promised myself then and there that I would be the one to bring it up, no matter how desperately I didn't want to.

CHAPTER 17
PHIL

My first date night without Amy was a stark reminder of how much I'd been struggling in the previous months. Ethel had her first-ever sundowning episode, which the specialist had supposedly prepared me for, but nothing could have made me ready. She knew who I was, but she kept pacing the room back and forth, shouting at someone who wasn't there. I tried multiple times to get her to sit down, or to take her to bed, but she fought me off every time.

I'd tried to keep myself busy by working on the costumes – specifically, I was stitching together the various components of Grey's chain mail armour – but I kept messing up and had to frog it twice, so eventually I resigned myself to sitting on the sofa and watching Ethel. The dishes sat unwashed in the sink, the data entry job I'd been ignoring all week sat undone on my laptop, and the chain mail sat unassembled on the coffee table. It took every ounce of mental energy I had to just make sure Ethel didn't hurt herself, and by the time we were both in bed, I was so tired that I didn't even do my usual nightly spiral about Amy.

DATE KNIGHT

I woke up from a fitful night of sleep the next morning, and I felt like I'd been hit by a truck. Ethel wasn't much better; she was in relatively good spirits, but she seemed exhausted, and I made the executive decision that we'd have to skip the Evans family dinner.

PHIL

> Hey, so sorry, but we had a really bad night last night, so I think Ethel needs a chill day. We'll have to wait until Tuesday to see each other.

I regretted it as soon as I'd hit send – it was unlikely she was constantly counting down to the next time she'd see me the way I was with her – but she saw it straightaway, so I didn't get the chance to edit it.

AMY

> Oh no! Everything okay? Why don't I come to you instead? I can hang with her whilst you catch up on things?

I honestly considered taking her up on it. I missed her, which was wild after just two days, and I knew seeing her would make me feel better. But she didn't deserve to be my emotional support crutch.

PHIL

> No, that's okay, thank you though.

AMY

> 👍

> BTW

> Let your mischievous side come out to play for a little while today.

It took me a moment to realise it was my horoscope. She'd taken to sending them to me most mornings, and it was the highlight of my day; not because I cared much what my horoscope said, but because it broke the texting seal so I could message her back without worrying if it was too much. As long as she kept sending them to me, I knew I hadn't scared her off.

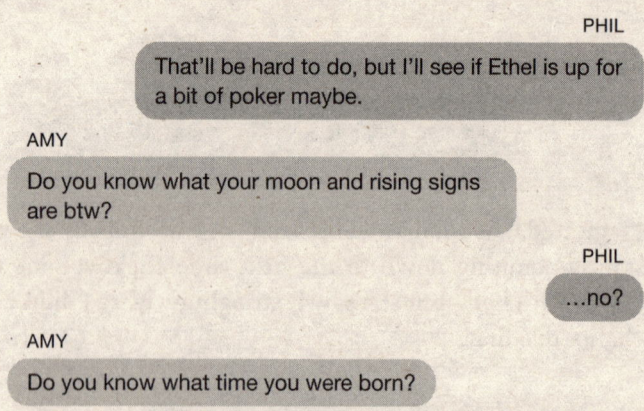

I did know, but only because a girl I'd dated in uni had asked me and I'd had to phone Ethel, who knew down to the minute. So instead of telling Amy, I opened my browser and found something that would calculate my moon and rising signs.

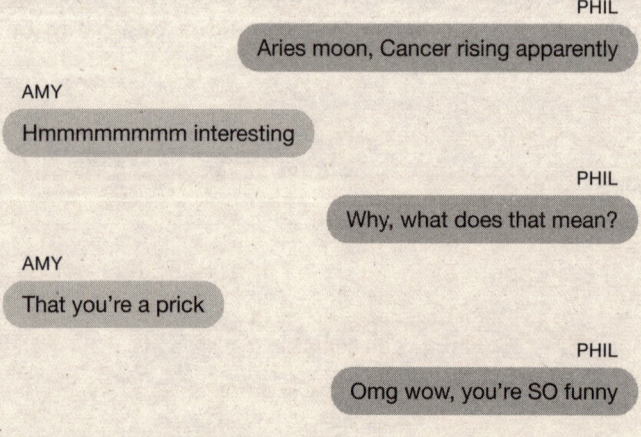

> **AMY**
> I mean, that's what the cards say, too. I don't make the rules.

> **PHIL**
> Maybe you need new cards.

> **AMY**
> Tell me about it.

This, of course, sent me down an hours-long rabbit hole trying to find a new tarot deck for Amy. I was pretty sure it was tarot, anyway ... actually there were loads of kinds of decks, including something called oracle decks, which were way more varied. I found a few good options, then got overwhelmed and decided to start looking later on.

But between looking up my moon and rising signs and looking for decks, and maybe all my googling of what the crystals on my windowsill actually meant when I forgot, I'd clearly told the internet gods I was into all that. I started getting ads everywhere for all kinds of tarot-themed stuff, witchy decorations, online courses, the works. Eventually, there was one ad that made me stop scrolling with how perfect it was. I bought it on impulse, even though Amy's birthday wasn't for about nine months, and like Christmas, we wouldn't be together anymore. Maybe it could be a breakup present?

Plus, I'd now told the internet I was happy to buy this shit from ads, so I'd get them for the rest of my life and never be allowed to go a second without thinking about Amy. I was pretty sure she'd love that, no matter how she felt about me when all this was said and done.

But no, I didn't want it to be a breakup present. More and more, I was certain that I didn't want to break up with Amy. I was also becoming more and more sure that she felt the same way, at least on some level. I knew I'd hurt her five years ago, but maybe she was further past that than I'd thought. Maybe what had happened with Niamh and Chris had put that into perspective for her. And maybe, just maybe, we'd grown close enough through all this for her to let herself feel something for me again. I could only hope.

But that wasn't right either. I could do more than just hope. I could pull my finger out and tell Amy Evans how I felt, for the first time in our storied history. Or better yet, show her. And this new deck was just the first step.

When Tuesday came, Anil called in sick, and I knew Amy was head down working on a big pitch for her dad, so I suggested we bail on the pub quiz and just see each other in a couple of days. I felt like I was running out of time – the festival was the following weekend, and Ethel was having more bad days than good in terms of how much care she needed – and I was trying desperately to buy myself more of it.

The irony, of course, was that I was running out of time with Amy, too; we had just weeks left until the ball. But it was easier to focus on the less confusing and more overwhelming things going on around me, like Ethel, so I tried to put it out of my mind.

Sure, I was drowning without her, but every time I looked around the house or took a mental inventory of what I had to deal with, it became easier to justify keeping Amy at arm's length. She was twenty-five, and so full of life. She finally had the job she'd wanted, and she'd gotten closer to the rest of our friends. She didn't need to be playing chauffeur to her fake boyfriend and his demented nan. She deserved to be getting something out of her relationships, and I just didn't have much to give her.

DATE KNIGHT

～

By the time Ethel's Thursday appointment rolled around, I cancelled on Amy again, claiming Anil was still sick, and that I would drive Ethel to physio myself. But I should have known she wouldn't just let me get away with it. Amy Evans had never let a single thing slide unmentioned in her life, and quiet quitting our fake relationship was apparently not the exception. So on Friday, when I told Jack I wouldn't be at film night, Amy, Jack, and Chloe showed up on my doorstep at seven with my go-to takeaway order.

Ethel was having a good day, actually, and as soon as they all walked in, she beamed. I expected her to go straight to Chloe, since they hadn't seen each other in months, and clearly Chloe expected that too, walking in with open arms. But Ethel went straight for Amy, wrapping her in a hug and asking why she hadn't been around that week.

Once Chloe had recovered from being jilted, she asked Ethel if she remembered how to play Hold 'Em.

"Remember?" Ethel asked, affronted. "I'm pretty sure I taught you lot how to play."

"Yeah, well, you also taught me how to drive," I said, "but I had to take your licence off you years ago when you forgot how roundabouts worked."

"You go the wrong way round *one* time," Ethel said to Amy, leaning in conspiratorially, and Amy dutifully scoffed.

"The cheek!" she said, smiling over at me, and my whole body relaxed. Seriously, why had I convinced myself it was better for her to be anywhere but here, with me?

"To answer your question, Chloe," Ethel continued, "these hands will remember how to play Hold 'Em long after my brain goes full veg."

Chloe sputtered a laugh; she clearly hadn't experienced how

candidly we joked about Ethel's condition. I had to admit it was seeming less and less funny to me.

"Well then," Jack said, producing a deck of cards from his pocket, "put your money where your mouth is."

Ethel scoffed. "You think I'm going to just take all your money from you? I'm far too kind for that."

"I think I can help with that," Amy said, reaching into her backpack and producing two family-sized bags of Galaxy Minstrels.

Just a few minutes later, the five of us were crowded around our tiny dining table, the lights low at Ethel's insistence. I watched Ethel closely as she dealt the first hand. It did take her a moment to remember what she was doing, but as she predicted, the moment she started shuffling, the muscle memory kicked in. She even attempted to do what we'd dubbed the "casino accent" growing up, which was essentially a bad mid-Atlantic American accent, though it melded more with her own accent the longer we played.

The only thing she struggled with was the concept of bluffing. Every hand, her bets matched almost perfectly with the quality of her hand, folding the moment someone else made a big move. I was overjoyed – it made her a less lethal opponent, for sure, but it also meant she was still able to process how good of a hand she had and make decisions quickly. Amy seemed to notice this too, commenting every time on how well Ethel had gauged the odds. I just wished nights like this weren't so rare these days.

At the end of the night, Amy paused in the doorway as Jack and Chloe left.

"You know I have Anil's number too, right?"

I gulped. "Oh."

"I'll see you tomorrow." The way she said it, it was clear it wasn't a request, or a platitude. She was letting me know that she knew Anil hadn't been sick, and that whether I wanted to or not, I'd see her tomorrow.

⁓

AND THEN IT was date night. I'd asked Anil if he could pretty please come over after his course, even though it would be late, both to make up for his lack of hours so far that week and so I could make things up to Amy. Not that I had to – there was nothing in our rules that said we'd do anything in particular, or see each other more than once a week – but I wanted to. She'd shown me the night before that she wanted to be there, and for now at least, I was done keeping her at bay.

PHIL

> I've got Anil tonight. What should we do?

AMY

> Leave it to me. I have an idea.

Amy showed up at half past seven, just a couple minutes after Anil did, with an actual picnic basket made of brown wicker, with a red checkered lining and a rolled-up blanket.

"Ooh, let me guess," I said after she'd greeted Ethel. I stepped out the front door, slinging a backpack over my shoulder. "Skydiving? Wait, no. Ice skating?"

"How'd you guess?"

Instead of heading back to her car, she started walking down the street; clearly we weren't going far. It felt good to be walking – it was hot as hell, but I'd been inside all day cleaning up after an isolated week so Anil wouldn't feel like he needed to do it. There was still a huge pile of tailoring work to do, and I hadn't finished a job all week, but at least the house was properly clean for the first time in ages. And now I was touching grass with Amy whilst Ethel was well cared for at home. Things were pretty good by my standards.

We walked out to the edge of town, about twenty minutes away, and across a big green meadow towards the river.

"You Evanses and your swimming spots," I said when I realised where we were headed. I was pretty sure Jack had pulled this exact move on Morgan when they'd gotten together, which was a weird thought. My stomach did a backflip at the idea that Amy was trying to make a move – was this what I'd been hoping for?

"Don't worry," she said. "I'm not expecting you to swim."

That was good, since I didn't have my swim trunks.

There were dozens of other people out here on the green, tossing frisbees and flying kites and having picnics of their own. It was late enough that the oppressive heat had lifted, and we passed the last of the swimmers walking in the opposite direction as they headed home. It took us twice as long as it should have to cross the meadow because Amy kept stopping to pet dogs that came up to us.

When we got to the river, the path diverging to either side, Amy didn't follow either route but rather took off her sandals and started fording the river, as if that were the most normal thing to do.

"Come on," she said. "I know a spot."

Okay, this was definitely starting to feel like a move. But my body was moving, my socks and shoes in hand, before my brain could question it.

Once we were across the river, we walked barefoot for a few minutes on the other side until we reached a secluded clearing just a couple of metres from the water. The sun was still very much out, so the shade from the surrounding trees made it noticeably cooler. It was golden hour, and the broad-leafed trees glowed around the edges. The light caught Amy's hair too as she rolled out the blanket, and I found myself frozen to the spot on the edge of the clearing as I watched her. She was so beautiful, and she'd made me a picnic, and she drove me half crazy. God, I was in trouble.

"Come on," she said as she sat down, waving me over to the blanket. I walked brainlessly over to her; I would have jumped off a bridge if she'd asked me to in that moment. Thank god she was too busy unloading the basket to pay any attention to the way I was gawking.

Except eventually my attention snapped to the blanket like a rubber band, because she'd produced a full-on charcuterie board, with at least half a dozen cheeses, just as many meats, fruit, crackers, and even a bottle of wine.

"I had to ask Jack for the pairing guide you sent him ages ago," Amy said, holding the bottle out to me, "but this should be a good all-rounder."

"You did well," I said, pretending to look at the bottle but knowing I would have drunk it no matter what it was.

She *had* done well though; I eventually found enough wherewithal to actually eat like a normal person, and it was delicious. The perfect meal for a summer's evening. I hoovered it up, half because it was so good and half because chewing meant not having to talk. And I didn't trust myself to talk like a normal person.

Amy, on the other hand, talked enough for the two of us. She picked at her food in between telling me about the rewilding trip with her mum, the ideas she and Fatima had for Eden's backstory, and the meeting she had coming up in a few weeks to present the pitch for the Kenchester job. Meanwhile, I sat there watching her, in awe of the woman she was, so full of life and so interested in everything and so fucking thoughtful. I needed to tell her how wonderful she was. How much joy she brought me. How around all the logistics and worries of my life, part of my mind was always stuck on her. I didn't know exactly what to say, but I was finally going to say it.

I opened my mouth and sucked in a deep breath for courage, just as she took a bite of her food.

"Amy, I—"

"Oh shit," she said suddenly with her mouth full, sending a few cracker crumbs spraying in my direction, and we both laughed as she tried to hold the rest in her mouth.

"I forgot to send you your horoscope for today," she said once she'd composed herself.

"I'm sorry, *that's* what was so important you couldn't swallow first?"

She held up her middle finger with one hand as she got out her phone with the other. "Here, look."

She held up the screen so I could see:

You are in charge of your own pleasure. Don't be afraid to take it, selfishly and often.

If it hadn't been in her astrology app, I would have thought she'd written it herself. That she'd somehow read my mind and was telling me to make my move. But no, it was right there on the screen.

"I have something for you," I said, my bravado evaporating under her gaze, grasping for anything I could do in that moment *besides* take my pleasure.

Amy's face broke into a grin. "Yay, presents!" She held out her hands in front of her, opening and closing them.

"Alright, close your eyes then," I said, but she pulled a face.

"If you give me something gross, Philip—"

"It's not gross, I promise."

"Fine," she sighed, then complied. I reached into my backpack and pulled out what I had ordered her earlier in the week, placing the small cardboard box in her hands.

I took a moment to look at Amy before letting her open her eyes. It would be so easy to lean in and kiss her right now; to do what I'd been wanting to for years, and what my horoscope was literally telling me to do. She looked so beautiful, with the setting sun filtering through the trees to cast orange streaks across her freckled skin.

"Okay, open," I said instead, and it took her a moment to process what I'd given her and read the front of the box, but when she did, she gasped in delight. God, I wanted to make her make that sound again and again.

"Phil," she said as she turned it over, her voice heavy with emotion.

"I went for an oracle deck in the end," I explained. "All the research I did implied that you can sort of bond with a tarot deck, right? So I didn't wanna just buy you a new one. But this looked cool."

It was cool, actually; I'd flicked through it when I'd opened it. It was an astrology-themed deck with a watercolour design style. All of the cards were heavenly bodies and houses, from the zodiac constellations to the planets to the phases of the moon. Most of it meant nothing to me, but given how astrology-obsessed Amy was, I hoped it would mean something to her.

"It's perfect," she said quietly, opening the box to see the cards. For a good five minutes, she flipped between reading the cards and paging through the accompanying booklet that explained their meanings.

"Do you wanna do it now?" she asked suddenly, and I was embarrassed at how long it took me to realise that she wasn't propositioning me, and to shake off the effect that misunderstanding had had on me.

"Yeah, go for it," I said, helping to clear space between us on the blanket. I was inexplicably nervous all of a sudden. I'd never done any kind of reading, and I just knew I'd manage to bungle it. I didn't even believe in all that, but I didn't want to mess it up somehow.

Amy held the deck out in front of her and had me put a hand

on top and focus all my energy into it. I didn't really know what that meant, so I just zeroed in my attention on the spots where my hand met hers on the edges, and the heat that passed between us. Amy had her eyes closed, and I supposed I should do the same, but I still couldn't take my eyes off her.

"Okay," she said with a nod, opening her eyes, and I quickly shut mine so I could pretend to be slowly opening them too. "Tell me when."

She started shuffling, and I wasn't sure what to look for, but I was pretty sure I'd done it wrong when she reached the end of the deck and I still hadn't said anything.

"Sorry," I said, but she shook her head.

"That's okay. Don't tell me to stop until it feels right."

When she started again, I tried to focus on the shuffling, having her stop about two-thirds of the way through. She drew the card that was on top at that moment and put it between us. It was a red circle with a constellation in it and the word "Sagittarius" written below.

"What does it mean?" I asked, and Amy laughed.

"I don't know," she admitted. "I mean, I know what Sagittarius is. That's Morgan's sun sign actually. But oracle cards are all different, so I need to use the book." She opened it up and flipped through until she found the corresponding page, squinting as she read through it.

"Hah!" she shouted, not properly laughing, just that one "hah". Then she kept reading.

"What?" I asked when she didn't explain, trying to lean forward over the booklet to read over the top, but she yanked it away from me.

"Let me read!" she said, then scooted a few inches away from me and resumed reading. Another few seconds later, she nodded and shut the book.

"So the good news is that this deck is amazing."

"That's good," I said warily. "What's the bad news?"

"The bad news, for you anyway, is that it's impeccably accurate."

I frowned. "How so?"

She cleared her throat and reopened the book, reading directly from the page. "This card could mean that you're spreading yourself too thin. Sagittarius is adaptable, but that doesn't mean you should try to do it all. If you do, you risk burning out, or possibly even losing yourself altogether."

Amy stared at me for a moment, her eyes wide as she gauged my reaction, but then she just burst out laughing, and I couldn't help but laugh too. It was, in fact, a little *too* accurate for my taste, but I had to laugh or I might cry.

"Well that's fucking spooky."

"Isn't it just?"

I reached my hand out for the booklet to have a look, and this time she handed it over happily.

"Can I ask you a question?" I asked, holding it up, and Amy nodded. "Do you actually believe in all this?"

Amy sighed and seemed to think about her answer. She narrowed her eyes, not angrily, but in consideration. Like she was judging whether she could be real with me. I tried to somehow convey telepathically that she could tell me everything; that she could admit to casting spells on me and I'd still be okay with it.

"Honestly?"

I nodded encouragingly.

"I'm not sure," she admitted, and she slumped slightly. "I mean, I believe in science, and Western medicine, and all that. And I don't believe that putting a rhodonite freeform under the full moon will cure Ethel's dementia, just like I don't believe I'm inherently self-centred because I'm an Aries."

"Good," I said, frowning. "Because you're one of the least self-centred people I've ever met."

We didn't often compliment one another without softening it with snark, and it took her a moment to absorb what I'd said.

"Thank you," she said, smiling. "But I do believe it can be useful. That if I use my birth chart to try to better understand myself, and better communicate with the people in my life, that's no bad thing. And if I use a horoscope as a prompt for looking at my life through a different lens, that's usually a good thing."

I didn't interrupt her – I could tell from the way she seemed to feel her way through the explanation that this was maybe the first time she'd articulated this out loud.

"And if I give Ethel a crystal as a gesture of love, and of care," she continued, "then that sentiment isn't wasted. It's a reflection of my intention to help her, which I follow up with other actions. Like helping you around the house, and driving her to appointments, and just keeping her company. I give her the crystals because I believe it will mean something to her to know I care, and it certainly means something to me. If there's some sort of magic to it too, that's just a bonus."

I sat there for a long moment after she finished, just nodding. She was right; she showed time and time again how much she cared about Ethel, in ways that went far beyond crystals and readings. In fact, I couldn't think of a single time she'd used astrology or tarot or crystals to communicate something she didn't back with her actions.

"What about you?" she asked, and I could tell my lack of response had made her uncomfortable. "You don't believe in fate, or the stars, or anything like that?"

I didn't like being put suddenly in the spotlight, and the retort was out of my mouth before I could stop it. "Well, I believe in the stars, obviously. Just step outside and look up."

Amy rolled her eyes. "Hardy har. You know what I meant."

"You're right," I said, dropping the instinctual smirk. "Sorry."

"It's okay," she said, looking at me so intently it was like she was trying to read my mind. And hell, after that oracle card, maybe she could. The thought made me squirm; I definitely didn't need her seeing everything going on in there.

"Not really," I finally admitted. "I think I stopped believing in that kind of thing – or stopped wanting to, anyway – when my parents died."

"Oh, shit, Phil," Amy said, bringing her hands to her mouth. "I'm so sorry. I didn't mean to imply anything to do with that."

I reached across the space between us to put a hand on her knee. "It's okay. I didn't take it that way."

"Good," she said, putting her hand on top of mine, making me breathe in sharply.

"In fact," I said, "I think it's nice that you believe that."

"It doesn't compromise your precious sense of free will, or seem like stupid people grasping at straws? That was what Chris always said."

I shook my head. "Well, first of all, you're far from stupid. And second of all, all this stuff with Ethel has shown me that free will only gets you so far. That damn card was right; I've never felt less in control of her wellbeing, or my own, than I do right now. I do everything I can, staying organised with her meds and consistent with her physio and informed about every new protocol and finding, but none of it stops her slipping away more and more every day. Some days I feel like there's nothing I can do at all."

Amy squeezed my hand and held it in place on her knee as she scooted closer to me, until we were just a couple inches apart, our legs nearly touching.

"You do so much for that woman," she said. "I know you feel like you owe her for raising you after your parents died, but you do more than anyone would ever expect. I don't think it's possible to have an easy experience with dementia. From what I've read, it's really normal to feel like you do as a carer."

"From what you've read?"

She shrugged. "Yeah. I'm subscribed to a few newsletters. I've ordered a couple of books."

I smiled. "I love how much you care about her. It means a lot to me."

"Of course I do. It's Ethel."

That might not have meant anything to anyone else, but it meant everything to those who knew her. For Ethel's whole life, she'd been a force of nature. And yeah, it was heartbreaking to see her losing pieces of that every day. But it didn't take away one bit of the impact she'd had on everyone in her life over the years.

Amy turned my hand over with hers and laced her fingers through mine, and suddenly the remnants of heat in the air collapsed in on that spot like a black hole. I couldn't look away from where we touched, her palm pressed firmly against mine.

We were linked in so many ways in our lives, and it felt more palpable than ever. After all my attempts to slow down time over the months and years that I'd been caring for Ethel, it was here with Amy where I felt like I could hold all of that at bay. Where time stood still.

Suddenly, I wanted nothing more than to make the move. But then I saw a flicker of uncertainty in her gaze, and my brain flipped from "fuck it" to just "fuck". So I pulled my hand away and shot up to my feet, pulling my top off over my head as I stood.

"What the hell are you doing?" she asked, looking up at me, and I felt a moment of smug satisfaction that she couldn't quite bring her gaze all the way to my eyes.

"Oh, come on," I said tauntingly, tossing my T-shirt to the side and starting on my belt. "As if you didn't want to go for a swim."

"I told you I wasn't expecting that."

"Wanting and expecting are two different things," I said with a grin.

"Yeah, well, it's so unexpected that I didn't actually bring a swimsuit."

"What a shame," I said, shrugging off my shorts so I was in just my pants. I could feel Amy's eyes roving over me, and I had to will myself to stay calm lest I give her something to gawk at. I decided the safest course of action was to actually get in the water so she couldn't see me at all, so I turned and stepped carefully over to the river's edge.

I'd expected the water to be cold, but the hot summer sun had warmed it through, and it was a pleasant temperature even as I got deep enough to hide what I needed to hide.

"Come on then," I called to Amy, who'd followed me to the edge but hadn't undressed. "Don't be scared, kiddo. The water's great."

I'd long since stopped thinking of Amy as "kiddo", but I knew it would rile her up. And I was right; she set her jaw and glared at me for just a moment before she stood and started unbuttoning her denim cutoffs. She tugged them off over her hips – with an effort I very much enjoyed watching – and they fell to the ground, where she kicked them aside unceremoniously.

My gaze roved up her tantalisingly long legs to where the tanned skin gave way to a thin, gauzy pair of underwear. Then I watched as she gripped the hem of her T-shirt, tugging it up painfully slowly, as if she knew I was watching with bated breath. But I couldn't tear my eyes away from the motion long enough to find out if she was teasing me, and in that moment, I didn't care. Her stomach wasn't as tanned as the rest of her, but I saw a peek of even paler flesh as her bra caught on her fingertips, and for a moment, my heart stopped. But she left it on as she took the T-shirt all the way off, revealing a thin white material that matched her pants. My brain skipped a couple of steps ahead, past the realisation that she'd worn matching bra and pants on our picnic, to the fact that she was about to get in the water in a white bralette that looked semi-translucent at best.

I swallowed hard. It was a good thing I'd gotten in first, I thought, or she'd be seeing just how appreciative I was.

She waded in, and I kicked backwards into the deeper water, making her come to me. But once she was in to her thighs, she dove in the rest of the way elegantly, and I lost sight of her in the murky water.

Then her hands found the sides of my thighs under the surface, and I tensed. She came up out of the water directly in front of me, her face appearing at my waist just before she surfaced, sending my imagination running wild. She stood, her shoulders just visible above the waterline. I couldn't help but reach out and tuck away the stray strand of her hair stuck to her face.

I wanted to pull her close to me, and for a moment, I wondered if my subconscious had taken over, because she seemed to float closer. But then I realised she'd stepped in just an inch or so. I did the same, bringing us so close we were practically in one another's arms. She didn't say anything, and I didn't either, but it felt like we were daring each other forward, playing a familiar game of chicken that I'd decided I wouldn't be losing again.

I held my breath as she stepped in again, bringing her close enough now that I had to look down between us to avoid her gaze. As I did, I could see her breasts in the water, and yep, that material was far from opaque.

She cleared her throat, and I was horrified to realise how obvious my ogling had been. So I looked up again, meeting her gaze with mine, all but withering under the intensity of her stare, even as she smiled up at me. There was a moment where it felt like we might kiss, and I wanted to so badly. I regretted not kissing her before, on our first date when we got back from bowling, or on that night five years ago.

I wouldn't make that mistake again. She was right here in front of me, damn near skinny dipping with me. It was terrifying and intoxicating, and I had never felt more turned on in my life.

Her smile faltered, and I watched her throat as she swallowed hard. Maybe she'd read the intention in my gaze, and she'd been anticipating this as much as I had. I was about to find out, because just like the horoscope had told me, I was in charge of my own pleasure. And if Amy would let me, I'd happily take charge of hers too.

I let my hand drift out in front of me until it found her waist, then slowly pulled her towards me. We were close enough now that the water treated us like one mass, flowing around both of us instead of cutting between us, the heat building quickly without the current to whisk it away. I felt my breathing grow shallower and shallower as her hands drifted to my arms, running over my biceps and through the hair on my chest. I wanted to watch her touch me like that, but I couldn't take my eyes off hers. The green radiating out from her wide pupils practically glowed in the golden hour light, and her eyes turned down at the corners as she looked questioningly at me. I was about to answer all her questions.

My gaze dropped towards her mouth as I began to lean in, but her light touch suddenly became firm as she pressed her palm to the centre of my chest and pushed me away.

"So, I was thinking," she said, and I blinked hard, confused. "Hmm?"

"We've been breaking one of our rules," she said, stepping back just enough that we were two separate objects again, the cool river water rushing between us. I pictured every time she'd put her hands on me over the last seven weeks, and vice versa, and all I could think was that we'd not broken that rule enough.

"How's that?"

I tore my eyes from her mouth and met her gaze again, and it was like running into a brick wall. I could immediately see that her defences had gone up, and I'd missed when and why. Suddenly, all the bravery and certainty I'd mustered leached out of me into the river, washing away downstream.

She sighed before she answered, looking nervously down at her hands as she lifted them above the surface, letting the water run off them.

"Because," she said, matter-of-factly, "we haven't agreed how we're going to break up. And I think it's time we figure that out."

CHAPTER 18
AMY

I hadn't really known what to expect from the fantasy festival. Sure, I'd looked at the website, but it was hard to tell what the vibe would be just from a list of vendors. The others had said it would be like a Renaissance Faire, like the one they'd been to the year before, but given that I hadn't been there, that was only so helpful to me. Plus, they hadn't actually been to this festival before, so they were really just guessing.

But after being there for less than five minutes, I fully understood the hype. In reality, it was probably only about half of the people we passed, but it seemed like nearly everyone was dressed up in varying levels of cosplay. There were people who looked like they'd been working on their costumes for years, like the full-on angel with massive, feathered wings and golden skin, and others whose had probably been store bought. And all of them were having an equally great time from the look of it.

The festival was in full swing by the time we got there, since we'd had to drive in that morning. We'd all met at Fatima and Morgan's house and piled into Jack's and my respective cars; they weren't the most economical on the road, but they had the most space for all of us and our bags, which were many given the sheer number of costumes. Phil rode with Chloe and me, but just like the other six days since our little river misadventure, things were off between us.

After I'd brought up the breakup strategy like I'd planned to, which felt nearly impossible with how close we'd gotten to doing something ill-advised, he'd just grumbled something about circling back after the festival and gotten out of the water. We'd walked back to his in relative silence, and he'd gone straight to his room as I said hello to Ethel and Anil. Both D&D and the pub quiz had been on hiatus for the week, so we hadn't actually spoken since I'd left his house that night.

He was obsessively glued to his phone on the way to the festival, which wasn't unusual when he was away from Ethel. But he didn't even try to keep up with the conversation I was having with Chloe in the back seat, despite the fact that I knew he had very strong opinions on who should play the next James Bond, probably based on actual factors instead of just who was hottest, which was the yardstick Chloe and I were using. And now that we were at the festival, Phil had paired off with Jack, and they walked several paces behind the rest of us as we explored.

The festival was set in the lush grounds of an impressive castle, adding to the fantasy vibes. Masses of people moved through the maze of tents and attractions, and groups formed every few paces to browse the offerings or admire one another's costumes. I'd never been much for people watching – I would always have preferred being in the heart of the action than on the outside – but I was mesmerised by everyone I saw. I knew I was annoying the shit out of Chloe by asking her every ten seconds to explain another costume, but I couldn't help it. I needed to be able to appreciate what I was seeing. And the more answers she gave me – "That's from *Rings of Power*"; "She's a playable character in *League of Legends*"; "I think they're just meant to be a normal jellyfish" – the more in awe I was of the vast swathe of nerd culture I'd never even dipped a toe into. I'd thought Jack and his friends – *they're my friends, too*, I reminded myself – were pretty nerdy. But it seemed they were just the very tip of the iceberg, and as it turned out, I didn't hate getting to peek under the surface. It had always felt painfully uncool, and my life's mission had been to avoid feeling ostracised, so I'd always avoided it. But here, surrounded by so many people passionate about their favourite things, I was definitely the uncool one.

We'd decided to save the *Shrek* costumes for the next day when it would be a bit cooler to spare Grey and Fatima having to sweat through their green body painting. Phil had asked what sort of other costume I wanted when I'd been invited along, and not wanting to give him more to do, I'd said to make whatever was easiest, or even just to tell me what to buy so he didn't have to make anything. But he'd clearly not been okay with that, and I'd ended up with *two* handmade skirts, the top one of which was a lovely brown and black tartan that he'd frayed slightly at the edges to give it a well-worn look. I had a pair of things called skirt hikes holding it up at the front, bunching it up with my underskirt, which had a raw linen look. He'd made me a plain black lace-up bodice, which I wore over an off-the-shoulder white blouse I already owned, and a tartan shawl that matched my skirt, which I could wrap over my shoulders to keep them out of the sun, wear as a hood if it started to rain, or tie around my waist for extra volume on my skirt if I wanted it out of the way. Chloe had loaned me a leather bag that clipped to my belt, big enough to hold my phone, my card, and the cash I'd stopped for on the way into town that morning. I'd offered to just bring a purse, but Phil had insisted that would have ruined the look, and he'd been right. Now I felt like I'd stepped straight out of *Outlander* or something – like I should be hitching up my skirt even further to run through a meadow – and after just fifteen minutes at the festival, I'd been complimented half a dozen times.

The others, however, were where Phil's creativity had really shone. I knew Jack's outfit was left over from the Ren Faire, but it was still amazing to see the intricacy of the brocade jerkin, a lopsided metal crown atop his head like some sort of wayward prince.

Grey wore the crocheted chain mail over a white tunic, their wrists wrapped in leather bracers, matching pauldrons on their shoulders. Phil hadn't made the leathers, but I knew how much trial and error had gone into that chain mail, and it looked perfect. It was hard to believe it was made of yarn, the way it shone in the sun, but I was sure Grey was grateful for the lighter material, as it was already quite warm.

Chloe and Fatima were dressed as slutty pink and purple versions of some *Lord of the Rings* villains – "Oh my god, *Nazgul*, it's not that hard," Chloe had said more than once – with big pointy helmets, semi-sheer corseted mini dresses, and knee-high platform boots. They looked fucking hot, and clearly I wasn't the only one who thought so, based on how many people stopped them for pictures.

Morgan had gone for a piratey look, with an off-the-shoulder top with huge sleeves, a waist cincher, three different skirts layered over one another, and a bunch of scarves and belts tied haphazardly around her waist. She'd topped it off with a tricorn hat, perched atop her mess of curls. All she was missing was a peg leg and a parrot.

Phil looked obnoxiously sexy, probably even more so for how aloof he was acting, which said a lot about my people-pleasing urges. He wore a dark brown pair of trousers with a fake sword holstered at his hip, a billowing white shirt, and a sort of cloak-shawl hybrid made of the same tartan he'd used for my costume, which hung bunched over one shoulder and long over the other. His beard and untrimmed hair only added to the effect, making him look like an adventurer who'd just stumbled into town, and I was but a lowly tavern wench swooning over him. Which annoyed the shit out of me, of course, so I tried my best to ignore him, focusing on everyone and everything buzzing around me instead.

The maze of tents opened up into different areas, some centred around stages with musical acts and comedians performing, and some holding activities, including people having literal sword fights in a little arena. I assumed at first, when I saw the battle, that the fighters were performers, but as I got closer, I realised that they were attendees like me, yet they'd apparently come prepared to have full-contact battles with one another. I really was in so much deeper than I would have thought possible after just a couple of months.

I was stood at the barrier watching them, marvelling at the difference between the brute force they were using and the swooping, elegant, choreographed fights I'd seen in films, when disaster struck.

One pair of fighters had positioned themselves just in front of me, and when one of them lunged, the other ducked out of the way, sending their assailant straight towards me. I shrieked and tried to dodge out of the way as he careened towards me, but the dull blade tore through the measly fabric barrier and caught my skirts, slicing straight through them. I fell to the ground, not because I'd been hurt, but because the tug on my skirts had thrown me off balance.

"Holy shit, are you okay?" Chloe asked, dropping to the ground next to me.

"Oh my god," the fighter said, pulling off his helmet to have what seemed like a full-on panic attack. He looked to be about my age, and his face went completely white. "I'm so sorry. I didn't mean to, I promise. The blade shouldn't be able to do any damage." He leaned over the barrier and grasped at my skirts, presumably looking for blood, but with his giant gauntlets and forearm guards on, and trying to move his sword and shield out the way at the same time, he was managing fuck all.

"Fuck off," Chloe snapped at him, glaring until he took a few steps back, then turned to crouch down next to me. "Are you hurt?"

"Out of the way," I heard from behind me. Chloe's eyes went wide as she stood up and took a step back, and then Phil was there in front of me.

"Did he hurt you?" he asked, his voice hoarse and angry as he looked over me, and I tried to ignore the way my breathing responded to his intensity.

"No, it just caught my skirt," I said. "I fell because I was trying to get out of the way."

"Fucking be careful, mate," he yelled at the fighter, who was stood a few feet away watching us, his hands fidgeting on the hilt of his sword.

"Sorry!" he called again, then resumed biting his lip anxiously.

"You're sure you're not hurt?" Phil asked me, and I nodded. "Can you stand?"

He held out his hand, and I took it, letting him pull me to my feet. As he did, the huge hole in the side of my skirts fell open, and I could clearly see my hip through it. I gasped.

"Phil, I'm so sorry," I said, looking up at him to see his gaze fixed on the hole, too.

"Why?" he asked, reaching out to grab the fabric, and I shuddered when his knuckles brushed against my exposed skin. "It wasn't your fault."

He bunched the hole closed and handed me the fabric to

hold whilst he stood back and looked at it, then nodded, seeming to make a decision.

"Put your shawl around your waist, and come with me." He held out his hand again.

I took my shawl from where it was draped over my arms and fastened it like he'd shown me, so it just about covered the giant tear, then took his hand.

I followed him as he pulled me through the festival grounds, back the way we'd come, towards the entrance. He paused a few times to check the festival map on his phone, but he never dropped my hand. Eventually, we came to a tent with a red hospital-style cross and a needle and thread on the side, and Phil pulled me inside.

There were a few other cosplay-clad festival goers inside, sat at the central table or stood on pedestals, mending their costumes. One side of the tent was lined with shelves full of plastic storage boxes, each labelled with a different item, from eyelets to thread to sheets of leather. In the middle of the table was a tray with scissors, needles, pins, and seam rippers.

Phil had me stand next to a table, then walked over to the section of thread boxes, scanning for what he wanted. Once he had the right colours – off white, and a brown that roughly matched our tartan – he came back and sat down next to me, bending so his face was level with my hip.

"Thank you," I said as he removed my shawl and began to pin the tear in the underskirt shut first.

"Don't thank me yet," he said softly around the pins he held between his lips, his brow pinched in concentration. "It won't be perfect."

"That's not what I meant," I said, shaking my head, which I apparently did with my whole body, because Phil put a hand on me to remind me to keep still, glaring silently at me. His hand pressed into the back of my thigh, so high that the tips of his fingers grazed my ass through my skirts. I wasn't sure if he could tell where he'd touched me, but I certainly could, and I definitely went still, which I supposed was the desired effect.

When he moved his hand and resumed pinning, I continued, careful not to move this time. "That's not what I meant," I said. "Thank you for coming to check on me. For caring."

"Of course I care if you're hurt," he said.

Which, true; it was pretty basic human decency, not any particular affection. But the way he'd rushed over, the urgency in his eyes as he'd scanned me for injury – it hadn't felt decent. It had felt almost desperate.

"You know what I mean," I muttered, though I wasn't sure he heard me, as he didn't respond. "Are you managing to enjoy yourself at least?" I asked, a bit louder this time, but again I must have moved.

"Hold still," he said, raising his voice slightly as if I were a disobedient puppy, and I rolled my eyes as I stilled, ignoring the shiver his stern voice sent up my spine.

"Yes, I was," he said as he threaded a needle and started stitching the underskirt. "But then you had to go and get stabbed."

"You literally just said it wasn't my fault."

"Doesn't mean it wasn't stressful."

As annoying as he was being, I knew Phil didn't need any more stress – he'd been head down on these stupid costumes for weeks, and I knew Ethel had been needing him more and more during the day. And it showed on his face; dark circles hung under his blue eyes, heavy with exhaustion.

"Are you okay, Phil?" I asked, willing him to look up at me – to tell me exactly what was weighing so heavily on him. Was it Ethel? Was it work? Was it me, and whatever had almost happened between us in the river last week? I'd thought I was doing the right thing when I pumped the brakes – doing what he would have wanted, too – but maybe I was wrong? I didn't want to think about the implications of that though when he had his hand up my skirt.

He didn't meet my gaze, and the pull of the fabric against my skin told me he was still hard at work down there.

"I'm fine," he said, almost robotically.

"Okay, but are *we* fine?"

That got a reaction, at least – Phil's fingers paused their work and he sighed, though he still didn't look up at me.

"Does it matter?"

I frowned. "Of course it matters."

He shook his head and put the lighter thread on the tray, picking up the brown as he started on the overskirt.

"I'm not so sure about that," he said. "But if you're worried about keeping up appearances, I'll be better. I'm just tired."

"Great, just what I wanted. I'm so grateful you're willing to rally yourself to be around me."

He didn't respond to that, and we stood there in heated silence – literally, my face got hotter and hotter as my annoyance stewed – until he was done, which he indicated by silently standing up and putting the thread back where he'd gotten it. The moment he moved away, I did too, desperate to put as much space between us as possible.

"How much?" I asked the attendant at the entrance, then handed her a fiver before I left. I heard Phil call my name as I walked away from the tent, but I didn't look back.

An hour later, I still hadn't found the others again. They had moved on from the fighting area, and despite my phone indicating full signal, nothing was going through. I was lost in a sea of costumes, looking for five nerds in a group of tens of thousands. I thought I saw Chloe and Fatima's weird helmets about a million times, but it turned out there were just a lot of pink and purple outfits, and even Jack's six-foot-whatever ass was nowhere to be seen.

Eventually, I decided I'd just have to eat lunch alone, so I made my way to a grassy area next to the ruined part of the castle. There was a cluster of food trucks and tents next to a large reflection pool, bordered on the other side by a stunning flower garden built into the ruins. Dozens of people wandered through it taking photos, and I made a mental note to look for some online after the festival. I was sure they'd look like they were straight out of one of those fantasy novels Morgan was always reading.

I ordered a whiskey pulled pork sandwich from a stand that was built to look like a steam engine, then took it to a bench that had just freed up in front of the reflecting pool, leaning forward as I ate so I wouldn't drop any on my outfit. I ate it in about five bites, licking my fingers clean of the sauce that had dripped down them.

"Is this seat taken?" I heard over my shoulder as I had my thumb in my mouth, and my heart jumped as I turned around, hoping to see Phil. But instead, there was a man standing there in what looked like full plate armour, a helmet tucked under one arm, the other behind his back. He had shoulder-length light brown hair and just a dusting of facial hair across his jaw, with deep brown eyes that turned down slightly at the sides in an endearing way. He was maybe a few inches taller than Phil, at least from what I could tell sitting down.

Something about him looked familiar, but I couldn't quite place it, until I looked closer at the sword, recognising it from where it had torn through my skirts.

"You," I said, trying not to sound overly hostile.

"Yeah, sorry, it's me," he said, grimacing. "But don't worry, I come in peace. And with a peace *offering*, no less."

He produced a brown paper bag from behind his back.

"I hope you like pain au chocolat?"

"I do indeed," I said, eyeing the pastry warily. I didn't make a habit of taking food from men I didn't know, especially those who had wielded a blade at me. But for some reason, there was something about him that felt trustworthy.

Famous last words before he buries you in the forest.

"I bought it from just over there," he said, pointing behind him at a coffee cart with a rack of identical pastries on display. "But I'll take a bite first if you'd like."

"That's okay," I said, scooting over to one side of the bench. He smiled and sat next to me, handing me the brown bag. He set his helmet on the grass at his feet before fumbling for the shoulder straps holding his shield to his back. I unwrapped the pastry whilst he did, pressing it lightly with my fingers. How it was still so crisp despite having been out for hours at a festival, I had no idea, but I wasn't questioning it. I took a bite, my eyes fluttering closed, a pleasured moan escaping my lips. It was heavenly.

My enemy-turned-benefactor laughed, and I opened my eyes, brushing crumbs off my mouth and chest as I chewed. "Sorry," I said, my mouth still half full.

"It's okay," he said, "it's nothing compared to almost skewering you on a dull blade."

I couldn't help but smirk. "In public, good sir?"

His cheeks went red, but he laughed again, a light and airy sound. It was nice.

"I'm Dan," he said, holding out his right hand between us. I shook it.

"Amy."

"Nice to meet you, Amy," he said, "and under better circumstances this time." His eyes were locked on mine, and I found myself grinning. He was actually quite charming when he wasn't bludgeoning me on the battlefield. Or, well, next to it.

"Thank you for the peace offering," I said, holding up the

rest of the pastry. "Offering accepted." I took what I hoped was a much daintier bite.

Dan threw his head back dramatically and brought his hands to his heart. "What a relief."

We spent a good few minutes chatting about where we were from (he lived near Bristol) and who we were here with (he was also with his D&D group, though he'd abandoned them to look for me). He was an ecologist by day, mostly evaluating new building sites for impacts on bat and newt populations, and a serial nerd by night. I learned that his costume wasn't just a standard knight get-up, but that he was meant to be a grittier version of a character called Sir Kirby from a kids' show called *Doc McStuffins*.

"I let my niece pick my costume," he explained. "She was obsessed with the show growing up in America, and she kept watching it when she and my sister moved back to the UK, even as she got older. I think it made her feel less homesick."

His sister lived not far from me, actually, just across the Severn in Ledbury, and he visited her a lot. There was a moment when I thought he was going to suggest we meet up – he looked at me meaningfully, scanning my face as if looking for the go-ahead – but he seemed to bail out, looking down at our feet instead.

"Oh shit," he said, as if remembering something suddenly. "I'm sorry about your skirt."

I gathered the fabric in my spare hand and turned to show him. "All fixed."

He nodded as he admired the handiwork, reaching out as if to touch it at one point before thinking better of it. "Impressive. You're good at that."

"It wasn't me," I said. "It was that guy who yelled at you to be more careful. Sorry about him."

He nodded. "I remember him fondly. Or, well, I remember

him, at least." I chuckled, then watched as Dan's eyes narrowed slightly. "Your boyfriend?"

I tipped my head back and laughed. A week ago, I wouldn't have thought twice about saying yes, and keeping up our charade, even to a stranger; that's what we'd agreed, after all. But Phil had been so distant for the past week, and so easily aggravated with me so far today, and I was annoyed. He'd felt like my boyfriend all summer, even if it was a ruse, but now? He really, really didn't.

Still, I wasn't quite prepared to tell Dan the whole truth, so I just settled for the truthiest truth I could manage.

"It's complicated."

Dan nodded, as if he'd been expecting that, but it wasn't a deal breaker. "The kind of complicated where you wouldn't want to give me your number?"

"Maybe I don't want to give you my number because you nearly skewered me."

"In public?" he said back to me, smirking. "I would never."

I felt genuinely conflicted, even putting aside whatever nonsense was going on with Phil. Under normal circumstances, I never would have met Dan. And yeah, him panicking after the whole stabbing debacle had been a bit of an ick. But I wasn't feeling the ick now. He seemed nice, and normal, and funny. And I wasn't ready to jump his bones, but that could have been the cosplay. He was definitely attractive, and if I squinted hard enough, I could even convince myself he looked a bit like Aaron Taylor-Johnson.

Not for the first time in my life, I felt annoyed at Phil for the irreparable damage he'd done to my ability to gauge attraction. I'd found other guys cute, and I'd even wanted to sleep with them, but there had never been the kind of electricity I felt with Phil. Even with Chris, it had been more about the social dynamic with the others than it was about him as a person. Was

I only capable of feeling palpable attraction to people I'd known for most of my life? Because if so, I was screwed.

But no, I refused to claim that. There had to be the possibility of something with literally anyone but Phil. If he didn't want me, I needed to learn to spread my wings – and maybe my legs – with other men.

I smiled, making a decision. "No, not that kind of complicated." Then I held out my hand for his phone, and he nearly dropped it trying to pull it out of his own leather pouch at his waist.

Just as I finished typing my number in and handed the phone back to Dan, I heard my name being called from somewhere behind me. I looked around for a few seconds before zeroing in on the figure striding purposefully across the grass.

It was Phil, again.

"What the hell, Amy?" he shouted as he came near. "I've been looking for you for more than an hour."

"Yeah, well, I didn't know the signal wouldn't work," I said, very intentionally not facing him. "Phil, this is Dan. Dan, Phil."

"Good to meet you, mate," Dan said, standing up and sticking out his hand, but Phil ignored it.

"Yeah, I fucking remember you," he sneered. "Now come on, Amy. The others are waiting."

"Don't be a twat, Phil," I said, standing, then turned to Dan. "I'm sorry about him. He's clearly forgotten how to be a human."

"Don't worry about it," Dan said, raising his hand. "I'll leave you to it. Goodbye, Amy." I smiled apologetically and waved.

"What the fuck is wrong with you?" I asked, turning on Phil. "He was apologising."

"It looked like he was doing more than just apologising," Phil said, pointing at Dan's retreating form. "Did you just give him your number?"

"So what if I did? What's it to you?"

Phil sighed, looking over his shoulder. "The others saw you, you know."

I looked back in the direction he had, where our friends were walking across the grass too, though tentatively, clearly trying to figure out if it was safe to approach. But I didn't care. I was so done with Phil's moodiness. He could be mad at me, but he needed to be a fucking grown-up and explain himself to me if so. Otherwise, what was the point? Why was I even there?

"Yeah, well, they also saw you ignore me the whole car ride," I said. "And my family saw me not come to yours at all this week because you wouldn't return my texts. So forgive me if I've stopped giving a shit."

Phil sighed again, but this time it seemed less exasperated and more just exhausted.

"Not here," he said, almost a whisper.

"Yes here," I said, so fucking done it wasn't funny. I wasn't exactly naming my future babies with Dan, but Phil didn't know that. If he was going to interrupt me meeting new people, acting all broody and possessive, but then still not kiss me or tell me what was wrong or anything else that an actual boyfriend would do, then we needed to sort it out *now*.

So I grabbed him by the arm and dragged him with me as I walked around to the other side of the retaining pool. The others shamelessly watched us as we went, so we rounded a crumbling wall into the gardens. There were couples and groups and impressively costumed people in every picturesque corner, so Phil and I stopped just in front of a roped-off path that led out the other side of the gardens into a copse of trees.

"Okay, that's enough," he said, wrenching his arm out of my hand. "If you wanna do this in public, then fine. Say what you want."

"Absolutely not," I said, shaking my head so hard I felt some of my hair come loose from the half-up style I'd so carefully done that morning. "You're the one who's clearly got a stick up your ass. What the hell is going on?"

"Jesus, you're not the only thing in my life, Amy," he said, his words full of annoyance. But his eyes went wide at the same time, and it looked as if he might start crying at any moment. He was clearly at his wits' end. "I've got other things I'm worried about."

"Then tell me," I said, stepping towards him and trying to grab his hand, but he pulled it away again. "Does none of this mean anything to you?" I gestured between us. "Shit, do none of the last nineteen years mean anything to you? Because if it's about Ethel, or work, or any of your friends, I care about that, too, regardless of our fake relationship status. I thought we'd established that."

"Of course we did," he said, holding my gaze. "It's not that, I promise."

"Because I don't actually need you to be okay," I said, desperate for him to understand. "You're dealing with more than any one person should have to. But I need to know that *we're* okay."

"Why?" he snapped, his lips pursing as he bit back words before choosing them. "Why is it so important to you that we're good, when you're just counting down the days until our breakup?"

Was he fucking serious? Was that what this was about? No, he couldn't mean that. There was no way that, after everything we'd been through over the years, *he* was mad at *me* for maintaining the boundaries we'd carefully drawn between us. My feelings for Phil had been an open secret since I'd been a teenager, and I was done pretending he didn't know. That it was somehow excusable for him to play dumb anymore, and that I had to be the one keeping track of where the line was, when he'd been the one to draw it five years ago.

"You fucking know why," I said through clenched teeth.

"Then say it," he said, stepping forward suddenly, his face close enough to mine that I could feel his breath on me; feel the tickle of his beard against my nose. He tilted forward and leaned his forehead against mine, and I could feel his words as he spoke, his voice strained and raspy. "Tell me, Amy. I'm begging you."

I closed my eyes and shook my head, gently this time.

"No," I said softly, my voice trembling. "I've put myself out there for you so many times. I won't do it again. Not without something concrete from you."

It was the closest I'd ever come to telling Phil how I felt, and I felt him swallow hard as our heads stayed pressed together.

"I fucking tried, Amy," he said, bringing his hand to my face, his fingers shaking against my cheek. He groaned, and it vibrated through my head and shoulders. "*You* shut it down. *You* made it clear you didn't want to have that conversation. I was ready."

"That's not fair," I said, clenching my eyes shut hard. "Don't do that."

Phil pulled his head back, but he didn't drop his hand from my cheek. I opened my eyes and saw a wretched, pained look on his face. He looked like he was about to break, and I knew the feeling.

And he wasn't wrong, either. Even if I'd been the one who felt ready five years ago, I'd also been the one to shut things down last week in the river. I'd been the one to bail this time. Sure, I'd had my reasons. But he'd never looked at me like this. Like I was his lifeline. His deepest need. Like he wanted me.

No, that wasn't true. He'd looked at me like this in the river, too. And maybe even before that, if I were being honest with myself.

And fuck, I wanted him too. So badly.

"Please, Amy," he whispered, sounding almost like he was gasping for air as he ran the pad of his thumb over my lower lip.

He clenched his own eyes shut. "I'm hanging on by a fucking thread here."

"Then snip that shit," I said, as calmly and evenly as I could manage, "and do something about it."

Phil's eyes snapped open and met mine, wide with surprise, his pupils blown so wide I could see my reflection in them. I saw the moment his resolve set, his jaw twitching hard enough that his whole beard shifted, and something bottomed out inside me.

I took in a deep breath to brace myself, but I barely caught any breath at all before he moved his hand to the back of my neck and pulled me into him, his mouth crashing against mine.

CHAPTER 19
PHIL

Five years ago, and then again one week ago, I'd nearly kissed Amy Evans. I'd actually done it almost two months ago, but just for show. Now that I was doing it for real though, it was somehow better than I'd ever imagined it could be.

The moment our lips met, she pushed herself fully against me, wrapping her arms around my neck and pressing her hips into mine, making me groan into her mouth. I felt her smirk as we kissed, which did me in even further. Her lips were soft and warm, even though the kiss was rough and desperate. A shiver went down my spine as her tongue met mine. Fuck, was this really happening? I strained against my trousers, but for the first time, I didn't try to hide it.

I nearly lost my balance trying to pull her in closer, feeling behind me for a wall to lean against, but there was nothing. So I broke away from her reluctantly, looking around desperately for somewhere we could go. But there were just flowerbeds everywhere, so I thought *fuck it* and ducked under the rope sectioning off the ruins from the path that led away from them.

Amy followed me, her fingers laced in mine, and as soon as

we were around the corner, I pressed her to the other side of the castle wall, ignoring the sign that clearly said **DO NOT TOUCH OR LEAN ON THE WALLS**. They had lasted hundreds of years so far; they could withstand Amy and me for a few minutes. For all I knew, we weren't the first in the castle's history to use that exact spot for that exact purpose.

She smiled up at me wickedly, and god, I'd wanted this moment for so long. I tried to savour it, leaning back to watch the way her chest heaved up and down as she panted beneath the bodice I'd hand stitched just for her – god, it was so hot to see her in something I'd made with my own two hands – but I couldn't stay away long enough to fully appreciate it, bringing my mouth hungrily to hers again.

She brought her hands to my beard, running her fingers through it, and then to the back of my head, playing with the hair at the nape of my neck, and I could have sworn I was in heaven. I pressed my hips harder into her, and she hitched up slightly against the wall; I felt her angling herself so she could feel me, and I couldn't help but smile when I pressed against her and she moaned.

Then her hands were tugging at my shirt, dislodging it from my waistband, and I grabbed them, pinning them against the wall over her head with one hand and holding her hip with the other.

"Not here," I said, between kisses to her neck and ear, somehow still aware of my surroundings. But even as I said it, I couldn't help but nibble at her ear, running my tongue along the back of her lobe. I ran my free hand over the rough fabric covering her chest, and she arched her back to press herself into my hand. She trembled as I rubbed, and I released her hands and kissed down the neckline of her stay, burying my face in her breasts, before she pulled me back up and kissed me deeply.

"Please," she whispered against my mouth, and Jesus, I could have come just from that word alone. And fuck it, I needed her somehow. The rest could wait until later, but I needed something. She needed to know how badly I wanted her. Wanted *this*.

I brought my other hand to her hip furthest from the path and started bunching at her skirts, cursing all the fabric involved in cosplay, working layer by layer until my hands were on her bare thigh. Goose pimples covered her flesh, despite the heat, and I loved that I'd put them there.

Amy brought one hand between us, helping me push her skirts out of the way. She brought the other to my hip and pulled me into her, and even through my own layers, I could feel where all of her heat had gone.

I inched my hand towards that heat, and she tipped her head back against the wall and sighed. Then she locked her gaze with mine, and I could see a flame burning behind her eyes that matched the one I felt, too. The one that had been burning for her for years, threatening to torch every ounce of sense I had. But I was done trying to keep it at bay. I was ready to let everything go up in smoke for this one moment with her.

"You say the word and I'll stop," I said, before bringing another, gentler kiss to her lips.

The tiniest crease appeared in the middle of her forehead, making me chuckle.

"Don't you fucking dare," she said, and I didn't need to hear anything else.

I ran my thumb over her pants, straining against my own even harder when I felt how wet she already was. I reached up to the waistband and tugged them taut against her flesh, relishing the groan she let out at the increase in pressure. I grinned, kissing lightly at her jaw, focusing as much as I could on what I was doing with my thumb. I stroked it ever so lightly up and down her crease through the fabric of her pants, taking care not to use too much pressure at her apex, but every time I reached that spot, Amy's hips bucked slightly into my finger, making her own pressure. She gasped over and over, as if she was about to come from that alone, so I eased off. This earned me an agonised moan.

"You bastard," she said through heavy breaths. "You've been edging me for the last five years."

I grinned as I kissed the tip of her nose, even as my hand brushed ever-so-lightly against her again. I laughed as she strained to press against it.

"No chance I'm letting you come," I whispered into her ear, "until I can feel you clench around me."

"Then what the fuck are you waiting for?"

She was practically begging, and whilst I knew better than to get my dick out in public, I wanted nothing more in that moment than to hear her moan my name as she tightened around my fingers.

"As you wish," I said, earning an ear-to-ear grin, and god, I wanted to make her smile like that every fucking day for the rest of her life. I felt my way to the edge of her pants, pulling them gently away from her skin, and she sighed in anticipation.

But just before I could press inside her, I heard a throat clear over my shoulder.

Amy and I broke apart so quickly that I nearly fell backwards trying to step away, and Amy desperately rearranged her skirts to disguise what we'd been doing. I was suddenly grateful for all those skirts, since they'd hidden the worst of it – or at least I hoped. I turned around to see a little old lady in a purple volunteer shirt glaring at us.

"Back in there," she said, holding up the rope and waving us back through. "And if I see you pulling that again, you'll be kicked out. That's what your hotel room's for."

I made sure Amy was appropriately covered, then took off back into the gardens. Amy rushed after me to keep up, whispering my name louder and louder, but I just kept walking. I couldn't believe I'd let myself do that.

"There you two are," came Chloe's voice as she came around the corner towards us, her headpiece in her hand, and I froze in place so suddenly that Amy ran into the back of me. We must have looked as dishevelled as I felt, because Chloe narrowed her eyes at me and smirked. "What have you two been up to?"

"Nothing," I said, probably too quickly, since Chloe pulled a smug face.

"Spoilsport," she said. "Now come on, I need another mead!"

The way she nearly threw her headpiece as she flung her arms out excitedly told me she probably did *not* need another mead, but she walked off anyway, and I let out a sigh of relief.

But when we rounded the same corner she'd disappeared around, all five of the others were staring at us with goofy grins on their faces, and I could tell from the way Chloe covered her mouth that she'd just told them what she'd guessed.

So far this summer, the others had looked at me differently. They watched closely as Amy and I acted the parts of boyfriend and girlfriend, which hadn't bothered me, mostly because it was an act. Or at least, that was what Amy and I had agreed on. But suddenly, knowing that things had shifted between us, the others' scrutiny felt new. Heavier. I wanted to squirm beneath it like a bug under a magnifying glass.

"Hello, lovebirds," Grey said, their own eyebrows bouncing up and down suggestively. "Good of you to join us."

"I can always give you the key to the rental if you need it," Fatima joked.

I tried to put on my most laid-back expression, actively relaxing my jaw and forehead and tipping my head back in laughter.

"Good one, guys," I said. "Don't worry, we were just trying to find a photographer."

They all nodded pacifyingly. "Yeah, okay," Chloe said. "Hope the pics turned out well."

I felt Amy's hand snake around my waist, and I saw Morgan tracking the movement. She didn't look sceptical, or upset, or anything like that. But still, I instinctively shimmied away from Amy's touch.

But then I turned back to see that she was looking up at me, her eyes wide and her jaw set, and my stomach sank. *Shit.*

"Got it," she spat once the others had turned away, and her lip started trembling. She bit it between her teeth, and I looked down to see her squeezing her hands into tight fists at her side. "I see how it is."

"Let's just keep it chilled around the others," I said, suddenly self-conscious of the hundreds of eyes we had on us as people milled around the reflecting pool, even as our friends walked back towards the festivities. "No unnecessary PDA, right?"

"Right," she said, nodding, releasing none of the tension. "I wouldn't want to embarrass you."

I opened my mouth to correct her, but I had no idea what to say to make it better. So I just watched as she followed after the others, knowing that somehow I'd had everything I wanted in my hands and still managed to fuck it up. Again.

FOR THE REST of the afternoon, Amy and I tried our best to avoid each other. There was a feeling, at least on my end, of having been caught doing something wrong, and whilst I definitely didn't regret that our feelings had finally caught up with us, I did wonder if perhaps we should have discussed what it meant before going there. Because the reality was that I didn't know.

So when we decided to split up to see a few different acts, I was slightly relieved that Amy went with her brother, Morgan, and Fatima to try out the archery range. Which meant Grey and I ended up babysitting Chloe the rest of the afternoon as she flitted in and out of the drinks tent, having apparently broken up with Lauren yet again and attempting to drown her sorrows in mead. She was a mead fiend at the best of times, but she was hitting it a bit hard, even for her, waving us off over and over so she could flirt with the bartender, even though she was clearly not interested. So Grey and I grabbed a bit of food from a nearby truck and found a table where we could keep an eye on her.

Grey asked pretty immediately how things were going with Amy, and I had no idea how to answer. But I'd known them since uni, including all through that summer five years earlier, and of everyone in our little group, they were the most objective.

I rested my head on my hand, running it over my face, smoothing down my beard. "Not well, mate. I think I'm really ballsing this up."

They laughed, which earned a glare, but they didn't give a shit. "Sounds about right," they said. "You never did know how to keep things casual."

I frowned. "I'm not trying to keep things casual."

"Yeah, right. If you weren't holding onto casual with all your might, you two would be shacked up by now."

"I don't know what you're on about," I said, stabbing a cheesy chip with a dull wooden fork.

They tilted their head and gave me an exasperated look. "As long as I've known you, even before I met Amy, it's been crystal clear what was bubbling under all that 'banter'," they said, using their fingers to make scare quotes around "banter".

"All that time?" I asked, incredulous. "No way."

"I mean, when was that summer you wouldn't shut up about her? Four or so years ago, maybe?"

"Five," I muttered.

"See? You know exactly what I'm talking about. And it's always been that way. So maybe don't try so hard. Maybe just admit that, as long as you've both been adults, there's been something there. Because if you keep fighting that history, you're gonna lose."

I sighed. "But that history is the exact problem. If we dive in headfirst and it doesn't work out, she's gonna get hurt. *I'm* gonna get hurt. And everyone else in our lives will suffer for it."

"I think we'll be fine," they said, but I shook my head.

"She's so important to Ethel already. I don't wanna imagine what would happen if Amy and I couldn't be around each other anymore."

"Well, helpfully you're adults," they said, as if it were that easy. "You'll figure it out. And besides, isn't it a bit late for that? You've been together for months. The damage is done."

I looked up at them guiltily, knowing that they didn't have the full story. But even so, they were right, weren't they? Even if Amy and I had fallen out weeks ago, before we'd decided to pretend to be together, Ethel still would have been devastated. I supposed that was the nature of having anyone in our lives who meant something to us.

Knowing that, of course, forced me to admit something that I'd known all along. That I wasn't worried about Ethel, or about Jack and Chloe, or Patricia and Alan, or anyone else. It was me. Because I was the only one who would end up more devastated if things ended after I let myself go there. I was the one who would suffer the emotional fallout if it all went tits up. And hadn't I had enough of that in my life?

"And I hope you don't mind me saying," Grey said, interrupting my thoughts by reaching across to pluck my last cheesy chip from right in front of me. I looked up at them incredulously as they popped it into their mouth. "You might as well go all in," they said, "because from the look of it, you're already fucked."

~

Eventually we had to drag Chloe away from the mead, and from the poor bartender just trying to do her job. We forced our little drunkard to get her face painted so she would have to sit still for a while, and by the time she had a flower design wreathing her face, she was a little less merry.

Next we headed over to the giant wicker stag they'd be burning later. We were meant to meet the others at the barrier surrounding it to get a good spot, but we were a bit early. There was a gap in the barrier, and people were walking up to the huge sculpture, taking pictures, and tucking little pieces of paper between the woven strands.

"You can write down a wish, or an intention," a volunteer said to me, beckoning me over to a table covered with pieces of paper and pens. "Whatever change you want to take place. Then, when they're burned, the magic of the stag will make it so."

I nodded, well practised from my time with Amy in going along with things that I didn't necessarily buy into. But something about the idea piqued my interest.

"So I can write down anything?" I asked, and the man nodded. "Like, if I'm afraid of something, and I write that down, will it help me move past it?"

He shrugged. "Sure. Why don't you give it a go? What's the worst that could happen?"

I walked over and accepted the paper and pen the man held out to me, then bent over to use the table. I stayed there for a long moment, wondering what exactly I should write, before it came to me.

I will let myself want things, even if I'm afraid of losing them.

I folded the paper in half and found a spot for it right in the middle of the stag's belly. It felt a bit silly, offering my intention to this wicker beast, but like the man had said, what harm could it do? And like Grey had said, I might as well go all in.

Just as I came out of the circle, the others arrived to meet us, Amy arm in arm with Morgan. I tried to pull her aside as she walked up, but she just stopped and shook her head, still facing the others.

"Let's not do this," she said quietly over her shoulder. "I think you've made it pretty clear that we don't actually want the same thing."

"It's really not like that," I said, but she shushed me and kept going.

"It's fine," she said, unconvincingly. "I'm fine. Just please don't confuse me like that again if it's not something you really want. It's not fair."

I opened my mouth to explain, but she shook her head and walked away. She settled on the side of the group furthest away from me, and as badly as I wanted to go to her and make her listen, to tell her that I was scared and that I did want her, I could tell that she was holding it together as best she could. And I didn't want to be the reason she couldn't do that in front of our friends.

So as the thousands of other festival goers crowded around the big stag, I instead settled in the grass next to Jack to watch the ritual unfold. When the stag lit, cheers erupted from the crowd, and I looked over at Amy, who was cuddled up next to Chloe, sharing her shawl around both their shoulders as the evening breeze blew through. I could see the orange light of the flames bouncing off her golden hair and reflecting in her eyes, which were wet and wide. I needed her here in my arms, not over there where I knew she was feeling like I didn't want her.

I swore I could feel the moment my paper burned, because that was it. I was head over heels for Amy Evans, and there was no going back. And soon she would know it. I was such an idiot. I'd berated Chris, both in my mind and to Amy, so many times for not knowing what he had in front of him. But it turned out, one could be acutely aware of the magnificence of what they had and still manage to let it slip through their fingers. I promised myself that if I got another chance, I wouldn't let it happen again. I would tell her exactly how I felt about her, consequences be damned.

CHAPTER 20
YORICK PROUDHOLLOW

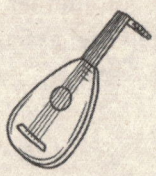

Laszlo's methods may have been strange, but he'd given them the name of the noble who had hired them to smuggle in the astral diamonds.

"Why is it always the nobles?" Calamity had asked. "Like, they've already got more than the rest of us."

"Perhaps that's precisely the point," Laszlo had responded. "I've met many a wicked man, and most were wealthy."

Regardless of whether her wickedness was caused by her wealth or not, Lady Nabora Nephrine had apparently been trafficking in materials from the astral plane for years. Laszlo had no insight into why she wanted them, or what she was doing with them, but they'd procured them for her in impossibly large quantities for years. When Eden asked how they managed to get their hands on so much, he'd looked at her as if she'd told an amusing joke.

"You would know, I suppose."

This comment had left Eden visibly flummoxed, even after they'd departed the camp the next morning; even days later as the party finally figured out how to get close enough to Lady Nephrine to investigate her.

Nephrine Manor sat perched on one of the only hills in the capital, looking down over the merchant district. There were rumours that beneath all of the hills that interrupted the sprawling cityscape, each home to a different noble family, were warrens of tunnels connecting the mansions atop them to the rest of the city, likely as escape routes for the nobles who lived there. In the case of Lady Nephrine's residence, it also would have made the perfect hub for smuggling. By Yorick's estimation, it was likely exactly that.

He and Eden had been watching the comings and goings for two days now, and they'd seen nothing of note. They had seen just one glimpse of Lady Nephrine herself, returning in a carriage from an unknown engagement. The only thing they'd learned was that Lady Nephrine was throwing a ball in honour of the city's bicentennial – the first celebration of many to happen over the next few months across the city's noble district. They weren't invited, but Yorick and Eden agreed that it would likely provide the best cover for them to access the manor, and also that Lady Nephrine would be distracted. Eden's star map had apparently held good omens for the day, and they were now slowly making their way up the hill towards the manor, having just cleared the gate at the bottom.

"I just don't know what he meant," Eden whispered as they passed through a small orchard. Yorick knew immediately that she was talking about Laszlo's reading; she'd spoken of little else during their stake-out.

"Maybe he could tell you're from the astral plane." This revelation had come more recently than Yorick would have liked, but he supposed they were still building that trust they'd talked about.

But Eden shook her head. "I genuinely don't think that was it. He made it sound like I was in on something. But I'm not, I swear."

Yorick did believe her – no matter how much scrutiny he applied, he sensed no deception. But somehow, that made it worse in his mind. If Laszlo knew or saw something about her that she didn't know herself, what did that say about her? He didn't like having so many unknown variables.

They snuck over the gate separating the orchard from what looked like a kitchen garden, ducking behind a row of raised beds just in time to avoid being spotted by a servant harvesting some herbs. Once the coast was clear, they crept along the garden wall to the side of the manor itself, diverting away from the busy kitchen and along the outside instead, careful to keep to the bushes lining the exterior so they wouldn't be spotted by anyone looking up the hill at the house the way they had been doing.

The first few windows they came to looked into areas that would either be too busy during the ball – the kitchens, the storeroom, the ballroom itself – or too risky, like the guardroom. As they passed below the open window to this last room, they heard two guards speaking to one another just inside, and they ducked down beneath the sill to eavesdrop.

After a lengthy discussion about what was for lunch – mutton stew, apparently, much to one guard's chagrin and the other's delight – their voices drifted away as if they had left the room.

"Let's go," Eden said, standing and lifting herself up onto the windowsill in one fluid movement. Yorick barely had time to understand what she was doing before she had disappeared inside. He tried to reach for her to stop her but just closed his hands around empty air instead.

What was she thinking? They had no idea if those guards had been alone in the room or where they had gone. She hadn't even run the idea past him first, just gone charging in without thinking. Had she forgotten that she could literally turn into an animal? Had she not thought about it at all?

If this was how she was on a mission, her reading was no mystery to him. She was a liability.

But he couldn't very well let her go in on her own, could he? So he looked around quickly and, seeing no one observing the window, stood to follow her. Only, it seemed he couldn't quite reach the sill. The bushes were too thin and scraggly to use for leverage, and there were no rocks nearby he could move into place.

He was just considering whether he should expend some magic to enlarge himself so he could reach when Eden's hand appeared, extending down towards him. He sighed and rolled his eyes, then took it and allowed himself to be pulled up into the window.

As his feet found purchase on the ledge, he looked around the room. The guards had not been alone, it seemed, or one of them had come back. Because at some point between leaving Yorick and reaching out for him, Eden had drawn her bow. And now, slumped against the wall just inside the door, Eden's arrow piercing his eye, was one of the guards.

CHAPTER 21
AMY

I could feel tears pricking at my eyes. Was it normal for roleplay to feel so ... personal? So real? The last thing I needed was to be airing my secrets to my friends and my brother in a thinly veiled exchange between fictional characters, and anyway, I wouldn't have thought it necessary considering where Phil and I had left things earlier. But maybe I was playing the fool yet again.

After I'd defended myself against the guard who had surprised me, and who was about to raise the alarm, I'd gotten an earful from Phil. As Yorick, of course, though it felt more personal than that. I was reckless. Thoughtless. Behaving rashly. And I got the message: he wanted me to back off and let him call the shots, both in game and out of it.

(I wondered when I'd started thinking of Eden as a part of me. Maybe when my in-character arguments had started to feel real?)

I excused myself from the table immediately after we finished, heading to the bedroom Phil and I were meant to share. It was the superking, but we hadn't unzipped the bed when we'd arrived and changed for the session, and even after how he'd acted at the festival, some part of me had stupidly taken that as an indication of what was to come.

It turned out a one-bed trope still caught me off guard, even when I'd been expecting it.

I pulled all the pillows and sheets off the massive bed and started looking for how to separate it, almost tripping over Phil's suitcase, which he'd left discarded on the floor on what I presumed he thought was his side. I stubbed my big toe hard on the wheel and let out a gasp of pain as I fell to the bed.

I grasped my toe as I sat on the mattress, clenching my teeth as the sharp pain radiated through my entire foot. It was the last straw apparently, as a tear finally spilled down my cheek and stung my jaw where it was still red from Phil's beard earlier. I used my free hand to lift the hem of the knee-length T-shirt I was wearing as pyjamas to dry my tears.

The door clicked open, and Phil walked in slowly, shutting the door behind him again.

"What happened?" he asked, a crease of concern appearing between his brows as he took in my hunched position, my hands in a death grip on my foot as I tried to control the searing pain in my toe.

"Just your baggage getting in my way," I said, clenching my jaw as I held back more tears. I was done showing Phil how much I cared what he had to say. "What a novel experience."

He let out a sigh that sounded as exasperated as it did pained. His eyes roamed from me to the bed behind me, landing on the pile of sheets and pillows half off the bed.

"We can share a fucking superking, Amy," he said. "You could build a wall between us if you'd like, and we'd still have plenty of room."

He bent down to toss it all back onto the bed, but as he bent in front of me, he must have noticed for the first time that I was crying. He put a hand on my knee as he crouched in front of me, and I brushed it off.

"It wouldn't be enough," I said, and I watched as hurt and what looked like fear flashed across his face.

"Amy, I'm so, so sorry about earlier," he said.

"About when?" I asked, crossing my arms in a gesture I knew looked petulant, but I couldn't help it. "When you were fingering me on a castle wall, or when you acted like you wanted nothing to do with me afterward in front of our— *your* friends?"

He ran a hand over his face. "I know," he said. "I'm sorry. It just happened so fast."

"I know that," I said, feeling my voice raise. "Don't you think I know that? I wasn't expecting that. I wasn't expecting *anything*."

"Me either," he said, tilting his head to catch my gaze. "But that doesn't matter. I shouldn't have brushed you off after, no matter how flustered I was. I get it."

"No," I said sharply, biting back my tears. "You don't get it. The problem is that nothing's changed for you."

"Amy," he started, but I shook my head, standing up and moving past him, taking care not to trip again.

"No, Phil, I can't fucking do this. I'm so tired of dancing around the truth. So let's just put it all out there."

He stepped towards me too, though not too close, and I was glad for it. I couldn't have done this if he'd been too close.

"I get it," I said, my voice breaking. I stared at the floor, knowing I needed to say this before I chickened out. But we needed to salvage what was left of this arrangement before we blew up our friendships in the process. "The proximity effect was in full swing, and we got carried away. I get that it doesn't mean the same thing to you that it does to me. In your mind, I'm still the desperate twenty-year-old home from uni, and you're still my brother's best friend who thinks I'm too embarrassing to be seen with like that. That's a lot to move past, and if you can't do it, that's fine. Let's just reset. We've only got a few weeks left, and we can ease off the physicality and the time together in the name of preserving a shred of shared dignity. We said that time would tell if this arrangement was working, and I know it's not working right now. But that doesn't mean we should throw it away entirely. I know you've gotten everything you wanted from me, but I still need this. Please."

He was quiet for a long moment. "Is that what you think?" he asked, his voice rasping. He stepped forward, narrowing that all-important space between us.

"I don't have to think it," I said. "You prove it every fucking day. Apparently you're perfectly happy to stare at my tits in the river or stick your hand up my skirt so long as no one else is around, but even the slightest touch in front of the others sets you on edge. It's humili—"

"Amy," he interrupted, his voice deep and stern like it had been in the repair tent earlier. He stepped forward again, robbing us of any remaining space, and closed his eyes. "Fucking hell," he said, and it was almost a growl. "You seriously have no idea, do you."

My breath hitched, and I tried to step back, but he grabbed me, and I froze. His voice sounded laboured, and I could tell even with his beard that his jaw was clenched.

"If your touch sets me on edge," he said, "it's because every nerve ending in my body is suddenly focused on you. And if I flounder in front of the others when I've just had my hands on you, it's because I can't even reconcile to myself how crazy you make me, much less to them."

"Because I'm your best friend's obnoxious little sister?" I asked, my eyes fixed on our feet.

"Shut the fuck up," he said suddenly, and I gulped in surprise. "You know damn well that's not true. It's because I know that the moment I give in to this, the moment we let ourselves go there, that's it. I'm done for. And given everything else I have going on in my life, that scares the shit out of me."

He brought his fingers to my chin, lifting it so I had no choice but to meet his gaze.

"Amy Evans, the only obnoxious thing about you is that no matter what I try, I can never get you out of my head."

He said it so smoothly that I was almost convinced it was a line, but he wasn't smirking anymore. He was giving me everything I'd ever wanted – what I'd wished for since I knew it was a thing one *could* wish for – after all this time.

"Do you *want* to get me out of your head?" I asked, hoping against all hope that this wasn't too good to be true. "Out of your system? Because that's not what I want."

"Absolutely not."

With that, I felt the insecurity that had been plaguing me all day – hell, all summer – fall away. I took a few steps back, breathing out slowly, willing myself to take what was finally being offered. I was done waiting. If he wanted me, he could have me. But he'd have to come to me. All the way this time.

"Then prove it."

In one fast motion, I pulled my nightshirt off over my head, showing him that I wasn't wearing anything underneath.

It took him less than a second to process what he was seeing before he was on top of me. He practically tackled me onto the still-dressed side of the bed, knocking a laugh out of me that continued as he shoved all the pillows and blankets out of the way, dragging me up the bed until my head found the cushioned headboard. His mouth pressed to mine with such force that it pushed me deep into the mattress, his weight on top of me just as I'd imagined all those nights at home alone. It was intoxicating.

I fumbled between the two of us as he kissed me, desperate to feel his skin on mine. I pulled his shirt off over his head, and it was like he didn't even notice, he was back to kissing me so quickly. Then it was time to push down his shorts, and I almost gasped when his length hit my belly, already hard. I felt a pulse of anticipation between my legs.

"Big boy indeed," I said, smiling up at him as he drank me in. But he didn't laugh, or even smile, just dropped his head to my breasts, taking one into his mouth so forcefully I couldn't tell if it hurt or felt incredible.

What absolutely felt incredible was the way his tongue flicked over my nipples, making me arch into him. I moved my hands to the top of his head to push him lower – I needed that tongue working elsewhere – but he was already on his way, and his mouth closed around me so suddenly that it made me bolt upright.

He pushed me roughly back down onto the bed as he sucked and lapped at me, his facial hair creating a whole new sensation as it tickled my sensitive skin. I bucked my hips against his face as it all became more and more overwhelming, and I could feel myself nearing the edge already.

My vision began to cloud with spots, and I was teetering towards the precipice, when all of a sudden he lifted away from me, leaving me cold and soaking wet.

I sat up incredulously. "I thought we talked about this, Philip," I said with a gasp. But when my eyes focused, I saw that he was on his knees, stroking himself as he watched me. And if I thought I'd been wet before, I was positively melting now, watching him watch me hungrily.

"Please tell me you brought a condom," I groaned, desperate for what was currently in his hand to be inside me instead. I nearly collapsed in relief when he grinned and leaned over, plucking one from the side pocket of his open suitcase.

"I thought you said you weren't expecting this?"

"Like I said before," he said, tearing open the packet and rolling it over his cock. "Wanting and expecting aren't the same thing. And fuck, Amy, I want you so bad."

"Then hurry up and take me."

I saw a flicker in his jaw, and then, an impossibly quick moment later, I was pressed firmly back into the bed, and he was nudging at my entrance.

He moved slowly at first, stretching me, easing in. But I was ready, and I wanted to feel him inside me *now*. So I put my hands against the headboard and pushed, bringing him all the way into me.

"Fuck, Amy," he said, pulling out slowly and pushing in again, and again I moved him faster, desperate for more of the fullness I got every time he bottomed out inside me.

"Yes, that's the idea," I said, bucking my hips. "Fuck me, Phil. I'm begging you."

He shook his head, his beard brushing my face. "I won't last. I need to feel you come first."

"Please," I whispered, making him look at me, and a pained look crossed his face before something hungry took over. I felt a flutter in my stomach at the intent I saw in his eyes.

"If you say so."

He pulled out of me, making me whimper, then flipped me over on the bed. He nudged my legs apart with his knee, then reached forward to wrap an arm between me and the bed, pulling me back to him. When he slammed into me from behind, I nearly cried out in delight, having to clamp my hand over my mouth to keep myself quiet.

His pace quickened, and with each feeling of fullness and release, I built closer and closer towards my climax. I knew he must have been close too, because he hunched forward over me, bringing his hand to my front and helping me along with his fingers. It only took a few seconds of that before I felt myself come undone, constellations forming in my vision, heat radiating outward from where he still pushed into me.

"Oh fuck, Amy," he said behind me as he felt me come

around him, just like he'd wanted, and I felt him start to move even faster. "It's so good. You're so good."

I brought my face to the mattress as I came down from my orgasm and pressed my hips back, changing up the angle, and he groaned. Just a few seconds later, he came too, pulling me back into him and wrapping his arms tight around me as he did.

There was a wonderful moment of heat and sweat and sweet relief as he collapsed forward over me, catching his breath, and I felt full in more ways than one. But the moment he pulled out of me to go deal with the condom, I felt myself go cold. Maybe it was from the lack of *Phil* around and in me, or maybe it was because part of me was bracing for what had happened earlier; for him to freak out and create distance.

But as soon as he finished in the bathroom, he was right there in bed next to me, spooning me from behind, nuzzling his face into my hair. I sighed in relief and let myself meld into him, entwining my legs with his and lacing our fingers together.

"That was incredible," he said, then pushed up onto his elbow and turned me so I could look at him. "*You're* incredible." Then he leant down and pressed a kiss to my mouth, smiling into it.

"Back at ya," I said, trying to mirror his enthusiasm, but part of me was still unwinding.

"Oh shit," he said, pulling back from me and frowning, clearly picking up on my lingering anxiety. "Did you not come? I'm so sorry, I thought you did, but I was so close, maybe it was just wishful thi—"

I lifted my head to silence him with a kiss, trying not to laugh at how panicked he sounded. It made me feel better.

"I assure you," I said with faux gravity, "I definitely came."

He smiled in relief before his brow pinched together again. "Wait, then what's wrong?"

After all that, there was no reason to mince words. I needed to assuage my fears once and for all.

"What does this mean?"

He twisted his face in confusion, like it should be obvious; as if I'd asked him for the answer to two plus two. "What do you mean, what does it mean?"

"Like, for us," I clarified, sitting up and pulling the closest sheet over my body as I wrapped my arms around my knees. Phil sat up, too, but he didn't look self-conscious at all. He just propped himself up against the headboard, his legs splayed out in front of us.

"God, this has actually never happened to me," he said, frowning as he thought. "Well, you're already my girlfriend."

"Your *fake* girlfriend," I reminded him.

"Ah, well there you go," he said, nodding and smiling as if I'd just handed him the answer. "We just drop the fake part, yeah?"

"Yeah?"

He nodded.

"And the breakup timeline? We just drop that, too?"

"That would be the idea."

I narrowed my eyes at him. "You sure you don't wanna think about this a little bit? Let the post-nut clarity kick in?"

Phil rolled his eyes. "Why, do you not *want* to be my girlfriend?"

"Oh my god," I said, sighing. "This is exhausting. Yes, I want to be your girlfriend, Phil. I've wanted to be your girlfriend since I was old enough to like boys."

Phil curled his lip as he nodded. "Okay, yeah, well, maybe let's not talk about being children whilst we're naked."

I laughed. "Sorry."

"But just to be clear, I also want you to be my girlfriend. I've wanted it for a long time."

I frowned. "Really?"

He nodded. "Really. Not quite as long, admittedly, but long enough."

"And you're not embarrassed by me?"

"Jesus Christ, Amy. You're fucking exhausting, yeah? No, I'm not embarrassed by you, and I'll prove it."

I swatted him on the arm as he rolled over to grab his phone off the nightstand. There were two messages waiting in the group chat:

> **CHLOE**
>
> When you two are done with your little couple's moment, could you please come back out?
>
> **JACK**
>
> Chloe's mad that she missed the flower crown workshop and would like to make a gameplan for tomorrow.

Phil smiled and typed out a reply.

> **PHIL**
>
> Tell her she should spend less time at the mead tent tomorrow then. And maybe you should start without us – I think we've got at least one more round in us.

I snatched the phone away. "You're not fucking sending that to my *brother*!"

But when I looked down at it, I saw to my horror that, in the act of snatching the phone away, I'd already hit send myself, though not before adding a few random characters and a potato emoji to the end.

Almost immediately, a GIF came through from Chloe of someone on Hot Ones throwing up in their mouth.

"I can't believe you just sent that to your *brother*," Phil mocked, grabbing his phone back and throwing it onto the floor on the other side of the bed before wrapping me in his arms. He pressed his mouth to mine again, and this time our kiss was sweet and slow. After years of dancing around one another, we were finally, blissfully, on the same page.

The kiss deepened over the next couple of minutes, and his hands began to roam over my body, making me shiver.

"I love making you do that," he said with a chuckle, but it cut off mid-laugh when I reached between us and took him in my hand.

"What was that about another round?" I asked.

He shook his head. "You're welcome to try for a bit if you fancy, but I'll need a while longer."

I pouted in response, and he narrowed his eyes.

"*But*," he said, and I smiled hopefully, "I feel pretty confident in my ability to get you there again, at least once. And I've been dreaming of you in a different position…"

He flipped both of us this time so I was sat on top of him. I could see the tip of him peeking out between us as I straddled him, and I grabbed the headboard with my hands. "Right here?" I asked, sliding back and forth along his length, but he shook his head.

"No," he said, then hooked his forearms under my thighs. He pulled me all the way forward, until I was hovering just above his chin. "Right here," he said, and I could feel the vibration of his voice and the tickle of his beard on my still-swollen skin.

Then he closed his mouth around me once again, and I tilted my head back and let myself go for good.

CHAPTER 22
PHIL

I'd been imagining for years what it would feel like to be Amy Evans's boyfriend, and now that it was happening, it was blissfully anticlimactic.

Well, technically, there was a *lot* of climaxing. But besides that, the whole thing felt surprisingly, wonderfully normal.

To be fair, we'd been practising the relationship side of things for nearly two months. She'd already become the person I texted when I had a random funny thought in the middle of the day, and she was the person I thought about first when I woke up. The only difference was that now I didn't have to keep my hands to myself, and thank god.

It wasn't just in bed, either. Our no-PDA rule had clearly just applied to the fake dating arrangement, and literally overnight we went from relatively hands-off to almost offensively hands-on. We walked around the festival the next day in our Donkey and Dragon costumes, constantly hand in hand or arm in arm, only breaking contact when we absolutely had to. She sat snuggled in my lap on the picnic blanket as we laughed along to a D&D-themed choose-your-own-adventure comedy set, tilting her head back to kiss my face through my beard every couple of minutes. We danced together in the rain as a pirate band played the last set of the festival, and I carried her on my back on the return walk to the rental at the end of the day, both of us with sore feet from dancing and sore cheeks from smiling.

One of the best parts of the day was seeing how willingly she threw herself into everything. She'd been so resistant to anything nerdy just a couple of months ago, and now she was buying sparkly dice and shopping for cloaks at a fantasy festival without a care in the world. I'd always thought of her as passionate and curious and excitable, but it was so satisfying to see that unbridled by insecurity and judgment.

She was more herself than ever, which meant I was more under her spell than ever. Which was fine for once, since we were finally on the same page.

BACK AT HOME, our routine remained largely unchanged, except now it felt like a given that she'd tag along everywhere. She scheduled the workload for her dad around Ethel's appointments – her car was better for that anyway – and she stayed over after date nights on Saturdays so she was already there to drive us to the Evans family dinners on Sundays.

To be clear, I was still exhausted. Over the next couple of weeks, Ethel still needed me more than ever, and I was filling the time I had spent working on costumes with more data entry jobs, trying to bring back up my scarily low bank balance. I'd also started working on something special for Amy for the fantasy ball, even looping Morgan in to help me sketch out the idea.

The difference was, I was exhausted and happy.

Amy would wake up with me for Ethel's morning routine at half five every morning she was there, until one morning she must have turned off my alarm, and I woke up at eight more refreshed than I'd felt in months. I panicked at first, thinking I'd overslept, and I'd stumbled out of my room as fast as I could. But when I did, I found Ethel fed, dressed, and sitting by the window, teaching Amy to crochet. It seemed Amy had managed Ethel's morning medications perfectly thanks to the notebook, and she'd even taken her for a walk around the block. Only then was I able to relax with a cup of coffee, a smile playing at my lips as I watched the two of them laughing together, backlit in the bay window: the woman who had raised me, and the woman I loved.

I'd never said the L-word to Amy, even platonically. But if I were honest with myself, I'd been in love with her before we'd even started this whole charade, and I was no less in love with her now. I couldn't imagine anyone in my position could avoid falling for her. She was gorgeous, obviously, but more than that, she was so unapologetically herself. And she fit so seamlessly into my life, probably because she'd almost always been a part of it. I wished so badly that my parents could have met her; they would have loved her just as much as I did.

But no matter how happy she seemed, and no matter how set she supposedly was against going to Niamh and Chris's wedding, she apparently couldn't stop thinking about it.

We were side by side in the kitchen one afternoon, the smell of cookies wafting over from the oven. Ethel had an extra-long physio appointment, so we'd come home instead of staying at the hospital, and I'd whipped up a quick dough whilst Amy worked at the table.

A while later, when we were doing the washing up together, she started telling me about the other friends who would be at the wedding. She sounded almost like she was changing her mind about going, especially as she talked about needing to show them how well she was doing away from them.

I handed her a baking tray I'd finished washing. "You don't have anything to prove to those assholes. You know that, right?"

"I know," she said with a sigh, running the towel over the metal to dry it. "But wouldn't it be nice to get a bit of closure?"

I shrugged. "I don't know, feels like the opposite of closure to me. Like you're just picking at the scab of what happened."

"But what about my friends?" she asked, almost wistfully, as if she were thinking aloud rather than asking me, so I paused a moment to let her, despite the voice in my head yelling *they are not your friends!*

"I do miss them," she said, and it felt almost like she'd managed to convince herself. "They don't seem to know I'm not going, and they've all sounded so excited to see me. I know things won't be the same – I don't wanna be friends with Niamh, and I don't live there anymore – but maybe it's worth it to salvage some of the few friendships I have that aren't tied to my brother?"

I frowned, setting down the mixing bowl I was washing and turning to face her. The summer sun was pouring in through the window in front of us, and I had to squint to look at her. "After all this time, despite everything" – I gestured between us with the brush I'd been using – "do you really still think of us all as your brother's friends?"

She pursed her lips and looked at me sceptically, as if searching for the answer. "Honestly, yeah," she said. "Maybe not you, not anymore, but the rest of them? Even Chloe? Yes. If Jack and I fell out for some reason, they'd all be his friends, not mine."

"You know that's not true," I said, feeling suddenly very defensive. "Remember when Jack went travelling for all those years? Chloe and I didn't ditch you. We were here for you."

"Yeah, and look how well that went."

I shook my head and turned back to the washing up, scrubbing hard at a dried-on patch of something. I wasn't sure what I could do to make her see how wrong she was. How integral she felt already to the makeup of the group. Ultimately, though, I wasn't sure it was possible for me to say something that would make her believe it. It would just take time, like everything.

"It's fine," she said when I didn't reply, wringing the towel in her hands. "And don't worry, even if I went, I wouldn't make you come with me."

"Oh no, I'd be going with you," I said, my gaze snapping back to her. "That prick deserves to see how good this townie looks in a suit."

This made Amy crack a smile, which of course meant I smiled, too.

"I don't think I've ever seen you in a suit."

"You're in for a treat." I winked, and she rolled her eyes.

"But you wouldn't be allowed to look better than I do."

"I assure you," I said, "that's not possible, even if you showed up in tattered joggers. But also, no girlfriend of mine would go anywhere of consequence without a Phil Owen original."

"Oh yeah," she said sarcastically. "Just whip up a black tie-ready dress in less than a month, why don't ya."

"I'm sorry, did you see how quickly I made your costume for the festival? I'd be fine." It wasn't strictly true – the design I'd been working on with Morgan for Amy's ballgown was pretty intricate, and making a wedding outfit too would be a bit much. I'd started on the gown weeks ago, as soon as we'd gotten back from the festival. The pattern was already cut in my craft room.

Not that she could do both. If she did choose to go to the wedding, she'd be missing the ball, and all that effort would be for nothing.

Amy's smile twisted into a wicked grin, and she stepped into me, turning me so my bum was pressed against the kitchen sink, her body against mine. She pressed up onto her tiptoes and leaned into me. "Does that mean you'd have to retake my measurements?" she said softly into my ear. "Because that might be reason enough to RSVP yes."

"Unlikely, since I'm now intimately familiar with every inch of your body." I desperately tried to keep my voice even, despite her running the tip of her tongue along the edge of my ear, making me swallow hard. I couldn't help but bring my hands up, running over the rough denim covering her hips, pulling her into me. I was already straining against my own jeans.

"Better safe than sorry," she whispered, then pressed a kiss to my mouth. I opened myself to her, and I felt her tongue run lightly along my lip. I traced up her spine with my hand until I reached her hair, wrapping my fingers through it and tugging, exposing her throat to me. I kissed the delicate skin there, feeling her pulse quicken beneath my lips.

"We have to finish this before we go get Ethel," she said, breaking my focus. Her voice was breathy, but I could still feel the vibrations of it in her throat. "But we have a few minutes, I suppose." She grinned up at me wickedly, bringing a hand between us, and it was everything I could do not to come undone at just the suggestion of her touch.

But I didn't want just a few minutes. I wanted to take my time with her. I wanted to stretch out every second of the next quarter of an hour we had together. I wanted to turn every heartbeat into an eternity.

I kissed her again, deeply this time. A moan escaped from between us, and I honestly wasn't sure if it was her or me. But either way, I decided it was my mission to make as many of them as possible before the oven timer went off.

I reached behind me and tugged the café-style curtains closed across the window. Then I dipped down and wrapped my arms snugly around Amy, lifting her up so her legs wrapped around my middle. She squealed as I spun her around, swiping Ethel's binder out of the way and propping Amy up on the worktop next to the pile of drying dishes.

She watched as I reached over my shoulders to grab my T-shirt, pulling it off over my head and letting it fall to the floor between us. Her eyes roved over me, reaching out to run a hand over my chest, tangling her fingers in the hair there like she always did, her eyes wide with pleasure. It could have been amusement, but honestly, I was perfectly happy being ogled by Amy Evans. I was just over the moon that she was so obviously happy to be there.

Speaking of which, my own happiness to be there was growing noticeably as Amy's hands began to roam, unbuttoning my jeans when she reached them. She tucked her fingers into the waistband of my pants and pulled everything down at once, and I sprang free as she did. She smirked up at me, clearly pleased with her own ability to turn me on so thoroughly, then ran a hand over my hip bone and inward.

But I reached down and pulled her hand away before she could spoil the fun too soon. I pulled her forward off the worktop so she was leaning against it instead and knelt in front of her. She wore denim cutoffs, short and loose enough that I could reach my arms around her and run my hands over her ass beneath them. I grabbed hard at the flesh there, pulling her apart with my fingers, letting them just skirt the next layer of fabric between her legs. She spread them further apart as she sighed.

She slowly untied the corset top she wore – it was probably unnecessary for the purposes of getting it off her, but it was mesmerising to watch. My eyes were glued to her chest as the top got looser and the swell of her breasts released, and it was all I could do not to stand up and bury my face in them. Instead I gulped as she finally tugged the top off over her head, her tits bouncing free from the fabric, and then I really couldn't help myself, tilting up and taking one of them in my mouth, earning another moan and her fingers in my hair. I closed my mouth around the tight bud of her nipple, sucking hard as I swirled my tongue around the tip, making her arch her back in response, her hair long enough to tickle my wrists where they disappeared beneath her shorts. I moved them to start unbuttoning the front, kissing the underside of her breast, then the pale skin just below it, then down her stomach. I reached her waistband just as my fingers tugged down the zip, exposing the pale pink cotton thong she wore beneath.

But instead of tugging them down immediately, I grabbed her by the hips and spun her around so her front was pressed into the worktop. Only then did I remove her shorts and her thong, letting them pool at her ankles.

"Shit," she sighed, trying to straighten, her hand reaching back for me. But I shook my head, even though she couldn't see me.

"Forward," I said, then put a hand firmly on her back between her shoulder blades, pushing her away from me until her forearms found the worktop. I felt her shiver as her bare skin met the cold tile, and I leaned to the side to see that she was smiling in anticipation.

I put my hands back on her hips and pulled them back into me, and she gasped as she felt my hard length press against her. I moved her forwards and backwards a couple of times, ever so slowly, spreading her with my hands as I did, her breath hitching as the air hit her wetness. I smiled at how turned on I could see she was.

"Tell me what you want," I said, my voice almost as strained as my dick, which was so taut that it tapped against her entrance with no help from me.

"I want you inside me," she said, reaching down for me, but I swatted her hand away.

"You sure?" I asked. "Because I feel like you could want it a bit more."

A perfunctory laugh burst out of her. "I beg to differ."

I smirked. "Oh, you beg, do you?"

She shook her head, even as she pressed back into me more. "Not a chance in hell."

I brought my right foot to the inside of hers, nudging her legs open even wider. She gasped as my hand found her clit right away.

"Yeah, well, we'll see about that."

∽

I MAY NOT HAVE UNDERSTOOD why Amy still felt anything but hatred for her Manchester friends, but I was determined to be supportive, especially when Amy told me a few days later that she wanted to get them a passive-aggressive wedding present regardless of whether we went or not. We were sat in the lounge during Ethel's afternoon nap, and she'd convinced me to do a Korean skincare mask with her. It had dried completely on my face, making my skin feel tight and pinched.

"You've never been more sexy to me than you are right now," I said, referring half to the green mask covering her face and half to the scheming she was doing, producing one bad gift idea after another. Maybe it was horrible, enjoying her bitchy side, but after the way they'd treated her – and the way they were still treating her, by trying to pretend nothing had happened – it was nice to see her stand up for herself, even if only in subtle ways.

Eventually, we landed on a tacky farmhouse-style wood carving with a chicken on it that could be personalised. Amy typed in "The Arden's, est. 2024."

I cringed. "You know there's no apostrophe, right? It should just be an S."

She smiled wickedly up at me. "I do know that," she said. "And Niamh does too. And it'll wind her up every time she looks at it."

I bit back a smile as she placed the order. "You're diabolical. Remind me to never get on your bad side."

Amy laughed. "You've been on my shit list more than

anyone else I know," she said. "If I haven't put you off yet, you're probably safe."

I grabbed her legs and pulled them around to drape over my lap. She kept looking at her computer like nothing had happened. I loved how casually intimate we were.

"We'll be sixty," I said, "and you'll be filling our house with grammatically incorrect signage every time I piss you off, and I'll still be besotted."

She kept the rest of her face completely neutral, but I saw the moment of recognition when her eyes stopped flitting across her screen, widening slightly. It was only then that I realised what I'd said.

Every time in the past few years that I'd tried to think about my future, even casually, it had felt impossible to plan more than a few months in advance. If I'd stopped to think about what life looked like years down the road, I would have had to confront the fact that Ethel probably wouldn't be there, at least not in the same way. And I couldn't do it.

But since Amy and I had gotten together – for real, at least – I'd been getting glimpses of what life could look like years down the road. It was usually inspired by the things already happening around me, which I was letting myself appreciate. Starting a veg garden out back like Patricia, getting a dog like Morgan, going on holidays and road trips, maybe going on a course like Anil or back to school like Jack ... it didn't faze me the way it always had. But this was the first time my brain had jumped that far into the future, and it was the first time I was saying it out loud. I wasn't sure how I felt about it. Part of me felt panicked and instantly regretted putting it out there, but another part of me felt almost relieved at my newfound ability to dream.

Amy didn't respond – though, was it just me, or was that a smile tugging at the corner of her mouth? – and we went back to our conversation as if nothing had happened. But I didn't forget about it. And later that night, when Amy was home and I was alone in my bed, my brain spun with all the unleashed visions of what a future together could look like. I could hardly picture one before my brain would skip to the next.

It wasn't real yet; I knew that. No matter what Grey said, no matter how much history we had as friends, the love I felt for her now was still too new for me to be latching onto the fantasies of domestic bliss playing out in my mind. But my imagination got carried away when I was alone, and I needed an outlet for it.

I took out my phone and tapped on my Notes App, scrolling past recent shopping lists and now completed costume to-do lists to Our Lore. I opened it and scrolled up – neither of us had edited it in over a month. And I figured that if she still looked at it, if she still liked reading through the life we concocted between us, maybe she'd like reading a bit more.

So I started typing.

CHAPTER 23
YORICK PROUDHOLLOW

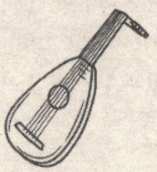

It took a lot of convincing, but despite the near-catastrophe on the stake-out, Yorick finally managed to charm his way into an invitation to the ball for the whole party. They debated for hours whether to take their weapons and wear their armour, knowing they could be walking into a dangerous situation, but ultimately, they knew it would cause more problems than it would solve, so they donned their finery and walked unarmed into Nephrine Manor.

The nobles had donned their own finery, too. There were magical fibres woven into garments, amulets that had no doubt cost the lives of countless adventurers to obtain, and ornamental armour so intricate it looked almost organic. The party had done their best, and Eden looked especially stunning in a glittering gown and cloak that resembled the effect of the astral diamonds, but they were nowhere near the calibre of the average attendee. Lady Nephrine was nowhere to be seen so far, but Yorick was sure she would look even more impressive than the rest when she did arrive.

As soon as they could, the party found as inconspicuous a gathering point as possible to confer.

"Shall we go over the plan again?" Morgana whispered. Yorick cleared his throat.

"Actually, I was thinking we could change it."

"How's that?"

"I think we need a lookout. Someone to stay at the party whilst the rest of us go looking for information. Someone who can alert us if there's trouble, or if Nephrine leaves too."

Morgana nodded. "It's not a bad idea. Are you volunteering?"

"As long as he doesn't get drunk and serenade them," Calamity said, and the others laughed. But Yorick didn't. He just shook his head.

"Actually, I think it should be Eden."

Yorick had been concerned about Eden since their conversation on the stake-out. As much as he'd grown to like her, she had proven to be a bit erratic. And maybe Laszlo's reading had gotten into his head, but there wasn't room for unexpected consequences.

Eden narrowed her eyes at him. "Why's that?"

He shrugged as casually as possible. "I just think it makes the most sense."

"I don't know," Morgana said. "I think Eden's knowledge of astral materials could come in handy."

"This is about the guard, isn't it?" Eden asked, catching Yorick's eye. "Or the cleric."

He sighed. "It's not *not* about that."

"Here we go again," she said, crossing her arms over her chest, covering her crystal pendant. "I don't know how many times I can apologise before you get over it."

"You can apologise," Yorick said, keeping his voice as level as possible to avoid attention from the partygoers swirling around them, "but that doesn't change the fact that you're reckless. And you heard Laszlo. That'll have consequences you haven't accounted for."

Eden smirked. "Oh yeah? You wanna talk about Laszlo's reading? Because I'm not the one whose card said I was a literal spy."

"You know that's not how that works, Eden."

"Then stop holding mine against me!"

Yorick huffed a cruel laugh. "I'm not. I'm going purely based on your actions."

She flung her arms out to her sides. "So that's it? You don't trust me. Not now, not ever. No matter what I do."

"I didn't say that," Yorick admitted. "I just don't think we're there yet, and this is too important."

"You don't think I know that?"

Yorick sighed. "It's not personal, Eden. It's about the mission."

"Feels pretty personal from where I'm standing. If you don't want me in the party, you should just say it." It took her gesturing to Yorick's friends for him to realise she didn't mean the ball, but rather the adventuring party.

Yorick's face fell. "Eden, that's not what I—"

"Forget it," she said, smoothing her gown. "Message received, loud and clear. I'll be your lookout, and you can all go complete the mission without me."

"Eden, wait—" But Eden had already been absorbed into the crowd.

Yorick looked around at the rest of the party, who stared wide-eyed at one another, avoiding his gaze. They began to filter away one by one, headed in the direction of the library Yorick and Eden had found during their reconnaissance mission.

"Calamity," he said, as the last of his friends lingered.

"I get it," she said. "Your name is Proudhollow. But that doesn't mean you can let your pride hurt the people that care about you."

"It's not pride," he insisted. "The Twelve targeted *me*. This is *my* responsibility. I'm just trying to keep everyone safe."

Calamity sighed. "Okay, yeah, they targeted you. But it was just a letter. A taunt, directed at all of us. This isn't just a *you* problem, Yorick. It's an *us* problem. And that *us* includes Eden now."

"Are we sure that's wise?" Yorick mumbled. Calamity looked back at him sadly.

"How's that for unexpected consequences?" she asked, then followed after the others, leaving Yorick alone in a crowded room.

CHAPTER 24
AMY

Being Phil's girlfriend came unbelievably naturally to me. And not just the touching, or the time together, but even just how normal it felt to combine those things with the dynamic we already had. We were pretty much back to our usual levels of antagonism in front of the others, since we weren't trying to put on a performance of being together. Except now, the heat simmering beneath the surface when we argued was clear. It wasn't rivalry or annoyance like I'd thought. It was raw attraction, and we had it in spades.

We actually got kicked out of Chloe's birthday party at an escape room when we found a secret room but, instead of solving the clues inside, used it as an excuse to snog the shit out of one another. And sure, it got a bit hot and heavy, but the others were too busy trying to fit some Tetris-esque block into a tabletop. And given that Phil had me propped up on the tabletop they actually needed to try, we knew they'd be a while. The camera operator, unfortunately, was less impressed, and we were asked to leave. Chloe didn't mind though, egging us on, firmly on-side after we gifted her a mead-making day course at a local meadery.

After one D&D session, Jack banished me to the kitchen to help Fatima and Grey with the washing up, feigning disgust over Phil and my PDA. Though I knew he secretly loved seeing Phil happy. And he did seem happy, didn't he?

But as I crossed the hallway towards the kitchen, I froze when I heard Grey say my name.

"Amy does complicate things, doesn't she."

"I mean, it's not a big deal," Fatima responded. "We just won't do the camper van road trip."

"But it's perfect. I knew you should have mentioned it before."

"There's too much in the diary already, and February's still so far out. I was waiting until after the ball."

I knew Fatima had been pushing for another US Renaissance Faire trip, but not as soon as February. And as far as she and Grey knew, Phil and I had been together for months now. I tried not to be annoyed that she hadn't factored me in.

"Well, what do you wanna do?"

Fatima groaned. "I did really want that one RV. It was so cool."

"Then we can get two, and I'll drive, too," Grey said matter-of-factly. "Or maybe someone won't be free."

"But I want everyone together. I've already got characters planned for a Western-themed session."

"Including Amy?"

"Well, no, not yet..."

I heard someone else push back from the table in the dining room, so I knew I couldn't lurk in the hallway anymore. But I didn't want to walk into that conversation, so I ducked into the downstairs toilet and pulled the door shut behind me.

I pulled out my phone and opened WhatsApp; I'd muted Niamh's hen do chat when I'd been added to it, but I'd been checking it obsessively all day knowing they'd arrived at the spa in Scotland at around lunchtime. And as I scrolled, I was surprised to see that I'd actually been tagged in a couple of messages.

> **SOPHIE**
> @Amy Evans, remember this??

That one was followed by a picture of Sophie, Maya, and Niamh, the latter with a veil headband on her head, holding up pink and blue frozen cocktails. I laughed to myself – they were a weird grenadine and curaçao concoction we'd created when already drunk one night, and they'd become our signature cocktail when we wanted to annoy bartenders. I replied to the message:

> **AMY**
> What did the poor sod do to make you so angry? 💀

The second message I was tagged in was a group photo of all of them in what looked like a circus tent, or at least a room draped with curtains on every surface. Behind the seven women was a table, where a fortune teller was sat with a crystal ball.

> **NIAMH**
> She could tell you were missing from the group @Amy Evans, so that's one reading she got right! Can't wait to see you at the wedding xxx

I tried to think of how to respond, but I heard someone call my name from the other room, so I pocketed my phone and flushed the toilet for effect, going as far as washing my hands before coming out.

When I walked into the lounge where everyone was gathered, I saw Chloe stood in front of the other five with a video queued up on the TV.

"Aren't we going to the pub?" I asked as Phil reached out a hand for mine. I took it, then he yanked it back when he felt that it was still a bit wet, wiping it on his jeans. Pablo trotted over and put his paws on my leg, so I bent down to pick him up, cradling him close and giving him belly rubs.

"No, we have homework to do," Chloe said, pointing to the TV, which was paused on two people in black spandex dancing together.

"Homework for what?" Jack asked.

"The ball," Chloe said, with an implied "duh" on the end. "There will be a few choreographed dances, and I think we'd be remiss to not learn at least one."

Fatima, Grey, and Jack all moaned. "Seriously?" Grey asked. "Choreographed dances?"

"Come on, it'll be cool," Phil said. "Like what they do in *Bridgerton* and shit like that. How there's a few dances that everyone just seems to know? It's for the vibes."

"Exactly," Chloe said, pointing a finger at Phil. "They've got them all up on YouTube, and I've found the easiest one, so there are *no* excuses!"

She pressed play on the video, which started walking us through the basics to the dance, which was set to an orchestral version of "Symphony" by Clean Bandit. She grabbed Pablo from me so I could dance with Phil, and I laughed as he twirled me around, completely ignoring the video's instructions despite his previous defence of it.

"Philip!" Chloe scolded him, and he sighed, straightening up exaggeratedly and following the instructions. But he was still smiling, and it was completely contagious.

Eventually we learned the dance – it was actually pretty easy, just lots of walking around one another in different positions – and Chloe let us leave. It was too late to go to the pub, so I walked back to the house with Phil, and he twirled me down the pavement all the way home.

~

I wouldn't have thought Phil and I had any firsts left – we'd known each other so long that there was no need to decide when to meet the family, go away together, or anything like that. But as it turned out, everything we did still felt like a first. Even things we'd done when fake dating didn't count, because it was the first time we were doing them as a proper *us*, like our first proper date after the festival.

And then there were our true firsts. Like our first actual dinner date, where we sat on the same side of the table, barely able to keep our hands off each other long enough to eat our food; our first overnight just the two of us, when I was housesitting for Jack and Anil was with Ethel; and the first time we talked about what we wanted for our futures and realised how aligned we were – on board with marriage, on the fence about kids, huge preference for relaxing holidays over adrenaline seeking ones. It made me excited for the firsts we would still have, like our first trip away together, and the first time we used the L-word. I could feel the latter brewing, but everything felt so new and exciting that it didn't bother me that it never came up.

Literally the *only* bad thing about being Phil's actual girlfriend, however, was that he made it very, very hard to get any work done.

One Thursday morning after I'd stayed the night, I let Phil sleep in like I had so many times. I got Ethel up and fed her, then we went for a walk together in the morning sun. But by the time I needed to wake Phil so I could go home and change for my Kenchester presentation, he proved unusually difficult to rouse. I couldn't just leave Ethel unattended, but Phil wouldn't budge from bed, even as I turned on all the lights and physically shoved him. He just pulled his duvet up over his head, holding onto it tightly so I couldn't pull it off him.

"Just two minutes of cuddles," he said, loosening his grip to reach for me.

"You and I both know that if I got in that bed, it would be much longer than two minutes before I got out again."

Phil smirked. "Damn right it would."

I knew he was naked under that duvet, and I could imagine exactly what was going on at the mention of me getting back in bed. But as tempting as it was, I truly did not have the time.

"Which is exactly why you need to *get* up, not get *it* up. Some of us need to go to work."

"You don't need to work," he said, reaching for me again, and this time I let him pull me down so I was sitting on the edge of the bed. He curled himself around me from behind, his arms around my waist.

"I do if I ever wanna move out of my parents' house."

"Just move in with me."

He said it sleepily, his eyes still closed, his mouth quirked up in a smile.

"You're absurd." I tried to get up again, but he held me tightly in place. "Despite what our friends and family think, we've only been together for three weeks. I'm not moving in with you after three weeks."

He opened his eyes and frowned, letting go of me to prop himself up with one arm. "What about four weeks?"

I rolled my eyes, even as I grinned. "No, Philip. Not after four weeks either."

"How long then?"

"Let's get through the initial trial period and then we can talk."

I meant it as a joke, but his smile faltered slightly, so I quickly leaned over and kissed him, making the smile reappear, if a bit less brightly.

"Now get out of bed, please, so I can go to work."

"I don't wanna," he moaned, flopping back on the bed, his naked body on full display, sporting a semi. *It wouldn't take much at all to bring that to full mast*, I thought, *and then maybe we could...*

The time on the clock caught my attention – it was already gone eight. I'd almost certainly be late at this point. So I had to pull out the big guns if I was going to get out of here.

"Oh Ethel!" I called. "Could you come into Phil's room for a moment?"

Phil instantly yanked the covers back up over him.

"What the fuck, babe?"

The doorknob turned, and Ethel poked her head in. "Do you two need something?" she asked. "Maybe a snack? Or a cup of tea?"

I smiled at her, trying not to laugh. "Phil just needs you to sit here with him for a few minutes," I said, standing up and pointing at the chair across the room. "He won't get out of bed. I think he's coming down with something."

"I'm fine, Ethel," Phil said frantically, grasping the covers close to him. "But maybe a cup of tea would be good?"

"I'll boil the kettle for you before I go," I said to Ethel, but I looked at Phil, winking at him as I walked back towards the door. "See you tonight."

He stuck his tongue out at me as I left, but he was already reaching for his shorts on the floor.

∼

By the time I boiled the kettle, drove home, changed, and made it to the worksite, it was nine-oh-six. I could see Dad glaring at me from the moment the house came into sight, despite the fact that Tim's car wasn't there yet.

"I thought that boyfriend of yours would be good for you," he said as I got out. "But here you are, AWOL on a Thursday morning."

"I'm sorry," I said. "Phil wasn't feeling well this morning, so

I had to get Ethel ready for the day." It wasn't completely true – okay, it was mostly untrue – but it worked. Dad's face softened at the mention of Ethel; he'd always had a soft spot for the woman.

"She doing okay?"

"She's got good days and bad days. Which is expected."

"What a woman," Dad said, just as a shiny blue Tesla pulled around the corner and into the drive. I unlocked my tablet and opened the file I'd prepared for today.

As I presented the full project plan to Tim, I couldn't quite let go of how similar he and Chris were. Not only did they look alike, down to their gelled-back hair and black gilets, but they had the same way of moving and talking, too, like everyone around them was just an NPC in their story, and they always had somewhere more important to be. I knew from experience that getting the full attention of someone like that could feel intoxicating, but it always passed. It was clear, now that I was experiencing the phenomenon in isolation, that I'd never been attracted to Chris's ambition or work ethic or charisma like I'd claimed. I'd just liked what it meant for the way other people treated me; like I was welcome in any room, and of course they wanted to spend time with me, because of who I was with. It was really quite sad when I thought about it.

But luckily, I was far enough past it that I could still nail the presentation. Today was a big day; we had to convince Tim that our approach, both in terms of the actual outcome of the flip and in how we'd manage it, was the right one for him. I'd spent so much time on the pitch that I could have delivered it in my sleep. Plus, I used all the new systems I'd been trialling for Dad, letting me give Tim a far more granular view of the process and allowing him to visualise the effects of any changes he wanted to make. I had every single image and link ready on my tablet so I could AirDrop them to him as soon as he had a question, and I knew every single figure down to the penny.

I actually found it quite exciting, and by the time I got to the end of my spiel, sat around a table we'd set up in the old meeting room just for the pitch, all comparisons to Chris were long forgotten, and I was fully locked in.

Tim asked about the rest of the team, and specifically who would look after the individual components whilst Dad managed the overall build. I ran through the foremen we'd have on site, mentioning before I could catch it that "my brother Jack" would manage the joinery. I saw panic flash across Dad's face, though I was sure he still looked pleasantly stoic to the untrained eye. As much as he loved running a family business, we knew that the other contractor in the running was a big corporate firm, and Dad was more than a bit nervous competing against them.

"You know who you're up against," Tim said as I finished, clearly reading Dad's mind. "They're bigger, so their materials costs are cheaper, but their management is more. They've got the track record on projects like this to warrant it. So why should I hire Evans Contractors?"

I exchanged a look with Dad, expecting him to take over. But instead, he just brought the corner of his mouth up ever so slightly and nodded at me. He was trusting me to close the deal.

I swallowed hard, wondering if I should go with the pitch I'd heard Dad make for years, or go with my gut, which was telling me that the very thing Dad was worried about was what set us apart. I took a deep breath and decided to trust my gut, very much not looking at Dad as I started.

"We're smaller than the other guys, there's no debating that," I said, holding eye contact with Tim. I knew from experience that he was the kind of guy who would admire assertiveness. "But that'll be a good thing on a job like this. It isn't a big high-rise project, it's a small-town conversion. We're locals, and we know the suppliers and the team and the area."

Tim nodded, encouraging me to continue, so I did, still not looking at Dad.

"We're a family business. This would be a big job for us, I won't lie. With a bigger firm, this would be bread and butter. And I'm sure that comes with apparent advantages. But it also means they wouldn't have their hearts in it the way we would."

I finally chanced a look at Dad and was surprised to see that his smile had grown, bolstering me. My instincts had been right – or at least he thought so.

"This job would be our biggest this year, and next year, too. And the year after when we win the rest of the work from you." Tim smiled; apparently he liked the confidence of assuming we'd win the rest, so I leaned into it, switching from "woulds" to "wills". "We won't have a dozen other similar projects going on simultaneously. Our hearts will be in it, and you'll be the most important client we have."

I was possibly going a little overboard on the ego stroking, and I worried I'd taken it too far, but Tim nodded enthusiastically at that last part, and I knew I'd nailed it. He brought his hands down flat on the table and pushed his chair back. I held my breath as I waited for his verdict.

"Honestly," he said, "I couldn't agree more. Let's do this, shall we?"

∽

WHEN WE GOT HOME, Dad gushed about the meeting as if he were giving the football highlights, relaying every single detail of the presentation to Mum.

"Amy was wonderful," he said, and I could have cried at how touched and surprised I was by his enthusiasm. "She had an answer to every question. She's really levelling us up, you know."

Mum beamed at me and pulled me in for a hug. "Oh, well done, darling."

"I'm so proud of you, Amy," Dad said, putting a hand on my shoulder as Mum pulled back. It was heavy and warm, rooting me to the spot. "And if you're up for one more big task this summer, let's set up a meeting with Jack and the guys to talk through the changes you want to make."

My mouth fell open. Dad had been fighting me every step of the way so far. "Really?"

He nodded. "You've proven that you know what you're doing, and you're not trying to change who we are at our core. So let's hear it. End of the month okay?"

It would be tight – there wasn't long left in August – but I needed to jump at this chance before his technophobia took over and he changed his mind. So I nodded, and Dad grabbed my hand to shake it. This time, I shook just as firmly as he did.

∽

Phil was so happy for me that he insisted on taking me out for dinner before D&D. I joked that Ethel should come with us since we'd be eating so early, but he said that Anil had the day off from his day job, so he could pick Ethel up from physio. So I took a shower and put on a nice dress before heading over to the hospital with Phil to get Ethel settled.

"Get in here," Anil said, wrapping me in a hug. I'd seen him more than ever in the last couple of months since I'd been around more, and I had to say, I loved him. We had a surprising amount in common – it turned out he was into crystals too, so we'd chatted loads about that, and he was a huge reality TV buff.

"We still need to arrange a MAFS date," I said.

"Hey, it's your boyfriend keeping me so busy in the evenings. Take it up with him."

We said our goodbyes, and Phil and I thanked Anil again for coming over early before we left. On the way out of the hospital, a beautiful blonde woman in an NHS uniform stopped Phil as we passed.

"Poppy!" he said, surprised, dropping my hand to step forward and hug her. "It's so good to see you."

"Yeah, well, it's been a while," she said, holding onto the hug for a long moment before stepping back. Then she saw me watching over Phil's shoulder, and her smile grew even wider.

"You leaving work?" Phil asked.

Poppy looked down at her smart watch. "Yeah, today was an early shift, and my little one needs picking up from daycare in a few. But it's right around the corner, so I've got a minute. Tell me what's going on here!" She pointed between Phil and me. I wondered why she would be so surprised that Phil had a girlfriend. I supposed he had been a serial dater, but was it so out of the question for him to have found someone?

Phil looked back at me and frowned as if he'd forgotten I was there, and then laughed. "Oh! Of course. Sorry. Poppy, this is Amy. Amy, Poppy."

"Nice to meet you," I said, holding my hand out. Poppy shook it, still grinning.

I tried to battle the instinct, but I was a basic bitch at heart, and I couldn't help but cuddle up to Phil when she dropped my hand.

"Well, good to see you," Phil said, draping his arm across my shoulders. "Hope you're keeping well."

"Good to see you, too," she said, smiling again, but she looked a bit confused. Phil hadn't exactly answered her question, and I wasn't sure why. But she clearly had bigger things to worry about – or littler things, from the sound of it – so she waved and walked off in the opposite direction from us.

"Who's that?" I asked as we started towards the car park again. Phil still had his arm around me, and it made it difficult to walk, so I shrugged it off to hold his hand instead, but he just let it drop altogether.

"Oh, that's Poppy."

"Yeah, I gathered that," I said. "It's pretty much the only piece of information you actually gave. How do you *know* Poppy?"

"We met on Hinge, I think? Or maybe Bumble? One of those."

I nodded. "Okay, so you dated. Just once?"

He shook his head. "No, a few times. Not in a row, though. Just when we felt like it."

"So she was a fuck buddy."

Phil shushed me as an orderly passed. "I mean, sort of. More like a date buddy?"

"So you didn't fuck?" I asked, no quieter than before. Phil sighed and stopped walking.

"Yeah, Amy, we did. Because we were single adults."

I narrowed my eyes as I rounded to face him. "I didn't suggest you weren't. I'm just trying to understand the nature of your relationship." *And why you didn't tell her I'm your girlfriend*, I added mentally, but it sounded petulant even in my mind, so I kept that part to myself.

But Phil had always been able to read me, and his face softened as he stepped forward to take my hands in his. "I was on a date with Poppy when you met up with Chris and Niamh," he said. "I ditched her without even saying goodbye to come and be with you because it was so important to me that you didn't feel alone. Trust me, she knows what you are to me. She probably recognised you, which is why she asked."

I felt myself soften as he spoke. It was still so hard to believe that even then, months ago, he'd felt about me the way he did now. How had we been so oblivious to one another for so long?

"I'm sorry," I said, squeezing his hands, and he stepped forward to press a kiss to my forehead.

"You've got nothing to apologise for. I'm just still not used to getting to show you off in public."

"Yeah, well, get used to it," I said. "And if you've got any more fuck buddies we're likely to encounter, let me know now, because I don't like surprises."

"Who do you think I am?" he asked, looking genuinely confused.

I shrugged. "I mean, Chloe jokes all the time about how you've been through half the town's population. I'm honestly surprised something like this hasn't happened sooner."

He tipped his head back and laughed – rather loudly, too, given how much shushing he'd been doing.

"Yeah, well, she doesn't know what she's talking about."

"Doesn't she? I've literally seen her swipe through your dating apps for you to find a date."

He waved his hand dismissively. "I almost never went on dates she picked for me. Most of the time I'd just go to the cinema on a Saturday night, or take myself out for a drive."

My mouth fell open. I couldn't believe what I was hearing. I'd spent every Saturday night for months trying to distract myself from what I knew Phil was out doing, and most of the time, he hadn't even been doing it. "You mean you had me sitting at yours with Ethel for months, and you weren't actually dating?"

He shrugged. "I mean, I went out with people sometimes. But yeah, it was especially weird when you started coming over, so I mostly didn't."

"And Poppy?" I asked, narrowing my eyes. "When was the last time you saw her?"

"Well, the day you went to meet up with Chris," he said, but I motioned for him to continue, and he creased his brow in thought. "Before that, I think maybe a month before you started coming over?" He snapped his fingers. "Actually, no, there was one week in the spring. But I didn't go home with her. In fact, I think it was the only time other than that last one that I didn't."

I shouldn't have felt as thrilled by that as I did – it would have been perfectly reasonable for him to go home with her before we got together, for real or for our arrangement. But the Aries in me liked the idea that he'd somehow been loyal to me even before that loyalty had been explicitly warranted.

"There's been no one," he said, reaching up to tuck a loose strand of hair behind my ear. "Not since you became a part of my life again. And if I'd thought I had a chance with you after that night five years ago, there probably wouldn't have been anyone in between, either."

I wanted to tell him the same had been true for me – that it had taken me moving away to be able to think about anyone but him. But everything was getting so emotionally hot and heavy so quickly, especially after his comment the week before about moving in, as casual as it may have been. And besides, a hospital corridor didn't feel like the most romantic place for a declaration of any kind.

"God, babe, don't be so dramatic," I teased instead, deflecting, and earning myself a firm smack on the ass. An orderly did stop to glare at us that time, and we giggled as we turned and rushed towards the car park.

LATER THAT NIGHT, when I was home in my own bed for the first time all week, I realised I hadn't done a reading about Phil and me since we'd gotten together. It felt scary, for some reason, as if the cards could somehow undermine how giddy I felt about us. But I pulled out the oracle cards Phil had bought me, deciding they would be the best possible deck to help me understand where we stood.

It wasn't that I doubted his feelings. But there was still, no matter how many times he reassured me, something slightly off. Maybe it was just a lingering feeling of insecurity on my part, the same that had fuelled what I'd said to Phil about our friends being more Jack's friends than mine. Or maybe there was actually something there that I was picking up on. Either way, the cards would help me get clarity.

I grabbed my amethyst pendant in my hand and unboxed the cards, pressing the stone into my palm to encourage my intuition, and held Phil's face in my mind. I decided one card should be enough, shuffling through the entire deck three times before stopping. Then I took a deep breath and pulled the top card, placing it on the surface in front of me.

A cloud of anxiety instantly fell over me as I looked down at the waning crescent moon, but I thumbed through the booklet anyway, wanting to be sure I wasn't jumping to conclusions.

What I read on the page made my mouth go dry.

The waning crescent moon is the final phase of the lunar cycle. It's time to wait things out and allow them to take their natural course. No matter what we do, we cannot change fate, and trying to do so will only make things worse. The best we can do is embrace the cycle of change and have hope for whatever comes next.

Your keyword: endings

CHAPTER 25
PHIL

It took ages, but the fabric I needed for Amy's dress finally arrived. I couldn't take full credit – it was Morgan's illustrations that had helped the idea come to life – but now that I could work on it properly, I knew Amy would love it. The deep violet of the satin, which almost perfectly matched the dress she'd worn on our first date, would bring out her emerald eyes, and the tiny stars already embroidered on the dusky purple tulle were even better in person. Once I added more stars in gold in her favourite constellations, it would be perfect. I didn't even need to look at the illustration to picture her in it; I knew she'd look downright ethereal. I even had my eye on a celestial halo headband that would look perfect with it.

Unfortunately, as perfect as it was, it was also expensive as hell. By the time I caved and ordered the headband, I'd spent as much on materials for the dress as I had on my tickets and accommodation for the fantasy festival. It was worth it, but I had to pick up a few extra data entry jobs to cover it, which was hard since I was also having to hide it away from Amy. I was mostly staying up late to work on it once Ethel had gone to bed, or taking advantage of the increasingly rare days when Amy wasn't at mine. I even put Ethel to work one day; her fine motor skills had worsened over time, but her draping skills were still far superior to mine.

Amy constantly tried to sneak a peek in my craft room, but I'd started keeping it locked, telling her I didn't want Ethel to pick up scissors or a needle without me knowing. I was pretty sure she knew I was up to something, but thankfully she didn't push it.

It was as tiring as it always was, trying to juggle everything. I was just about keeping my head above water, mostly because of Amy, but I knew eventually something would have to give. Especially when I noticed that, despite the injection she'd gotten, which should have eased the pain for months, Ethel was still compensating for the arthritis in her back, leaning to the side when she was sitting down and using the walls and furniture for support when she walked. I didn't deal well with that, spending a solid hour after she went to bed one night pacing the lounge in front of Amy, wondering what I was missing or doing wrong, and blaming myself and everything I had going on for distracting me.

I didn't think I ever implied that Amy was counted among the things distracting me, as much as she might have been; at least I tried not to insinuate that. But she seemed to go there herself, always offering to be there more or less, or whatever I needed, and I had to reassure her more than once that I wanted as much of her as I could have.

Maybe I needed to take a break from the crafts and the baking, or maybe look at a meal delivery service. But all that cost money. And not to mention, I was already only making dinner maybe three days a week, relying more and more on frozen ready meals and leftovers, and I hated it. Every time I took a bite of something I hadn't prepared myself, no matter how good it was, I felt a sense of disappointment. I was failing to be and do everything I needed to be and do, and every cut corner I noticed or ball I dropped just made my deficiency more evident.

~

We arrived at the Evanses' house one Sunday for dinner, about an hour before the meal as usual, so I could help Patricia cook. Amy asked Ethel if she wanted to go see the cows again, and I wasn't convinced she remembered what Amy was talking about, but she seemed enthusiastic enough. So whilst I went inside, off they went to the farm.

I'd lost risotto stirring privileges years ago for forgetting to stir for approximately thirty seconds – five years ago, actually; I'd been distracted by a certain leggy blonde, if I remembered correctly – so Patricia put me on chopping duty for the salad. Alan came in at one point and asked me a few questions. We'd always struggled because I didn't watch football or listen to death metal, and he didn't watch *The Great British Sewing Bee* or listen to podcasts about dementia research, but he always made time for a conversation, and he always asked after Ethel. Now we talked about Amy too, apparently, as he bragged about how well she'd done with the big pitch.

"She worked really hard on that," I said, knowing she'd hate me saying that, but it was true. "I think she's really chuffed it paid off."

"Yeah, I know the feeling," he said, just as Amy and Ethel walked in through the back door.

"What feeling?" Amy asked, skipping over to kiss me on the cheek. That was new to our real relationship, too: PDA in front of her family.

"Being proud of you, essentially," Patricia said from the hob where she stood stirring, probably knowing Alan would never admit to it.

Amy frowned, then started wiping at my face. "I take that kiss back. You weren't really talking about me, were you?"

I shrugged as I sliced through a pepper. "You'll never know, will you?"

Amy unhooked a tea towel from the cabinet pull and wound it up before whipping at my legs with it. Luckily, she missed by a hair.

"Watch it!" I yelled. "Sharp knife here!"

"Not in the kitchen!" Patricia shouted. "Alan, take over the chopping so Phil and Amy can spend time together."

Alan huffed his disapproval but ultimately complied. "As if they don't spend enough time together," he said, taking the knife and pointing it at me. "I knew you were trouble."

I thought about insisting he let me continue for my own safety, but Amy was already pulling me out the door.

"Did you two get to see the cows?" I asked as Ethel followed us. Amy let go of me and rushed to her side to help her over the threshold, which jutted up slightly.

"No, we got distracted by the ducks at Jack's. Wanna go now?"

"Dinner in twenty!" Patricia called as we left through the back gate, and I gave her a thumbs-up through the open window.

We walked up towards Amy's Uncle John's land where the cows were, but I suddenly understood why she and Ethel hadn't made it there earlier; Ethel was so slow that we barely made it up the hill halfway to Jack's before needing to turn around again. I was sure the walking was good for her, but I could tell with every step she took how badly her back was hurting. I thought I might need to get her using her walker more at this rate.

Jack, Morgan, and Pablo caught up with us a couple hundred metres from the house and walked the rest of the way with us. Amy helped Ethel steady herself so she could bend down to pet Pablo, and I felt a surge of affection for how well she looked after her. She was so attentive to what Ethel needed, and I noticed that she was correcting her posture the way we'd been taught by the physiotherapist.

"Whatcha looking at?" Jack asked, nudging me in the side, and I looked up to see him and Morgan staring at me, dopey grins on their faces.

"Shut up," I muttered, then motioned for all of us to keep moving. The last thing I needed was Patricia having a go at me for the risotto going cold.

Maybe I was in a sentimental mood, because I couldn't take my eyes off Amy all through lunch, even when she was ribbing me about the quality of the salad. I insisted she should take it up with her dad, who jokingly warned me not to be insolent. Even Ethel joined in, holding up a rather large chunk of cucumber to Alan, saying "What the hell am I supposed to do with that?"

Just as we were finishing our food – which had been delicious as always, unevenly chopped veg notwithstanding – Alan cleared his throat and looked at Patricia, who took his hand on top of the table.

"We have an announcement," Alan said matter-of-factly.

"What's going on?" Amy asked. "You're not pregnant, are you?"

This elicited an eye roll from Patricia and a guffaw from Alan.

"No, Amelia Celeste, I am not pregnant."

Amy sat back, thoroughly chastised. She hated having her full name used, and I took a mental note of that for later.

"Ooh, I know," Morgan said. "I've been here before. They're selling the house to go travelling." Morgan's own mum had bowed out of regular society to live in a van in the US a few years back.

"Warmer," Patricia said encouragingly, and Morgan's eyes went wide.

"I was joking!"

"Yeah, where am I supposed to live?" Amy asked, and despite what I'd said to Amy in the confines of my bed, I glared at Jack when he looked straight at me. Ethel seemed to be sharing a brain cell with him, though, and she had far less of a filter.

"Well, you already spend enough time with us," she said, "so as soon as Phil finishes that big project, we can clear out his craft room for you."

Everybody else at the table cracked up at the idea that Amy would move into my craft room, whilst Morgan and I exchanged a panicked look that Ethel had nearly given up the game on Amy's dress.

"Calm down," Alan said, holding up his free hand. "We're not moving. You're all so dramatic."

"Get on with it then," Ethel said. "I'm not getting any younger."

"Right," Alan said, nodding at Patricia to take over.

"Your father and I have been thinking," she said, "we'd like to go on holiday. All of us, as a family."

"Sick!" Jack said, up for anything as always. "Where to?"

"We were thinking a cruise to the Norwegian Fjords."

Jack and Morgan exchanged an excited look. "I'm definitely up for that," Morgan said.

"Yeah, amazing," Amy said. "When?"

"Well, that depends," Patricia said. "The trip would be about a week and a half, maybe two weeks, but when we go depends on what works for everyone involved."

Then everyone turned to look at me, the only person who hadn't responded. Well, besides Ethel, but she was looking at me, too. *Thanks a lot, Nan.*

I coughed lightly into my napkin. "Well, that's really kind,"

I said, "but I don't think that's feasible for me. I couldn't be away from Ethel for that long."

"Oh!" Patricia said, bringing her hands up in front of her. "I'm so sorry that wasn't clear. Of course Ethel's invited too. That was part of the reason why we thought a cruise might be a good fit, because it's so accessible. We can even get one out of a UK port."

I nodded as if that made sense, but inside I was panicking. I wanted to be literally anywhere else, but everyone was looking at me, and I could tell they were expecting an answer, or at least an indication, now.

Amy grabbed my hand under the table, and I took that as a sign of solidarity, so I finally replied.

"That's so thoughtful," I said, "and thank you again. But I just don't think it's sensible for us, or for Ethel especially."

"Bollocks," Ethel said, proving exceedingly unhelpful. "Maybe I haven't been on a cruise in a while, but it's the classic old person holiday for a reason, right?"

I shook my head. "Ethel, I don't think you're thinking it through." *And this is the most lucid you've been in months,* I didn't add. Maybe if she'd been her usual self, it would have been clearer why I was so resistant.

"She's not wrong," Amy said, and I spun to look at her, shocked that she wasn't on my side.

"What do you mean?" I asked, genuinely not understanding.

She shrugged. "Well, they are pretty accessible, and even if she did have different needs by then, we could adapt. Maybe stay on the ship instead of going into the ports."

"I don't think she'd be up for that," I said, but Ethel smacked my upper arm hard enough that it stung.

"Don't talk about me like I'm not here. I may be old, but I'm still a person."

I turned around to face her. "I know you are. Of course you

are. I'm just trying to look out for you. Think about your back. Can you imagine walking on the deck of a moving ship? Much less one that's crossing the North Sea?"

Ethel frowned, and I could tell that, at least on some level, she understood. But honestly, that wasn't even the half of it. I could picture her waking up and forgetting where she was, and panicking, and maybe hurting herself. Or getting disoriented walking down a long hallway of identical staterooms. Or having an irritable moment and smacking the arm of someone who wasn't me and getting in trouble for it. It would be a nightmare, probably for both of us.

"That's okay, let's park it," Amy said, smiling, clearly trying to defuse the tension. "We can talk about it later."

"We don't have to talk about it later," I snapped, and I saw her wilt, but I couldn't help it. It felt like no one was listening. "Thank you so much for the offer. It means a lot, really. But it's just not a good idea for us. Sorry."

Alan and Patricia both nodded, but Amy just looked up at me, a wounded expression on her face. I couldn't handle it. I was trying to do the right thing for Ethel, which was usually her priority, too. So why was she trying to gang up on me?

I pushed back from the table and excused myself, aware that I was being rude, but I just needed a minute. I found myself upstairs in the hallway, not sure where to go. My first instinct had been to go into Jack's bedroom – the last time I'd been upstairs in the Evanses' house I'd been nineteen at most – but it was clear when I opened the door that Patricia had turned it into her office, so I backed out again.

I heard a creak on the stairs and turned to see Amy step into the corridor. And as overwhelmed as I felt, as on edge as I was, seeing her felt like letting a little bit of air out of the situation.

"We can go in here," she said, nodding me towards her room. It felt weird to follow her in there, but where else was I supposed to go? And I supposed if I couldn't have a moment alone, at least I could clear the air with her.

Stepping into her room was like stepping back in time. Her walls were the same pink they'd been since she was a kid, there were height markings on the doorframe, and there were glow-in-the-dark stars I knew Jack had helped her put up when they were younger. But other than that, it looked completely unlived in. There were boxes everywhere, and the wardrobe, which was open, was empty except for a dozen or so dresses and jumpsuits on wire hangers. Amy appeared to be living entirely out of the dresser, which was covered in her crystals and incense and card decks.

"Wow," I said dumbly. "It's different in here than I would have expected."

"How so?"

"Well, you haven't exactly made yourself at home. You've been back a year now, haven't you?"

She sat down on the bed and shrugged, patting beside her. But I didn't join her.

"Sorry about that downstairs," I said instead, standing in front of her. "I didn't mean to snap at you."

"It's okay," she said, smiling. "We can go over things together later. I get that it freaked you out, so we'll do as much research as needed so you feel good about it."

I frowned. "Amy, I'm not apologising about not wanting to go. I was apologising for how I spoke to you. But I'm not going without Ethel, and Ethel absolutely cannot go."

Amy held my gaze as she took a deep breath, and I felt my jaw set in anticipation of an argument. Heaven knew I'd had enough of them with her over the years, but not usually about something that actually mattered.

"Why don't you want to do this?" she asked, crossing her arms. "Why don't you want to come on holiday with us?"

I sighed and rolled my eyes. "You know that's not what's happening here. Don't be like that."

"You're right," she said. "What's happening here is that you seem to have zero interest in finding a way to make things work. The first suggestion offered didn't fit your idea of what was achievable, so instead of having a fucking conversation, you just shut it down."

"You and I both know I can't just pack up and go away for two weeks, no matter what the holiday looks like."

"A week and a half," she said, as if that made a difference. "And isn't that what carers are for? If we plan around Anil's schedule, we could—"

"*No*, Amy!" I said, my voice raised now. "I'm not leaving her for that long, and that's final. What if something happened? And I don't even mean the worst thing. I mean, what if she started sundowning and Anil got hurt? What if she fell again? The only reason I can go away for things like the ball and the festival is because I can get back in an emergency if I need to. I can't very well be airlifted back from some fjord if I'm needed, and that's assuming I could get the call to begin with."

"So let her come with us!" Amy shouted back, though I could tell even she knew that wasn't an option. "Or let's think of something different! Don't just write it off. It doesn't have to be a yes or no."

"It's very much a yes or no," I said. "We're going on a two-week Norwegian fjords cruise. Wanna come? Yes or no."

"They said they were *thinking* about Norway, Phil." Amy rubbed her face, and for a moment I thought she was wiping tears away, and I softened slightly. But there was just frustration in her eyes when she looked back up. "They want to take all of us on holiday together, and they were trying to be thoughtful."

"And I appreciate that, I do. But I just can't do it, Amy."

"And when will you?" she asked, flinging her arms out to the sides. "When she's gone? Because that's not fair to you, Phil, and it's not fair to her either. You're taking on too much, and she wouldn't want you giving up things like holidays and nights out. You've already given up your twenties to care for her."

"Don't you dare speak for her," I said, pointing a finger in Amy's face, my voice low and rough. She didn't balk, but I did see surprise flicker across her expression.

"Something's gonna have to bend, Phil," she said, bringing her hand to wrap around my finger, lowering it. "Otherwise something's going to break, and that something will probably be you."

Or us was the unspoken end to that, and I knew it.

I felt my lip start to shake, and before I even knew why, Amy's face softened, and she reached up to wipe away the tears that had started slipping down my face. She pressed up onto her toes and kissed my face – each cheek in turn, each eye, my forehead, my mouth – and then wrapped me in her arms. I tried to swallow the tears, but they wouldn't stop, and before long I was sobbing into her shoulder.

"I'm just so tired," I said through the sobs. "I don't know how much longer I can do this. It's not fair."

"I know," she said, stroking my hair. "I know it's not."

At some point my knees started to go weak, and she squeezed me tighter to keep me up.

"It's okay," she said, her breath hot against my ear as she spoke. "I'm here. And I always will be."

CHAPTER 26
AMY

Against my better judgment, and against the advice of every horoscope I saw in the following days, I followed Phil's lead when he brushed the holiday incident under the rug. Moments after he was crying in my arms, he was walking downstairs for dessert like nothing had happened. I expected there to be at least *some* awkwardness, but he was instantly back to his usual playful self: debating the ideal crumble topping with Mum, arguing with Ethel and me about the best *Pride and Prejudice* adaptation (he preferred the 2005 version, like a weirdo), and later, in bed, waking me up in the night with kisses on my ear and a hand already roaming up my thigh. It was like he'd just needed to get all the stress out of his system, and now that he had, he could slide back into the status quo like nothing had happened. Like he'd just decided to compartmentalise, and it had worked.

But still, it had scared me. He hadn't said it, but I'd been able to read between the lines: our relationship and the things he thought it demanded were making his burden heavier.

So over the next week, I took care to need nothing from Phil. I didn't ask about plans for the ball, despite the fact that we were getting close enough to necessitate more detailed logistics. I asked to cancel the bonus date night we'd planned in favour of hanging out at his, knowing it meant one less shift he'd have to pay Anil for and several hours fewer to worry about Ethel. And all the while, I wore my amethyst pendant every day, even buying a handful of tumbled sodalite and amazonite, dropping stones in his pockets each day, desperate for anything that could encourage honesty and understanding.

Meanwhile, I had plenty of my own shit to worry about. I was trying to get the presentation ready for my dad, spending actual time at the job sites so I understood how he and his team worked. I asked them questions about how they got their schedules, what annoyed them about the processes they used, and what they would change if they could. I knew I'd be asking for a lot – I was going to try to strike whilst the iron was hot and get him to implement a bunch of integrated upgrades at once – so I needed to be just as on it as I had been for Tim. All around making sure my boyfriend didn't crumble into dust under the weight of ... well, everything.

But things weren't getting better. If anything, I could see Phil fraying further and further. And by the time Sunday dinner rolled around again, I suggested he stay at home to catch up on things, and when I joined him at around seven, he fell asleep on the sofa almost immediately.

So I was surprised when Tuesday came and he didn't want to skip the pub quiz.

"Of everything you could skip, the pub quiz is the easiest," I said as we waited outside the physio. Phil was texting Anil to confirm for the evening. "We only ever get second place, and I can go by myself."

"I know you can," he said, and despite the fact that he was smiling, I could hear the exasperation. "But you like going, don't you? So I do, too." He pressed a kiss to my temple.

I narrowed my eyes at him, sceptical at best, fearful at worst.

"I know I've been tired," he said in the understatement of the millennium, "but I feel like I've been neglecting you. So let's just do the quiz tonight, yeah?"

"I don't feel neglected," I lied. Though it wasn't his fault; I was insisting upon my own neglect. It was temporary ... wasn't it?

Although, come to think of it, what was the endpoint? What arbitrary milestone was I waiting on that would make everything better? I didn't like where that train of thought led.

"It's a done deal," he said, hitting send on the text and holding it up to show me. "Also, you didn't send me my horoscope today."

"No, I guess I didn't," I said, frowning. "Why, do you want it?"

"Of course," he said, lacing his hand through mine. "Like I said, I care about the things you love."

"You've literally never requested a horoscope from me before."

"Probably because you've always shared them with me by lunchtime."

He wasn't wrong; I'd sent him his horoscope religiously. I'd omitted today's on purpose because it was a bit *too* relevant. But he held out his hand as if I would physically hand it to him, so I couldn't exactly deny him one. I thought about making one up off the top of my head, but I couldn't very well lie to him whilst hoping he'd be honest with me. So I opened the app on my phone and read it out to him, as if I were seeing it for the first time.

"Failure is inevitable, but the best jesters turn dropped juggling balls into part of the show. When things don't go to plan today, focus on how to stick the landing."

He frowned. "That's a bit ominous."

I shrugged, hoping to play it off. "Sounds to me like we need to make sure our pub quiz team name is good enough to make everyone laugh when we're listed in last place."

Phil looked at me like I'd just stabbed him, his mouth falling open. "You don't like Presti-quiz-itation?! You wound me, Evans."

I rolled my eyes, but inside I was heaving a huge sigh of relief that I'd managed to stick *that* landing. The only thing that worried me was the niggling feeling in the back of my mind that his horoscope had been about much more than just the pub quiz.

As we sat around the table at the pub later, marking down our last answer, we collectively held our breath. We'd been confident about nearly everything, and, based on the muttering around us, we were pretty sure the other teams had not. But it was the busiest it had ever been for the last pub quiz of the summer, with a dozen different teams and at least fifty people in the room.

Phil was as relaxed as I'd seen him since we'd gotten together properly. He'd let himself have not one but two beers, and he seemed back to his usual self, which mostly meant making innuendos for every question and propositioning me to meet him in the toilets at least three separate times. I'd brushed him off, but he ran his thumb up and down my spine as we looked over our answers before marking, and I crossed my legs tighter, wondering if maybe it wouldn't be such a bad idea to pass the time until the results were announced in a more *intimate* way ...

"Is it jinxing it to say that I think we've got this one?" Chloe asked as she looked over Fatima's shoulder at our paper.

"Absolutely yes," I said, pointing at the table. "Touch wood immediately."

"I'm literally leaning on wood," Chloe said, indicating her elbows on the table, but she knocked it with her fist obediently anyway.

"Let's not get our hopes up," Morgan whispered. "None of you knew the answer to the Stephen King question, and that one was worth a lot of points."

"Hey, Chloe's right. We've got this," Phil said, smiling and nodding as if trying to make his optimism catch. But we were more stoic than ever, desperate to win first place just once before the summer ended.

We exchanged answer sheets with the team at the table next to us, called "Quiz Khalifa", and it was almost comical how little we spoke whilst the answers were being read out. We all exchanged relieved looks every time our answer was revealed to be right, and smug ones every time Fatima crossed out a wrong answer on the other team's paper.

We swapped papers back and were pleased to see we'd gotten seventy-six of a possible eighty points, compared to Quiz Khalifa's sixty-one, though we had no idea how well the other ten teams had fared.

"Results time!" The host said into the mic once the results had been tallied, and all fifty-plus people packed into the pub cheered. I grabbed Phil's hand, surprised at how nervous and hopeful I felt. When Chloe, Fatima, and Morgan grasped hands too, and Fatima reached out for mine, we closed into a circle around the table.

"In fourth place, with sixty-two points," the host said, and we all exchanged incredulous glances – that was a massive points gap from what we knew we had, which was a good sign – "we have I Wish This Microphone Was A Massive Cock. Hardy har, boys."

The table of six twenty-something lads to our left roared

with cheers and laughter – clearly they were impressed with their own sense of humour – as the rest of the teams clapped politely.

"Shouldn't it be I Wish This Microphone *Were* A Massive Cock?" Chloe asked. "I'm not exactly an expert, so I'm not sure."

"And at third place, with sixty-nine points—"

"NICE!" yelled nearly everyone in the pub at once, including the host himself.

"We have Quiz-Team-a Aguilera!"

A table of forty-somethings across the room cheered and high-fived, and I felt both Phil and Fatima tighten their grips on my hands. Or maybe I was the one squeezing them. It didn't matter; all our hands would go numb for all we cared if it meant we could somehow manifest the win.

"Our top two teams," the host said, "are Presti-quiz-itation, who have basically been paying rent on their second place position this summer, and newcomers Les Quizerables."

I made eye contact with someone a few tables over whose group looked similarly expectant – a group of eight shoved around a tiny table for four. If we lost to them, I'd still chalk it up as a win; they had almost twice as many people as we did.

"So let's reveal our winner, shall we?"

Amidst cries of "Yes please!" And "Get on with it!" from the crowd, Phil suddenly dropped my hand and reached for his pocket. He pulled out his phone and stared down at it, then flashed me the screen, his face white as a ghost.

Anil was calling.

"Yeah?" he said, answering, his voice dry and stilted. And if I'd thought he looked scared before, I hadn't known what was coming.

Over the next five seconds, as the others in the pub started a drumroll on their tables, I watched as Phil's eyes widened ever so slightly, his mouth fell open, and then his jaw twitched as he clamped it shut again.

"I'll be there in twenty," he said, then hung up and met my eye. "I have to go."

We shot up at the same time as our friends, but whilst they cheered and high-fived and hugged, we just took off towards the exit. I followed Phil as he literally sprinted out of the pub, but I realised halfway to the door that I'd left my bag. I would have just left it behind, but it had my phone and keys, so I ran back to grab it off the chair, offering a quick "Sorry, guys," to the others before running off again.

But when I got outside and looked around, trying to figure out where Phil had gone, he was nowhere to be seen.

CHAPTER 27
YORICK PROUDHOLLOW

The security was much tighter than they'd expected, but eventually the party were able to slip past a guard distracted by a young woman in a revealing dress and make their way down the dark corridor he was meant to be guarding.

"Men are trash," Calamity whispered, and Morgana shushed her, but Yorick could hear her breath stutter with laughter as she did.

Eventually, they made their way to the library, which was almost half the size of the ballroom, lit by an ornate brazier burning in the middle of the room. As planned, Calamity cast a spell on Liam and herself, allowing them to levitate so they could more easily check the higher shelves. The spell would only last ten minutes, but they only needed three in the end before Liam called out.

"Hey, check this out," he said, dropping a book down to Morgana where she stood below him before guiding himself back down to the ground. She turned the midnight blue leather book over in her hands. The cover was embossed with the twelve-pointed star that had become all too familiar to them over the past months.

"Let me see," Yorick said, snatching it from Morgana's hands.

"Hey, chill out," she said, but she didn't take it back from him.

Yorick ran his finger over the symbol before turning the book on its side and letting it fall open. It opened directly onto a page marked with a small piece of parchment. The text told of an artefact called the Diadem of Dominion, which had been destroyed centuries ago but could be rebuilt with the right materials.

"What do you wanna bet those materials are astral diamonds?" Calamity asked as Yorick relayed the information to the rest of the party. "What does it do?"

"The gleam of the diadem," Yorick read aloud, "once powered, proves irresistible to all who gaze upon the visage of the wearer once, engendering complete loyalty and obedience to any instruction the wearer bestows. This loyalty persists until the wearer or the loyal subject dies, or until the diadem is destroyed, which can only be done by magical means equal to those which created it."

"It's always mind control with these assholes," Morgana muttered. "Okay, so we have to find the diadem and destroy it before Nephrine can wear it and turn us all into drooling minions, yeah?"

Yorick nodded and clapped the book shut. "That sounds about right."

"Good luck with that," a honeyed voice said, and the party spun around to see a shadowed figure in the doorway.

No, two figures.

Lady Nebora Nephrine stepped into the light, dragging a handcuffed Eden with her by the arm. Nephrine's robes were the same midnight blue as the book in Yorick's hands. They flowed over her shoulders and down her body, held tight to her waist by a matching leather belt. At the centre of the belt was a golden buckle in the shape of a twelve-pointed star.

The noblewoman also wore the elf's star crystal around her own neck, and suddenly it all made sense. The diadem was infused with astral diamonds, so the only thing that could power it was something else from the astral plane. Something like Eden's crystal. Yorick felt so stupid. The Twelve hadn't been targeting him, they'd been targeting Eden. But going after her would have been too obvious, so they'd plucked the string they knew was most likely to snap. Him.

"Let go of her," Yorick demanded, taking a half step forward, but he stopped when he saw Eden shake her head.

"I wouldn't be so reckless if I were you," Nephrine said through a sickening grin. Yorick swallowed the bitter taste that flooded his mouth at the reflection of his own words from earlier. His eyes flicked to the place where Nephrine gripped Eden, noticing for the first time the dagger she also held. "But thank you," Nephrine continued, "for hand-delivering me exactly what I need to power the diadem. Come forward, my child."

Yorick tried to look around, confused, but he realised with horror that he had lost control of his own body. He took one step towards Nephrine, then another, and another, until he stood directly before her. She nodded down at him, and even as he fought against the movement, his arms reached out in front of him, slipping the book into the pocket of her robe. He tried desperately to will himself to cling to the tome, to not deliver it to her, but her control over his body held.

As soon as he surrendered the book, Nephrine snapped her fingers, and the flame burning in the centre of the room snuffed out. A loud clicking noise bounced around the room, just as a thick black smoke began to fill the space. Yorick regained control over his body, and his arms recoiled so suddenly that he hit himself in the gut.

Calamity uttered a spell in between coughs, and a magical light began to radiate from the now-extinguished brazier, illuminating the dense but already dissipating smoke. The party looked around in confusion, trying to see where Nephrine and Eden had gone, but they had disappeared.

CHAPTER 28
PHIL

I hadn't meant to leave Amy behind. At least, it hadn't been an intentional choice. All I'd done was focus on putting one foot in front of the other as quickly as possible. For the first half of the journey to the hospital, I didn't even notice she wasn't with me, because the only thing I'd been thinking was *I should have been there.*

When I realised she wasn't with me, my initial reaction was relief, because it meant I didn't have to worry about explaining things to her when I still didn't know anything myself. My second reaction, of course, was to feel guilty about being relieved. But I had to focus on what was happening, because I'd had too much to drink to go back for my car. Which meant I needed to get there on foot, and fast.

All Anil had said was that Ethel had fallen, and she was conscious and mobile, but he was taking her to the hospital in his van because something didn't feel right. I wished as I ran that I'd asked more questions, but Anil's phone went to voicemail when I tried to ring him again en route. And it was probably for the best, given that I was so winded from running for the first time in years that he would have struggled to understand me.

By the time I arrived at A&E, I was drenched in sweat and felt like I might see my beer again soon if I wasn't careful. I saw a predictably long queue at the desk, and I desperately looked around for someone who could just tell me where Ethel was. I saw a nurse and grabbed him by the arm as he passed, and he looked down at my hand in shock as if I'd punched him.

"I'm sorry," I said, holding my hands up, "but I'm looking for my nan. She's been rushed here."

"Join the queue," he said dismissively as he walked away, gesturing towards the mass of people I'd been trying to circumvent.

I joined the back of the queue as instructed, not sure what else to do. I probably was standing way too close to the person in front of me, even tapping my foot impatiently, but they were scrolling through TikTok on their phone, which I could just about hear, thin and tinny, through their earbuds. Okay, yes, I was definitely standing too close.

I took my own phone out of my pocket, dislodging a blue crystal as I did; Amy had been dropping them in my pockets all week. I knew it wasn't the same one as earlier, either, because I'd been piling them on my bedside table. I knew I should look them up to see what they meant, maybe figure out what she was so desperate for me to feel or not feel, but I'd had too much on my mind to remember.

I woke my phone screen and saw a slew of texts come through, mostly from Amy.

> **AMY**
>
> Where did you go? I'm coming
>
> Seriously, where are you? I'm at the house, but it doesn't look like you're here?
>
> Are you at the hospital?

> Phil please let me know that you and Ethel and Anil are okay when you can.

There were messages from Chloe, Fatima, and Morgan, too, all in the group chat, similar to Amy's, asking where I'd gone and hoping everything was okay. Jack chimed in too, seeing the activity, and he must have been with Patricia, as he was offering any help we might need on her behalf.

But none of the messages were from Anil, and the line was moving painfully slowly, so I took my chances grabbing another person in a uniform as they walked past. I barely registered the tied-back blonde hair before I grabbed their arm.

"Phil?"

"Oh my god," I said, wrapping Poppy in the biggest, sweatiest bear hug. "You're a sight for sore eyes."

But she pushed me off her. "What are you doing here? You're not sick, are you?"

I shook my head. "No, it's Ethel. Her carer said she'd had a fall and they were coming here. I need to find her."

"Oh, I can help with that," she said, pulling me out of the queue.

The person in front of me groaned. "Not fair," I heard them mumble as I walked away.

Poppy took me through the triage area and ducked into a room, motioning for me to wait in the hallway, before emerging with a tablet. I tried to look over her shoulder, but she glared at me until I backed off.

"It's Ethel, right?"

I nodded. "That's right."

"Surname?" she asked.

"Same as mine."

She stared at me guiltily, and it took me a moment to realise she actually didn't know my surname. If it had been any normal circumstance, I might have teased her for not remembering it. But I didn't have it in me.

"Owen," I offered. "No S."

Poppy flashed a thankful smile at me then finished typing in her search.

"Damn, that carer of hers must know somebody."

"Why do you say that?"

"Because she's been here less than half an hour and she's already having scans done," she said. "Here. I can walk you."

ETHEL'S BACK WAS BROKEN.

After waiting hours for the CT and X-ray scans to come back, it turned out that the "arthritis" we'd been treating in her back for the last month hadn't been arthritis at all, but an S2 fracture they'd missed in their initial scans.

"It's a good thing I ordered that angle," Dr Mulling said, "and that Mr Agha here told me about her back pain."

I nodded gratefully at Anil, but I was cursing myself. I should have noticed something bigger was wrong. I'd made it my life's mission to make sure Ethel was comfortable and cared for, and yet, whilst I'd been making googly eyes at Amy and playing silly games, she'd been hobbling around with a broken back. I would never forgive myself for missing it.

"I'm not surprised it's been painful, Ms Owen," Dr Mulling continued, directly to Ethel this time. "That must have been really uncomfortable."

"The jab helped, I think," Ethel said. "Can't I just have another?"

"You'll get painkillers, yes," Dr Mulling said, nodding, "but those shots were because we thought the problem was your arthritis. We wouldn't prescribe it for a fracture."

"So we've been missing this for years, since her hip?" I asked. "Why after all this time is it just now giving her pain?"

Dr Mulling frowned. "Oh, this isn't from that fall. It's far newer than that."

Anil and I exchanged an alarmed look, and I racked my memory for when she could have hurt herself that badly.

"When, then?" Anil asked, but he didn't need to. Realisation sank over me.

"About a month ago," I said, looking up at Dr Mulling for confirmation. She nodded. "She fell out of bed at night. Then she started having that pain. I just thought it was the arthritis like they said. I figured the fall must have made it worse."

And it was the first and only time she didn't know who I was, I thought. At least her CT scans had come back clean, so I knew she hadn't acquired a spinal fracture *and* a traumatic brain injury all in one night.

"Now, Mr Agha," Dr Mulling said, turning to Anil, "you're specialised in home adaptations, right?"

Anil nodded. "I'm two weeks off my certification."

She nodded. "Then as far as I'm concerned, you're the best person to advise Ms Owen and her grandson on some changes that may help prevent this in the future."

I frowned. Changes? Like, to the house? Anil and I had worked hard to make sure the house was as safe as possible without making Ethel feel like a patient. I was worried anything else would make it start to feel like a hospital, which I knew she didn't want. And frankly, neither did I.

But Anil nodded back. "I think there's a lot we can do."

∽

I WAS nothing if not a master compartmentaliser. And as hard as I'd worked to let Amy build little doors between my compartments, as much as I'd invited her into each one, I knew I'd have to go through and lock those doors one by one. There would be too much to keep track of: changes to Ethel's medication, new physio routines to implement, adaptations to discuss with Anil; hell, the binder would need a complete overhaul. And if I thought too much about Amy, if I left those doors open, I was afraid the whole thing would crumble.

So I tried my best not to think of her as we discussed referrals, went through the discharge process, and loaded Ethel and her new wheelchair into Anil's big van.

But as we pulled up to the house and I saw Amy on the bench beside the hawthorn tree, it was clear my compartmentalisation was doomed to fail because of one crucial thing I'd failed to consider: just how persistent my girlfriend was.

She snapped her head up as soon as we'd pulled onto the street, watching us as we pulled up at the end of the drive.

"Talk to her," Anil said as he put the van in park. "She's a good egg."

"I know she is," I said, more to myself than to him. And I did know. But that was part of the problem.

Anil unloaded Ethel and wheeled her up the path whilst I walked directly through the grass. Amy didn't stand up from the bench to greet me, she just scooted a couple of inches to the right so I could sit down beside her.

"I'm glad to see you're all alive and accounted for," she said, and I didn't miss the bite in her words. "It was hard not to think the worst when you didn't even text to tell me she was okay."

It was as if an elephant had sat on my chest. I hadn't even realised what she must have thought, though I was sure I would have if I'd spared her even a moment's consideration. "I'm sorry," I said weakly. "She's okay. But she has broken her back."

Amy's eyes went wide. "What? How?" The alarm in her voice matched mine from earlier, and I felt a surge of affection for her at how worried she was for Ethel. But then I felt my own fear sneaking in the door behind her, and I couldn't have that.

There was no space for me to let fear and emotion creep in if I was going to do a better job of keeping Ethel safe.

"She fractured it a while ago, but they only just found it on the scans. It seems today's fall didn't really do anything."

"Yesterday's," Amy corrected, and when I frowned in confusion, she showed me the time on her phone. "It's almost two in the morning. Yesterday's fall."

"Right."

"I've been out here since half eight, you know. I nearly broke a window so I could use the toilet and charge my phone."

"You can go now if you want," I said, but she didn't move, and I didn't repeat myself. We sat side by side in silence for a solid minute, and as much as I would have liked to be thinking of how to apologise for making her wait, for making her worry, I couldn't. My head was already swimming with next steps for Ethel, and what that meant for me. I'd need to upgrade the car, for sure, and I'd need to rethink the sched—

"So what's the plan?" Amy asked, interrupting my train of thought. I looked at her in confusion, thrown.

"The plan?"

"For Ethel," she said, with an implied "Obviously". "Presumably there's more physio now, and I'll need to retrofit the back seat of the car to be accessible, but I'm sure there are companies that can do that. And will she be in the wheelchair all the time? If so, we should think about looking for a more comfortable one for her, because those NHS ones can be a bit..."

It was all too much, this echo of the concerns swirling around my own mind, and I couldn't listen to it. Not just because it was overwhelming, though it certainly was, but because as I watched Amy, I saw her slipping into the role of caretaker. She was a twenty-five-year-old with a beat-up old Land Rover, and she was talking about retrofitting it for a wheelchair for my grandmother. She'd worked so hard to build the life she wanted since moving home, and here she was willing to reshape it literally overnight for Ethel. For me.

In that moment, I'd never felt more tired in my life. I wanted desperately to be in her shoes; to have the world at my fingertips, and be bold and beautiful and clever enough to have any of it that I wanted. She was one of the most amazing people I'd ever known, and she always had been. And she deserved an equally amazing life.

But my life? It wasn't fun or bold or carefree. It hadn't been for a long time, as much as I enjoyed pretending some evenings and weekends that it was. That I could still be that guy. And as much as I desperately wanted her with me, as much as she made things better just by being there, I couldn't keep subjecting her to that. She'd said it herself, that I'd given up my twenties to Ethel, and I was fully prepared to give her my thirties too. She deserved every second of my time. But I wouldn't take the best years of Amy's life from her.

So I slammed all the doors inside me shut and locked them tight.

"Anil and I have the plan covered," I said. "Thanks for the offer, though."

Amy's face fell. "Oh," she said, swallowing hard. "I mean, maybe let's get some sleep and we can talk about it tomorrow? Come on, let's go inside."

She reached out to me, and I could see in her face and the tremble in her hand that she was pleading with me. But I just shook my head.

"Honestly, I think we should just call it," I said. "This was never part of the deal."

She recoiled as if I'd slapped her, and I suppressed a wince at how cold I sounded.

"The deal?"

"Yeah, the deal. I know it's not been three months, but I

think we both got what we wanted from it, right? You've nailed things at work, and everyone's off our backs about dating."

I saw her lip begin to quiver before she bit it back, and the part of me still locked in the room labelled "Amy" banged at the door, yelling for me to go kiss the quiver away. To tell her I was sorry, and stupid, and didn't know what I was saying, and to take her inside and find sleep together.

But that part of me had had his fun, and there was too much to be done to let him out again.

"What about the ball?" she asked as she crossed her arms. "That *was* part of the deal."

I shook my head. "I can't leave Ethel for the weekend now. Hell, I may not even be able to leave her for the evening. But maybe that's for the best so we can get a bit of distance."

"Distance," she repeated, her mouth pulling into a smirk. *Don't do that*, I thought. *Don't dig your heels in*. But this was Amy we were talking about, and I'd learned five years ago how she reacted to feeling hurt.

I'd also learned five years ago how to drive her away. And despite everything in me desperate to do the opposite, I knew that was what I had to do.

"Even without the ball, though," I said, already hating myself as I formed the words, "you got what you wanted, didn't you?"

"Oh yeah?" She tilted her head to the side, and I could tell she was biting back tears. "And what was that?"

I summoned the worst version of myself, smirking up at her and rolling my eyes as if I weren't dying inside. "You know," I said, as if we were in on a secret. "You've always had a thing for me, right? So you got to see that through, and same for me. Win-win."

I watched as the last hope of repair left Amy's eyes. She sucked a deep breath in through her nose – I could see her nostrils flare with anger as she did – and just nodded.

"Got it," she said, her voice matching mine now. "Lucky me. I'll go tick that off my bucket list then."

She lingered for a moment with her eyes narrowed, as if expecting me to try to have the last word, but I didn't want it. I just wanted her to go, and take with her the risk that I would choose to be selfish and trap her in this mess with me. So I stayed quiet, trying to keep an image of nonchalance on my face as her bravado slipped for just a minute, letting a tear slide down her face. She wiped at it, embarrassed, and took off running down the street.

It wasn't until she turned the corner that I let my own tears fall.

CHAPTER 29
AMY

I didn't need the cards to tell me what Phil was doing; I'd seen the warning signs when he'd broken down in my arms just over a week ago. Had I imagined it would happen so quickly? No. But part of me had known it would happen eventually, and it hurt just as badly as I'd known it would. It felt like something inside me, maybe the version of me that had always loved Phil, was trying to claw itself out of my chest. And the last thing I wanted was to spend my time crying about a boy in bed, even if that boy was Phil.

Still, I couldn't stop myself from doing a reading when I woke up late Wednesday morning. There was something comforting in the shuffle of the cards; something cathartic about letting the tarot tell me how to feel.

I opted for a three-card spread to represent past, present, and future, focusing all my energy on Phil. Which wasn't hard, given that his smug face when he'd driven me away was all I'd been able to think about since it had happened.

For the past, I drew the Hanged Man, upright. It stood for sacrifice. Martyrdom. Phil had been sacrificing his entire life for Ethel since her first fall years ago. I tried not to let my mind go to the place it wanted to – thinking that he'd been playing the martyr by pretending to be with me all along.

For the present, I drew the High Priestess in reverse. Since she normally represented intuition and being in touch with one's feelings, the opposite was repression. Lack of centre. And based on how easily Phil had shoved his feelings down last night, this didn't surprise me either. He hadn't even seemed scared or upset. Just resigned. Cold. Completely *un*feeling, even.

Finally, for the future, I drew a reversed Two of Pentacles. Upright, it would have symbolised balance and adaptation. But reversed, it foreshadowed the opposite. Disorganisation, loss of balance, overwhelm. The things I'd seen coming a million miles off for months, but which now seemed more inevitable than ever.

I tried to find it in myself to feel empathy for him; to remember that he was slowly, cruelly losing Ethel after having already lost his parents. I knew that on some level it was his trauma from their death causing his reaction now.

But still, he'd been so horrible to me, and so easily. I knew he was probably scared shitless, but it didn't make it okay that he'd said those things to me. If anything, it made it worse, because he'd made the deliberate decision to say what he knew would hurt me the most. He knew how to get under my skin – he always had – and he'd pushed the exact right buttons to make me hate him.

And I did. I hated him more than I ever had. So no, there was no room in my heart that morning to feel sadness for his future. At least I'd been right, I supposed, even if it was at the expense of my own happiness.

～

On Thursday, Phil finally texted the group back whilst I was trying to distract myself with work, and I flung my laptop aside onto the bed to read his message as soon as it came through.

> PHIL
>
> Hey everyone, sorry for the radio silence. Ethel had another fall on Tuesday, which was why I rushed out. Sorry for not updating you sooner. She's mostly okay, but it's gonna be a bit intense around here for a while, so I'm going to have to bail on the fantasy ball. Anil's forcing me out of the house to play D&D, so I'll be there tonight, but probably without any snacks, sorry.

The responses from the others came in thick and fast, including relief that Ethel was okay, understanding about the ball, and offers to help however they could. Jack was the last to reply, still only a couple of minutes after the initial message, and I knew exactly what would happen.

About five minutes later, I heard a knock at my bedroom door. I knew I wouldn't be able to fend him off forever, so I took a deep, centring breath in, letting my eyes close, telling myself I could do this.

"Come in."

The knob twisted, and Jack's face appeared in the growing gap in the door. "You got a minute?"

"For you, always," I said, hoping I was appropriately communicating my sarcasm. "What do you want?"

"You wanna tell me what the hell is going on?" he asked, settling onto the mattress at the foot of the bed. "Mum says you've been here all day today and yesterday, but I would have thought you'd be in town. What happened to Ethel?"

I recounted what Phil had told me, and Jack's face dropped in worry.

"Jesus," he said. "Phil must feel awful."

"Well, it's not his fault," I said, not sure why I was defending him, but still.

"I know, I know. But he's almost certainly blaming himself."

"That he is," I said under my breath.

"So why aren't you there then? He must be freaking out."

"Because your darling friend Philip broke up with me, that's why."

Jack recoiled in shock before almost immediately softening again, and the reactions were so contrary and in such quick succession that it made me snort.

"Yeah, well, I mean, obviously he doesn't mean it," he said.

I sighed. "Whether he meant it or not, he did it."

"Yeah, but you know how freaked he gets about Ethel. He feels like he owes her everything, so he gets a bit tight-fisted about making sure everything's perf—"

"Do you not think I know that?" I snapped, more angrily than I'd intended. But come on, of course I knew all that. As far as Jack knew, I'd been dating Phil for months. And whether we'd been calling it that between us or not, we basically had been. And I'd been the one helping him look after her before that. I'd seen exactly how far his loyalty to Ethel went.

"Then maybe cut him some slack, yeah?"

I felt my eyes prickle with angry tears, and I swallowed hard, desperate to keep them at bay. "Sure, I'll just let him say horrible things to me and treat me like I'm the least important thing in his life, because he doesn't mean it."

Jack's face fell. "No, Amy, that's not what I meant—"

"And while I'm at it," I continued, feeling myself get riled up, "I'll just keep showing up for him in every possible way when he can't even show up for me in the one way I asked him to. I'll just accept that being left outside on a bench in the dark for *five plus hours* with no contact comes with the territory of being with someone who's a caregiver."

Jack's mouth fell open. "Did he really do that?"

I couldn't keep the tears back any longer, as fed up as I was with the amount of crying I'd been doing. "I know you love him, Jack. I know he's part of the family. And I know you've been pushing for us to be together for a long time. But I'm so—"

"No," he said firmly, interrupting me, then leaned over to put a hand on my shoulder like Dad often did. "You're right, I love him. He's my best friend. And yeah, I think you two are good for each other. But you are my *sister*. You are my flesh and blood. And if he's being a dick to you, then he's a colossal idiot."

I felt the ire leach out of me, as if Jack's hand on my shoulder was absorbing all of it through my skin. "You mean that?" I asked, my voice breaking through my tears.

"Of *course* I do," he said, scooting closer to me. "You're the best of us, Amy. You always have been, even when you haven't believed it yourself. And I won't tolerate anyone, not even Phil, making you feel otherwise."

I smiled and let out a soft sigh. "To be fair, like you said, he didn't really mean it." And I knew he hadn't; still though, he'd said it, knowing what it would do to me. He was fully aware of how hard it had been for me to accept that he actually liked me for me, and he'd thrown that back in my face so easily.

"Hey," Jack said, "if I'm not allowed to defend him, neither are you. Now come here." He pulled me in for a hug, and I let him squeeze me tight like he had when we were kids.

"Thank you," I said. "You have no idea how much that means to me, actually."

"Probably about as much as having you around means to me," he said as he pulled back. "Now come on. You need a cup of chamomile tea and a puppy cuddle."

My eyes went wide. "You have a puppy for me to cuddle?"

He nodded. "I've got him today whilst Morgan's at a work event."

"Why didn't you lead with that?"

"I figured you were upset, but I wasn't sure if it would be a crying sort of upset or a throwing things sort of upset."

"Throw things? *Moi*?" I joked as I followed him out of the room.

"Hah!" He laughed over his shoulder as he headed down the stairs. "Says the Aries."

～

THE PABLO CUDDLES DID HELP, and the chamomile surprisingly did too, but I had a lot of hard things still ahead of me that day. The first was to let Niamh know once and for all that I wouldn't be at the wedding. It was ridiculous that I'd let it go on so long without RSVPing, really.

But just as I unlocked my phone to message, Sophie sent a message through in an old group chat from a birthday dinner for Maya a couple of years ago, with a few other people in it, including Niamh.

> SOPHIE
>
> What are everyone's plans for the morning after the wedding? We're thinking brunch at the country club if anyone's in? @Amy Evans that includes you and your new man!

My heart sank at the reference to my "new man", but I wasn't about to admit in a text that we'd broken up. I did need to bite the bullet though.

> AMY
>
> Hey! So weird, I was just about to message Niamh. Phil and I actually can't come anymore unfortunately; his nan is having health problems. But we send our congratulations.

I knew Phil would hate me sending congratulations on his behalf – "Send them a middle finger emoji from me, would ya?" he would have said instead – and the spite I felt at responding in a way he'd hate did a surprising amount for me mentally. Though that boost lasted only a few seconds before I was reminded that Chris was also in that group chat.

> **CHRIS**
>
> Hah, I knew that townie couldn't hack it. Good try though, Amy. Better luck next time.

I felt my teeth grind together as I clenched my jaw, feeling like I might hurl my phone across the room. In fact, Jack's joke about me throwing things was probably the only thing that kept it in my hand. Genuinely, what had I ever seen in Chris? Had I been that desperate to make my friends happy that I'd been with a guy like that for months?

"Better you than me, Niamh," I said to myself, then smiled as I saw the responses that followed.

> **MAYA**
>
> Genuinely Chris, you can be such a twat. Niamh, run away with me instead! Save yourself! 🏃, 💨

> **NIAMH**
>
> Don't listen to him, Amy, he's just kidding I'm sure. Give Phil and his nan our regards and best wishes. We'll miss you on the big day.

> **AMY**
>
> Thanks Niamh, I'm sure they'll appreciate that. Oh and Chris, here's your response from both of us: 🖕

The other hard thing I had to do was face Phil at D&D. I'd been mildly annoyed that he was coming at all – surely he wanted to give me some space after literally *just* breaking up with me? – but once I accepted it I became determined to make him regret coming along. Sure, I was the newest joiner, but it was my campaign now, too. I was contributing to the story, I was enjoying spending time with everyone, and I'd be damned if I let his lack of ability to feel his feelings ruin that for me.

So I dug through my wardrobe until I found the outfit I'd been looking for: the sage green playsuit I'd been wearing the night he'd rejected me five years ago. The night he claimed he'd been so desperate for me he could hardly breathe.

He may have thought he was capable of shutting his feelings off, but I was coming at that shit with a wrench.

Jack rode with me, and we made a pit stop for snacks at the supermarket. We rolled the windows down on the way and shouted along badly to Kelly Clarkson's "Since U Been Gone" when it came on the radio, even if it didn't quite ring true. Then I walked into Fatima and Morgan's house with my brother at my back, determined to be unapologetically present.

I could tell the moment I walked in that the others knew we'd split up. Phil and Fatima were sat at the table having a chat, Grey and Chloe were playing video games on the sofa, and Morgan was coming out of the kitchen with a jug of water. And the moment I stepped through the door, they all turned to look at me at once, everyone and everything going quiet.

I tried desperately to avoid eye contact with Phil, but he was looking at me with his mouth open – scanning me, actually – and I could tell he recognised what I was wearing. I should have felt smug at the sliver of hurt I could see in his expression, but instead I had to force myself to keep up my smile. I looked away from him before I could let my empathy get the better of me.

And plus, I'd brought a trump card.

"I brought cheesecake!" I said, holding up the two different flavours Jack and I had bought on the way there.

The others cheered, and I saw Morgan head back into the kitchen and open the cutlery drawer, but best of all, I watched as Phil's face set into a hard line. I set the cheesecakes in the middle of the table and put my things down in Jack's usual seat – he'd suggested we swap so I wouldn't have to deal with Phil – and then went into the kitchen to help Morgan.

"Can you give us a minute?" Phil asked just as Morgan was handing me a stack of plates. I spun around to face him, almost dropping the plates as I did, and narrowed my eyes.

"Is that really necessary?" I asked.

"Please, Morgan," Phil said, looking over my shoulder, and I was shocked when that traitor tiptoed past me.

"Sorry," she said. "Just shout if you need me." Then she pulled the door shut behind her on her way out, and Phil and I were alone.

"Cheesecake?" he asked. "Really?"

"What?" I asked faux-innocently, shrugging as I put the plates down on the worktop. "I figured everyone would be hungry since you weren't bringing anything, and this game is played at the least convenient time ever. So excuse me for acquiring sustenance."

"Please don't be like this," he said, his face pleading.

"Like what?" I crossed my arms. Seriously? He was going to lecture me about reacting poorly?

"You know," he said. "Petty. Vindictive." I could guess the last word before he said it, but I urged him to stop before he did. "Childish," he said anyway.

"Childish," I repeated. "You think *I'm* being childish."

"Um, yeah," he said. "Bringing cheesecake. Turning Jack against me. Wearing..." He waved vaguely at my outfit but fell short of acknowledging it.

"I didn't turn Jack against you."

"Oh yeah? What did you say?"

I shook my head. "Honestly? Almost nothing. I didn't tell him the worst of it. Not by a long shot."

"Well, if looks could kill, then I would have dropped dead the moment he walked through the door."

"Maybe you should leave then."

Phil looked taken aback by that. "You want *me* to leave? *My* D&D game?"

"*Our* D&D game," I said. "And if you can't handle being around me, then yeah, *you* should leave."

I picked the plates back up and stepped closer to him, pausing when I was just a couple of inches away. I was hoping the heat that usually pulsed between us would have burned off after the other night, but it hadn't. I could still feel every breath he took as if it were my own. So I just used it the way I always had before this summer: as fuel for my hatred.

"Because I'm not going anywhere this time," I said, pitching my voice low, trying to keep it soft and even. "I'm not running off to another city, or avoiding anything because of you. So if you can't handle the outcome of your decisions, maybe you should make better decisions."

"That's not fair," he said, and I refused to let the wobble in his voice mean anything to me. "You know why I did it."

"And I don't fucking care," I said. "You've made your bed. Now you get to lie in it."

Then I pushed past him and through the kitchen door, plastering the smile back on my face as I did. I had cheesecake to serve, and an upper hand to maintain.

CHAPTER 30
YORICK PROUDHOLLOW

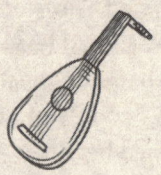

Yorick looked desperately around for where Nephrine had taken Eden, but they were gone. He'd been looking directly at the door, so he was certain they hadn't left that way. Which meant they had to still be in the room somewhere. He spoke a spell of his own to see any invisible creatures around, but there were none. He cast another to detect any magic at the nexus of the smoke, which turned out to be not the brazier but the bookshelves in the corner of the room. The smoke itself began to shimmer slightly with transmutation magic, which was no surprise, and Calamity's magical light was a well-known evocation. A few spell books on the shelves glowed as well, but nothing else appeared to be magical in nature.

Yorick pinched his eyes shut; he needed a deep breath, but there was still smoke in the room. This was all his fault. He'd insisted Eden stay behind, and she was now paying the price for it. And in the end, it had been his card that had rung true – he'd been puppeted right into giving over the clue they'd risked their lives for.

Surely he could still fix this. Surely it wasn't too late. Otherwise, he'd never forgive himself.

Yorick pulled his robe up over his mouth and plunged into the smoke, fighting the burning in his eyes as he scanned the shelves for another clue. The smoke was gone by the time he found it, but eventually he noticed another twelve-pointed star – this one crude and hand-drawn – at the base of an unrelated book: a history tome he recognised from his training at the bard college.

As he reached out to examine the book, it refused to come away from the shelf, simply tipping backwards instead. And as it did, a deep clicking and groaning emanated from the bookcase – no, from beyond it – and the shelves swung open to reveal a dark staircase leading down into the earth.

They couldn't be certain, of course, that Nephrine and Eden had gone this way. Not without magic, of course. So Yorick cast another spell, this time holding the image of Eden's star crystal in his mind's eye, grimacing as he pictured Nephrine wearing it. He would tear it from her neck if it were the last thing he did.

As the spell manifested, Yorick could sense the crystal descending bumpily beyond the secret door.

"She's this way," he said. "I'm sure." Then he pulled Calamity after him, gesturing to himself until she transferred the light from the brazier to his cloak. The library plunged into darkness behind him as he started down the stairs, forcing the others to follow, though not without grumbles. Nephrine moved faster than they did, but this was her home, after all.

"Yorick," Calamity whispered as she followed close behind him, "we need to talk about the book later."

"It wasn't me," he said. "I tried to fight her, I swear."

"I know you did," she replied instantly, and Yorick felt a pang of gratitude for her trust. "But we don't know *how* she was controlling you. And that could be a problem."

"We'll have to worry about that later," he said.

"Eden's down there, and it's all my fault. I'll never forgive myself if something happens to her."

The staircase wound down into the earth, deep enough that the cold, damp air chilled their bones, and their ears began to pop. Yorick's spell ended after ten minutes, and as desperate as he was to keep sight of Eden, he didn't know what they were walking into, and he needed to save his magic. Without their armour and weapons, without his lute, they'd need it. And besides, they'd yet to encounter any branches or junctions. Just the one winding staircase the whole way. So there was only one way they could have gone. Yorick only hoped there was another way up; he didn't relish the idea of ascending all these stairs later. Though he supposed he'd be lucky to get to do so, given that he was charging unarmed into a confrontation with a member of The Twelve.

A few minutes after the spell ended, Yorick slowed and motioned for the others to do the same. Calamity dropped the spell illuminating his cloak, and they stopped in the darkness to listen.

Well, near darkness; there was a strange glow emanating from just around the next bend, and as they stopped, Yorick could hear chanting up ahead. *Wonderful,* Yorick thought. *Just what we need.* At least the diadem was likely to be there, he supposed.

The party conferred for a long moment, but there wasn't much to be agreed. They had no idea what they were walking into, and they had no weapons. Hell, only three of them had any magic. All they could do was creep forward, hoping beyond hope that there was something – anything – they could do.

They finally came to a landing at the bottom of the stairs, just in front of a large ornate door, the eerie purple light filtering out around it, with a twelve-pointed star carved into it. The same star symbol that had enraged him so much months ago. It was time to end this.

He knew it was reckless; he'd chastised Eden for doing just this only the day before. But there was no more strategising to be done, and every moment he didn't act was a moment she was in danger. So he pressed the door open and walked forward.

It took his eyes a moment to adjust; there was a bright purple light in the centre of the chamber he'd entered. He looked across the room instead as he blinked, and as he did, his eyes focused on Eden. She was chained to the wall there, her glittering dress torn where she'd clearly been searched. Her eyes met his, and there was just a flicker of relief before her face collapsed into agony.

Yorick held her gaze and reached out to her with his magic, forming a telepathic bond between them. It was probably a reckless use of magic, but he couldn't stand seeing her so powerless.

It's okay, he said to her in his mind. *You're okay.*

None of us are okay, she thought back. *They've already started the ritual.*

Sure enough, when Yorick looked at the centre of the room, there was Nephrine. She stood on a tall dais surrounded by hooded figures, the source of the chanting, one of whom held the book Yorick had hand-delivered just minutes before. In one hand she held aloft Eden's star crystal, which was catching the light from a skylight above. Only that didn't make sense; they were hundreds of feet underground. It wasn't a skylight, it was a crystal of some sort, powering what Nephrine held in her other hand.

The diadem.

CHAPTER 31
PHIL

Every time I thought I was at the end of my rope, it just kept going, like an amateur magician's crappy handkerchief bit.

I knew I'd become the worst version of myself with Amy, telling her she was being childish for responding in a perfectly normal way, but I couldn't help it. If I wasn't actively pushing her away, I would start reaching for her, and I couldn't afford that. If I had to hate myself but keep her safe from the spiral of shit my life was turning into, then so be it.

I practically sprinted home after D&D. It was the first time I'd left Ethel since the fall – I'd even slept on her floor the first couple of nights so I'd know if she got up in the night – and even then I'd only left because Anil had practically forced me to.

I didn't see Anil for a while after that. I had plenty to worry about at home. Or, well, increasingly *out* of the house, as in a flurry of worry I'd signed Ethel up for every single thing I could find locally that was mentioned on a list of ideas Anil sent me. Apparently, keeping her active – more active than I'd been managing – was an important part of her cognitive health, especially with her reduced mobility whilst her back was healing.

The next couple of weeks were incredibly regimented but somehow still passed in a blur. Every day I would get her up at five-thirty as usual, make us both tea and breakfast, and then get a couple of hours of work in whilst she watched TV or sat in the garden. Then we would take the bus to the arts centre, packed lunch in hand, and I'd do more work whilst Ethel participated in (or sometimes just watched) whatever they had on. She'd always loved the actual art classes, but they also had bingo, cross stitch, and ballroom dancing. She insisted she would just watch the latter, but I looked up from my computer at one point to see a volunteer spinning her around the dance floor in her wheelchair.

We'd then get back on the bus to the hospital, where most of her appointments were. Every journey time had to be doubled just in case, because the local buses were terrible about keeping their wheelchair ramps functional, and more than once we relied on there being someone able-bodied who could help Ethel on and off the bus whilst I lifted her wheelchair in and out. Then we'd eat lunch by a fountain Ethel loved around the corner from the hospital before her afternoon appointments.

We had something every weekday now – physio on Tuesday and Thursday hadn't changed, but we now had an occupational and speech therapy referral for Monday, and her water aerobics on Wednesday, and I had decided to pay out of pocket for cognitive stimulation therapy on Friday. I still wasn't sure how I was going to afford all of it, but I had to throw everything at the wall and just blindly hope it would all add up to being helpful.

I let myself go down rabbit holes I never had before since her diagnosis: food for cognitive health, playing soothing music in the house any time the TV wasn't on, and even resorting to charging the crystals on the windowsill. I wasn't taking any chances.

Another thing I wouldn't let myself sacrifice under any circumstances was cooking Ethel a nice dinner every day. I'd always tried to cook her favourites – Patricia's lasagna recipe, tuna pasta bake, toad in the hole – but now I'd switched to brain-healthy options like grilled salmon with quinoa and kale, even if it hurt my soul to eat like a gym bro. She complained once or twice that she wanted an old favourite, but I brushed it off. *As far as she knows*, I told myself more than once, *we had lasagna yesterday.*

And she was fading, quickly. I knew from experience that falls could escalate things, but it was startling to me how much she seemed to change in the space of a few days even. She could still mostly have a conversation, but she rarely initiated them. She wasn't angry or oppositional – at least most of the time – but her warmth had noticeably dissipated. It was like she'd gone from being a main character to an NPC, with an increasingly limited dialogue menu. But I couldn't let myself be sad about that, because every time I looked at her and missed the old Ethel, I felt guilty for not appreciating the grandmother I still had sitting in front of me.

Ethel's evening TV time became shorter and shorter – our full days were tiring her out, and the sun was setting earlier, too, so her bedtime moved ever forward. But that worked out nicely for me, because then I had the rest of the evenings to clean up after us, plan the following day, and deep dive into whatever tiny throwaway comment a doctor or therapist or volunteer had made that day that had burrowed into my brain. If I had time, I'd do more work after that until I couldn't keep my eyes open anymore, and then I'd go to sleep and do it all again. I left her for D&D and nothing more.

My life was like one big puzzle I had to put together just so, every piece in its perfect place, over and over again, every single day. And if I didn't, it was Ethel who would lose the big picture.

Every moment of every day, I missed Amy. I missed sitting

next to her at Ethel's physio appointments, chatting shit. I missed the heart and light she brought to even the heaviest and most practical conversations. I missed working around the house with her, each doing separate things but orbiting around one another as we got on with whatever was in front of us. And god I missed her touch – the casual way she'd fling her legs over mine when we sat together, the way she always reached for my hand, the way she would mindlessly fiddle with my beard as we lay in bed together, not wanting to fall asleep and miss even a second together. The intention she'd brought into our lives – the happy, healing energy, as corny as it felt to admit – was so noticeably absent that it felt like a light had been turned off in the house, no matter what else I tried.

It was usually just before midnight that the buzz of a full day wore off, and the loneliness set in fully. Just a couple of weeks ago, I'd had a girlfriend I was falling in love with, a group of friends that felt like family, and a grandmother who was declining but still present. And I'd been exhausted, and it had been hard, but I'd at least felt like myself.

But now, I felt like an island in a way I never had before. I knew it was an island of my own making – everyone but Amy reached out over and over again, and I was the one who refused their help – but it felt like the only way I could stay afloat. Like if I dared to hope that any of them could help me, dared to pull focus from the extreme juggling act that was my life, everything would come crashing down. *I should know*, I thought. *It already happened once.*

One night, just as I was sinking into my nightly spiral, I walked into my craft room for the first time all week to find a sea of purple tulle and satin all over the place, Amy's dress half finished. I stared for a long time at the raw edges and the pins and the embroidery thread. Part of me wanted to set it on fire and let it burn the way I had with our relationship. But with everything else unspooling around me, the only thing I could think was, *now here's one puzzle I know how to solve.*

⁓

ON THE LAST Saturday in August, there was a knock on the door at around five, and my heart leapt.

"It's not her," I muttered to myself as I shut my laptop and set it aside on the sofa.

"Not who?" Ethel asked.

"No one," I said, walking towards the door, but I could still feel my heart in my throat. The curtains were drawn – the late afternoon sun was apparently offensive to Ethel all of a sudden – so I had no idea who it was. And it should have been date night, after all; the last one before the ball.

When I opened the door and found Anil, my heart sank.

"Uh, hey," I said, stepping aside to let him in. "Did I have you booked for tonight, and I forgot to cancel?"

Anil shook his head as he slipped off his shoes. "Nah, don't worry, mate, you were pretty clear that you were gonna do it all yourself." He didn't sound angry or bitter, but there was a tightness to his voice anyway.

"Oh, okay," I said as he walked into the kitchen and leaned back against the worktop. "Well, is everything okay?"

Anil laughed. "You mean, what the hell am I doing here?"

I smiled and leaned against the sink across from him. "Not that I'm not happy to see you." But then I realised something. "Wait, aren't you meant to be at your class?"

"Finished it," he said proudly. "I'm all certified now."

"Wow, that's amazing! Congrats."

"Thanks," he said, then brought his arms up and crossed them. "Actually, though, that's part of why I'm here."

I frowned. "Because you're done with your course?"

He nodded. "And now I'm looking at getting a day job.

Which probably means I'm looking at shift work, meaning I wouldn't be able to look after Ethel on a regular schedule anymore."

It was like a punch to the gut. Which didn't make sense – I'd already decided to take a step back from the things that meant I'd need him in the evenings – but the idea that he wouldn't be there if I did need him? That now, without Amy as well, I was well and truly alone in caring for Ethel? It scared the shit out of me in a way I hadn't been expecting.

"Got it," I said, staring down at my hands.

"But Phil, I could have told you that on the phone. I came here because I wanted to talk to you about your plans for Ethel."

I looked back up at Anil and narrowed my eyes, my brain going into defence mode before I even really processed what he was saying.

"What do you mean, my plans?"

Anil took a deep breath and repositioned against the worktop. "Let me guess. You feel guilty about her fall, so you've cut yourself off from everything that might distract you. You've jumped in at the deep end with all the activities and therapies and all that, and you're trying to do everything for her so nothing bad happens to make it worse. Am I right?"

Well, that was spooky. "You put a nanny cam in the house or something?" I asked, trying to sound casual and joking, but Anil just smiled sadly at me.

"I've seen it before, more than once. It's a really normal response. But it's not healthy, mate."

I dropped my joking tone and shook my head. "I'm fine," I said. "Seriously, don't worry about me."

"Well, I am worried about you," Anil said, "but that's not what I meant. I meant that it's not healthy for Ethel."

I blinked at him. "Sorry?" *How is me giving her every possible resource and assistance not healthy for her?* I didn't ask.

He nodded. "It's coming from a good place. I know that. I've seen how much you love her and how well you look after her. I'm not suggesting you're not doing your best. But it can actually cause a faster decline to approach things the way you are."

I could feel my breathing grow shallow, and I sat back to try to deepen it. I fought the instinct to shut it down – to tell him to leave me to my juggling and we'd both be fine. But I pictured Ethel in the other room, listening to an audiobook, and I thought of how Anil had worked so hard to help me get my feet under me after her diagnosis. And I figured if I could let anyone help me, it should be him. We wanted the same thing, after all, which was the best for Ethel.

"You're gonna have to walk me through this," I said, and I could hear the strain in my voice. "Because I swear, Anil, I'm trying my best to do the right thing. So what am I doing wrong?"

He chewed his tongue as he stared down at his hands, clearly considering something. "How honest do you want me to be?" he asked eventually.

"Completely honest," I said without even thinking, and the moment it was out of my mouth I regretted it. I knew I wasn't going to like whatever he said next.

Anil took a deep breath. "I think you need to consider moving Ethel into a care facility."

I stood up straight before he'd even finished the word "moving". I shook my head as I paced back and forth across the kitchen.

"That's not an option," I said, instantly feeling my breath quicken again.

"Why, Phil? Please, genuinely, tell me why."

"Because it's not," I said, more forcefully than I intended, and then brought my hand to my mouth.

"Is everything okay?" I heard Ethel call from the lounge.

"Yes, sorry," I called back. "Just speaking with Anil."

Ethel didn't respond, which told me she either hadn't heard

me, hadn't cared to hear me, or didn't currently remember who Anil was.

"It's not an option," I said, pointing towards the other room. "That saint of a woman took me in when I was eight years old, becoming a mum again at sixty. She came out of early retirement to provide for me and gave me everything I ever wanted or needed."

"I know that," Anil said, his hands open in front of him, pleading. "And believe me, it's so clear to anyone who meets you both how much you love Ethel. How grateful you are to her. But Phil, I've seen this happen before with others I've cared for. There are usually more people to share the load, but when there aren't, it's always one person thinking they need to do everything, even if their loved one doesn't want that for them. And I can say *so* confidently that Ethel doesn't want you sacrificing everything to care for her."

"Don't fucking speak for her," I said, instantly right back in that pink room with Amy, pointing my finger in anger.

But Anil wasn't Amy, and he pushed up away from the worktop. "Then who will, Phil? Because I don't think you are."

My mouth dropped open. "What the hell is that supposed to mean?"

He put his hands up in a kind of surrender, as if he felt he'd gone too far. "I mean that, if you're the one speaking for her, then be honest. Do you think, if she woke up fully lucid tomorrow, that she'd be happy with the way you've shut yourself off from everyone and everything in your life to care for her? Genuinely, do you? Because if so, maybe I'm wrong."

But he wasn't wrong. I knew he wasn't. Because if Ethel woke up fully lucid, the first thing she'd do after telling me off for how I'd treated Amy would be to check herself in. And I knew it.

But I also knew that as soon as it happened, that would be it. It wouldn't be Ethel and me against the world anymore, the way it had been for as long as I could remember. It would be just me, away from her. And if I didn't have Ethel, then who was I? I'd never existed in the world outside of the context of who I was to her.

"You're not wrong," I admitted, sitting down in the closest chair, across from Anil this time. "But she's not there yet."

"She's closer than you think."

"Okay, well, *I'm* not there yet."

"And that's okay," he said, leaning back again. "There are lots of middle ground options. But they all involve you letting go and investing in a bit more care for her. Because looking at you, you're not gonna make it much longer. And if you think she wouldn't want you giving up everything to care for her, imagine how pissed she'd be if you flamed out because of it. You can only do your best, and that doesn't mean ignoring your own health and limitations and sanity for her sake."

Anil made sure I was looking him in the eye before he continued.

"Phil, if you shoulder all of that burden yourself, and then you break, she breaks with you."

"Then I won't break," I insisted, though I knew I sounded less confident than I'd intended.

"I mean this with all the love in the world, mate," he said, pinching his brow sympathetically, "you look pretty cracked to me."

I both knew he was right and hated him for saying it at the same time. Because even if he had a solution, it didn't change the fact that I was the one keeping all the balls in the air in that moment. And I was worried that even the slightest suggestion of passing some or all of them off would make the whole lot come crashing down.

Anil and I made plans for him to come over again on Monday. He'd send me some articles to read the following day, and then we could talk about what the middle ground options were. But for now, he said I should focus on having a restful weekend, as much as that was actually possible.

I waved from the front door as he climbed into his van, then poked my head back inside to confirm that Ethel was still happily sat in front of the television. Then, instead of shutting the door, I went to sit on the front bench.

I didn't really believe Mum and Dad were smiling down on me or anything like that, of course. The only reason I felt close to them sitting there was because I'd seen their ashes go into the hole where we'd planted the tree. I tried to channel my inner Amy and suspend my disbelief long enough to think they might be able to hear me if I spoke, but I felt nothing.

I wanted to tell them how badly I needed them. How much I wished they were here so I could keep my crappy little car instead of buying a van, or spend my money on something stupid instead of worrying about paying for Ethel's care, or go on holiday with my girlfriend's family without a care in the world.

But unlike usual, when I tried to speak, I couldn't make my mouth form the words. I was too tired, and I was more certain than ever that there was nobody there. And maybe Anil was right and I had options, but as much as he wanted me to rest, none of those options were going to let me take the evening off. So I stood up and went inside so I could start on our brain-healthy dinner.

CHAPTER 32
AMY

As much as I hated to admit it, I knew that the key to my survival would be to take a page out of Phil's playbook and compartmentalise. I spent the rest of the week after our breakup wallowing, fuelled by a great playlist Jack sent me, and it got to the point where I couldn't bear to look at myself in the mirror anymore. Every time I did I saw the pink walls of my childhood bedroom and the matching pink of my skin from where I'd rubbed my eyes raw trying to wipe away my tears. Tears I was crying over Philip fucking Owen, just like I had when I was a teenager, and up until that night five years ago when I'd decided I wouldn't let him matter to me anymore. If I'd done it then, I could do it again, right? Even if I did struggle to summon the resentment I knew would help me move on.

I definitely didn't struggle to resent him, however, when I finally had to break the news to Mum and Dad. I was nervous about telling Dad, as my trial period was part of why Phil and I had entered into this whole ridiculous thing to begin with, but in a rare demonstration of empathy, he just wrapped me in a hug and told me Phil was an idiot.

Mum, on the other hand, I was more worried about. When

Chris and I had broken up, she'd been beside herself for months. I now suspected that was only half about the breakup and half about me being far away from her whilst I went through it, but still. By Jack's account, it had been an overreaction either way.

But as I stood over her in the garden and told her as she harvested tomatoes, she seemed wholly unbothered.

"You two will work things out, I'm sure."

My brow pinched together, half in a frown and half in a squint as I shielded my eyes from the bright sun.

"No, Mum, you don't get it. It wasn't a fight. He broke up with me."

I had half a mind to tell her we hadn't even actually been together for most of our supposed relationship, but even now, even after everything Phil had done, I didn't want to undermine what we'd had. Even then, there had been something.

I watched as Mum leaned over her raised beds, pushing one plant out of the way to get to another. Was it just me, or was she smiling? She was certainly relaxed, anyway, as she plucked a perfectly ripe heirloom tomato from its vine. She was so nonchalant that I couldn't do anything but laugh.

"How can you be so calm about this?" I asked, crossing my arms, incredulous. "Last year you were tearing up the front garden beds because you were so upset on my behalf."

"Yes, well, that was rather silly of me, wasn't it."

"Sure," I said, "but aren't you angry now?" I certainly was – in fact, I was angry enough for both of us.

Mum must have heard the edge in my words, because she finally stopped harvesting. She brushed her dirt-covered hands off on her dungarees and stood.

"Do you want me to be angry?" she asked, her gaze inscrutable behind her sunglasses. "Because if you need to feel justified in your anger, I've got a few summer squashes that need pulling. I could put on a real show of it."

I stared at her open-mouthed, feeling a traitorous heat behind my eyes.

"Do you really not care about this?" I asked, my lip quivering. Mum's face softened instantly, and she brought a hand up to my face. She pulled off her glasses, and I could see that her own eyes were indeed wide with concern.

"Of course I do, Amy," she said, and I pressed into her hand, the tears slipping from my eyes and running down my face, no doubt mixing with the dirt on Mum's fingers and making mud on my cheek. But I didn't care.

"I care that you're hurting, darling," she said. "But last year, you didn't have us. I wasn't upset that you and Chris broke up. I was upset that I couldn't be there for you. That none of us could. I know you had your friends. But they weren't good to you. That was clear from the day you moved there."

"Was it?" I asked, huffing a laugh. "Because I didn't know until everything fell apart."

Mum removed her hand and grasped both of mine in hers. "The point is, I love you. And of course I was sad for you. But more than that, I was scared for you."

Her voice quivered slightly at this admission, and my own frown deepened.

"But these last few months, especially this summer, you're like a different person." She frowned, then shook her head slightly. "No, not a different person. But like a more mature, more confident version of yourself. And I'm not scared for you anymore."

As annoyed as I was at her lack of reaction, I didn't disagree with her on one point, at least. I felt more like myself than I had in years, maybe ever. But I did disagree with her on another point. I swallowed and looked down at my bare feet in the grass.

"I'm scared for myself," I admitted. "I don't know how much of that confidence was because of things with Phil."

"Precious little, I'm sure," she said, tipping my chin up so I met her gaze again.

Her smile wasn't nonchalant now; it was calming, like a flight attendant catching your eye during turbulence. *Don't worry,* that smile said. *You're not about to drop out of the sky.*

"How do you know?"

"Because I know you," she said. "As much as it will pain you to hear it, you and I aren't that dissimilar. And I can tell that you're growing into the person you're destined to become."

It didn't pain me, actually, to think of myself as being like Mum. Maybe it would have before – when I was a teenager, desperate to prove myself. But I'd seen more of Mum lately. Or at least I'd noticed more. The passion she had for her work. The care she gave to Ethel and to all of us. And the lightness she seemed to embody all the time. I wasn't sure I'd seen much of that last quality in myself, but I'd found my nurturing side and my passionate side in a way I hadn't before, and I was proud to come by it honestly.

"Thanks, Mum," I said, smiling weakly, and I meant it. "But whilst that's all well and good, Phil still didn't want me. Not the version of me I was years ago, and not the version I am now."

Mum pressed her mouth into a line as she considered this, letting a slow breath out through her nose.

"I have a sneaking suspicion that all this has a lot less to do with you and a lot more to do with Ethel. Especially after what happened at family dinner when we brought up the holiday."

I knew she was right. But that didn't make it any easier.

"But still..."

I trailed off, not sure what to say. But still, he didn't want to try? But still, I was part of that area of his life, too? But still, how was I supposed to see him and hear about him if I couldn't be with him?

"Still, you have us," Mum finished for me, and I smiled.

"Still, I have you," I agreed. And I did.

But that didn't make the Phil-shaped hole in my chest close up any faster. And eventually, I would need to figure out how I could keep having all of them without being with Phil. Because as much as I needed them – Mum, Dad, Jack, Morgan, Chloe, all of them – Phil needed them too. Probably even more than I did.

Dad tried to push back our big meeting in the name of "giving me some time", but I immediately changed it back in the diary, not wanting to give him an excuse to kick the can down the road. As hurt as I was, I was also raring to go at work. So I threw myself into preparing for the big proposal, making up for the time I'd spent wallowing by putting in a full week's worth of work in just three days.

When the day came, Dad brought Jack, along with his foremen Jerry and Luke, into the house for the meeting. Dad sat in his usual chair in the lounge, the others on the sofa, all facing the TV so I could deliver my presentation. Jack smiled encouragingly at me the whole time, but Dad kept his face neutral if a bit stern, and I had to rely on all the work I'd put in over the past three months to win him over.

The plan was straightforward enough. Dad was taking on more and more jobs with increasing amounts of overlap, so I was suggesting a professional license of the project management software I'd been trialling. The business was also growing financially, and with Dad eyeing retirement and the admin burden bigger than even I could manage, we needed an integrated cash flow, payroll, invoicing, and P&L system. This would mean paying for software that could handle all of that, as well as paying for the integrations between that and the project management tool so we could automate it.

"Sounds expensive," Dad said, and I clicked immediately to the next slide I'd prepared, which covered the costs. I tried very hard not to look smug, but I must have failed, because Dad narrowed his eyes at me.

I'd taken the amount we would save by not outsourcing payroll and accounting, then scaled that up to reflect the thirty per cent increase in revenue Dad wanted to achieve in the next three years. After removing the amount we'd still need for end-of-year filing help, the remaining savings more than covered the cost of the solution I was proposing, as well as my own salary. It all meant we wouldn't have to turn down work because of the admin burden, *and* we wouldn't have to hire anyone else on the admin team to help us manage it. This meant Dad could focus on hiring skilled tradespeople instead, and still have profit to spare.

"Or ..." I said, interrupting the impressed nodding the foremen were doing. Dad still looked inscrutable, but he wouldn't for long. This next bit was the least important suggestion for the business, but I was pretty sure it was the most important for him.

"Go on," he said, nodding.

"Or you could start a formal apprenticeship programme," I said, clicking to the next slide. Covering the screen entirely was a photo of Jack using the circular saw, Dad watching over his shoulder. I remembered that day perfectly; it was shortly after Jack had moved home, right after Dad had agreed to take him on. Mum had been so proud that she'd snuck out to the workshop to watch them for a while through the window, snapping the photo when neither of them was looking.

"As you all know, trade careers have become less and less popular with young people over the years. As a result, finding junior workers and apprentices is harder than ever. And as a family business with a reputation for excellence, there's no reason why we shouldn't be leading the charge with the next generation of tradespeople."

"Agreed," Dad said. "But it's a lot of work, otherwise we'd have done it already."

"I can help," I said, moving to a breakdown of my time. "If I come on full-time, I would be able to manage the new admin systems *and* help with the apprenticeship programme."

Dad read over the slides as I spoke – I'd thought about the budget needed to promote the programme, the additional wages he would need to pay to be more attractive than office-based apprenticeships, and the extra workload of training and assessing them. It was risky; I was showing my cards that there wasn't actually a full-time role's worth of work in managing the systems I was recommending. But I hoped he saw the vision enough to bite.

There was a long moment of silence when I finished, ending on a slide summarising everything I was proposing. Dad, Jerry, and Luke's eyes all darted back and forth as they leaned forward, taking it all in. But Jack just smiled dopily up at me, throwing me a double thumbs-up. He was so unserious sometimes. I ignored him, knowing this was a time I couldn't afford to be unserious with him.

"I'll think about it," Dad said. "But no matter what I decide, you've done good work, Amy. You should be really proud."

He led the others back out towards the workshop, and Jack leapt up from the sofa to pull me into a hug. "You did so well," he said, squeezing me tight. "Dad's right. You should be proud."

"I am," I said, and I meant it. I'd worked really hard on the presentation, but I'd also bought into all of this myself. I was actively excited about bringing it all to life – even the apprenticeship, where I knew I'd have to deal with annoying teenagers who thought they were far cooler than they were.

But as soon as I admitted how proud I was, that sense of accomplishment was quickly followed by the realisation that I couldn't celebrate it with the one person I wanted to.

"Thanks," I said, but as soon as the word was out of my

mouth, I felt my lip begin to tremble. I bit down on it, willing it to stop, but my eyes began to sting.

"Hey, hey," Jack said, pulling me in again. "It's okay."

"I just wish I could ring him, you know? See how he is."

"Yeah, well, you and me both," Jack muttered, and I pulled back.

"What do you mean?" I asked, then frowned. "You know I don't need you to ignore him for me, right?"

"I know," he said. "I've tried to reach out. We all have. But he's not responding. Mum even tried the landline, but Ethel didn't answer."

"She's probably in a wheelchair all the time now," I said, remembering what I'd read about sacral fractures. The fact that she'd been walking at all was no small miracle.

I hated how quickly my heart ached for Phil. How immediately my empathy kicked in, after he'd shown no hesitation to hit me where it hurt. Had he done it to try to protect himself and Ethel? Yeah, probably. But it didn't make it okay that he'd treated me like I was disposable. Like the nearly three months we'd shared had meant nothing to him. Like the two decades before that had meant nothing, either.

Still, I knew exactly what he was doing, and if I could have teleported over to him before thinking through the consequences to my own well-being, I probably would have. He was isolating himself, and it was only a matter of time before he buckled under the weight of everything he insisted on carrying. Even he couldn't compartmentalise himself out of that one; trying to do so would just make it happen faster.

It made me especially angry because he hadn't just excised me from his own life. He'd excised me from Ethel's, too. And I missed her. I missed the way she would pat my hand every time she saw me. The way she always knew just that little bit more than she was letting on. And I wasn't the only one – I was sure Mum was foaming at the mouth wanting to help out. It was who she was; I supposed I came by it honestly. And how dare he not let us do that? How dare he be so selfish that he would keep people who loved Ethel away from her in the name of looking after her?

"Don't do that," Jack said, and I snapped back into the lounge. "Don't spiral."

"Easier said than done," I muttered.

I was just opening my mouth to suggest maybe we could do a drive-by, force a little wellness check, when the front door opened again and Dad walked back in, alone this time.

"Jackie, give me a minute with your sister, will ya?"

I PULLED up outside Fatima and Morgan's house the following night, parking behind Jack's new car on the street just as he left through the front door. They looked so similar, except one looked a little worse for wear. The same could be said for Jack and me, I supposed; I had the dark circles under my eyes that would let the girls know immediately just how badly I'd been Going Through It. But I didn't have it in me to care.

Dad's full buy-in for my plan couldn't have come at a better time. He'd signed off on everything I'd proposed, including the apprenticeship programme, and he'd officially invited me on board full-time. It had given me the excuse to throw myself immediately into starting the ball rolling with the software solutions, which was good since I didn't have D&D to distract me; Fatima had taken the week off for her first non-teaching day of the term. I'd thrown myself into work on Friday, too, only paying enough attention to know that Phil's car never appeared in the driveway for film night at Jack's.

But now I had girls' night, which, true to their word, they'd invited me along to when they'd rescheduled after the rewilding expedition. I could picture them whispering amongst themselves inside, speculating whether I'd be okay or not. But being pitied by my friends was better than losing them in the breakup, so I wasn't about to look a gift horse in the mouth. And at least it would take my mind off what should have been the last date night before the ball.

The other three were already getting snuggled up on the big sofa when I walked in, and when I went to sit in the armchair off to the side, Chloe yelled at me to come join them, so I squished in between her and Fatima instead. We watched a bunch of YouTube videos Chloe had queued up until dinner came, only one of which was about the queer inclusive sex scenes in *Baldur's Gate 3*, which I knew showed serious restraint on her part.

Apparently takeaway sushi and cheap wine was a sacred girls' night tradition, so once Morgan had brought in far too many bags for the four of us – "It's fine," she said, "I'll happily eat this for days" – we all sat on the floor around the coffee table to eat. This included Pablo, who begged constantly but wasn't quite brave enough to jump up and take any.

"It's perfect heartbreak food," Chloe said, before putting a gigantic piece of a tempura-fried salmon roll in her mouth. When she saw me staring in disgust, she shrugged.

"Uhh? Assowayooeeingahan," she said around the food, which I was pretty sure was supposed to translate to "What? That's how they do it in Japan."

"I'm pretty sure that doesn't apply when the piece of sushi has the same circumference as a tin of beans," Fatima said, popping a tiny piece of cucumber maki into her own mouth. She was vegetarian, so she had her own mini platter. "You've got to be dainty."

"Uckgheingainny," Chloe said. "Fuck being dainty," I was pretty sure. We all laughed.

"Anyway," Fatima said, "I thought we weren't acknowledging the heartbreak? Is that not the case? Because I've got something to say."

I froze with a piece of nigiri halfway to my mouth. It fell out from between my chopsticks as I stared back at Fatima.

"I hate having elephants in the room," she said, then turned to me. "We don't have to tiptoe around it, right?"

"Uh, sure?" I said, bracing myself for the "something" Fatima clearly had prepared. Chloe cleared her throat, finally having swallowed.

"I mean, I was talking about *my* breakup," she said. "But sure, let's get into it."

"Great," Fatima said, sitting forward and setting her tray down, then rubbing her hands together as if brushing off crumbs, though there weren't any, of course. If any of us could actually be described as dainty, it was probably her.

"Hit me," I said, sitting up straighter, trying to sound as casual as I could.

"Right," Fatima said, nodding. "Amy, I just have to say, I think you can do *so much* better than Phil. I love the guy, but you are a literal goddess. What the hell did you see in him?"

"Hey, that's not fair," Chloe said, jumping to Phil's defence. "Not about you being a goddess, Amy. That's absolutely valid. But Phil's a good guy."

"Right, but that's exactly what I'm saying," Fatima said, speaking more to Chloe now than to me. "He's a *good* guy. And listen, god knows I'd take a bullet for him. But I've known Amy for all of five seconds, and she's so far out of his league it's not even funny."

"Okay, that's true," Chloe admitted, shrugging at me.

I felt my cheeks burn with self-consciousness, but I was determined to play it off. I flipped my hair over my shoulder dramatically. "Thank you."

"Now, I'm still happy to set you up with my new colleague,"

Fatima said. "We start work next week, and I can put in a good word."

"Oooh, yes," Morgan said, "date Hot Teacher!"

"He is *way* hotter than Phil," Chloe said.

"Your opinion there means very little." I squinted at her. "I couldn't pay you to lock lips with any man." *And plus*, I didn't add, *you're also wrong*.

She pulled a face. "That's true."

"Or that guy from the fantasy festival?" Fatima asked, looking at Chloe for confirmation.

"I mean, he did almost get her killed," Morgan said, "but yeah, he was pretty hot."

Dan had texted me, actually, but only to apologise again. And I'd been with Phil at the time, so I'd just said thank you and let it taper off. If I forced myself to remember sitting next to him, I wasn't opposed to the idea of seeing him. But try as I might to banish Phil, he still plagued my every waking moment, and I didn't see that changing any time soon.

"Thank you," I said earnestly, "but I think it's a bit soon."

"Of course." Fatima held her hands up. "But the offer stands."

I stood up to go pour myself another glass of wine – I was staying the night, so I figured I could drown my sorrows in bottom-shelf Savvy B if I needed to. But as I headed towards the kitchen, Morgan came with me.

"Hey, I'm sorry about that," she said. "I did ask them not to bring it up. But I feel I should warn you, Chloe's picked *When Harry Met Sally* as the film. So I don't think they really got the memo."

I sighed, immediately thinking of the lore drop about watching it with Phil. Of course Chloe had chosen that exact film. I would have almost certainly teared up at the best of times, but tonight was almost guaranteed to be full of waterworks if the ultimate friends-to-lovers film was on the docket.

I unscrewed the wine and poured myself a generous amount, finishing the last few sips directly out of the bottle once my glass was full.

"But I also wanted to say," Morgan continued, "that I get it. I was kidding about Hot Teacher. I know the kinds of feelings you had for Phil don't go anywhere overnight."

I pressed my mouth into a thin smile. I didn't want to think about what had happened to all the feelings I had for Phil. I was pretty sure I'd successfully smushed them down somewhere inside me, and I was worried that identifying where would compromise the structural integrity of whatever was holding them there.

"It's been almost a year since your brother and I broke up," Morgan said, and I couldn't stop a laugh escaping me, causing me to blow bubbles in my wine as I took a sip.

"Don't I know it," I said when I surfaced. I'd had to help him through that particular gauntlet. "Jack's always been a drama queen, but god was he miserable when you guys split. But at least things worked out there."

Morgan shrugged, quirking her eyebrow in a way that implied she was trying to draw a parallel. I frowned and set my glass down.

"I don't really think it's the same though, if that's what you're implying."

"No, I know," Morgan said. "Jack and I were each standing in our own way. You and Phil have much more tangible hurdles in your way."

"There is no Phil and me," I said, maybe a little more forcefully than I needed to. "Not really. He made that crystal clear when he said that at least I'd finally gotten to live out my fantasy of being with him."

Morgan winced. "Ew, he said that to you?"

I nodded. "I'm pretty sure he only said it because he was trying to drive me away. But it fucking worked."

"Well, I'm sorry he was such a dick. For someone who's such a good friend, it sucks to know he was such a shitty boyfriend."

I wished that had been true. If he'd been horrible to be with, it might have been easier to rid myself of the feelings I'd harboured for so long. I could have resented him, like I resented Chris and Niamh, knowing that they had never been good for me. But no, I couldn't even have that satisfaction. Because up until that last moment, he'd been perfect. And losing him hurt all the more for it.

We carried our wine back into the lounge and curled up on the sofa again to watch the film. But before Chloe pressed play, Fatima cleared her throat.

"Just one more thing before I forget," she said. "I know it's a few months away still, but I've been thinking about the next Ren Faire trip. I know we talked about Arizona, but if we're happy to wait until a bit later in the year, I found a really cool Airbnb for the seven of us near the grounds of one in California. It's supposed to be haunted, and it has a great dining room for some D&D sessions. What do you think?"

"Ooooh, sounds creepy," Chloe said, steepling her fingers together.

"Count me out of anything creepy," Morgan said, "but I'm definitely up for some games!"

The three of them turned to look at me, and I tried my best attempt at a smile.

"You sure?" I asked, thinking back to the conversation I'd overheard between Grey and Fatima a few weeks ago. "Obviously Phil and I aren't together now, and I'm sure there are more options for six. Don't feel you have to invite a tagalong just because I'm Jack's little sister."

"Ew, shut up," Chloe said, wrapping her arms around my neck and pulling me into her so forcefully I wasn't sure if it was meant to be a hug or a headlock. "You may be Jack's little sister, but that doesn't mean you're not part of the group."

"You're like the little sister *of* the group," Fatima said. "Keeping us young."

"Just like Fatima is group mum," Morgan said. "She's not actually our mum, but we let her herd us as if she were."

Chloe snapped her fingers as she released me. "Mother is mothering."

Fatima pulled a face. "You are nearly thirty, Chloe. Act like it."

"Yes, mommy."

Fatima grabbed the pillow from behind her back and jumped at Chloe, threatening to smother her with it. They crashed into me and then both dissolved into giggles, and I just held Chloe's head in my lap as it turned as red as her hair.

"See?" Morgan asked from the other end of the couch, and smiled at me. "You're right where you're meant to be."

"I'm starting to see that," I said, smiling over at her. "By the way, I never did say thanks for bullying Fatima here into letting me join the D&D game."

Morgan's smile dropped as she pinched her brow together. Fatima and Chloe sat up suddenly from their tussle.

"What are you talking about?" Morgan asked.

I dropped my chin and looked slyly up at her, like we were sharing a secret. "Come on, I know it was you. You told Jack to invite me camping, you told Fatima to add me to the group..."

She shook her head. "I'd love to take credit for that but—Okay, I did tell Jack to invite you camping, but he forgot to do it, apparently. After we found out you and Phil were together, Phil just told him you were coming."

My own smile fell as well. "Wait, that was Phil?"

Fatima sat forward. "Yeah, and honestly, Amy, he was the one who pushed for you to take Lauren's spot when she left the game. Jack too, a bit, but Phil pestered me about it for weeks until I sent you a message."

"Oh," I said, looking down at my thumbs as I twiddled them in my lap. Even after all this time, after everything that had happened, it was weird to hear how badly he'd wanted me around, even then.

"But I'm glad he did," Fatima added. "You're part of the group now, like we said. And it's weird, because it feels like you've always been here."

"Agreed," Chloe said, sitting forward and wrapping her arms around my shoulders before planting a sloppy kiss on my cheek.

"Ew!" I screeched, wiping at my face. Then we dissolved into laughter and throwing pillows at one another again in the most ridiculous cliché of a girly sleepover, but I didn't care.

We eventually got around to watching the film, too, and it was surprisingly bearable. I only teared up a little bit when Harry told Sally that he loved her, and then again when he said he wanted the rest of his life to start as soon as possible. But mostly I just laughed, and joked with my friends, and drank probably too much wine.

I'd have to figure out how to coexist with the man I'd thought would be my Harry, but I could do that. Because unlike what I'd thought before, this wasn't his life I was hitching onto. It was my life, too. And at some point, without me even realising, I'd come to love it.

~

That night, I didn't sleep. And as much as I wanted to blame it on Chloe's snoring next to me in the guest bedroom, it wasn't her fault. Or it was, but more because of her choice of film than anything.

Because of Harry and Sally, I couldn't stop thinking about

New Years. Not one full of love declarations and passionate kisses before the credits roll, but one of a hundred occasions where I would have to coexist alongside Phil whilst we drank champagne and hung out with our friends. The question remained: could I do that? Did I *want* to do that? And if I did, what did I want that to look like?

This was all assuming, of course, that Phil didn't cut himself off completely. But I thought about the way Chloe had stood up for him; the way Jack and even Mum had been trying to get in there to help. I was pretty sure that no matter what, he wouldn't be allowed to just retreat into caring for Ethel. He had too many people who cared about him.

When he'd rejected me five years ago, I'd wanted nothing to do with him. We'd only re-entered each other's lives because I'd moved home, and enough had happened in the intervening period that I was willing to overlook our history.

But as badly as he'd hurt me, and as angry as I was at how he'd lashed out when he'd felt cornered, I didn't want that this time. As hurt as I was, I didn't want to have nothing to do with him. If I never saw him again, sure, I could avoid awkwardness, but I would be sad. Because the nature of our stupid fake relationship meant that – whilst to the rest of the world it looked like we'd been falling for one another, and maybe on some level we had been – we had actually developed a real friendship, probably for the first time in our long history. Sure, we'd known one another for most of our lives, and we'd spent time together. But it was the first time we'd had a relationship that didn't hinge on other people.

And as much as I missed what we'd had romantically, I missed our friendship even more. The way he'd always known when to listen to me without teasing. The way he'd taken even the most outrageous parts of me seriously. The way he'd fought to include me in every way he could, apparently. The thoughtfulness he'd shown at every turn.

And that wasn't even accounting for Ethel, whom I missed so badly I'd actually thought about crashing a physio appointment just so I could see her.

So yeah, I was hurt and angry and a little embarrassed. But I also missed my friend. And the difference between the me of five years ago and the me who lay awake in that bed worrying about her friend was that I didn't *want* to dig my heels in anymore. I didn't actually *want* to teach Phil a lesson or keep the upper hand, no matter how angry I felt. Life was already bashing him over the head enough. And if that meant swallowing my pride so I could show up for him when he needed someone the most, I could do that now. At least, I thought I could.

My oracle deck had told me the waning crescent signified endings, and I'd assumed that meant our relationship was over. But just as a new moon cycle came each month, maybe our relationship was just entering a new cycle, too. One that didn't look like I'd hoped, but could be just as impactful if I let it. If I cultivated that impact.

As the sun crept up and filtered in through the window, I knew what I needed to do. So I packed up quietly and snuck out through the front door whilst the others were still asleep, waiting until I was outside to ring someone I knew would be up.

"Everything okay?" Jack asked when he picked up, sounding awake but alarmed.

"Yeah, it will be," I said. "Are you at the house?"

"Just making breakfast," he said. "Do you need me at Morgan's?"

"No, that's okay," I said as I climbed into the Defender. "I'm on my way. But clear your morning if you can. I need your help."

"Intriguing. What with?"

"With Phil," I said, and I heard a sharp intake of breath on his end. "I think he needs an operations manager, and I know just the girl for the job."

By the end of the day, we had what we needed. I'd egregiously abused my access to Anil's number, and I'd gotten all the intel I needed to pull everything together. Mum was on board, Dad would be helping, and the rest of our friends had jobs to do, too. Now it was just down to Anil to get us in.

Jack left for Morgan's as soon as we finished, but I rejected his offer of a ride. I opted to walk back up the path to Mum and Dad's house instead. It still didn't feel like home, even though I'd been back for a full year now; even though I'd grown up under its roof. But as I was beginning to understand, that didn't mean I didn't belong here.

I'd always had a sense of restlessness; of waiting for something interesting to happen. I'd felt like that starseed soul, on an alien planet. And as I'd tried and failed over the years to make myself fit with other people, I'd become even more restless, probably because I'd known that my fate couldn't possibly find me if I wasn't even being myself.

But it turned out that I didn't need to figure out exactly who I was in order to be myself. I just had to let myself feel the love and passion I'd always had; to let the spiky bits of me exist instead of chipping away at them, even if that meant getting stuck from time to time. And as I walked up the dirt road, for the first time in a long time, I felt like I was being truly faithful to myself and what I wanted. And I didn't feel like an alien anymore. No, "home" didn't feel particularly like home, but god did it look beautiful as the sun set behind it, casting the sky in pinks and lilacs and fiery oranges.

So as I reached the old stone farmhouse, I stopped in the kitchen to give Mum a long-overdue hug, headed upstairs to my room, opened all the curtains to let the light in, and finally started unpacking.

CHAPTER 33
PHIL

It took Anil and me nearly a week to take full inventory of what Ethel would need changed. We looked at everything in the house from the flooring to the clocks, and we mapped out what her next couple of years might look like in the best and worst cases so we could figure out if there were any major changes we needed to make. I'd had to start parking my car in the street so we could get the wheelchair past the cars, and I knew the Healey was likely not long for this world.

No matter how we sliced it, it was going to be expensive, and it was going to be a lot of change all at once. And as much as that change worried me for Ethel, I was worried for me, too; the more switch-ups I needed to manage, the more likely I was to mess something up. And given that I'd been treading water for months now, I knew I wasn't operating at top form.

Anil seemed oddly optimistic, but I just chalked that up to professional encouragement.

It was Wednesday afternoon, and Ethel was out with Anil for her appointments. The plan was that then they'd come back for dinner, and he and I would figure out what to tackle first.

But that all hinged on me doing what I needed to do on my own.

I'd avoided tapping into Ethel's money for so long, but I also knew from the last week of discussions that I was going to need more than what I had left in my trust. This was more than a new boiler or a car service, and as much as I hated it, I'd need to start taking Ethel's available funds into account. I'd resisted the idea in my conversations with Anil, but he'd helped me realise that, in my desperation to care for Ethel without taking from her, I was quite possibly holding her back from getting the best care she could have, and for what? So that one day, when she was gone, I could point to a pile of money and feel good about not having spent it? No, Anil was right. It was her money, so it should be spent on her.

I settled myself at the table with my fourth cup of tea of the day and my laptop, determined to get the lay of the land before Anil and Ethel got home later. So I took in a deep breath and entered the login information I'd dug out, bracing myself for whatever it showed. I reminded myself that, even if she didn't have much, we had options.

Once the account loaded and I saw the balance, my entire body ran cold. How had I let myself go this long without checking?

Before I could sink into a proper spiral, the doorbell rang.

"Coming!" I yelled as I stood up, not even bothering to peek through the now permanently drawn curtains, figuring it was the postie with the new clock I'd ordered. So when I opened the door and saw Amy standing there, after how many times I'd imagined her showing up, I thought maybe I'd conjured her somehow.

Except, it wasn't just Amy. She was flanked by Jack and Patricia, with Chloe, Morgan, Grey, and Fatima behind them. Alan was even there, looking like he was wondering how he'd gotten roped into whatever was going on, and Pablo, who sat obediently at Morgan's feet on the pavement. They all held clipboards and notebooks in their hands, except Pablo of course.

My mouth fell open in surprise, and I just stood there staring for a good few seconds, until I felt my phone buzz in my pocket.

"Sorry, just a sec," I said, pulling it out to see a text from Anil.

> ANIL
>
> You can be mad at me later, but please let them in.

I looked from the text back up to Amy, who was smiling sheepishly at me.

"Can we come in?" she asked. "We come in peace."

I knew what this was. It was an intervention, because I'd been ignoring all of them. And honestly, I wasn't sure I had it in me to be sat down and told how much they all cared about me. I knew they did, but that didn't change what was happening. And given that Anil and I were finally making a plan, why did he choose now of all times to arrange this? Couldn't he have waited until I had something helpful to share with them? Or at least until he was here to face what he was subjecting me to?

But Amy was here. And as much as I didn't want an intervention, god I missed her. It took every ounce of willpower I had not to reach out, pull her into me, and slam the door in the rest of their faces so I could show her just how *much* I missed her. But being the paragon of restraint apparently, I just pressed my mouth into a line and nodded.

Clearly taking that as an invitation, Pablo stepped forward and trotted into the house and started sniffing around. We all watched him, and I was pretty sure it was Chloe who started laughing first, but pretty soon it was everyone cackling at the dog.

Everyone except Amy, who just watched me closely.

"Guess I'd better put the kettle on," I said, and it was like I'd raised the gates at a horse race. Everyone but Amy pushed past me into the house. Patricia and Chloe went straight through the hall to the back garden, Pablo trotting after them, whilst everyone else took their shoes off. Jack and Alan went towards the bedrooms, and Fatima into the kitchen, whilst Grey and Morgan pushed open the door to my craft room. My eyes widened in a panic as I remembered what was on the dress form, but I saw Morgan notice it too, and she turned back and winked at me, so I knew she'd get rid of it before Amy saw it.

I'd kept working on Amy's dress. Of course I had. In a week of adaptation plans and care option evaluations and chaos, it had been the only thing that made me feel like myself. Would I have preferred Amy herself be there? Of course. I'd taken out my phone to text her too many times to count, especially when I was tired and broken and spent. Even just being near her had always made me feel better – like she was a campfire, and I just needed a little bit of warmth. But I'd had to channel that longing into something more productive. Something that didn't involve dragging her down with me. Because even at my least certain, when I doubted whether I was doing the right thing, I knew she deserved more than the version of me I had to be in order to get by. So I'd stitched and embroidered every night until my fingers were sore and I couldn't keep my eyes open, and that had to be enough.

Except now she was here, in my house. Or, well, outside it – she was the only one who hadn't come in after Pablo. I could see now that she had a backpack slung over one shoulder.

"May I?" she asked, and I stepped aside, waving her in. *Be cool*, I told myself. *Don't act like a starving man seeing a roast dinner.* And by some miracle, I kept my shit together as I followed her into the lounge. She went straight for the TV, setting her backpack on the floor and producing a computer and an adapter cable, which she connected together before plugging the other end of the cable into the back of the TV.

"What's this?" I asked as Fatima came in with cups of tea. I thought about pointing out that I already had one, but despite it being my home I got the sense I needed to just come along for the ride, so I just accepted it gratefully.

Morgan and Grey came into the lounge, too, Morgan throwing me a subtle thumbs-up. Fatima stopped them in the doorway, having a quick, hushed conversation before taking the clipboards off them and following them back down the hallway.

"What is this?" I asked Amy when we were alone again. I sat down in Ethel's armchair facing the TV, whilst Amy perched on the edge of the sofa closest to it, holding her laptop. If this was an intervention, why was everyone scattered around the house? Were they looking for a secret stash of drugs or something? I heard the distinct sound of a measuring tape withdrawing into its case. *What the hell?*

"Listen," Amy said, sitting up straight, all business. "I'm sorry to have sprung this on you like this, but you weren't answering anyone's calls. Mum even tried to come by yesterday, but you weren't in."

I nodded. I tried to reach for something cavalier to say, but the last week had drained me, and I didn't have any bravado left. Especially not for Amy. "Sorry, it's been a bit mad."

"I've heard," Amy said, and I remembered Anil's message. I may not have been answering their calls, but clearly someone had been.

"Now listen," she continued. "We've been working on something, and I need you to promise me you'll hear me out."

I nodded – what choice did I have, really? And honestly, I missed her so much that I knew I would listen even if she pulled up a PowerPoint comparing me to actual war criminals. I probably deserved it.

But when she pressed a button on her laptop, the screen

was suddenly filled with the words "Ethel Owen Home Care Plan."

"Shit, Amy, what did you do?"

"All of us," she said. "*We* did this. Not just me. I'll be honest, it would have probably been better – easier for *me* at least, in the long run – to just let you cut yourself off. But…"

She swallowed hard, and I knew I had so much hanging on whatever she said next.

"But you have a lot of people that care about you, Phil. And Ethel, too. And we can't sit aside and let you isolate yourself. *I* can't sit aside whilst you do that."

I could feel tears pricking at my eyes already, and she hadn't even started her presentation. But when I made eye contact with her, she didn't mirror my emotion back at me. She was shutting herself off from me, the way I had from her. And that was okay, really. Good for her. I could take it.

"Anil gave me the breakdown of everything he thought needed changing in order for Ethel to stay here," she said, changing to a slide that listed everything Anil and I had discussed over the last week. The new car, the widened doorways, changes to the garden, lowering part of the worktop in the kitchen to be wheelchair accessible … it all seemed to be there. But I caught on the last item: "Accommodation for live-in care."

"I haven't decided on that last one," I said, pointing.

"Anil told me," Amy said. "And we'll come to that. But for now, I'm leaving it on the list, okay?"

I had no idea what that meant, but I nodded anyway. "Sure."

Over the next few minutes and a dozen or so slides, Amy broke down exactly how they all planned to help with Ethel's care.

Alan and Jack would do all the adaptation and conversion work for free, bringing spare materials from the Kenchester job, which was starting later in the week, so I wouldn't have to pay for new versions of everything. Anything that did need to be bought, we could go through their suppliers to get the best price.

Patricia and Chloe would convert the garden. As much as I was sure it broke the Rewilding Queen's heart, they would pave over the patch of grass so it was even with the back door and therefore wheelchair accessible, and they'd put in raised beds and a small lean-to style greenhouse. Then Patricia would bring by a selection of bulbs for them to plant together before the first frost.

Patricia would also be donating a second freezer, which she insisted on filling with brain-healthy meals once a week. This would go in the kitchen, which would mean we would need to shuffle things around, but we needed to do that anyway to adapt it for Ethel's wheelchair. And since Fatima, Grey, and Morgan were currently taking inventory of everything in there and in my craft room to figure out better storage options, that shouldn't be a problem.

Which brought us to care.

"I think you need to sell her Healey," Amy said matter-of-factly. "You can't just keep taking on more and more work without it becoming a full-time gig, and you know you'll get at least a few months' worth of care out of that thing."

She wasn't wrong – I'd filled out a valuation form online just a couple of days ago – but I shook my head anyway.

"I can pay for a relief carer out of what I make now."

Amy sighed, exasperation peeking through. "Phil, please, I need you to be so fucking for real right now. You know you're past needing just a relief carer."

It was what Anil had been saying, too, but the thought of leaving Ethel with a stranger all day, every day? I couldn't handle that.

"It's okay, I thought you might say that," Amy said when I told her as much. "So here's where things get logistical."

She flipped to a slide that said "Option 1", which was a list of specifics for a live-in carer. They'd need a private bedroom and bathroom, which meant I'd need to give up my craft room. And whilst Alan and Jack would do the bathroom conversion work for free, the materials cost for splitting the existing bathroom in two would be extensive. The carer would also need set hours, which would mean I would likely still need a relief carer if I wanted to do anything in the evenings or on weekends.

I'd always railed against that idea, and seeing everything it required should have solidified that for me. But I couldn't stop looking at the line that said: "Suggested hours: 7am-7pm 4 days per week." I thought about being able to actually do the weekly shop in person, instead of settling for some teenager's acceptable substitution for cultured butter. I imagined going to work at a coffee shop instead of the dining table, and not having to interrupt it every few minutes to remind Ethel what day it was or that she'd already had lunch. I thought about being able to come home and talk to her about her day without having been next to her for every single second of it. Being able to enjoy her company again, in the way she deserved, for as long as she had.

"But I get that you're not sold," Amy said, "so I've got another option for you."

The next slide said "Option 2" across the top. It had a week-long calendar on it, each day divided into AM and PM. And in every slot, there was someone's name – Amy's, Patricia's, and even Chloe's and Jack's. There was also the word "carer" in some of the slots, but fewer than I would have expected. I counted the slots where I saw my own name; there were only four.

It was astounding to me that the Evanses and my friends – my family, really, all of them – were willing to wrap themselves around Ethel and me so tightly that I would have less of a care burden than if I had a live-in carer. I could hardly believe my eyes.

Except, was that true, that I couldn't believe it? I *could*, actually, if I let myself think about it. The way they'd shown up for me time and time again, I should have been expecting this. Hell, maybe I *had* been expecting it, and that was why I'd shut myself off before they could insist on it.

"I couldn't let you do this," I said, my voice catching, but I choked back the emotion.

"You absolutely could," Amy insisted, her voice firm; she'd clearly prepared for that response. "In fact, all of us – even Grey and Fatima – have signed up for a course Anil recommended for carers. We're taking it the weekend after next, after the trip."

The trip. The one to Manchester for the ball. The one I wasn't taking because I had to care for Ethel. According to Amy's little schedule, Chloe was doing Sunday mornings; would she not be able to take those kinds of trips anymore? Or what about Patricia, who was down for Thursday nights AND Sunday afternoons? Could she not go on holidays with her family to sail the Norwegian fjords because she needed to look after Ethel? Could none of them go to the Ren Faire because of me?

No, this didn't solve anything. As lovely a gesture as it was, and as tempting as I found it, if only for the knowledge that I wouldn't lose these wonderful people, I couldn't let them do it. It would be bringing them down with me, which was exactly what I'd been trying to avoid all this time.

"No way," I said, shaking my head. "It's really kind of you, but I can't let you all do that. It's too much."

"It's really not," Chloe said from the doorway as she took off her shoes and followed Patricia into the room. "We wouldn't have offered if we didn't want to do it."

"You're family, Philip," Patricia said, walking up beside me and squeezing my shoulders. "This is what family does."

As the others filtered in – first Jack and Alan, then Fatima and Grey and Morgan, and finally Pablo, presumably having sniffed every inch of the house – they all offered some sort of confirmation that they wanted to be there. Wanted to help. Even Pablo jumped up onto my lap and started licking my hand.

"When I moved home," Jack said, "I was so useless, but you came and sat with me all the time whilst I built my house, even when I didn't speak to you."

"And when *I* had to *leave* home," Chloe said, "you came in the middle of the night and moved me out, no questions asked."

"You've fed us family dinner as much as I have over the years," Patricia said, which was an egregious exaggeration, but she squeezed my hand in such a motherly way that I was incapable of arguing.

"When Jared and I broke up," Fatima said, "you sent me a meme every day for a month. Always at the same time, as if you'd set a reminder to check in on me. That was how important it was to you."

Grey cleared their throat. "Then there's all the brownies, cookies, lemon bars, and birthday cakes, and not to mention the costumes you've insisted on making for us all, even though we know you've been burning yourself out to finish them."

Everyone looked at Alan, who shrugged. "You take amazing care of Ethel," he said. "And for every good thing you've done, she's done ten over the course of her life. We owe her a great debt of friendship, which means we owe you that debt too. Because you've kept her here with us."

I wouldn't have thought Alan Evans could make me cry – at least not from being nice – but his words were ultimately what sent the tears streaming down my face. I gripped Patricia's hand tighter as I sniffed, trying to stop them from coming. But I couldn't.

Which was unfortunate, because I had something to say.

"You're all so lovely," I managed, "and I understand why you want to do this. But I can't let you. I've been doing it for long enough to know how thankless it is."

"We don't need your thanks," Patricia said. "We just need you to let us help. We love her too, Philip."

"You can help," I said, nodding. "I promise, I'll let you do all the rest of this. I graciously accept your offers to make us food and renovate our bathroom. But not this. I can't let you do this." I pointed at the care schedule on the screen.

I looked up at Amy, whose face was set in anger as she stared down at her hands. She'd worked so hard on this; I could tell. If her presentation to her dad had been anywhere near as well thought out and earnest as this, I was almost certainly looking at the new full-time Operations Manager at Evans Contractors. But now I was telling her no, despite all that hard work. And she looked angry.

"You selfish, scared idiot," she muttered. "You know none of that other stuff will make a difference if you don't let someone share the load with you."

Alan put a hand on her shoulder and shushed her, but I wished he wouldn't. She had every right to say that to me after the way I'd treated her. And I was scared. I spent every moment of every day terrified that I was screwing things up.

But I refused to be selfish anymore, or to act from my fear, especially where Ethel was concerned.

"I choose option one."

It took Amy a moment to process what I'd said, but her eyes slowly lifted to mine as she did.

"You what?"

"I choose option one," I repeated. "I think you're right. It's time. Being so fucking for real."

This earned me a smile, and I looked up to see the others smiling, too. Alan didn't even call me out for my language.

"You're making the right call," Patricia said, crouching down next to me and squeezing my arms, but I couldn't look away from her daughter, who was still holding my gaze, her own eyes dampening.

"We can start the work next week," Jack said, "so you're ready as soon as possible for someone."

Amy swallowed hard. I could feel my restraint fraying, desperate to leap out of my seat and across the room to her. I could hold her face in my hands and kiss her freckled cheeks and wrap her in my arms and not let her go until she forgave me for being so selfish and scared, just like she'd said.

"Can you give us a minute?" she asked, and I nearly jumped out of my skin.

I still didn't look away from Amy, so I couldn't see people's reactions to her question, but I saw them leave out of the corner of my eye, and I felt Patricia pull away from my side.

"You sure?" I asked as the others retreated. *Because I don't know what I'll do once we're alone*, I thought.

"I'm sure," she said, then just sat there watching my face until the door clicked shut.

I was barely an inch out of my seat before she started speaking, freezing me to the spot.

"So, I've been doing a lot of thinking," she said, then smiled as if she'd told a joke. "And it's important to me that I say something to you."

"Yeah?" I asked, sitting back down. "What's that?"

She let out a deep breath and closed her eyes, clearly bolstering herself, then continued without opening them again.

"I love you."

My mouth went instantly dry. "You ... you what?"

"I love you," she said again, more confidently this time, opening her eyes and finding mine again. She didn't look terrified or embarrassed or desperate, all of which I was sure I looked in that moment. She looked ... calm.

"I don't know what to say," I admitted, but she shook her head.

"Say nothing then. I just wanted you to know. I love you. And I don't mean that I'm in love with you, to be clear."

She frowned and looked off to the side as if considering that, then shrugged and carried on.

"Well, okay, what I mean is, loving and being in love are two different things. You know that. Everybody knows that. Right?"

"Sure," I said, on board with that in theory, but where was she going with this?

"I've been *in* love with you since I had even an inkling of what that meant. And I always hoped that ours was going to be the twin flame, soulmate, two sides of the same coin kind of love. But that was because I never really knew you well enough to just love you."

Part of me wanted to argue – she knew me better than anyone else, I was sure of it. But she was right; that hadn't always been the case. As many times as she'd accused me of seeing her as just my best friend's little sister, until recently, I'd mostly been her big brother's best friend, and little else.

"Until this summer," she continued, "when that deep, human caring for you came out of nowhere. So the way all those other people have loved you for a long time? I love you like that now, too. I've loved you almost my whole life in one way or another, and regardless of what I've felt, or what I've hoped, I'm not about to stop. I can love you like a friend if that's what you need."

Screw what I needed, that wasn't what I *wanted* at all. But I didn't say that. I didn't want to confuse her – or myself – any more.

"And I think," she continued, "and feel free to keep it to yourself if I'm wrong, that for you it was the other way around."

I frowned. "How do you mean?"

"I mean that you loved me as a friend long before this summer. You knew who I was in a way I didn't know you. I don't know how, but you did. And then maybe this summer was when the 'in love' part started to build for you."

"You're wrong," I said without thinking, but she held up a finger, and I snapped my mouth shut before I could explain.

"Keep it to yourself, big boy."

I bit back a laugh and nodded for her to carry on.

"The point I'm trying to make," she said, "is that people fall in and out of love, but I've got that other kind of love for you now. And it's not going away. You may be able to push me away from being your lover, but you can't make me go away entirely. So that's why I'm here. It's why we're all here. Because you may have really hurt me, but I'm still your friend. And I refuse to let you do this alone."

She was crying now, too, and I pushed out of my chair before I could stop myself, coming to sit next to her on the sofa. I reached my hands up to wipe her tears away, but she held her palm up to stop me.

"Don't," she said, her voice croaking. "I'm okay. Or at least I will be. But not if you do that. Just please let us help, okay?"

"Amy, I'm so—"

"No," she said firmly, and I clamped my mouth shut. "Just nod. You'll let us help you, yes?"

I could feel my own tears run down into my beard, but I didn't move to clear them. I just nodded, like she'd asked. Amy smiled and collapsed back into the sofa, visibly relieved.

"Thank you," she said, shutting her laptop and unplugging it, putting everything into her bag. I wanted to tell her to stop.

"What made you change your mind, by the way?" she asked.

"About what?"

"A live-in carer."

I chuckled lightly, remembering what I'd seen moments before they'd all arrived. "Just before you got here, I was sitting down to work on the financial side of things," I said. "I finally got access to Ethel's online banking."

"Oh yeah?" she asked, standing up at attention. "And?"

I smiled, glad to have some good news.

"Well, let's just say I won't have to sell the Healey."

CHAPTER 34
YORICK PROUDHOLLOW

They were too late. Eden was bound on the other side of the chamber, the chanting seemed to be reaching some sort of crescendo, and Nephrine was beginning to bring the diadem up as if to place it on her head. It was now or never.

Liam and Morgana had clearly had the same idea, running up to disrupt the circle of chanting figures, but they encountered some sort of protective barrier as they did.

"Ignore them," Nephrine called from her dais to her minions, who were beginning to glance over their shoulders. "Finish the ritual." They turned back to face her obediently.

Unlike the barrier at Laszlo's encampment, Yorick could actually see this one once he knew it was there. It glimmered slightly where it broke the air, a couple of feet beyond the circle and extending up nearly to the ceiling, leaving just a small gap. A half-sized gap, one might say.

It was a very, very bad idea. Very unlikely to work. But without their weapons, Yorick knew he had to try. So he turned to Gorlag, extended his arms, and puffed out his chest.

"You ready, bud?"

"For..." Gorlag looked down at Yorick hopefully, their eyes going wide. Yorick nodded.

"That's right," he said. "Toss me."

Gorlag's mouth split into a wide grin as they bent down and put their enormous hands under Yorick's arms, hoisting him into the air. Yorick felt jostled as Gorlag repositioned him so their hand was somewhere they wouldn't speak about, but he tried anyway to point himself in the direction he wanted to go, and a moment later he was flying through the air.

Catch, he said to Eden.

I'm literally tied up! she replied, but not before he found himself just narrowly making it over the barrier. Nephrine's eyes went wide as she saw him coming, and he saw her hand tighten protectively around the diadem to keep him from it.

But Yorick wasn't after the diadem. They'd need to destroy it, but they couldn't do that if they were powerless. And he could think of only one way to bring a bit more power into the equation. So he snatched Eden's star crystal from Nephrine's other hand and lobbed it as hard as he could over the barrier towards Eden.

The light in the room dimmed suddenly, the crystal in the ceiling emitting only half of what Eden's crystal had projected. Yorick hit the barrier hard on the other side from where he'd overcome it, ricocheting into some of the hooded figures, disrupting the circle. One of the ones he hit turned on him with a dagger, and he ignored the shooting pain in his hip to roll out of the way. It was only as he continued to roll that he realised the barrier had dropped, and as Gorlag's foot came down hard beside him that he realised his friends had seen it come down.

Yorick leapt to his feet and looked around as the circle devolved into a brawl. His friends took slashes from the daggers on their arms as they fought the hooded figures, each of whom Yorick could now see wore amulets of twelve-pointed stars. Nephrine stood at the centre of the fray, clutching the diadem, looking around for where the crystal went. Yorick looked around too, desperately hoping his aim was true and it had found its way to Eden.

A hideous noise tore through the room, as if the air itself were ripping apart. Across the chamber, a black hole had appeared in the stone wall, reality seeming to swirl into it. Some of the minions closest to it lost their footing and found themselves sucked in, their screams inaudible amidst the roar of whatever was claiming them.

Yorick looked over his shoulder to see Eden, nowhere near where she had just been tied up, holding out the crystal as Nephrine had done just a moment ago, her body full of stars just as it had been in the forest, only this time in the shape of the dragon constellation. It was clear she was using all her strength to maintain the black hole. Yorick felt just a moment of triumph that he'd managed to get her crystal back to her, if nothing else.

The fight was getting desperate. Gorlag front-kicked one of the hooded figures into the black hole, but one of the others did the same almost concurrently to Liam, and Morgana barely managed to grab onto his hand before he was taken. Orange light flared into Yorick's vision as flames roared around Calamity, protecting her from a spell Nephrine fired at her. A hooded figure ran at her with a dagger, but the flames consumed them before they could reach her.

Yorick's hand reached instinctively for his lute, but it wasn't there. So instead, he cast an illusion of colour onto the ceiling with a spell he'd used against another member of The Twelve, charming two of the hooded figures into going after Nephrine, who had to use some of her magic to defend herself from her own minions.

They weren't losing. But the diadem was still there, and Nephrine was clearly very powerful. She easily fended off the two figures Yorick had sent to her, then turned Calamity's preferred type of magic back on her, the flames licking up her body until she collapsed. Liam rushed over to help her just as Morgana took a dagger to the neck, falling to her knees. Gorlag had four hooded figures on them. One of the figures lost their dagger to the force of the black hole, and it nicked Gorlag's cheek as it was sucked into the darkness.

Yorick cast a basic charm spell on Nephrine, but she shrugged it off as if it were nothing. He tried a more advanced one too, but again, she refused to succumb. Yorick wondered if she had some sort of protection against it. She seemed to be holding her ground against the force of the black hole, too, despite Eden's efforts.

He knew one other spell that could help, but it would take all the magic he had left in him. If it didn't work, he'd be as useless as a puppet. But he had to try. He'd gotten them into this mess, after all. So he threw everything he could into the spell, ready to pay the ultimate price if he needed to, staring directly into Nephrine's eyes as he did.

Slowly, her gaze iced over with fear. Just as Yorick had experienced too many times for his liking, her body was betraying her. Freezing up, refusing to fight, as swirls of arcane energy held her in place. Her hand still gripped the diadem, but she could no longer move. It had worked.

Yorick ran forward, dodging Liam as he staggered backward after a hit. He ducked around Calamity, back on her feet, and lunged for Nephrine. Her eyes widened slightly as Yorick approached, as dark as the gaping black hole behind her.

His plan had been to dislodge the diadem from her hand so it was sucked in as the dagger had been, but the moment he connected with her, he knew he'd miscalculated. The slightest touch sent both of them in that direction as well, powerless against the force of Eden's spell.

In the space of a single second, Yorick swung from confusion to terror to resignation. This was the price for his folly. His pride. And he would happily pay it. He looked directly into the black hole, surprised to find that there were no stars beyond. Nothing at all. Just darkness. And that felt fitting, really. The only stars he needed were behind him.

He watched as Nephrine and the diadem were consumed, blinking out of existence, and smiled. Even if he had to give his life, he'd done what he'd come to do. He could be at peace.

But just before the darkness took him, he felt a tug at his neck, and he dropped suddenly to the floor. It knocked the wind out of him, and he closed his eyes for a second, trying to figure out if he was still alive. He thought he must be; he was in too much pain for this to be the peace he'd been headed for.

He opened his eyes, and stood over him was a dragon made of stars.

CHAPTER 35
AMY

The holiday let in Manchester was abuzz with activity when I arrived. It felt weird to be in the city and not see any of my old friends, but they were all several miles away at the wedding on Chris's family estate, and I felt better than ever about my decision not to go. I'd taken the train up – without Phil, there had been just one too many people to ride in one car, so I'd sacrificed myself in the name of some alone time – but now I found myself genuinely excited to be there. I walked through the door Chloe held open, letting the chaos of my friend group envelop me.

"Thank god you're here!" Chloe squealed as she shut the door behind me. She pulled me in for a hug, forcing me to drop my duffel bag. "No one else knows how to curl long hair."

"I tried!" I heard Fatima yell from the other room. Chloe just rolled her eyes and pulled me down a long corridor, presumably towards her room. I barely managed to grab my bag again before I was yanked away.

"Grey would come say hi," she said, "but they're currently dyeing their buzz cut gold."

"Oh good, you're here!" Jack called as he appeared through another doorway. "I have something for you."

"Oooh, gimme!" I said, holding my free hand out. But Jack just pointed further down the hall.

"It's in your room," he said, and I followed his direction to the last door on the right.

I creaked open the door to find a small double room – when we'd booked, we'd obviously thought I'd be sharing with Phil. But I wasn't mad about having the bed to myself, even if I would rather have had Phil with me.

Though it was probably good he wasn't there, because there wouldn't have been room for him. There was barely room for me around the giant white box sat on the bed. Actually, maybe Phil was inside it – it certainly looked big enough to hold a body.

I turned around to look at Jack for an explanation, but he was pulling the door shut behind me, fending off Chloe and her curling wand in the hallway.

I turned back to the box, which was so big I wasn't sure how Jack had managed to get it through the door. There was an envelope taped to the top with my name on it. I opened it and pulled out a folded white card, four stars embossed in gold leaf on the front in the shape of the Aries constellation. It was beautiful. Elegant, even. Perfect.

I flipped the card open, not at all surprised to see Phil's chicken scratch handwriting inside.

> Amy, I've been dreaming this up for you since before you were truly mine, and I don't believe in letting a good dress go to waste, especially for someone as beautiful as you.

> *I'm sorry for everything I've done to hurt you. I hope you know that you deserve a knight in shining armour, not a fool.*

My breathing hitched as I put the card back in its envelope, then set it aside on the bed and lifted the lid of the box to find the dress he hadn't wanted to go to waste.

I gasped. It was so stunning that it literally took my breath away for a moment. If I'd thought the card had been beautiful and elegant and perfect, those words had entirely new definitions now. This would certainly beat the dress I'd brought with me.

I hadn't been able to bring myself to buy a new dress for the ball after what had happened with Phil, opting to bring along my outfit from the festival instead. It wasn't very formal, but I'd hoped Chloe could help me spruce it up a bit. Now, though, I was relieved I hadn't bought anything else, because no matter how wonderful it was, it would have paled in comparison to the piece of art inside that box.

There was a knock at the door, and they'd barely rapped a second time before I yelled for whoever it was to come in. Chloe rushed into the room and pulled the door shut behind her.

"Ooooh, let me see!" she said, peeking around me. When she saw the dress, she gasped just as I had, her hand coming to her mouth. "Holy shit, Amy, that's incredible."

"Isn't it?" I said, sounding breathy as I kicked off my sandals. "Help me get it on."

Chloe lifted the dress delicately out of the box – or dresses, it turned out, because it was actually in two separate parts. The strapless sheath under-layer was made of a deep violet satin that felt buttery soft against my skin, and I felt certain he'd chosen the fabric because of how similar it looked to that other purple dress.

Chloe held out the tulle overdress, which was a slightly lighter colour. She'd loosened the corset lacing at the back, and I dropped down to my knees and stretched my arms up so she could lower it over me. Then I stood and prepared myself to have to hold my breath whilst she laced me up, but it wasn't necessary; the dress fit perfectly.

The moment I stood and saw myself in the mirror, I felt tears well up in my eyes. The soft tulle was covered in delicate gold embroidery – stars of different shapes and arrangements. There were at least four different layers, each with stars stitched into them, creating a sense of depth, as if an actual galaxy lay hidden in the layers. I gathered part of the skirt and pulled it up to see closer, and I gasped yet again when I realised that the constellations weren't just any old ones; they were ours, Aries and Gemini. I'd need smelling salts if things kept going this way.

The overskirt was much fuller than the sheath beneath, falling in a big puff over the satin like a princess dress. The corset laced at the back with a long satin ribbon that matched the under-layer, and a swathe of tulle wrapped around my arms and across my chest, creating an off-the-shoulder neckline that made my windswept hair look intentional rather than incidental. Not that I'd be keeping it this way. A dress this stunning needed a stunning hairstyle to complement it.

"I have no idea what to do with my hair or makeup," I said to Chloe, who had been fawning over me in the mirror, but now she was staring down into the box again.

"Well, I can do them," she said, reaching in and pulling out something else – something gold and rigid. "But I think Phil's coming in clutch with the hair."

She held a gold headband – a halo headband, I was pretty sure it was called, meant to look like a normal headband, but floating just above my head. The outer circle was covered in delicate stars, swirls and gems that perfectly matched the dress. It was a celestial dream.

Chloe slipped it onto my head, and even over my plait it looked phenomenal. I looked like I was made of stars, just like Eden. It was obvious even at a glance how much time and energy Phil must have put into it, despite famously having no time or energy to spare.

I turned on Chloe suddenly. "When did he do this?" I asked. "And why? We broke up weeks ago. This is too much."

Chloe shook her head. "I don't know. I only found out about it today because he had Jack pick it up on our way."

"It was done when we all went over there earlier this week," Grey said, poking their now completely golden head in, making us jump. "Sorry. Thin walls."

"But that doesn't make any sense," I said, more to myself than to anyone.

"Well, you look fucking incredible," Grey said, and I smiled at them before they disappeared again.

"They're right, you know," Chloe said, stepping back to look over me from head to toe. "You look fucking incredible."

"I just don't understand why he did this."

"What did you guys talk about the other day?" Chloe asked. "You know, when you kicked us all out?"

"Just that we were gonna be friends," I said, though that wasn't really true. "I said I was going to be his friend, whether he liked it or not. That he couldn't freeze me out just because we weren't together, and I wasn't going to run away with my tail between my legs like I did last time."

"Well, maybe this is him saying he accepts?" Chloe said, though it sounded more like a question. "I mean, he's made outfits for all of us before. Though this is one hell of a dress."

On one hand, I hoped she was right. It would hurt sometimes, but going back to being Phil's friend was almost certainly better than being iced out in the name of protecting me. I didn't need his protection.

But on the other hand, I wasn't so sure. Couldn't we have just reconciled in person? Why the dress? Why the note? Why the radio silence?

I decided to put it to the test. I picked up my phone from where I'd discarded it on the bed and typed out a message.

CHAPTER 36
PHIL

By the end of the week, I'd made all of the big decisions I'd needed to. For starters, I had a big van with a wheelchair ramp, parked right next to my Ford Fiesta. I hadn't *needed* to sell Ethel's Healey, but when I asked about it and she didn't even remember that she had it, I knew it was okay to say goodbye. And at least now I got to keep my own car.

Anil had lined up interviews with five different carers he knew for the next week, though I was still trying to convince him to take the job himself, and Jack and Alan would start work on Tuesday. The binder would get a complete refresh once we knew exactly what the new setup would be. I'd gotten a head start on packing up my craft room, having been able to take some time off work after seeing just how big Ethel's nest egg was. I only regretted that I hadn't found out about it sooner so I could have invested it; we could have been paying some of our bills off the interest alone. I was still determined not to use it for myself if I could help it – she was still relatively healthy, and her care would only get more and more expensive over the years – but it felt really good to have it there just in case.

Plus, we'd finally gotten a dishwasher, and it was as life changing as I'd thought it would be.

It was the end of the first week of September, still sweltering outside, and the hawthorn berries had started to emerge on the tree out front. It would be a while before they were ripe, but it felt good to see them there anyway, knowing I could harvest them and make something that meant so much to me.

Ethel was having a good day, too. She wheeled herself slowly through the front door and down the makeshift ramp we'd created, parking herself next to me where I sat on the bench soaking up some sunshine. I tried not to rush to help her; Anil had said to let her take the lead on when she needed help. Once she was in place, I let myself close my eyes and enjoy the warmth again.

"Enjoying yourself?" she asked, and I nodded. It was amazing how true it felt, too. I was still just as busy as I'd always been – I'd finished Amy's dress the night after she'd brought the cavalry, but I'd replaced that workload with getting started on changes around the house. But just knowing what my next steps were had made a bigger difference than I would have thought possible.

"You?" I asked, intending it as a throwaway comment, but I opened my eyes when Ethel didn't respond and saw her frowning.

"I miss Amy," she said, and I couldn't help the gasp I made.

"Amy?" I asked, wondering if she was remembering the right person, but she just looked at me like I was the senile one.

"Amy? Your girlfriend?" She laughed. "I'm not that far gone yet."

Not today, I thought, but obviously didn't say. "Amy and I broke up," I admitted. I'd told her this at least once before, but clearly she didn't remember, since she reeled back in shock.

Then she smacked my arm out of nowhere.

"You're an idiot if you let that one get away."

"Don't I know it," I said, pretending her strike had actually hurt. "But what's done is done."

"God, you're thick," she said, and I couldn't help but laugh.

"Really, Ethel?" I asked, incredulous. "Says the woman who can't remember what day it is?" It had been a while since we'd joked like this; it was dark, sure, but I missed it.

"It's Saturday, thank you very much, which I know from that handy new clock you got me."

The new wall clock in the hallway was an aesthetic abomination – it was about two feet across with big red LEDs displaying the day, date, and time – but it did seem to help Ethel orient herself.

And it was in fact Saturday. Until a few weeks ago, I'd planned to be halfway to Manchester with Amy right now for the wedding, and then the ball.

"You don't seem happy," Ethel said, examining my face.

"Don't I?" I asked, genuinely surprised. I was the closest to happy I'd been since I'd driven Amy away.

"You don't," she said, pressing the pad of her thumb to the centre of my forehead. "You look just like your father. He got the same wrinkle right there when he was upset."

I smoothed my forehead with my hand as if that would undo all the frowning I'd been doing these last weeks. Hell, these last years.

"I'm not upset," I muttered.

"Could have fooled me."

"That's not saying much."

"Shut your dirty mouth," she said, and I burst out laughing. God, I missed sharp-tongued Ethel. Getting glimpses of it was such a rare treat these days.

"What I'm trying to tell you," she continued, "is that you're just like your father was, like it or not. He worked so hard for you, and he left you with a lot, but he didn't know how to be present."

I frowned. She'd never said anything critical of my parents before, not once that I could remember.

"Learn from his mistakes, Phil. Be present. Don't let life get away from you."

"But what about you?" I asked. Because that was reality. If I was too present with Amy, with anything else, I'd miss the time I had left with Ethel. And there would never be enough of that.

She sighed. "I'm so grateful for everything you've done for me."

"It's nothing compared to what you did for me."

"That is my job, darling boy."

"And this is *my* job."

She huffed, indignant. "Oh, I'm a job, am I? Does that mean I can fire you?"

I frowned. "*Are* you firing me? Gonna check yourself into a home?"

She chuckled and patted my leg. "No. But one day I won't be here anymore, and you'll be out of a job then."

Jesus, I hated when she got all macabre like this. "That's not happening any time soon."

"And I don't want it to," she said. "But it's an inevitability. I'm old now. I'm going to have bad days. I'm going to get hurt."

"Not if I can help it," I said quietly, but she carried on as if I hadn't spoken.

"And one day I'll be gone. And if you blame yourself for the natural circle of life, or you double down on trying to stop it, you'll have nothing left at the end. If you want me to be happy, if you want me to be at peace, then have a life. Give me some sort of reassurance that you'll be okay when I'm gone. Because right now I'm not convinced."

My mouth pinched together at the thought of Ethel being

gone. Without Amy to pin all my hopes and dreams on, I genuinely couldn't imagine my life without Ethel; when I tried, there was nothing there. Maybe I needed to revisit Our Lore and remind myself what I'd once been able to picture for myself. But that was all tied up in being with Amy; with a future I'd made impossible.

"I won't be okay when you're gone, no matter what."

"You're sweet," she said. "But you're wrong. I've seen how happy Amy makes you, and I refuse to be the reason you don't get to have that."

"It's not you," I insisted. "I screwed that up all on my own. I don't deserve her. Or, at least, she deserves more than me. More than this."

I didn't specify what "this" was; I didn't want to make Ethel feel she was the reason I couldn't be with Amy.

Just then, my phone buzzed with a text.

AMY

> Got the dress. It's incredible. Thank you. But I'm a little confused.

I started typing back straightaway, a smile on my face as I thought about her seeing it for the first time. Maybe it was arrogant to think so highly of my own work, but I knew it was an amazing dress. I'd poured everything I had into it, after all.

PHIL

> Don't be. It's just a gesture. An olive branch, if you will. Enjoy the ball. 🦋

The message showed as read straightaway, and I stared at the phone, willing her to say more. To give me even a tiny glimpse of how she was. What she was feeling, besides confused. I hated that I'd made her feel anything but loved. Anything but wanted.

A painstakingly long moment later, she wrote back.

AMY

Thanks, Phil. Wish you were here.

I smiled down at my phone, hoping she was doing the same. More than anything, I wished I were there with her. Not so I could change things between us – maybe we were too far gone – but just to see her. To know she'd be okay despite me, since she'd rejected my attempts to make sure she'd be okay without me.

"Do you love her?" Ethel asked, snapping me back into the moment.

"Yeah, of course I do," I admitted. It was surprisingly easy, actually, admitting that to Ethel.

"If you love her, then you deserve her," Ethel said, as if it were that easy. "And she couldn't do any better than a man who knows her and loves her well."

"I disagree," I said to my hands. "I was pretty horrible to her."

"Well then," Ethel said, slapping her hands on her legs, "you know what you have to do."

I laughed. "Yeah? What's that?"

"Grand gesture," she said, doing what passed for a shrug, given that she didn't quite have the shoulder mobility for a proper one anymore.

I hated how quickly my heart leapt at the idea that there was a way to get Amy back. That we could just ride off into the sunset together despite everything that had happened between us. That it was as easy as telling her that I loved her, and that I was sorry, and that I wanted to be with her.

But then again, hadn't Amy done essentially that? Minus the part about wanting to be with me, of course, but the grand gesture part? She'd spent days working on a plan, had come here with everyone who loved me, and had put herself out there. As far as she'd known, the cold way I'd spoken to her was what had been waiting for her here. As far as she'd known, I would roll my eyes and lob a "Thanks but no thanks" at her before kicking her out. But she'd come anyway, and told me she loved me, and made me promise to let them all help.

So the least I could do was put myself out there for her just in case ... right?

Except I had no idea how to do that, and I couldn't just ignore the reality of my life. I had Ethel with me, and Anil wasn't here, and Amy was in Manchester.

In Manchester, in a perfect dress, in a literal castle. If I'd been looking for the perfect ingredients for a romantic gesture...

I shook my head. I was clearly getting carried away sat in the sun. I stood up to go inside and get some water, but Ethel grabbed my hand.

"So?" she asked, looking up at me expectantly. "Are you really not going to do anything?"

I looked down at my wonderful, generous, hilarious grandmother. My life had revolved around her for so long, and I didn't regret that even one bit. She'd done the absolute best she could to take me in after the worst had happened, and I'd had an amazing life. No part of me resented her for what I'd had to give up to take care of her in return. Did I hate the disease eating away at her mind? Of course I did. But Ethel herself? She was still my world.

But she was right. She wouldn't be here forever. And if I thought about what my world looked like – maybe not *after* Ethel, because I still couldn't fully picture that, but *outside* of Ethel perhaps – the only thing that mattered to me was Amy, and showing up for her the way she'd showed up for me.

Something focused inside me, and resolve settled over me. I'd have to be fast, but if we left now, we could make it happen.

"Let's do it," I said, and Ethel squeezed my hand and squealed. I'd never seen her so giddy.

"What can I do?"

"Start packing," I said as I helped her up the ramp and inside. "We're gonna need to stay away overnight."

I pulled the door shut behind us and picked up my phone off the hall table where I'd left it, googling the number for the animal rescue. "You've got twenty minutes," I said as Ethel wheeled herself down the hall, suddenly more spry than I'd seen her in months. "I have some phone calls to make."

CHAPTER 37
AMY

Once we were all dressed and ready, we headed out for the evening. First we stopped at a gaming supply store Morgan had apparently designed the logo for – they were closed, but Morgan and Fatima knew the owner Greg, so he let us inside for a bit – and between us we left many sets of dice richer and many pounds poorer. Then we made a pit stop for a fine dining experience at McDonald's, which involved tucking napkins into our gowns to avoid getting Big Mac Sauce all over Phil's handiwork.

Four hours, a tram ride, and multiple Chicken McNugget Shareboxes later, Chloe placed my crown of stars on my head, and the six of us finally arrived at the castle where the ball was being held. There was a huge queue of people waiting to get inside, everyone dressed beautifully in gowns, suits, tunics, and more, including a group dressed as the gargoyles on the actual castle. Everyone was stopping everyone else to compliment their outfits and ask where they were from, and it felt bittersweet every time I responded with "My friend made it".

I'd been to the castle before – it was usually open as a museum – but they'd completely transformed it for the ball.

Most of the light in the entrance hall came from LED candles suspended from the two-storey ceiling, or from uplighting showing off full suits of armour and banners with fantasy insignia on them. We were offered champagne as we stepped inside, the bubbles in our glasses catching the flickering light from above. It was like walking through the night sky.

The lights were brighter in the dance hall, where a sweeping staircase on one side led to a gallery overlooking the room. A stage stood at the far end of the space holding a small ensemble. As we entered, they played what sounded like a strings-only version of Taylor Swift's "Wildest Dreams".

We made our way to the bar where Chloe made us all order mead, then stood on the periphery watching people arrive. After a few minutes, the speakers lining the walls began to thump with a beat, and the dance floor immediately filled up. I looked up to see a DJ on the gallery level wearing a wizard hat. Morgan pulled me onto the dance floor, and for the next several songs, all six of us danced together until I was dizzy from joy.

At one point Jack seemed to flag very suddenly, walking off to the side of the dance floor. I followed him to find him staring down at his phone.

"You okay?" I asked, and he looked up at me, looking slightly alarmed at first before smiling.

"Yeah, just tired," he said. "I can hike a Munro no problem, but a few tracks in and my legs feel like they're about to fall off."

I narrowed my eyes at him – he looked rather too upright for someone supposedly so exhausted.

"Let's go check out upstairs," he said, pointing at the grand staircase. People stood at the bottom taking photos, but it was plenty wide enough for us to get past. So I followed him up and along the gallery, overlooking the entrance, where they'd shut the doors we'd come through. They were huge wooden doors, at least fifteen feet tall, and it was comical watching latecomers squeeze through the gap between them as if they were tiny faeries instead of full-sized humans.

The people-watching was sensational. There were couples who were clearly living their romantasy dreams, making out on the dance floor; there were people who were clearly just there for the social media content, posing in front of every possible backdrop and queueing for the 360-degree camera; and there were people who had clearly been dragged along, or not known what they were getting into.

"I'm really glad you came," Jack said as we watched the revelry. "I was worried you'd bail on us a for a second there."

"You kidding? I'd already paid for the ticket and the holiday let. I wasn't gonna let that go to waste."

He shook his head. "I mean in general."

I frowned. "Why would you think that?"

"Because of what happened with Phil right before I moved home. I know that was part of why you were so anxious to move back." He gestured around as if I'd moved into the castle itself.

My mouth opened and closed again – I didn't know what to say.

"I didn't know you knew about that," I said eventually.

"Chloe told me," he said. "I'd wondered why you were so averse to hanging out with them, when you'd loved being around us growing up. So she filled me in. Sorry."

I felt my face flush slightly. This whole time I'd thought Jack had been oblivious to my feelings for Phil. Sure, he'd known I had a crush on his best friend growing up, but adult feelings were different.

"I can't believe you've known all this time."

"Yeah, well, I notice when you're not there."

"Yeah?" I pouted up at him. "Really?"

He nodded solemnly. "Really. I like having you around. We all do. And it's not the same when you're not there. Why did you think I was so keen for you to move home last year?"

I shrugged. "Because you hated Chris?"

"Well, that too," he said, and we laughed. "But I missed you. And I wanted you home. And I know things went a bit wobbly with Phil there for a bit, but I'm really glad you're still here. I know you're my sister, but you're my friend, too. And that makes me really happy."

I could hear a slight croak in his voice, and I glared at him sternly. If Jack cried, I would almost certainly cry, and Chloe had worked too damn hard on my makeup. I took a deep breath, flapping my lips as I breathed out, shaking back and forth, trying to let the emotion roll off me.

"It makes me happy too," I said, warming up to a cringeworthy "I love you." But then Jack frowned and pulled his phone out again, and the moment was gone.

"What the hell is so important you're interrupting our sibling bonding moment?" I joked, but then he winced and looked up at me guiltily.

"Sorry," he said, then held out a hand. "Just do me a favour and don't move for a minute, yeah?"

"Okay," I said tentatively, but he was already walking away. Then he paused on the steps, looked up from his phone, and then back at me again.

"By the way," he called, "what did you and Phil do on your first date?"

I blinked at him, confused, and not just because the question had come out of nowhere. I almost said we went bowling – that had been the first actual date night of our arrangement, after all. But I couldn't remember what we'd actually agreed to tell people. I wasn't sure it mattered anymore, but it bothered me that I couldn't remember.

"I'll be back," he said, despite the fact that I hadn't answered, then turned and skipped down the grand staircase.

I pulled my phone out of my dress – because yes, Atelier Owen gowns had pockets – and opened the Our Lore note for the first time in ... weeks? Months even? We'd stopped using it so quickly, I couldn't be sure.

I didn't have to scroll far to find the answer – we'd agreed that our first date was actually just an angry makeout in his front hall because we'd fumbled asking one another out so badly. But why had Jack asked me that?

I scrolled back up to the top before closing the note, but as I did, I saw the "last edited" date, and my heart stopped. It was today's date, just a few minutes ago.

I scrolled down desperately, trying to see what he'd added. Before long, I reached what had been our last entry – one I'd written joking that Phil was a terrible driver – but it was far from the last entry now. There were dozens of pieces of lore that had been added since then, separated from the rest by the selfie we took on our first date – both of us drunk out of our minds, Phil's eyes glued to me, full of love even then.

I read through the new additions, my mouth falling further and further open as I read.

> I'm 60, and you buy me a 30th anniversary present. It's the 30th iteration of the same sign: The Evan's-Owen's, est 2024. I hang it up anyway next to all the others.

> You finally unpack and redecorate your bedroom, and the next day I ask you to move in with me for real. Not coincidentally, either. I waited until the exact moment you were happy with it to ask you. Because I'm a prick, remember?

> Instead of shutting down the holiday idea, I hire a carer for Ethel and spend two weeks in your arms as we sail through the fjords. Your parents have to move rooms because of how loud you are when I make you come.

I don't say horrible things to you, or leave you sitting outside on a bench. Instead you come to the hospital with me, and we deal with things together, and I act like a fucking grownup instead of a scared child.

We never start our fake dating arrangement. You marry the cute knight (yeah, I know he's cute, I have eyes) and have lots of dumb cute babies with him. I pretend to be thrilled for you, because I want you to be happy more than I've ever wanted anything.

Somehow my mum and dad are still here, but I also still know you. They love you.

I make your wedding dress. You insist that it's too much work, and that it breaks tradition, but I convince you it would be fun for YOU to be the one who doesn't see your dress until the wedding day, and for some reason you're up for it. It looks a hell of a lot like the one you're wearing right now, actually.

I looked up from the note, then leant over the railing, searching for a familiar face; *any* familiar face. What the fuck was going on?

I finally found Morgan in the crowd, just as she ran up to the stage. She tapped the emcee on the leg and said something to her before running back towards the stairs, where she started shooing people off of them.

The emcee signalled for the DJ to stop, and the room went suddenly quiet, collective gasps rising from the dance floor as people wondered what was happening. The heavy groan of the doors sounded, and I looked over to see Jack pulling one open. Every head turned to look.

Through the door walked a knight. And not just someone

dressed as a knight, though obviously it was – it looked like one of the suits of armour against the wall had come to life. The silver plate mail was covered in gold filigree, and pops of purple showed through at the arms and waist. A plume of gold feathers flowed from the back of the helmet, and a purple cape almost the same colour as my underdress billowed behind him as he walked – nay, strode – across the stone floor. The string ensemble started up again, this time playing "Symphony" by Clean Bandit, and the knight stepped forward almost perfectly on tempo with the music.

"As is our tradition," the emcee said, "we'll now join in one of the choreographed dances we like to do. So if everyone could watch our demonstration, you should be able to follow along. Feel free to join in from the second round if you know the steps."

The knight reached the centre of the dance floor just as she finished speaking. And when he pulled off his helmet, combed through his beard, and looked directly up at me at the top of the stairs, my stomach dropped, even though I'd known who it was the moment I'd seen him walk in.

CHAPTER 38
PHIL

Five years ago, I'd nearly kissed Amy Evans for the first time. This summer, I'd finally closed the deal, and it had been better than I'd ever imagined it could be, but I'd stupidly let her slip away. So now, I watched her descend the stairs and walk towards me, vowing to never let her go again if she could forgive me.

The dress was even better than I'd dreamed, but I could barely look at it. All I could focus on were Amy's green eyes and the way they shone brighter and brighter the closer she got to me. Maybe it was the lighting, or maybe … no, I didn't dare let myself hope yet.

"You're here," she said, stopping just a couple of feet away. It was still too far.

"I couldn't miss it," I said. "And thank god, because you look incredible. Not seeing you in that dress would have been the worst mistake of my life."

She narrowed her eyes. "The worst?"

I shrugged. "Second worst. Maybe third."

The music paused for a moment, and the ensemble started the last section over again, and I remembered that I'd promised the emcee, via Jack and Morgan, that I'd demonstrate the dance. So I stepped towards Amy and raised my left arm. She met it without hesitation, stepping around me just like we'd practised.

"Well, I've got a few things I wouldn't mind doing over," I said.

I had to tear my eyes away from her so I could walk to the edge of the dance floor and deposit my helmet and gloves, but the moment I could spin around, I was admiring her again. How had I ever let myself stop doing that? It turned out I could be both a knight *and* a fool.

"Where did you scrounge up a suit of armour?" she asked as we moved towards each other again.

"Lauren's friend. But they're a bit shorter than I am, so I'm not sure how long I'll last to be honest."

I brought my hand to her waist and guided her in a circle around me. I hadn't touched her like this in weeks, and I let myself press into the dip in her side.

"You look heavenly," I said as we pulled in closer, our faces just a few inches away as we spun.

"It's the dress," she said, smirking. "It's rather well made."

My cheeks burned. "I mean, I'm pretty sure it's you. You could be wearing a bedsheet and you'd still be beautiful. Actually, come to think of it..."

I trailed off suggestively, but I wished I could take it back when I saw her smile falter.

"You can't say things like that to me anymore," she said as I grasped her right hand with my left, bringing my other hand to her waist.

"You're right. I'm sorry."

The round ended, and we stepped apart, and she lifted her skirts and dipped in a curtsy as I bent forward in a bow. The crowd clapped, and several people, including Grey and Fatima, stepped onto the dance floor to start the next round.

This was the moment – this was why I was here. I looked

over Amy's shoulder as we danced to see Ethel in her wheelchair by the door, Chloe stood dutifully behind her. She and Ethel were both giving me identical thumbs-up.

Amy stepped forward with her arm raised, ready to dance the next round with me, but I couldn't do it. We'd danced the same steps so many times over the years, and it had gotten us nowhere. So I swallowed hard and stepped forward, ready to lay it all on the line. I shook my head, and she dropped her arm.

"Phil," she said, and hearing the strain in her voice when she said my name made my heart feel like it might beat straight out of my chest, through the breastplate and onto the ground in front of us. Though I supposed that was the idea of all this.

"Amy," I said back, smiling. She could stomp on it if she wanted to. It was hers to do with as she wished.

"I read the lore—"

"It's a lot, I know," I interrupted, stepping in close, needing her to hear me. "And I'm not trying to ask for anything you don't want to give. I just thought you should know how I really felt. *Feel*, still. Because the thing is, I love you too, Amy."

Her eyes went wide. "What?"

"I love you," I continued, right over the top of her reply. If I stopped, I might not start again. And I needed to get this out. "And yeah, I love you like a friend, and I want the best for you, yada yada. But I'm also *in* love with you. I have been for years. And I'm sorry I ever let you feel like I wasn't."

I watched as her face melted, her eyes growing wide and wet, her brows quirking up in the middle, her lower lip falling slightly away from the other.

"And if I fucked things up too badly," I said, "if you can't forgive me, that's fine. I'll be your friend. But if you'll let me, well, I'd really like to carry on being in love with you."

Amy bit her lips and took a shaky breath in. "But what does that change, Phil? If you were in love with me yesterday, and last month, and last year, but you still pushed me away."

"It changes everything," I said, gathering her hands in mine and bringing them to my face. "*You* changed everything, just by being yourself. By bringing the magic to anything and everything you touch. By forcing me to realise what I really want, which is this."

I pressed a kiss to each of her hands in turn. The corner of her mouth quirked up slightly, but she didn't give just yet.

"Why couldn't you do this before?" she asked, her voice small and quiet.

"I was scared," I admitted. "Shit, I'm still scared. Everything around me feels like it could fall apart at any moment. And I was stupid, too, because I thought focusing on you was what *made* everything fall apart.

"But that wasn't true, Amy. Everything else was already falling apart. But you were holding *me* together. And if everything's going to shit anyway, I want to be standing there side by side with you, if you'll have me. I want to spend every moment of every day showing up for you the way you've shown up for me. Not every *spare* moment, because we both know there would be nothing left to give. I want to put you first like you deserve. I want to be your knight in shining armour."

I stared into her eyes, willing her to see how much I meant it. How badly I wanted to not only be present – be *her* present – but be her future, too. God knew we already had the past covered.

She didn't say anything for a long time, just kept staring at me, as if she were trying to work something out, too. People moved around us, but it was like we were in a little bubble, as if the rest of the ball wasn't there around us at all. But somehow, I heard shouts from somewhere in the room.

And clearly Amy heard them too. I saw her frown and look around, and only then did I listen to them properly.

"Kiss her, you fool!" Ethel yelled again, and I looked over to see Chloe keeping her hand on Ethel's shoulder so she didn't jump out of her wheelchair and come towards us.

In the past I might have worried about the uneven floor or the way she was leaning, but I let myself be present, turning back to Amy instead.

"Is that Chloe's Fairy Godmother dress?" she asked, still looking over at Ethel. "A bit campy, no?"

"She wanted to dress for the occasion," I said, relieved as I watched a smile creep over Amy's face. "It was the only thing I had that felt appropriate."

"Not the yassified Witch King of Angmar?"

"Oh, we tried it. Let's just say the way it fit made me a bit uncomfortable as her grandson."

"You've really gone all out, haven't you?" she said, turning her attention back to me.

"For you? Every time." I brought a hand to the side of her face, running my thumb along her cheekbone. Her smile dropped instantly, but she didn't look upset, or even afraid. Just ... frozen. Disbelieving, maybe. Hell, I could hardly believe it myself. "What do you say?"

"You mean it?" she asked, her voice thick with emotion. "Because Phil, I really don't think I can take it if you push me away again."

"I really mean it," I said, bringing my other hand up so I was cradling her face in my hands. "I don't know much, as is well established, but I know that I love you."

I nearly fainted with relief when she smirked up at me. We were *so* back.

"Well, that's really embarrassing for you," she said. "Maybe I should find someone who knows more things. Some fun wildlife facts, maybe?"

I stepped closer, shuffling my feet under her skirts, so that her chin tilted up in my hands to meet my gaze, our mouths just a whisper apart. "Yeah, well, your brother's around here somewhere if you want wildlife facts. This is the best I've got."

"Christ alive, Phil, will you shut up and kiss me alr—"

I closed my mouth over hers, needing no further encouragement.

The moment we kissed, it was like coming home. Her lips were soft and warm as always, and I could feel her smiling as I kissed her over and over. She pushed up onto her tiptoes and brought her hands up between us, running her fingers through my beard, tugging at it lightly as if she could pull me even closer. I wrapped my arms around her, and she burrowed into my embrace, smiling up at me from the crook of my elbow.

I could hear Ethel cheering from the side, and was it just me, or was that Jack and Chloe joining in too? But I didn't look. I kept my eyes on the centre of my world – the burst of starlight cradled in my arms.

"This is twice now that you've been my knight in shining armour," she said. "Though the last time was a bit less" – she scanned the armour, reaching up a hand to brush across the breastplate – "literal."

"Baby, I will live and die in this armour if that's what makes you happy. That's my life's mission now, remember?"

"I don't know," she said, walking her fingers across the metal. "I'd quite like to take it off you later."

I quirked a brow at her. "Later?"

"Well, that depends," she said. "Tell me, mister dressmaker of dreams."

I looked up wistfully towards the ceiling. "Ooh. I like the sound of that."

"Eyes on me," she said, tugging at my beard again, less lightly that time, so I looked back down at her.

"I'll never look away again. What can I tell you?"

"If you made this dress," Amy whispered, her brows

bouncing suggestively, "does that mean you're especially good at taking it off?"

She shrieked as I reached down and looped my hand behind her knees, sweeping her off her feet and cradling her in my arms.

"Alright, it's bedtime for you," I said, and she tipped her head back and laughed as I carried her carefully towards the door. When we reached Ethel and Chloe, I let Amy down gently, moving her skirt out of the way so she didn't step on it.

"It's about damn time," Ethel said, reaching up to grab Amy's hand and give it a firm pat. Amy bent down and pressed a kiss to her cheek.

"Thank you for helping him see the light," she said, "because I feel pretty certain he didn't get there on his own."

"I'm sorry," I said, feigning offence, "do you want me to leave?"

"Only with me," she said, standing up to press another kiss to my mouth. "Now let's get out of here."

I retrieved my helmet and gauntlets from Grey, who rushed them across the room to me, then reminded Chloe to text me if she and Ethel needed anything at the hotel I'd gotten them down the street.

"You ready, m'lady?" I asked, bending my arm and offering Amy my elbow. But she took my hand instead, lacing her fingers together in mine as we walked side by side into the night. Despite the bright lights of the city, when I looked up, I swore I could see every single star.

EPILOGUE
CALAMITY

Calamity and her friends were heroes. Just ask anyone in the Capital. Word of their success defeating Nephrine had spread, and they were invited to banquets and ceremonies night after night. Yorick's ballad about the whole affair was being sung by every bard in every tavern across the realm.

But Calamity didn't feel like a hero. She felt like a fraud. Because she was lying to her friends.

Well, not lying. Not explicitly. She'd never told them she *wasn't* the daughter of a demon lord prophesied to destroy the very kingdom they fought to protect, after all.

After Laszlo had drawn the Dark Lord card for her, she'd thought someone would ask her what it meant. Luckily, Yorick and Eden and the rest of them had been so wrapped up in their own cards, and then in the whole Lady Nephrine situation, that they hadn't remembered to ask. Unluckily, it had been weighing on Calamity ever since. So despite the fact that she wanted nothing more than to enjoy the adoration and gratitude the city wanted to bestow on her, and despite the fact that The Twelve still had ten chances to take over, she decided to confront her history once and for all before it came back to bite her.

Which was how she found herself in the astral plane, standing in front of the portal to Pandemonium. The immense vortex of colour and light swirled into the abyss in front of her, casting pink and blue and orange glimmers across her purple skin. She'd seen visions of the astral plane – Eden had shown her before projecting Calamity here so she would be prepared – but being there, standing in front of a portal to another dimension, was ... well, it was another thing entirely, and not one she thought anyone could ever fully prepare for.

Her body was back on the material plane under Eden's careful protection. If anyone else found her in Calamity and Eden's room, they would think she was sleeping. Astral projection was cool, Calamity could appreciate that even now, but it was also scary as hell. Or, she supposed, scary as Pandemonium. Any mistake here could kill her body, too, connected to her projected self by a thin silvery cord that disappeared behind her. The only material possessions she had in her lighter-than-usual pack were her spell focus – the broken tip of a horn wrapped in thin leather – and the scroll of astral projection she'd need to get back. Whilst she'd never been to Pandemonium, she knew this could be a one-way trip if she didn't do things exactly right.

That said, it was now or never, so Calamity grabbed onto the straps of her pack and stepped forward. She expected to experience the feeling of being sucked into the vortex, and even held her breath in anticipation, but the moment her foot connected with the swirls of colour, she stepped not into the abyss but onto the hard, dusty ground of Pandemonium.

As if he'd been waiting for her – and knowing him, he probably had been – Calamity looked up from her feet to see Trulnuroth, the demon lord in exile, standing before her. Feather-like obsidian scales covered his body, lying upwards rather than down. Sharp talons protruded from the tips of his fingers and toes, and his eyes glowed silver as they took in Pandemonium's latest intruder, who would have wanted to look around at her new surroundings, had Trulnuroth not been taking up her entire field of vision. He stood more than twice as high as the tallest of her friends, and that was without the long, curled horns atop his head, one of which was broken off at the tip.

Calamity sighed and waved up at the demon, annoyed but not surprised when all she saw in his returned gaze was disdain. She took a deep breath in, preparing to greet him, trying to lace her words with the same sentiment.

"Hey, Dad," she said. "Long time no see. Sorry to drop in on you, but I need your help."

ACKNOWLEDGEMENTS

Coming back to this world and these characters was such a joy. Thank you to Jennie Rothwell and Charlotte Ledger – and the rest of the One More Chapter team – for letting me tell more stories about this lovable group of nerds. Let's do it again, shall we?

Speaking of lovable groups of nerds, I must thank my own adventuring party for showing up for me both literally and figuratively in my writing journey (and in life in general). To Cate, Steph, and Jim in particular, I'm so lucky to have you in my corner. Let's keep up the support so that one day I'll sell enough copies for that commune we want.

Thank you to my mom, Lisa, for your help with this book. Dementia isn't easy to write or speak about, especially given the impact it's had on our family, but your expertise was invaluable to me. Thanks for always being my cheerleader, though I really do wish you would skip the spicy scenes.

To my incredible partner Alex: thank you for the cups of tea, the desk dinners, and the attempts to lure me away from my desk and out into the real world. Your love is a constant source of inspiration to me. And to our fur baby Kirby, let's put my gratitude into words you can understand: treato?

To my writing group, thank you so much for the sprints, the check-ins, and the motivation. My writing career only looks the way it does today because of your support and community.

And finally, to the wonderful community of people who

follow me online and encourage my writing: thank you, thank you, *thank you*. I love sharing this journey with you. Chat, we did it!

The author and One More Chapter would like to thank everyone who contributed to the publication of this story...

Analytics
James Brackin
Abigail Fryer

Audio
Fionnuala Barrett
Ciara Briggs

Contracts
Laura Amos
Laura Evans

Design
Lucy Bennett
Fiona Greenway
Liane Payne
Dean Russell

Digital Sales
Laura Daley
Lydia Grainge
Hannah Lismore

eCommerce
Laura Carpenter
Madeline ODonovan
Charlotte Stevens
Christina Storey
Jo Surman
Rachel Ward

Editorial
Kara Daniel
Charlotte Ledger
Laura McCallen
Jennie Rothwell
Tony Russell
Sofia Salazar Studer
Caroline Scott-Bowden
Helen Williams

Harper360
Jennifer Dee
Emily Gerbner
Ariana Juarez
Jean Marie Kelly
emma sullivan
Sophia Wilhelm

International Sales
Peter Borcsok
Ruth Burrow
Colleen Simpson
Ben Wright

Inventory
Sarah Callaghan
Kirsty Norman

Marketing & Publicity
Chloe Cummings
Grace Edwards

Operations
Melissa Okusanya
Hannah Stamp

Production
Denis Manson
Simon Moore
Francesca Tuzzeo

Rights
Helena Font Brillas
Ashton Mucha
Zoe Shine
Aisling Smyth
Lucy Vanderbilt

Trade Marketing
Ben Hurd
Eleanor Slater

The HarperCollins Distribution Team

The HarperCollins Finance & Royalties Team

The HarperCollins Legal Team

The HarperCollins Technology Team

UK Sales
Isabel Coburn
Jay Cochrane
Sabina Lewis
Holly Martin
Harriet Williams
Leah Woods

And every other essential link in the chain from delivery drivers to booksellers to librarians and beyond!

When life goes rogue, roll for romance...

Avid role-playing gamer Morgan is on a quest – to step out of her comfort zone and become her own knight in shining armour.

Jack, the group's loveable cleric character, is also looking to rewrite a more exciting story for himself.

When they and their friends plan a Renaissance Faire adventure, Morgan and Jack embrace the magic of their alter egos – is it possible they might just fall for each other in real life too?

Available now in paperback, ebook and audio!

One More Chapter is an award-winning global division of HarperCollins.

Subscribe to our newsletter to get our latest eBook deals and stay up to date with all our new releases!

signup.harpercollins.co.uk/join/signup-omc

Meet the team at
www.onemorechapter.com

Follow us!

@onemorechapterhc

Do you write unputdownable fiction?
We love to hear from new voices.
Find out how to submit your novel at
www.onemorechapter.com/submissions